Disillusioned Love

Disillusioned Love

by
Amy Lee Peine

To my beautiful family, thank you for your patience and support. To my husband, thank you for showing me what true love is and being an inspiration.

This book would never have made it to the end had it not been for the unconditional love, support and critique of my best friend Bethany. This is as much your novel as it is mine.

To Renee, your belief in me astounds me every day. You continue to push me to reach my full potential.

Contents

CHAPTER ONE

I Think They Like Me

Thursday May 25, 2006

"Dude, it's like nine o'clock at night, do you really need coffee right now?" Alex moaned from behind the wheel of the rented Chrysler. Even though he was distracted by his search for some kind of late night café he still caught Matthew's shocked and offended expression. Matthew had developed a coffee addiction early on in life, but it was to be expected; with their late night sessions in the studio, the tours and crossing time zones and the expectation for them to be chipper and happy when dealing with fans or interviewers. Alex raised his hands in defense with a quick laugh, "Okay, okay!"

"Well we *are* in Chicago, there has to be some kind of cafe open late. I refuse to drink cheap gas station coffee or restaurant coffee. That stuff is like sludge it--" Alex was thankful Matthew's dramatic rambling was cut short by his sudden left turn which threw Matthew slightly into the side of his door. Derek, the eldest of the three men and Alex's brother, stifled a laugh in the backseat as he undid his seatbelt. Matthew huffed and shot a smoldering glare in Alex's direction.

"Found one!" Alex proclaimed with the biggest, cheesiest grin he could muster as he, too, undid his seatbelt. It brought Alex joy to ruffle Matt's feathers, especially when it was so easy to do.

They proceeded to a small cafe nestled below one of the massive office buildings on Michigan Avenue. It seemed out of place, like the person who still carried a notebook and pen within the seas of laptops and smartphones. The bell above the cafe's door announced their arrival but the handful of people inside didn't look up; Alex released a breath he unknowingly held as they stepped in. Nine years ago he, Matthew and Derek had released an album that took the world by storm and made D.M.A. a household name almost instantly. While things had changed over time, D.M.A.'s fan base was large and loyal. The fans settled some as they grew older but that didn't mean the guys didn't occasionally run into some sticky situations when out in public.

It was a quaint coffee shop; artsy and quiet. There was a quiet hum of conversation, clicks of keys and a soft call of instrumental guitars from the surround sound. They were met with the sweet and overpowering scent of espresso and pastries; a scent that undoubtedly set Matthew's heart at ease. It was cozy, a few couches scattered about with tables made from large butcher blocks. There was a fireplace in the back and a diversified collection of art that adorned the walls. Most of the patrons were of their early to mid-twenties and engrossed in books or laptops. It appeared to be a college crowd. Matthew collected his caramel macchiato and returned to Alex and Derek.

"Hey," he started, "let's stay for a bit. This place is kind of neat." he finished as he strayed towards a print of a face disintegrating against the background. He stood there silently as he examined the painting. His jeans hung loosely off his small hips while his t-shirt clung to his thin, yet firm, torso with a knit hat snugly placed over his layered locks.

"It doesn't look like we have a choice." Derek commented as he and Alex followed behind Matthew. To anyone who didn't know their relationship they looked like an unlikely group of friends. Matthew was a tall, thin, Hipster type with fair features. Alex; a sturdy, well-built darker skinned man, with harder, edgier features and a laid back style and Derek; a shorter but thinner version of Alex with a bit of curl to his dark hair with a style as classic as a 1950s Chevrolet. As they wandered around the café and admired art they later discovered was done by local students, a group of women caught their attention. The women's backs were almost to them, they were closely nestled on one of the couches and a large overstuffed chair by the fireplace. They hadn't caught the guys' eye; more like their ear.

"Well I don't think sex appeal is always in direct correlation with looks." one of the women declared.

"Even though so many people put them together." another interjected.

"Right, almost as if we've been taught we should only be attracted to quote unquote good looking people." the first continued. A quick flick of gazes to each other confirmed that each of the guys was intrigued.

"It's sad because people stay stuck in the mindset for so long, no one really teaches them to look beyond that; for someone that meshes with you in other areas. Maybe people care too much of what other people think. I mean, God forbid you try and explain to shallow people why you're partnered with a quote unquote unattractive person." the blonde bemoaned. The guys knew it was her because she actually used air quotes. Alex looked over at Derek and Matthew and raised a brow. Matthew smiled and motioned to the nearest table. It was wrong to eavesdrop, but the discussion at hand had drawn them in too much to ignore.

"I, for one, do not like how everyone associates conventional good looks with sex appeal." a new voice commented. It was light and feminine with a Canadian accent. Derek smirked as he noted the accent provided its own unique element of sex appeal. "I think sex appeal is so much more than looks. It's more about how they carry themselves, how they interact with other people--"

"A guy can be hot but if he's an ass, there goes the sex appeal." The Canadian was interrupted but they all laughed and agreed. Alex smiled from his place at the table behind them.

"No, I totally agree." the blonde interjected.

Alex started to notice the blonde talked a lot with her hands and she waved about to bring the discussion back to the topic at hand. "I've seen drop dead gorgeous people, society standard perfect pretty people, but had no attraction to them at all because of how they carried themselves. Whether they were stuck-up, ignorant or whatever. Regardless of how they may have looked, they didn't compare to those people in my life who go above and beyond what looks could ever do for someone else."

"Ignorance is an instant turn off. Like Josh and his--"

"Wow you have a lot of books." they all mocked.

"And 'You must have to know big words to be an editor.'" the Canadian mimicked.

"Because I used eclectic!" the curly dark haired one exclaimed exasperatedly then leaned back as she laughed. All three of the guys tried to contain their own laughter.

"That's horrible. I'm so glad you got rid of him." the Canadian patted the brunette's shoulder. "You know what I want to know? Who is it that determines who's societally 'perfect pretty'? Because personally I think it's a load of shit. People come in so many shapes, sizes, and colors who's to say what the standard is?" she implored, pretty riled up.

"Ri said its biology."

The blonde raised her hands in defense, "It's not all biology." she retorted as she revealed her identity as Ri. "Although studies have claimed there are things which historically have caught people's attention. Symmetry is one. People claim the more symmetrical a face is the more aesthetically pleasing it is." She was eloquent, articulate and spoke with such an authority it left little room for argument.

"So that's why you're so obsessive about your piercings!" the Canadian giggled.

"No! I'm just...ugh, shut up!" Ri laughed. "But other biological things play into it. It's also been claimed on the most primal and basic level men notice blondes because it's been theorized blonde hair is a sign of fertility--"

"You would say that; Miss 'I'm naturally blonde.'" the brunette teased.

"Right, like I enjoy the attention I get from morons that don't have a clue." Ri snipped. "But aside from biology and primitive psychology, a large part of who is considered perfect pretty comes from society."

"Wait!" the Canadian yelled. "Before the Almighty Riana gets started on her area of expertise, does anyone need more coffee? Because you *know* this will take a while." Everyone, including Ri, laughed as they shuffled around and got up for a refill. At the mention of "Riana" a flicker of recognition passed over Matthew's face, but it was gone as fast as it appeared to Alex and Derek. Matthew knew the name, had known it for years. The chances of it being the Riana he thought it was would be slim, almost non-existent. Matthew couldn't help but think back nine years though, when the letters started, and the attachment he formed for her. He reached in his pocket and stroked the beads that always rested there, ever since he was eighteen and the necklace he had worn for three years finally got too small.

As the women walked back up to the counter for refills Matthew leaned in to Alex and Derek and commented in a hushed tone, "This has got to be one of the most interesting things I've heard in a long time." Alex nodded in agreement.

"I think it's about to get more interesting if this Riana lady is truly an expert on society." Derek predicted. Alex contained the urge to roll his eyes, Derek was always the skeptic. Derek had formed a fairly cynical view on the world through D.M.A's success in the music industry. Much of the attention from fans and media was always focused on Matthew, and it had left Derek somewhat jaded.

The girls ambled back to their places and the guys tried to pretend like it didn't matter. Not that they had to, it didn't seem the women knew the guys were there. Once the three women got together and started to talk, the rest of the world didn't matter, time didn't exist; only their friendship and passions.

"I'm just saying I've talked about it before, in my lectures, classes, even Lexi and I have butted heads on it at times."

Alex quickly looked at Matthew and Derek, worried they missed her explanation of social complexity in standards of beauty.

"Society very frequently sets the standard. This can distinctly be seen through the eras of art, and even modeling. For a long time curves, meat, and weight were all seen as intricate parts to sex appeal and the standard for women to meet. Back in the 18th century heavy women were considered the ideal because...well frankly they had the money to eat, and therefore were of good childbearing because men knew they'd survive a winter. It then went into looks of tiny waists but big hips...hips again giving signs of how able the woman was to bear children. They didn't advertise it of course, that's simple biology and psychology speaking. Trends fluctuate a lot. Look at Marilyn Monroe who was a size fourteen by today's sizing--a six by her days sizing. And yet, we're told today that she was a six, leading us to believe she was petite and she wasn't. They don't tell us that sizing had changed. Then over time, the trend just kept getting smaller. Towards the early 90s it became the sickly thin, waif look, and slowly we're heading back to healthy curves. What's sad is one, we will never be able to live up to the media standard because nothing is actually real and two, and the complex we form when we don't meet it screws our perception of ourselves." Derek raised his dark brows, impressed. "It's unfair, the backlash we get when we aren't the standard."

"Or even if you are." the brunette interjected.

"Nothing you ever do is good enough." the Canadian sighed in disappointment.

"Which is why I think people just need to pull their heads from their asses and realize people are beautiful beyond looks, and ugly despite them. They need to start treating people accordingly. They need to give people a chance, and they need to take perfect pretty people off their undeserved pedestal." Ri concluded. Alex resisted the urge to applaud.

"Perfect pretty people piss me off." the Canadian huffed. "They get shit handed to them simply because they're attractive. They don't know what it's like to have to prove their worth because people already fight to get near them. They're treated in higher regard. They take advantage of it too, and never form human compassion because they don't know what it's like not to get it." Ri leaned over from her spot on the couch and rubbed the Canadian's leg. "It's not fair."

"It's not but…" the brunette started. "On the other side of it, very frequently perfect pretty people get the shaft in the way that so many people think they're nothing but their looks. Sometimes that's the case of course, but other times it's an injustice to them that they're viewed as ditzy or stupid."

"I can attest for both sides." Riana confessed quietly. The fact was she probably could. It was true; her blonde hair was natural; long and flowing. She was short, and curvy. Her eyes often startled people in how blue they were, they gave somewhat of an unnatural effect to her face when her eyes ended up intensely locked on someone. Riana loved to smile and laugh and the combination lit up her slightly round face. She had tastefully picked piercings, funky ear pieces and one feminine, small barbell placed strategically in the middle of her lower lip. She had an unusual balance between beauty and brains, which given the current discussion, could bring a mixture of treatments to her.

"Just look at Matthew Sullivan." the brunette started. The men quickly looked around, worried they had been discovered. Matthew realized they hadn't noticed him; they were using him as an example, which startled him even more. He knew people talked about him, it was one of the tradeoffs for their success, but to actually overhear it was totally different.

"How many years did the fans call him ditzy simply because he was good looking? He had to fight that, and he shouldn't have had to, they as quote unquote loving fans should have listened to him from the beginning. And Alex, the fans and their inability to let him grow out of the 'crazy kid' he was when D.M.A. started. He was eleven. He's twenty now. The only reason they accepted him growing up was because...well because he's hot. Not to mention how much I want to kick them for their judgments on Derek, not listening to him or giving him the props he deserved as a brilliant musician simply because he wasn't as pretty as Matt, even though I mean really, the man is sexy in his own right."

"I want to talk to them." Matthew declared.

"Are you sure?" Derek asked as he quickly glanced between Alex and Matthew. Alex remained quiet and thoughtfully chewed the inside of his lip as he contemplated the idea. "They obviously know who we are."

"It could be refreshing. They don't seem to be typical fans." Alex observed with a raise of his eyebrows.

"I'd say! They don't even *like* our fans." Matthew laughed. Alex and Derek grinned in response. However, no one moved. They eyed each other and wondered who would make the first move. For the first time in a long time for the guys it seemed the roles were reversed; they were the fans of the spoken brilliance they'd been eavesdropping on and didn't want to be rude by inviting themselves over.

Alex released his lip from his teeth. "Let's do it." he blurted as he stood up and pushed his shaggy black hair from his face. Matthew looked at Derek and they reluctantly followed Alex's lead. The women were hunched over in hysterical laughter as the guys approached; the conversation had obviously taken a much lighter turn.

"Oh it hurts! It hurts!" the brunette laughed as she held her stomach. The Canadian wiped her eyes and Riana tried, quite unsuccessfully, to catch her breath.

"Um, excuse me?" Matthew ventured from where he stood on the other side of the low table that separated him, Derek and Alex from where Riana and the Canadian sat on the couch and the brunette in the overstuffed chair to the left of him.

The Canadian waved him away without looking up, "Just a damn minute." Riana laughed harder, the brunette looked up and, upon seeing the members of D.M.A in front of them, choked on a quick intake of breath, then laughed again. The Canadian looked over at the brunette, "What?" she questioned between giggles.

"I don't...think...Matthew has ever...had someone...tell him...to wait." the brunette wheezed.

"Where did that come from?" Riana inquired as she obliviously took a sip of her coffee, which was immediately shot out her nose and half choked on when she looked up towards the men who stood before them. Having been fans for the last nine years, it didn't seem possible to see Derek, Matthew and Alex, right there, attempting to talk to them. Riana's round cheeks grew red and hot, her hands started to tremble and she thought she might even forget how to breathe. Cool under this kind of pressure she certainly was not.

"Bloody hell!" the Canadian half yelled, half laughed as she rushed napkins to Ri's aid. The scene was total chaos. Matthew quickly knelt down and helped wipe up spilt coffee. A sense of panic and embarrassment grasped him as he quickly regretted his hasty idea to meet them.

"Oh yeah, just perfect. Should have known I'd look like an ass in front of D.M.A." Riana mumbled as she shook her head and mentally scolded herself for appearing so incompetent.

The Canadian tried to hide a giggle. "Hey, it's kind of like when you called Ryan…" Riana closed her eyes and groaned. "the dead sexiest guy on campus!" the brunette finished along. They both fell back into a laughing fit, though Riana was reluctant to join. Riana's boyfriend of the last three years, Ryan, had struck her fancy immediately but the beginning of their relationship wasn't the course they had together at the university, it was the moment in which he overheard Riana deem him the dead sexiest guy on campus. Riana knew in that moment, much as in this moment, she could either face the music and talk to Ryan after she realized what he heard or run away with her tail between her legs, never to look back.

Riana finally broke, "That bastard still won't let me live that down." she laughed. Matthew stood back up and looked at Derek and Alex in disbelief. He couldn't fathom that they were being ignored; it was practically unheard of.

Riana quickly appeared to compose herself, though her mind still reeled from being face to face with some of her favorite musicians. "Now," she started and cleared her throat. "Who's going to replace my wasted caramel macchiato?" she asked as she stood up and looked in the direction of Matthew. A perfectly arched eyebrow was lifted in expectation over her stern, brilliant, cobalt eyes. The brunette snickered.

"I, um," Matthew started as he reached for his wallet. Ri raised her hand to silence him.

"I'm kidding. It's fine, there's more." she smiled and lifted her still half full, large, lavender porcelain cup for him to see. Her smile was bright and friendly as her ultramarine eyes danced playfully. She placed her cup back on the table. "Hi." she offered while she extended her hand to Matthew. Matthew smiled back as he grasped her petite hand. "I'm Riana, this is Samantha," she motioned to the Canadian with clearly unnatural blonde hair with deep red tips and thick rimmed black glasses after she released Matthew's hand "and this is Lexi." she finished as she nodded towards the curly haired brunette who had a large, contagious smile. After a quick exchange of greetings there was a moment of awkward silence. Heavy uncertainty filtered around them as they glanced at each other.

"Hey, didn't we meet you in Minnesota?" Alex asked Lexi. He figured if all else failed, start with something familiar. Lexi smiled.

"Yeah, I didn't think you'd remember." she blushed lightly and Alex smiled at her.

They had met, briefly, before one of their concerts. It was a memorable moment for Alex. Lexi had come in with a group for a meet and greet, she was polite and soft-spoken but when she got to Derek she couldn't even bring herself to look him in the eyes. Derek, ever the gentleman, never wanted fans to be uneasy around them so he attempted to bend down, catch her eye and engage her in some kind of conversation. He failed miserably.

"Well, sometimes faces are easier to remember than most people think." Alex explained.

"Yeah, but then sometimes you get people coming up to you asking, 'Don't I know you? You look awfully familiar' when you know, they don't know you." Ri rambled quickly. "That's annoying." she finished as she sat back down and gathered more napkins to clean up her mess. Her hair drifted down in front of her face and she gave a little puff of air through her lower lip to move it out of her way.

"Yeah…" Matthew slowly agreed. He eyed Riana as she finished wiping off the table. He hadn't seen a picture of the girl from his past in so many years; it was difficult for him to decide if the angles of her face were the same as the woman in front of him. It just didn't seem possible.

"I'm sorry if we disturbed you guys. Riana here can get pretty obnoxious." Samantha quipped as she cleaned her funky glasses. She had a wonderfully quirky style, bright colors and patterns graced her clothes and satchel. She was just a touch taller than Riana, but with oddly similar features. They were both blonde, curvy, and their smiles mirrored each other but Samantha had adorable dimples deep in her round cheeks where Riana didn't. They could have passed as twins, or at the very least sisters. Ri quickly snapped her head in Samantha's direction, set on defending herself.

"No, no, you didn't disturb us." Derek quickly insisted before Ri's offended look transitioned into words.

Lexi's brow furrowed as she tilted her head to the side. "Um, then.." she started as she glanced between Riana and Samantha.

"Why'd we come over?" Alex offered. They nodded.

"We sort of overheard you all talking," Matthew started. Lexi was the first to drop her head as she felt caught in their exploits of the guys and their fans. "And it was really quite intriguing and--"

"Really?" Samantha questioned. Matthew looked at Derek and Alex while they nodded.

"Did you want to sit down?" Ri offered as she motioned to the empty spots around them. "I'm feeling shorter than usual with all of you standing around me." At a mere five feet tall, the difference between Riana and the guys was drastic. Each of them had at least a foot on her.

"Is it possible for you to feel any shorter?" Lexi teased with a grin. There was obviously a special and unique dynamic between Riana and Lexi. Lexi was the odd one out of the group of women, much as Matthew was the odd one out with the guys. Riana and Samantha shared the same features that Lexi was almost completely opposite of. She was quite a bit taller than both Riana and Samantha; she had dark, curly hair that was pulled back off her longer face. She had large, bright, carob colored eyes, her nose was more petite than Riana's, and lips that were just a touch fuller.

Riana gave a deliberate smile as she cocked her head to the side. "Lick it." Matthew's jaw dropped, Derek and Alex gasped and the women broke into laughter. Alex pulled up a chair next to Lexi's and Derek sat on the other side of Samantha on the couch. Matthew took the chair across from Riana and continued to gaze at her. He was still attempting to decide if he had found the woman he'd grown so attached to all those years ago without ever having directly conversed with her.

They easily fell into conversation. It was refreshing for the guys; to find people who didn't seem to treat them differently due to their status. The women were filled with what seemed like endless topics; from random trivia facts, to mind-boggling questions of life, to stories that got everyone wheezing through their laughter.

Hours later, their small world was disrupted by the barista from behind the counter when he informed them the cafe was closing. Riana checked her watch as if she didn't believe him. "Damn, it's like midnight." The rest of the group also checked for the time. "I'm going to be absolutely dead for my meeting with my publisher tomorrow." Riana complained as she stood up and grabbed her purse. The rest of the group followed suit, Lexi and Samantha with concerned looks on their faces. Riana left hastily, she didn't even turn to say good-bye. Lexi quickened her pace to catch up to Riana as she burst out the door and onto the sidewalk. Samantha grabbed Alex's arm to get him and the other guys to follow.

"Ri! Wait!" Lexi yelled as everyone got outside. Despite the time, the street pulsated with people; street artists, groups of friends, and couples on dates. Chicago wasn't exactly known as the city that never slept, but it certainly kept up with New York City.

Riana turned around about thirty feet from the door, her hand buried in her purse. The imposing skyscrapers surrounded her, made her appear smaller, almost lost in the bustle of the city. "Honey, I have the keys." Samantha called from Alex's side. Riana let out a sigh of relief as she shuffled back to the stunned group outside the cafe. Lexi was at her side and rubbed Ri's back comfortingly.

"It'll be okay Ri. Your meeting will be fine. You can function on less sleep than this." Lexi assured.

"Yeah, but..." Riana stopped as she reached Alex, Derek, Matthew and Samantha. "I'm sorry." she expressed softly. Her head was dropped and she glanced up at them from hooded lids. The misting of rain which had started left what looked like fresh dew drops on her cheeks and along her collarbone. As they gathered in the hollow of her throat the coolness brought goose bumps to the surface of her skin. It was in that moment Alex decided she was truly beautiful. "...didn't mean to leave so quickly. It's just I have an important meeting with my agent and publisher in the morning and I have to be on top of my game."

Matthew reached out and stroked Riana's arm. She looked up at him quickly, shocked at the small sign of affection and he smiled. "Hey, no, it's totally okay. We remember what those kinds of meetings are like." She smiled back at him. "Go, get some sleep. You'll do wonderfully." Riana nodded. Alex looked over at Samantha and she smiled at him; a way to apologize for Riana's running off and to relay that Matthew's gesture was sweet.

As Riana turned to finally leave with Lexi and Samantha, Alex reached out and gently grabbed her upper arm. He grinned and bit his lip lightly. "So, if you have time or whatever tomorrow..." He was nervous, there was no reason to be nervous, was there? "Um, you could, well, I'd like it if you'd call and let me--*us*--know how your meeting went." A look of shock barely passed over Riana's face before she smiled.

"Okay." she simply replied as she took out her cell. Alex dictated his number and she grinned again as she saved it. "Thanks. I'll call you tomorrow." Alex smiled again as Riana turned and jogged to catch up with Samantha and Lexi.

"Wow." Derek gushed from Alex's side as they headed towards their car. "That was..."

"Awesome?" Matthew finished.

"Definitely awesome." Alex agreed.

CHAPTER TWO

I Write Sins Not Tragedies

Friday May 26, 2006

Riana found herself underneath the safe canopy of a huge magenta umbrella at one of the sidewalk cafes in downtown Chicago with Lexi and Samantha. She stared at the screen of her cell phone as the new entry "Alex Cell" taunted her. She had wanted to call sooner; her meeting had been over for almost three hours. She had the time to call before she met Lexi and Samantha for a late lunch but she simply couldn't. She wasn't sure if she needed encouragement, all she knew was she just couldn't bring herself to hit that one, tiny, insignificant green button to dial his number.

Roughly four miles away Alex was restless in the hotel suite he shared with Derek and Matthew. "She said her meeting was in the morning, but she hasn't called yet." Alex complained. There was no specific reason as to why it bothered him so much. Although Derek seemed to have a theory.

"Just because you're Alexander Jennings doesn't mean every woman in the world considers your number to be a gift from God." Derek quipped from the couch in the living area of the suite. Alex stared at him with his mouth agape.

"I...never...said..." Alex started. Perhaps it was true; Alex was used to getting a bit more attention. Of course that didn't mean he believed giving Riana his number would somehow possess her to call at her earliest convenience. However, he also didn't think she wasn't going to call at all.

"Alex, relax." Matthew spoke from behind Alex with his head half in the refrigerator. "You know how long, not to mention stressful, meetings with any kind of executive can be. Whether it be producers, management, accountants..." Alex began to inwardly groan as he tuned him out. Matthew had a habit of rambling. Alex always thought it was because in D.M.A. Matthew always got the majority of the attention in any public situation. He had to learn how to carry the conversation. It was rare when the questions were directed at anyone but him. The sudden sound of Alex's phone brought him back to the present time and also thankfully stopped Matthew's rambling. Alex grinned excitedly as he picked up, "Hello?"

"Riana just *call* him." Samantha ordered. Riana sat at the cafe with Lexi and Samantha; her phone in her trembling hands. "He gave you his number for a reason." Riana knew it may have been true, but calling him was too real for her. She worried it would go badly, she might interrupt something, or he might get annoyed. Riana nervously glanced up at Lexi and Samantha. Lexi gave her a reassuring smile. There was something about Lexi's smiles that brought comfort to Riana. No matter what the situation, Lexi gave Riana a sense everything would be okay. Given the eleven years of their friendship, it was a logical feeling to have as Lexi had stood by Riana's side through absolutely everything.

"Besides, Ri, you have some pretty fantastic news to tell him." Lexi encouraged. Despite the lack of sleep, the meeting with Riana's publisher had gone better than expected.

Riana looked between her two best friends and nervously spun the barbell placed in the middle of her lower lip between her teeth and tongue. She took a deep breath, "Okay, here it goes." She highlighted "Alex Cell" and hit talk.

Alex hopped onto the kitchenette counter and smiled. Matthew looked at Alex and laughed at the ridiculously happy look on Alex's face. He mouthed "say hi" and waved. Alex rolled his keen, dark eyes but nodded in compliance.

"Hey Alex, it's Riana." her voice had an edge of nervousness to it.

"Well how are you this afternoon?" Alex asked in an almost sing-song kind of way, his lame attempt to ease her nerves.

"I'm good." Alex could hear in her voice she was smiling. Alex smiled in silent victory that his lame attempt worked. She apologized for not calling sooner. She explained her meeting ran pretty late then she met Lexi and Samantha for lunch.

"Hey, no problem." Alex assured. Matthew walked by and hit Alex's arm. "Ow! God Matt you can be such a bitch sometimes!" Riana started to laugh on the other end of the line. "Sorry about that." Alex apologized coolly. "Matt says hi." Riana was still giggling and it elicited a deep laugh from Alex.

Riana attempted to reply through her giggles. "Well, make sure you tell the diva I said hi back." Alex smiled and lightly shook his head in disbelief. He wasn't quite used to dealing with someone who didn't get tongue tied and star struck when interacting with the Golden God of D.M.A. Typically Matthew, with his shaggy, silky blonde hair that fell perfectly above his incandescent cerulean eyes, stunned women into some kind of muted stupor. "Oh, and Sam and Lexi say hi to everyone as well. And make sure you tell Derek we all say 'what up dawg, holla back.'" She started to laugh deeper and again Alex joined her. "No, seriously, tell them." she encouraged. Alex laughed harder as he hopped off the counter.

"Okay." Alex relented with a snicker as he skipped into the living area of the suite. "Hey Matt; Lexi and Samantha say hi."

"Sweet." he smiled triumphantly. "Wait, what about Riana?" he pouted. Matthew had the pout absolutely perfected. Not only was his hair perfect and well suited to frame his eyes, but his face was blessed with long, even lines, a strong jawline, perfectly groomed and arched eyebrows. A pull of his lower lip and sadness to his eyes made his pout flawless.

The pout had no effect on Alex after nine years and he fought to remain calm as to relay Riana's message to Matt. A light giggle escaped before he could say it, "She said, and I quote, 'Tell the diva I said hi back.'" Alex let go of the full force of his laughter once he got the whole statement out.

Matthew's jaw dropped in horror. "She. Did. *Not!*" Alex lost all control and grasped the edge of the couch as he laughed the hardest yet and practically fell into Derek's lap.

Derek laughed along with Alex and agreed, "Well Matt, your reaction supports the diva theory." That topped it off for Alex and he snorted, which set off Riana into another fit of giggles.

"Wait." Alex called as he waved his hand in front of himself and tried to catch his breath. "She also said she, Lexi and Sam all say 'what up dawg, holla back.' to you D." Derek laughed and held up the peace sign. Alex laughed a bit more and proceeded to his room, and left Matthew stunned in the living area; complete with his hand defiantly on his jutted hip.

"That, was perfect." Riana complimented.

"Thank you, thank you. I aim to please." Alex grinned. "So tell me, how did your meeting go?" he asked as he plopped down on his bed.

"Wonderfully." Riana sighed happily.

"Oh yeah? That's great Ri!" Alex exclaimed with relief, she seemed so worried last night. Alex laid back on the cool comforter of the king size bed and stared up. He attempted to keep his eye on one spinning blade of the ceiling fan above him. The conclusion--don't try, it was surprisingly difficult.

"To say I was relieved it went so well would be a drastic understatement. We'd been butting heads quite a bit about how we were going to market my book now that it was transgressing local markets to national. I think my lack of sleep actually helped. I was more stubborn than usual." she laughed.

Lexi and Samantha were inadvertently ignored by Riana, but Riana felt it was their own fault as they were the ones who pushed her to call. They were happy she finally called and when she would find their eyes with a smile on her face they returned the gesture. "So what's this infamous book about?" Alex probed light-heartedly. Riana dropped her head and wished desperately for a light-hearted answer.

"Well," she began to play with the vertical labret barbell which rested in her lip. It was a habit—a nervous habit more precisely. Lexi's eyes grew concerned when she saw. Lexi knew Ri better than Ri knew herself sometimes, which was often simultaneously comforting and frustrating. "It's kind of… the story of… my life." Riana took a deep breath. "Not all of it of course, just…"

"Ri?" Alex interrupted gently.

"Hmm?" Ri replied with the barbell firmly held under her upper teeth against her bottom lip.

"This seems hard for you to talk about. I'm sorry, I didn't--" It was clear in his voice he truly didn't mean for it to be such a difficult question.

"Alex, no. No, you didn't know. I know you didn't mean to ask such a hard question. And I usually don't have such a hard time talking about it. I really don't." Riana almost laughed at the irony of it being a difficult question for her to answer. She was a renowned author and national speaker on the very topic her book dealt with. It should have been an exceptionally easy question to answer. "I just, didn't want to have to tell you my sob stories quite yet." She tried to laugh to lighten the mood but wasn't exactly successful.

"Everyone has their sob stories, Ri." Alex breathed.

"I know." Riana murmured, defeated. She knew if he kept going he was sure to break through walls she had meticulously built. Riana watched a bead of sweat roll down the side of her glass of iced tea. Samantha leaned over and urgently tapped her. "Hold on Alex." She covered the bottom of her phone and turned to Sam. "What's up?"

"It's almost four Ri, you have your lecture at University of Chicago in two hours." Sam hinted quickly. Riana gave a quick expletive as she started to gather her stuff. She heard Alex question what was going on.

"Alex, I am so sorry." Riana gushed as she stood up and slung her bag over her shoulder. "I have to go. I lost track of time. I have a speaking engagement to go to." Alex assured her it was okay, despite his slight disappointment in not being able to talk to her more. "Can I call you later?" she questioned.

Alex couldn't stop the smile that spread over his face and squinted his eyes up. "Of course." He bid farewell, hit end and continued to save Riana's number into his phone. He sat on the edge of his bed and smiled to himself as his eyes lost focus of anything specific. It was unusual for him to be so naturally comfortable with Riana. Alex was usually pretty guarded when it came to new people, call it an after effect of becoming famous at perhaps too young of an age. There was something about the three women that relaxed him, while simultaneously excited him. Who knew what the next conversations would bring; life stories, tears of laughter, political discussions, questions about religion? Alex shook his head to slow the thoughts. It was only one night and one phone call, surely he was getting ahead of himself.

Lexi and Sam shared a smile and a deep breath at the cafe table before they got up to desperately try to catch up with Riana, who was on a mission to get to campus on time. The afternoon traffic on the streets and sidewalks were not helping Ri however, and Lexi and Sam caught up to her as she waited at the corner for the walk sign to illuminate and give her the okay to cross. "Ri?" Lexi hailed. Riana turned around. It appeared she only then remembered she had been with two other people at lunch.

"Hey. Sorry. I just really have to go, you know? We still have to get back to my place so I can change and grab my notes." Lexi and Sam nodded as they all stepped off the curb. They knew all too well how frazzled Riana got before her speaking engagements, especially seeing as Riana also had a hard time staying within a timely schedule.

"How'd your chat with Alex go?" Sam asked, attempting to get Riana to relax just a bit. Riana smiled, and Sam knew she succeeded.

"Lovely." Ri sighed. "I'm going to call him later." Lexi and Sam were glad to see her happy. Not only were Riana's speaking engagements more frequent and expanding all over the country; her book was going national and now she had the phone number, and attention, of a man she'd been enthralled with for years.

Alex sighed as he went back to the living area of the suite. Disappointment crept in when he realized his company for the day would be his big brother Derek and their best friend, and bandmate, Matthew. He threw himself sideways into the huge armchair in the corner.

"Off the phone so soon?" Derek quipped. Alex pursed his lips as he glared at him.

"She had a speaking engagement to go to." Alex explained. "She said she'd call me later." As Alex smiled he fought to keep the slight blush that threatened to take over his cheeks at bay. It was one of the times he was thankful for his darker skin. Derek nodded from his place on the couch.

Matthew checked the time on his phone. "So, guys, are we just going to sit here and numb our brains for the next three hours before we grab Rebecca for dinner or are we going to do something productive?" Alex bit his lip in contemplation.

"Was that today?" Derek questioned. *Thanks man for reading my mind.* Alex thought as he threw his head back over the arm of the chair to look at Matt.

"Um, yeah. Remember, she was going to see that speaker and then we were going to steal her for some long overdue brotherly love and bonding." Matt smiled. Rebecca wasn't actually his sister, she was Alex and Derek's but being as D.M.A. had been together for so long, they were all family.

"Otherwise known as obnoxious teasing and undeniable embarrassment." Alex laughed. "What do you guys think, want to hang here or maybe investigate her campus while she's attending that thing?"

"Let's check out the campus. The University of Chicago has some amazing architecture I'd love to photograph." Matthew offered. He seemed giddy at the prospect of looking like a horrible tourist or maybe a creepy peeping tom taking pictures through windows.

<u>CHAPTER THREE</u>

Waiting On The World To Change

Lexi, Sam and Riana got to U of C with about a half hour to spare. It was the perfect amount of time for Riana to have a coffee to calm her excited nerves. She knew it was contradictory, to use a stimulant such as caffeine to relax, but it was habit. It's not that she had any fear of her speaking engagements, only too much excitement. It calmed within the first ten minutes of her being on stage. Riana stood to the side of the stage and took in her surroundings as the heavy red curtain blocked her from the view of the steady stream of people that were beginning to fill the auditorium. She smiled to herself and embraced the feelings that took over her. She was aware she would change the life of every person who entered the room. Each person took something different from her story, but they all left changed.

Lexi came up behind Riana and softly called her name as to not draw attention to them. Riana turned to her and smiled softly, her excitement and joy clearly bounced off her bright eyes. Lexi brought Riana's coffee to her, just the way she liked it; without the annoying cardboard sleeve around it. She took the cup from Lexi's hand and thanked her quietly. She turned back around to watch the auditorium fill up with students, faculty and community members. "It's going to be a great audience, Ri." Lexi commented from her side. Riana took a sip of her coffee and hummed in agreement.

The U of C campus was absolutely beautiful and Matthew was having a glorious time photographing it. Being as the University first opened its doors back in 1892, the historical nature of much of its architecture was immense, and right up Matthew's alley. Rebecca had told Matthew her lecture would take until about seven, which gave the guys an hour and a half to explore and hope their presence went unnoticed. "So was this lecture thing for a class?" Derek asked from a bench as Matthew ventured off to snap more pictures.

"I don't think so. She said something to the effect of her school had booked some public speaker, author woman and she was really interested in going. Which is why were are here, waiting." Matthew distractedly replied, too focused on capturing angels and perspectives most people wouldn't think to look for in photography.

"Hmm, so what's this person giving a lecture on anyway?" Alex wondered as he precariously walked along the stone edge of a pond in the courtyard they were currently in.

Matthew pulled his face away from his camera and tried to remember exactly how Rebecca explained it. "Rebecca said she was a woman who had lived through some terrible things, abuse and rape. She now speaks about the healing journey she took and what she learned through those experiences. I think Rebecca is so interested because of the work she's been doing with the campus Women's Center here. Apparently this woman is pretty big in the area of sexual violence and how society kind of encourages and allows it."

"You know," Derek started, "that sounds like something Riana, Lexi and Samantha might be interested in. What with their interest in society and such. Alex, why don't you call Ri and see if she wants to go?"

Riana was giving herself one last check in the mirror before starting when her cell phone began to ring. "What the hell?" she mumbled to herself as she fished her phone out of her bag. "Alex Cell" flashed before her and she couldn't help but smile despite her initial annoyance. "Hey there." she answered as she nestled the phone on her shoulder.

"Well hello." he greeted. Riana could tell he had that contagious grin again.

Riana waited a moment but when Alex didn't continue she asked, "So, what's up?" As much as she enjoyed talking to the boy, she did have some important things to attend to.

"Well, you see… my sister is attending this lecture...thing on her campus at U of C and we thought it might be something you and the girls would be interested in. Something about societal effects on women and the problems of rape and stuff." Riana almost laughed, but stopped herself. "Oh, but wait, you said you had something to go to yourself right? Oh man, I'm sorry." Alex quickly apologized. He had been so excited at having a reason to call Riana again that he had spaced her own prior plans.

"Oh Alex, it's fine. I am doing something, but that was pretty cool of you to think of us, it does sound really interesting." She grinned as she again approached the side of the stage. "It'll be something I'll look into another time."

"Sweet. Well, I'll let you go. We're just going to hang out for a while then take Becca out for dinner. So I'll give you a call later, if that's okay?"

"Of course Alex, that's fine." At the mention of Alex Lexi and Sam gave Ri knowing grins. Riana playfully rolled her eyes and stuck her tongue out at them. "Have a good evening, I'll talk to you later." She turned her phone off after Alex hung up and put it snugly back in her bag before she handed it to Sam. The director of the U of C Women's Center did Riana's introduction and Riana excitedly bounced in her place as she waited to take center stage.

Matthew continued to snap pictures around campus as he, Alex and Derek explored while they waited for Rebecca. Alex and Derek ventured off a bit on their own, afraid to be categorized with "the weird guy taking pictures of things." Instead they chose to talk about Alex's quickly developing friendship with Riana. "So you really like talking to her huh?" Derek questioned. Alex chewed his lip for a moment.

"Well, yeah. I mean, we haven't gotten a chance to really talk much one on one, but she's wonderfully interesting. C'mon D, you were there last night as well." Alex grinned. Derek smiled in response and nodded.

"So, do you think you two will stay in touch after we leave?" D.M.A was only in Chicago for a short stay regarding business. It was a harsh reality that a fair amount of distance was about to separate the new friends.

"I haven't really thought about it, but I suppose it'd be cool." Alex started to wonder if Riana hoped they'd stay in touch as well. It had been a long time since Alex had connected with anyone the way he had with Riana, Lexi and Sam. It was invigorating, exciting and oddly comforting.

As Riana's speech closed she was once again moved by the tear-streaked faces in the audience, the heartbroken souls, and the massive applause thanking her for her time and story. She stayed behind as she typically did after her engagements. She spoke with the workers from the center who worked so tirelessly to get her there. She shook hands and shared hugs, then started her walk outside. As was also typical, she was stopped a few times to chat quietly with people who had similar stories. She took her time to offer them reassurance and optimism for the future. As she ascended the stairs one of the women from the center stopped and called out to a young woman who sat solemnly in a seat by herself, "Rebecca, you okay?" The lady looked up. Long, wavy, dark hair parted way to show a pair of red, swollen and teary eyes. Riana's heart instantly broke. The young woman sniffled, wiped her eyes and nodded.

"Yeah," she started as she cleared her throat. "I'm okay. I'm just so moved." she finished as she stood up, and grabbed her things. She approached Riana and gave a weak smile. Riana smiled softly in return.

"Hi." Riana greeted and offered her hand. The young women looked down at Ri's hand tentatively before she took it.

"Rebecca." the young woman stated simply as she released Riana's hand. "It's so amazing to meet you." Riana often had a hard time with compliments; she didn't find herself amazing. Her experiences were not unique, or rare, she just happened to be one of the few women in the world who had the strength and passion to speak out about it. Riana thanked her anyway. "Your story is so inspiring and so heartbreaking. I can't believe you've gone through all of that and became the woman you are."

"Ah, that's the thing Rebecca. I am the woman I am today *because* of what I've gone through." She smiled just a bit. "It's all about perspective." Rebecca nodded thoughtfully and for a moment she reminded Ri of someone though she couldn't place who. They began their walk to the back of the auditorium and the doors to lead them outside when Lexi and Samantha came up behind Riana. "Well hello kittens." Riana cooed. They smiled and praised Ri on yet another speech done beautifully. Riana looked around to introduce them to Rebecca and the other women from the center but they had gotten ahead of them.

Alex realized the time had come; Rebecca should be finished with her lecture at any minute. "Hey guys, it's time to go get her!" he cackled maniacally as he ran in the direction of the auditorium. They reached the auditorium as a steady stream of people exited. "Damn, guys, how are we supposed to find her in this?"

"Let's just stand back and watch for her, if we don't see her we'll just call her cell." Derek offered as he sat down on the edge of a landscaping wall across from the exit. Alex and Matthew hopped up next to him. The rush of people slowed to a trickle, yet they still hadn't spotted Rebecca. Just as Derek started to pull out his phone to call her she came out with a small group of other women. She looked distraught. Matthew called out to her and her face instantly brightened as she smiled and waved. She turned to her friends to say goodbye then hurried to the guys.

Alex got up and met her halfway, wrapped her in a tight hug and swung her around. "ALEX!"

she squealed and laughed. Alex put her down and grinned.

"Becca, you okay? You look upset." Matthew inquired. He had always been a natural father type.

"Yeah, I'm okay. It was just a hard speech to sit through, but it was amazing." Rebecca continued to tell her two brothers and her surrogate a rough outline of the story she had just listened to. The guys were heartbroken. The issue of sexual violence was no secret, but to sit and hear the gritty details of being repeatedly hurt, even second hand, was difficult.

"Alex!?" a voice shrieked from the auditorium. Alex froze for a second and feared the worst, like a mob of crazy fans. He took a breath and braved the outcome of lifting his eyes to the direction of his name.

"Ri?" he called out when he saw her, Lexi and Samantha come down the steps outside the auditorium. Riana smiled and quickened her pace. "What are you doing here?" Alex exclaimed as he wrapped her in a hug. *A hug? Why did I hug her? It was a reflex I swear!* Alex felt a moment of panic when he realized his mistake but Riana didn't seem to mind as she hugged him tightly and pulled away still beaming. "I thought you had that speaking... engagement..." The pieces came together. "...thing." Alex looked from Riana to Rebecca then back to Riana.

"Alex," Rebecca started, "that's her." Alex looked back to Riana and she gave him a shy smile. It hit him all at once; what Rebecca had told them about this woman, everything she'd been through. He wanted to hug her again. Riana saw the comprehension in Alex's eyes and knew what he was thinking. She took his hands in both of hers.

"Alex, it's okay. I know what you're thinking and it's fine, I'm fine." His eyes were glassy as he fought to keep the tears at bay. He took a deep breath and tried to dry out his tear ducts. He refused to cry in front of her.

"It was amazing Alex, you should have been there. She's amazing." Rebecca gushed.

Riana could see Alex was still processing everything. She attempted to lighten the mood as she gave a smile and a shrug, "Eh, it's what I do." Alex just shook his head in disbelief. His mouth opened slightly as if to say something but he closed it with a soft exhale of air through his nose. Riana admired his features as they stayed locked in each other's gaze. His skin was tan and smooth. His rich, dark eyes were framed by his even, heavy, black eyebrows. The breeze blew his black hair in every direction. Riana felt a smile creep back onto her face and she quickly looked away before she blushed. She looked over to Rebecca, who had overcome her tears, but still looked confused. "So, you're Alex's sister then?" The question shook Rebecca from her thoughts and she grinned.

"I try not to claim him but sometimes he doesn't leave me a choice." Her eyes lit up as she looked at him and laughed.

"Oh, hey, I'm not that bad of a deal when it comes to big brothers. I mean, you could have been left with just Derek or something." he laughed.
Riana said a silent thank you for the change in focus.

The change was short lived though as Rebecca turned back to Riana and implored, "So how do you know Alex?" Alex and Riana looked at each other and laughed. Riana grabbed her vertical labret barbell between her teeth for a moment and thought of how to respond, but Alex beat her to it.

He started with a giggle, "We met after Matt, D, and I overheard her and her two friends over there insulting our fans in a coffee shop downtown." He nodded towards Lexi and Sam who were joking around with Matt and Derek. Riana looked down. She found the ground in front of her boots suddenly intriguing as she tried to will the blush off her face.

Riana heard Rebecca laugh and she quickly lifted her head, determined to defend herself, "There was more to it than that and you know it Alex!" She playfully pushed him. "It's not like that was the main topic of our discussion, it just led there eventually."

Alex raised his hands in defense as his smile grew, his perfectly straight and bright white teeth accentuated. "True, true. But that was the moment I decided to go over there and meet them." Riana tilted her head to the side and gazed at Alex. She had thought it would have been Matthew who would have decided to head over. She wasn't sure why, just an assumption.

Just as she thought of him, Matthew sauntered over with the rest of the crew. Matthew didn't just walk, he definitely sauntered. His lanky six foot frame approached them with a airiness Ri didn't think was possible. "So what about dinner?" Matthew asked as he draped an arm over Rebecca's shoulders.

"Oh man, I'm sorry. I didn't mean to keep you!" Riana stumbled over her words. Alex caught her eyes and without a word or a lift of his perfect lips assured Riana that it was more than okay. She quickly dropped her eyes from his.

"Actually, we were wondering if you'd like to tag along with us." Derek said. "That is, if it's okay with Rebecca." Riana looked at Samantha and Lexi and they smiled excitedly. She then looked to Rebecca, who had a large smile on her face and nodded in agreement.

"Um, sure, that'd be great." Riana conceded, though she still felt a touch guilty for having intruded on their family time. "So, where to?"

They gathered together and moseyed towards the parking lot. Discussion took place as to how to best make it downtown from Hyde Park. Lexi mentioned public transportation would be best with the parking situation downtown; however, the point was made that given the current company, public transportation might be deemed risky. "Time to split up kittens." Riana observed. "I'm driving though!"

she exclaimed while she scampered off to her black Audi A4. Alex was instantly impressed by her taste in cars.

The rest of the group hesitantly stood there for a moment. Alex looked around, afraid to make the first move to ride with Riana. "Hey Matt, can I ride with you?" Samantha asked. "Riana has a tendency to dance around to Motown in her car after speaking engagements." Matthew laughed and accepted the request.

"Motown eh?" Alex smiled. There was his in. "I'm with Riana!" he yelled as he chased after her. Rebecca hollered something to the same effect and trailed after Alex. The split ended up with Alex, Riana and Rebecca in the Audi and Matthew, Derek, Sam and Lexi in the rented Chrysler.

Alex hopped in the front seat as Riana put in a CD, presumably Motown. She looked up and her eyes lit up. "Hi." she grinned. The back door opened and shut and Riana turned around. "Hey." she smiled at Rebecca.

"We heard about the Motown and simply couldn't resist." Alex explained.

"So you think you can handle it?" Riana teased as she revved the engine, turned up the Alpine and shifted into reverse.

CHAPTER FOUR

Why Don't You And I

"I totally knew that was going to happen." Matthew snorted as he pulled up behind Riana's car.

"Knew what was going to happen?" Lexi asked from beside him.

Matthew pointed in front of him. "That!" he laughed. "I knew Alex was going to ride with Riana." He was immensely amused by how excited Alex got when he was around Riana or talked to her.

"Hmm, yeah, I knew too." Samantha agreed from the back seat with Derek. "I think it's cute."

Derek's face revealed resistance. "Yeah, cute until reality hits." he mumbled. Matthew found Derek's eyes in the rearview mirror and questioned him with a raise of his eyebrows. "Alex seems to have forgotten that Kim is back home waiting for him."

"Oh he has not Derek, stop being dramatic." Matthew scolded. "It's okay for him to have female friends you know."

Derek sighed as he contemplated Matt's words. "I guess. I just don't remember ever seeing him quite so...instantly drawn to someone."

"That might be so, but despite noticing a smile on Ri we haven't seen in a long time we know she won't forget about Ryan back home either." Sam commented. "Regardless, I'm happy to see them happy. So," she turned towards Derek with a serious look in her eye, "let's just be happy." It wasn't a suggestion, more a demand. Matthew looked over at Lexi and tried not to chuckle.

Riana led the way downtown and found a parking spot, but she and her comrades didn't exit the car right away. Instead, they continued their hilarious rendition.

Samantha came over to Riana's car and knocked on the window. The whir of the window could barely be heard over the music and their obnoxious singing. The look on the faces of Sam, Matt, Derek and Lexi were priceless. The three in the Audi burst out laughing and exited the car.

"So how long are you guys in Chicago for?" Lexi asked as they awaited their dessert. They had talked endlessly through dinner, with more laughter than most would think possible. Riana couldn't help but feel happier than she'd felt in a long time. It was a perfect ending to a perfect day.

"Three more days I think? Yeah, today is Friday, right?" Riana smiled as Matthew figured out the answer the same way she would; by talking through it aloud to himself.

"We're looking at a local band to work with and possibly sign to our label."

"Ah, very exciting." Samantha grinned. Riana looked into her glass of Asti and silently thought to herself how sad it was they'd be leaving in three days. She glanced up at Alex and he seemed to have an expression that matched her feelings. She tried to smile.

"What about you? Do you all live in Chicago?" Rebecca inquired as she spun her straw in her strawberry lemonade.

"Well, kind of." Riana replied with a small laugh. "I mean, Lexi lives here. I live here part time seeing how my publishing company is here and I have so many meetings with them and my agent. I have a condo about four blocks from here actually. And Sam, well, she's a free spirit who ends up wherever her heart is at the time."

"Which includes a lot of traveling to be by Ri's side for her speaking engagements."

"So, where does that leave you the rest of the time, Ri?" Alex asked.

Riana laughed as she knew the answer would seem contradictory. "You'd never guess it, but when I'm not at my condo here I'm at my ranch in Arizona."

"Downtown Chicago living to a ranch?" Derek exclaimed with a hearty laugh. "You're absolutely right, we wouldn't believe it." He pursed his lips for a moment in thought, "I guess it keeps it balanced though."

"Exactly." Riana grinned as their desserts were finally placed in front of them.

"So Ri, are you staying at your place tonight or mine?" Lexi questioned. Typically Riana would stay at Lexi's after a speaking engagement as it took quite a while for the rush to burn down enough for her to relax.

That night, however, she decided to head back to her place to do some writing. Inspiration came at the oddest times and she had to catch it before it passed in a fleeting moment. "That's fine, Ri. Sam and I can take the El home if you wanted to get going."

"Oh you will not." Matthew declared. "I can take you back, I'm heading that way anyway with bringing Rebecca back to school."

Riana stretched her arms over her head and twisted her neck with a sigh. "Well, with that all taken care of, I do believe I shall get going." she asserted as she stood up. Everyone else followed her lead and gathered their things. Hugs were shared, and smiles danced along faces that hurt from too much laughter.

"Hey Ri?" Alex beckoned from behind her as she reached the large glass door at the front of the restaurant. She turned and smiled at him with her eyes, anxious to see what he might want. "I think I may have left my keys in your car."

"Well then, come on Sparky." Riana laughed. They meandered out of the restaurant and across the street in silence. After she got into the car and searched all the obvious and then not so obvious places Riana started to think the boy had lost his

45

mind. "Alex, I don't see any keys." She looked up and out the back driver's side window and noticed Alex leaned against the car. She twisted herself back out of the car. "There aren't any keys are there, Alex?"

Alex looked down and shuffled a foot, "No."

Riana closed the door and leaned against it next to him. Despite the passing of cars, and the heavy beats of street musicians, there was a soft solitude to the moment as Riana and Alex stood in their own version of silence. "Get in." Riana commanded as she turned around and opened her door. He followed her instruction without question. Riana pulled out and drove down a few blocks and parked her car in the underground parking garage of her building. After she disengaged the ignition Alex turned and looked at her. "Want to go for a walk?" she offered. He nodded.

The garage was still; no air movement to disperse the oppressive scent of exhaust. Their footsteps echoed off the cold, damp cement blocks as they proceeded to the side stairway. Alex pushed opened the heavy steel door and the silence was broken. The bustling sounds of Chicago greeted them. The stale, still air was quickly replaced by warm breezes. Alex and Riana fell into step once on the sidewalk, both of them immersed in their thoughts; a comfortable moment that didn't need words.

"I don't want to go back to New York in three days." Alex finally admitted.

"Can I be honest?" Riana asked. He nodded. "I don't want you to leave in three days either." They walked for a few more steps before she continued. "It's just so surreal. There's something about you, Matt and Derek that feels so familiar, so comfortable. It's rare to find that in anyone, let alone someone of your stature." A small smile danced along Riana's lips.

"Hey now, I'm not the only famous one here." Alex quipped as he nudged Riana with his side. He had known she was brilliant when he overheard her eloquent assertions about society; her book and speaking engagements proved it to the rest of the world.

"Right." she laughed with a small roll of her eyes. "I'm not exactly known the world over and I'm pretty new in my career compared to you. Besides, you weren't a fan of me before we met like I was of you. Makes it just slightly unbelievable." Alex nodded. "I just feel like if you leave so soon, we might lose this odd familiarity."

Alex shook his head quickly, his black locks tossed by the movement and the warm breeze that danced around them. "No we won't." he proclaimed. "I won't let us." Riana blushed as she dropped her head and focused on the dirty, cracked cement before their feet. She knew why she was drawn to him, but she couldn't comprehend why he was so anxious to stay in touch with her. They continued to walk in silence until the shrill ring of Riana's phone shattered the moment. She looked at the screen and knew she couldn't ignore it.

"I'll make this quick." she promised to Alex. "Hello?" she answered as a mixture of pure joy and shielded defense passed over her face. Alex took in the city lights as he tried to provide Riana some privacy for her call. She stayed close by him though, and provided Alex with a perfect one-sided conversation.

"Hey honey." Riana greeted. "It went really well. I had an amazing turnout for an audience." The other person must have asked about her speaking engagement. Alex couldn't help but smile a little as he was reminded of the impact she obviously had on everyone leaving the auditorium. "I guess I lost track of time. We went for dinner afterwards." She looked over at Alex. "Lexi, Sam, Rebecca, Alex, Matthew, Derek and me...just some friends." Riana suddenly halted. "Oh hell Ryan, you can't be serious." Alex also stopped but stayed at a bit of a distance as he sensed a turn in the emotion of the call. "No. It was not a date." Riana barked firmly. "You are so delusional Mr. I Don't Get Jealous." Her eyes turned steely. "Wait, how does this work? You can freak out because I went to dinner with a group of friends and I have to just sit back and be okay with the fact that you go on trips with Nicole lasting two weeks without so much as word from you?"

Riana had always been suspicious of Ryan's relationship with his best friend Nicole but he constantly assured her nothing was going on. It didn't ease any of her concern however. She put up with it, year after year, because she loved him. She was sure she loved him.

Riana sighed angrily as Ryan went on the defensive. "I'm not doing this again Ryan. I refuse. I refuse to ruin my fantastic day with this." She paused again. Alex became increasingly uncomfortable as he watched Riana get more upset. "Yes. Yes, you are ruining it. The man that is supposed to make all my fantastic days that much better is ruining it for me! I don't even know why we're doing this again. Seriously. If you can't trust me I don't see why we're even trying—I do trust you!" she shouted. "I was just simply pointing out that you were blowing a dinner out of proportion when I have been so accepting of your trips with Nicole for the past three years Ryan!"

Riana became silent and Alex noticed tears welled up in her eyes. He decided he couldn't just be a bystander anymore. Alex approached Riana and rested his hand on her shoulder. Riana instantly leaned into him and sighed. "I do love you Ryan, you know that. I've always loved you. I just can't do this right now. I hate fighting with you. Yes, Ryan, we're fighting. I need to not do this right now. I'm going to finish my walk and I'll call you later." Alex rubbed her shoulder and upper arm in silent comfort. Alex heard Ryan say he loved her and a wave of tension washed over him. "I know you do Ryan, I'll call you soon." She ended the call then turned her whole body towards Alex and fell into his embrace. He didn't dare ask about it.

Riana couldn't decide, as she felt Alex's arms around her, if the call from Ryan was the last thing she needed or the one thing she needed. The last as it ruined her wonderful day, but perhaps the best thing because it broke the undeniable draw she felt for Alex. Of course, the sensation of Alex's strong arms as they held her tightly to his chest as the breeze wrapped itself around and through her hair didn't curb that uncontrollable feeling any.

Riana took a slow, deep breath and found she trembled as emotion coursed through her veins from Ryan's venomous words. She also found that Alex smelt delicious.

Riana pulled away from Alex and looked up at him. His eyes were warm and caring despite the fierceness of his features. Riana looked back down to prevent herself from saying or doing something she wasn't sure she'd regret.

They resumed their walk without a word. Riana felt the need to explain, though if she had learned anything from the past three years with Ryan it was that there was no explanation anyone could understand when it came to their relationship. It had been volatile from the very beginning. She tried anyway, "He's not usually such a jerk." Alex nodded silently. "I don't know," she sighed. "I think the time apart strains the relationship. But really, I don't see how he finds the right to freak out on me as I've only been touring with my speaking engagements for a year, and he...well he's had a habit of disappearing out of my life a lot for the two years before that." Alex's heavy black eyebrows furrowed together, he couldn't quite understand. Why would Riana stay with someone so flaky, why would anyone disappear on her and then just expect her to be there when he returned? "Sometimes I think he deserves to be worried and jealous. I had to deal with those feelings too often. It's his turn." she decided with an angry pout. She sighed and leaned into Alex again. He wrapped his arm back around her.

"I can't say I completely understand as I know nothing about this guy or your relationship with him but I do understand how being away from your partner can strain the relationship. Kim and I deal with that a lot too." Riana scolded herself for not remembering Kim sooner. Alex and Kim had been together for almost five years. She was soft spoken, sweet, and always incredibly friendly to the fans. "Sometimes," Alex continued "it's like no matter how much you love them, when they get into that place where all they need is to be with you, nothing but you actually being there will make it better." Riana nodded against him. "Then when you can't... well then you feel terrible that they're angry, lonely and insecure. Of course, if they continue to push it, then the roles reverse and you're the one that's angry they can't simply understand how important it is you're away from them at that moment to do something that could potentially make your lives together better."

"Hmm, at least I'm not the only one struggling with this kind of set up." Riana observed. Alex agreed softly. They headed east, towards Lake Michigan on Monroe Street. Riana glanced down and smiled when she noticed their steps were in sync.

"Hey!" Alex's excited tone startled Riana out of her trance-like state and she looked up at him quickly. "Let's go for a carriage ride!" His giddiness was adorable and even though Riana had done the carriage ride through downtown before, she couldn't help but share in his excitement as she agreed. Alex reached down and grabbed Riana's hand as he took off in a light jog across Millennium Park over to the horses. Riana shook her head and laughed as she struggled to keep up with him.

Alex slowed as they approached the line of carriages. He made soft, contemplative hums as he examined each horse. Riana cocked her head to the side as she watched him. He finally stopped by a black Arabian Quarter cross. Riana watched quietly as he deliberately reached up and brushed the long black hair away from the horse's huge, dark eyes. "I like this one." The horse reached his head forward and sniffed Alex's sweatshirt.

"I think he likes you too."

"Then it's settled. He shall take us around downtown." Alex asserted firmly with a quick nod. He turned to smile at Riana and she, too, nodded in agreement. "Now, what's the proper way to do this?" he questioned. "Do I get in first and help you up or stand by and lend you my hand?" Riana laughed quickly, but when she saw how serious he was she wished she could have prevented the laugh that had escaped her.

"Sorry." she deplored with a quick scrunch of her nose. "How about, you get in first and I'll follow?"

During the hour and a half ride around downtown Riana and Alex talked endlessly. "I just can't believe you were able to turn so much torment into something so...powerful." Alex expressed as Riana dug deep to give him the raw story of her past and how she came to be an author and speaker about it.

"I guess I had no choice. I'm not exactly the type to stand idly by and let outside events dictate my life journey." She thoughtfully chewed her vertical labret. "From the very beginning I fought it all, but in different ways. First I fought him, I fought the legal system, then I fought to be normal. Just when I thought life could move on I had to fight the second, I fought to heal, then I fought for other victims. Now I use my drive to fight for those who haven't experienced assaults, but are immersed in the hidden rape culture of our society that makes such disgusting things possible. I fight to educate. I was truly blessed with an ability to articulate things well, explain things in a way that people get it, and blessed to personally connect with people. I couldn't let that go to waste." She looked over at Alex and grinned. "Much like you didn't let your God-given musical talent go to waste." She winked.

Alex was thankful for his dark skin again as a slight blush warmed his cheeks. He questioned what it was about her that flustered him so much. "Oh, not even a close comparison." Alex reached his arm up and behind Riana to pull her into him. "I didn't need to go through such a personal hell."

"Ah, well, life goes on." Riana murmured modestly. "And hey! I've *met* your fans. I'd venture to say that dealing with them could very well qualify as a personal hell." she looked up at him and giggled.

Alex laughed deeply next to her. "Touché, my dear."

Matthew glanced at the clock in the bottom right corner of his laptop screen and sighed when he saw it was already 1:15am. Alex had been with Riana for over four hours. He hadn't called, and Matthew didn't want it to appear like he was checking up on him by calling, but he couldn't help but wonder what they were up to. He knew Alex would never cheat on Kim, but he could also see something between him and Riana that placed a small whisper of doubt in his heart.

Just as he pulled his phone from his pocket he heard the hotel door open. "Well hi." Matthew greeted as he turned his head over the back of the couch.

Alex gave him a goofy grin as he flopped down next to him. "What are you doing up so late?" Alex asked.

"Oh, not much, watching movies, surfing the web, you know, the usual." Matthew quickly rambled.

"Ah. Waiting up for me." Alex laughed.

"I...certainly was...not." Matthew defended. As their eyes met they both laughed. They knew the truth. "Yeah, okay, fine. So what did you and Ri end up doing for four hours?"

Alex's face softened and he smiled. "We took a carriage ride around the city, talked, got ice cream, talked, walked around, talked. We did a lot of talking." he laughed. "We are most definitely keeping in touch after we leave."

Matthew smiled back at him as he got up and patted his shoulder. "Good."

CHAPTER FIVE

Where'd You Go

Sunday May 28, 2006

It was D.M.A.'s last day in Chicago and Alex wasn't faring well with it. He should have been happy to head home, Kim was going to visit him in New York that upcoming weekend, but he had become so sucked into Riana's story, life and spirit he had a hard time imagining not being surrounded by her energy. "She is coming right?" Derek asked as they waited for Riana to meet them for lunch. They picked the historical Atwood Cafe as it was placed strategically in the middle of downtown, with plenty of opportunity to people watch.

"Of course she's coming, D. She just called Alex and said she'd be here in about five minutes. Order another drink and relax." Matthew advised with a slightly annoyed sigh. Alex kept his eye down the street and watched for Riana. As he saw her round the corner he couldn't help but light up. "Ah, see, she must be coming." Matthew laughed as he quickly noticed Alex's change in appearance. Alex couldn't help but laugh as Riana shuffled her foot back into her heel after it slipped off as she tried to run. She looked up towards the cafe and she, too, lit up. Riana continued a half jog until she was about ten feet away, her face was flushed and her forehead was dotted with bits of perspiration. She pursed her lips and let go of a heavy breath.

"I. Am. So. Sorry." she huffed as she reached the table. Derek was the first one out of his chair to wrap her quickly in his arms.

"No problem lady." Matt assured as Riana was passed to him.

"I may not have known you for long dear, but, I think you may have a problem with punctuality." Alex teased as she finally fell into his hug. He laughed deeply as she sighed against him.

"You sir, are right." she confirmed as she pulled a seat out and took her place between Alex and Derek. Riana knew it was selfish to feel the way she did, but she didn't want the guys to leave yet. It'd been so long since she'd connected with anyone the way she'd connected with all of them; especially Alex. She spun her vertical labret ring around as she churned everything in her head.

She half listened to Derek and Matthew carry on about hitting the studio when they got back to New York. She glanced over at Alex. His strong chin rested in the palm of his hand as he watched his bandmates. Riana reminded herself of boundaries and the fact both she and Alex were quite seriously involved with other people. He was beautiful though.

"So when does your book tour start?" Derek shook Riana from her daydreaming. "Maybe we'll intersect again." Riana grinned brightly at the idea of being able to see them while she was on her own tour.

"The plan right now is to hit the road in eighteen days." She raised her eyebrows in mock nervousness. The truth was, she was dying to get on the road.

"Pretty sure the world won't know what hit them." Matt laughed as his blue eyes squinted against the sun beams that broke through the skyscrapers.

"Exactly." Riana winked as she took another sip of her iced tea. "So you guys will be recording for a while then? Should I call when I'm heading to New York?"

Alex turned to look at her, with an exaggerated look of offense on his face. "Um, of course!" Riana grinned around the straw in her mouth, happy to know it was expected of her to let them know if she was ever nearby.

Tuesday July 18, 2006

As Riana attempted to pack her suitcase in her hotel room in Philadelphia she heard an all too familiar ring come from her cell phone on the dresser. She stuck her tongue out at the misbehaving suitcase and hopped over to pick up the phone. "Hey Alex." she greeted happily.

Riana had been on the road for five weeks. She worked her way from the west coast to the east coast. She had hoped to start east and work west so she could stop and see the guys right away. The tour had been amazing. She met so many wonderful, inspirational women—and men. She knew she was finally on her way to change the world.

Alex made sure to call her fairly often, every other day or so. Sometimes, when she was lucky, she'd get to talk to Matthew and Derek. She had decided early on that Alex was a bit of a Riana hoarder.

Things between Riana and Ryan had unfortunately gotten worse since she started the tour. It helped her immensely to be able to talk to Alex about it. Lexi and Samantha were over-protective of Riana and held a lot of resentment towards Ryan. Alex, though, listened to Riana intently, kept any negative opinions to himself, and supported her in how she felt. It helped tremendously that he could relate to so many of the issues she faced with Ryan.

"Hey lady, what are you up to?" Riana loved Alex's voice. His deep and happy voice.

She groaned, "I'm attempting to convince my suitcase that yes, all my belongings will fit in there. He apparently doesn't want to listen to me."

"He?" Alex questioned with a full laugh. Riana knew he was probably sitting somewhere, shaking his head at her.

"Of course!" she exclaimed. "It couldn't possibly be female, a female would never give me so much attitude!" The way Alex made Riana laugh was more genuine than most of her laughter; rivaled only by laughter shared with Lexi and Samantha. He brought laughter out of her that siphoned the joy of life from all around and inside her and allowed it to burst through.

They continued to chat about her tour and how things were going in the studio with D.M.A.; all the while Riana was distracted by the frustration of figuring out the physics of packing. Surely if it all fit on her way to Philly it should fit on her way out of Philly. "So, next stop is New York. You guys going to be around to catch dinner?"

"Absolutely!" Alex boasted without any attempt to disguise his enthusiasm. "I kept Thursday open for you."

"Oh, how nice of you." Riana teased. "Will Matt and D be keeping their schedule open as well?" She twisted and wrapped two shirts together and barely squeezed them into a tiny corner of the suitcase as she precariously dragged the zipper across the tight seams. "A ha! You little bastard!"

"Riana!?" Alex's voice called out in bewilderment.

"Sorry Alex, I just conquered the suitcase."

Alex laughed whole-heartedly at her. "You are the best. I can't wait to see you Thursday."

Thursday July 20, 2006

The time that passed between when Alex got off the phone and when he got ready to meet Riana for dinner went painfully slow. Even at times when he was sure the time had to have flown by, he would find the clock seemed to have gone backwards.

Derek kept a watchful eye on him and never allowed Alex to forget about Kim. Alex couldn't understand; he could never forget about Kim. He loved her, she'd been with him through so much. It wasn't that Alex was losing sight of his love for Kim, it was that Riana brought a light to him; a craziness and a joy he thought he had lost.

Alex knew it was rare to find friends who understood their crazy schedules and lives. So for them to have found Riana, someone with her own crazy schedule; their natural friendship couldn't be passed up. Their conversation the second night in Chicago summed it up well; sometimes other people just don't understand they simply couldn't be there. Riana and Alex both understood phone calls, texts and online chats had to be enough when it wasn't possible to physically be there. What saddened Alex was the man Riana loved didn't seem to understand the dynamics of such a hectic schedule. She put up with so much from him, she always took what little he gave to her but the moment she wasn't able to give him everything he expected, all hell broke loose.

"Come on, seriously, let's go!" Alex yelled down the hall to Matthew who was deep in his diva ways, getting ready for dinner. Often times Matthew was worse than a high maintenance woman when it came to getting ready.

"Calm down Alex," Matthew muttered nonchalantly as he strolled down the hall. "I mean seriously, we don't have to be there until--" he glanced down at his watch as he entered the living room. "Shit, we have almost ten minutes to get there."

Alex's eyes grew large and indignant. "Like I said!" he yelled as he grabbed his keys from the granite countertop in the kitchen and stormed out of the condo.

Riana took another sip of her Asti and glanced at her watch. She pursed her lips in worry. "Relax sweetie, they'll be here." Lexi assured as she patted Riana's leg.

Lexi, as a freelance editor, had freedom most people only dreamed of. It provided her with opportunities to travel with Riana, volunteer with organizations close to her heart and pursue passions that would otherwise be unobtainable. Riana hadn't told Alex that Lexi would join them, she loved surprises and thought it might qualify as a good one.

As Riana went to take another sip she heard them, "I swear Matt, if she left because we're late, I'm kicking your ass." Riana smiled, stood up and went to meet them in the middle.

"Now, now, no need for violence kittens." she teased. All three of them lit up as they saw her. She was all business in her flattering yet professional pants suit with sequin tank under a modern cut black blazer. She gasped for air as she was suddenly wrapped in an Alex sized bear hug. She sighed when she found he smelt more delicious than she remembered. "Hey buddy." she mumbled against his chest; that strong, warm, comfortable chest. She quickly chastised herself, the only man she should find delicious and comfortable was Ryan. Alex released her and she turned to Matt and Derek. She felt love in each of their embraces. "I've missed you guys."

"Us too." Derek echoed as Riana led the three of them back to the table where Lexi waited. Everyone else's dinner was quickly interrupted when Derek shouted out in surprise when he saw Lexi. Riana looked around with a smile and a touch of embarrassment when she saw annoyance on the faces of other patrons. She quickly ushered the guys to their seats.

Seeing Riana and Lexi together was an absolute joy for the guys. They created their own little world between them, those lucky enough to be invited in like Matt, Derek, and Alex got to experience joy and happiness that stood the test of time. They were beautiful together; Riana and Lexi. Their friendship and love brought a light to them that could only be created through authenticity. They found joy in each other, comfort in each other's understanding, and hope in each other's dreams. They'd always been there for each other, no matter what. That kind of devotion couldn't be falsified and it was inspiring to witness.

Riana enthusiastically told them about the book tour, mostly of the people. Anyone could see when it came to what she did, it had nothing to do with her, it was all about the people she could touch with her story. There was a distinct sense of selflessness to her; she didn't care if she made money off any of her books or speaking engagements. If she could help bring peace, hope, or comfort to anyone that's what she'd do for the rest of her life. Alex's admiration for her grew immensely as he listened to her, and watched her. She beamed with pride, not in herself though, for the people who she had helped to find their voice; the people whose first time breaking their silence was to her.

"I can't believe we did it again!" Lexi laughed. Derek looked around and realized the place was practically empty. Alex looked down at his watch and realized once again, they had talked all the way to closing. Some things never seemed to change. That was the thing with people like them, with crazy lives and schedules, they couldn't seem to break away from the moments in which they truly felt understood and appreciated.

Alex draped his arm over Riana as they walked out and into the thick summer air of New York City. "So how long until you think we'll cross paths again?" she asked.

"That depends." Alex replied simply. She looked up at him with her brow wrinkled. "How much longer are you here?"

"Saturday. I planned for a slightly longer stay here." she grinned proudly.

"Hmm." Alex pursed his lips and feigned contemplation. He didn't have to think about anything specific, he just enjoyed making her wait. "Would you and Lexi like to come by the studio tomorrow and watch some magic happen?" He winked with a wiggle of his heavy, yet beautiful, black brows.

Lexi giggled beside them as they stood on the sidewalk. "Oh you are dirty!" Riana squealed with a playful swat to Lexi's arm. She turned her attention back to Alex. "Yeah, we'll come watch some magic making goodness. Give me a call tomorrow."

Alex began to wonder, as he laid in bed that night if maybe Derek did have reason to keep a cautious eye on him. He couldn't escape the thought of Riana; her smile, her laugh, her passion, or her sweet scent. He thought maybe it was because it was new and exciting, or maybe because he hadn't seen her in so long. However, there was a quiet murmur of something beneath the friendship. Alex vowed not to mess it up, not his friendship with her, Lexi, or Sam. He definitely didn't want to ruin things with Kim. He was lucky to find someone he could relate to so well, and felt comfortable with. He would do whatever he could to keep it, without messing everything else up in his life.

Friday July 21, 2006

Riana pulled into the lot of the building D.M.A's recording studio was in and Lexi shook her head in disbelief. "Seriously Ri, how many times did we dream of being exactly where we are right now?"

Riana looked up at the imposing building and laughed lightly. "Oh, I don't know, about a hundred times a day for at least three years straight." She found Lexi's eyes and smiled. "I'll tell you though, it's better than I ever imagined. You know how sometimes you build something up in your mind, or expect people to be a certain way and then you're inevitably let down?" Lexi nodded. "So not what happened with these guys."

As they entered the building and stepped into the elevator Riana checked her text messages quickly to find out exactly where they were heading. "Alright, so apparently if the red light is on above the door we're to just wait a minute." They exited the elevator and anxiously walked down the rich blue hallway that was decorated with pictures and records of musicians past and present.

They found room 653 and noticed the red light was indeed on. Lexi also noticed Riana grasped her labret anxiously. "I'll shoot Matt a message and let him know we're here." Lexi offered. Riana nodded. Before she got a response back the light was off and the door was swung open. Matt greeted them in all his beautiful splendor. His smile was bright, and it accented the slight crow's feet at the corner of his blue eyes.

"Hey!" he greeted happily. "Come in. D was just finishing up." He wrapped his arm around Riana as they entered and she gave him a tight side hug. D.M.A. had always been very open to sharing their studio experiences with fans via live streams, but being able to fully experience the studio gave those streams no justice. From the lighting to the faint scent of incense, there truly was something "magical" about it. Lexi and Riana attempted to take in as much as they could; the art on the walls, the scraps of paper littered about with lyrics and sketches on them, the endless coffee cups and the overstuffed furniture.

"This is pretty sweet." Riana commented as she plopped down in one of the overstuffed armchairs. She continued to scan the room, then unconsciously pursed her lips.

"He's getting snacks." Matthew stated as he noticed the musing on Riana's face. She blushed as she felt exposed by her less than discreet search for Alex.

Derek entered the main area of the studio from the recording section, oblivious to their guests as he stared down at his guitar. "I don't know Matt, seemed there was something missing. It should have a heavier groove or something..." he trailed off then finally looked up to find Riana and Lexi. "Ladies."

he commented as he gestured a grand bow. Lexi laughed and tipped her head towards him, thankful he was just as amusing in day to day life as he was for his fans.

CHAPTER SIX

Speed Of Sound

"Damn, Alex sure is taking his sweet time isn't he?" Matthew observed after he and Derek had shown Riana and Lexi around a bit. "Ri, you want to come with me to look for him? Maybe we'll stop and make sure we have enough coffee and other drinks to go with the snacks he brings." Riana smiled, Matthew and his coffee. She forced herself out of the comfortable suction of her chair. She gave one last grunt, stood up and laughed. "That chair is evil you know." Matt teased with a chuckle.

"I see that now." Riana eyed the chair suspiciously. "Lexi, you cool to hang with D?" She knew the answer, but liked to poke a little fun every now and then.

"Of course she is." Derek answered before Lexi could.

Matthew opened the door and placed his hand on Riana's lower back as he escorted her through. Something had endlessly ate at him ever since their first night in Chicago. He figured this might be his only chance to get Riana alone, he knew once Alex got back she'd be all his.

She was so familiar to him that night in the coffee shop; a comfort he felt he'd known forever. He couldn't imagine it could be her, but the more he thought about it, the more it all clicked. The similarities between what he knew for certain was Riana's story and the stories he'd been told nine years prior were too much to ignore. And her eyes; Matthew felt he'd know those eyes anywhere.

"So you've been a fan for quite a while huh?" he asked impassively.

"Oh yeah, for sure." she smiled. Matthew couldn't help but grin at her undeniable Minnesotan accent. He knew there wouldn't be many Riana Grahams out there, but it was imperative he knew for certain.

"Since you were about fourteen, right?" Her eyes quickly shot over to Matt and her footing faltered for a second, but she recovered quickly.

"Assuming I was an original fan I see." she teased. She silently hoped he wasn't leading into what she feared he was. Despite her smile there was deep apprehension behind her blue eyes.

Matthew chuckled a bit in an attempt to ease the uneasiness that lurked in her eyes, "Well I was hoping!"

Riana settled back into her stroll as they journeyed to the main level of the building to where a small shop was located. "Yeah, I'm an original." She didn't meet Matthew's eyes so he figured he'd take a deep breath and jump right into it.

"Those were some crazy years back then. Crazy fans. Sometimes, it was hard for us to find some resemblance of predictability, stability, or comfort." He saw Riana nod but she continued to avoid his eyes. "The guys helped of course, but I had something else for a little while too--"

"Oh Matthew, don't tell me the drug rumors were true!" she taunted playfully.

"No," he laughed and nudged his shoulder into her. "I had this girl who wrote to me, like all the time. Only it wasn't typical fan mail. She didn't go on and on about how much she loved me or how she made her parents take her to ten of the shows on the last tour. She told me about her family, her dog, school, friends. She was funny and smart..." Riana didn't look at Matthew or say anything so he quickly rambled on. "She was so alone though, lost and struggling. I never knew what to say to her, so I never wrote back. I always made sure to get her letters and packages though, somehow hoping she'd know or feel someone was listening to her. She was a genuine person, loving, compassionate, spunky though too." Matthew smiled as he remembered the words that brought him into her world, her pain, her love, and her humor. Her letters were filled with life. "I still have this thing she gave me, years and years ago..."

He anxiously reached into his pocket, "It's crazy; as it hasn't fit in years," he saw Riana's eyes flick over to what was within his hand and heard a quiet, quick intake of breath and it seemed his suspicions were confirmed. "but I still keep it with me, hoping she found her way, that she was able to embrace her life, find friendship, love and strength. She stopped writing after about three years or so."

He trailed off and Riana finally turned towards him with tears in her eyes. "I'm so sorry I never wrote you back, Ri." She couldn't hold them back. She choked on ragged breaths and tears fell as she threw herself into Matthew's embrace. "I'm so sorry." he whispered again. Matthew felt his own tears break through as he let go of pain he had held on to for her. They held on to each other through a long and intense moment. He smoothed Riana's hair down as she buried her face in his chest as sobs continued to heave from her. Bystanders and patrons gawked at their tumultuous moment. They had searched for that moment for almost a decade though, they were unconcerned with anyone's judgments.

Finally, Matthew felt Riana take a deep breath and she pulled back to look at him. She wiped tears from her face. He grabbed her wrists and brought her hands down between them. He opened one of her hands and placed the red and black beaded necklace she made him when he turned fifteen into it. "I don't need to carry this with me anymore now that I know you're okay. That you found your way, and your strength." She lost the battle against more heart wrenching sobs; they broke through as she closed her hand around the necklace and nodded. "I think I knew, deep within me it was you that first night. People change over the years, but your eyes, your smile and your soul were all so familiar." The fact was, he was pretty sure it had been her over the years at concerts, glimpses of her he wanted to believe were real; moments that passed by too quickly to be caught.

"I could never prove you read my letters, but you're absolutely right, somehow I did feel I was being heard." Riana sniffled and wiped the remnants of tears from her face. "And then, when I saw this on you," she paused as she ran her fingers along the beads she had put together so many years ago. "even then I didn't know for sure you were reading them, but I sure had hoped you were." She smiled softly as she looked up at Matt. "The moment I saw you wearing it... It broke a depression I thought would never end. Seems dramatic I know, but I was sixteen, it was one of the biggest moments of my life at that point." she admitted, then laughed a bit. She grasped her vertical labret ring under her teeth and churned the moment over in her mind.

"Life plays out in mysterious ways, Ri." Matt maintained as he gazed at her. He felt terrible for having made her cry, but he was relieved to know it was definitely her. "I'm just... I'm so happy our paths finally crossed. It's my fault they didn't cross sooner--"

Riana quickly shook her head in disagreement and cut him off. "No. No, Matthew, our paths crossed exactly when they were supposed to. I needed to go through every atrocious thing I did to get where I am now, and you... you needed to find your way too. I needed that outlet for those three years, to write to someone without ever actually receiving a response. I needed to put the words out there and not get judgment, pity--anything in return." Matthew admired her wisdom. "Everyone plays a role. I gave you a resemblance of predictability and you gave me a muse and comfort in the words I envisioned were written for me--or people like me; struggling and feeling alone. You, Derek and Alex gave me laughter and joy. And a dream that life could be better than the one I was living." Matthew pulled her into his arms again.

"Now you don't need to dream, right? So many things have worked out for you." he asked as his chin rested on the crown of her head.

She pulled back from his embrace. "Life is definitely better than a dream now. Between finding true friendships, a career I love, a healing I worried would never come, and now this," she motioned around her and smiled at him. "life is definitely good."

Matthew turned and placed his arm back over Riana's shoulders. "So, what do you say about those drinks?" Riana laughed and made sure there were no final traces of her tears.

As Alex pulled into the parking lot, he realized one of the unfortunate things about Riana being on tour was he had no idea what she might be driving; therefore he had no way to scan the lot to see if she and Lexi had arrived yet. He exited his car, proceeded to gather the bags upon bags of snacks then tried desperately not to drop them all as he shuffled to the building. He was thankful to see the light above the door wasn't on so at least he wouldn't have to stand there and continue his balancing act as he waited. He chewed his lip as he reached two fingers out to grasp the doorknob then thrust his foot inside the few inch gap. "You know, it would have been really helpful if, oh I don't know, someone would have come with me." he grumbled as he stumbled through the door, still careful not to drop anything.

"Oh, but then who would have been here to greet us when we arrived?" Lexi teased as she lifted herself from the overstuffed couch. Alex couldn't stop the full grin that crossed his face, no matter how ungodly awkward the bags were in his arms. Lexi came up next to him and grabbed a couple from his embrace.

"Thanks dear." Alex gushed as he dropped the last couple bags on the table then threw his arms around her. "How'd that track for 'title pending' lay down, D?" he asked as he sank into the overstuffed chair next to the mixing board. Unlike Riana, he was well aware of the firm grasp the chair would soon have on him and he settled in happily.

"I don't know man, it's good, but it's missing just a little something." Derek grumbled as he sat on the arm of Alex's chair and plinked the guitar strings.

"Wait! Derek, that's it!" Lexi shouted from across the room where she explored the abundance of snacks. She turned away, with a bag of peanuts in her hand and hurried to the guys. "Do that again." Derek twisted his lip a bit, thought back to what he had just done and gave his guitar another groovy tweak. "Ah, yes, it's perfect! Get in there and lay that down right at the beginning." Lexi pulled him off the arm of the chair and practically pushed him through the door to the recording area. Derek shook his head and laughed. He did as he was told and went in to lay Lexi's brilliant new idea down.

"Nice, Lex, very nice." Alex complimented as he forced himself out of the chair to man the mixing board.

Riana remained stunned from her moment with Matthew. There were no words to describe the overwhelming amount, and kinds, of emotions that engulfed her whole soul after he put the pieces together and broke her down. She probably would have ventured it brought her back to being a teenager; to when she felt so alone, and yearned for some connection to keep her going. There it was, that something. Someone who kept her going without knowing. Riana had thought she was an insignificant young woman nine years ago, but she had been immensely significant to him. It created a spine-tingling sensation within her.

She ran the beaded necklace through her fingers and smiled to herself as she and Matthew approached the studio door. "He better be back by now, I'm positively wasting away." he proclaimed dramatically.

Riana giggled at him and pushed him through the door. "You have got to be one of the most dramatic queens I have ever met." Riana taunted. She was greeted by a deep belly laugh as they entered.

There was Alex, his finger pointed at Matthew as he caught his breath through his laughter. "A queen!" He leaned over with his hands on his knees. "Oh dammit I wish I had that one on video!" Riana stood by the door and grinned at both of them. The dynamic between the two was relentless, but it was easy to see they wouldn't have it any other way. Alex finally gathered himself, looked up and met Riana's eyes. His deep, chocolate eyes held her there for a moment. The rest of the room faded into the background. Riana felt a flutter, a paused moment in her breath. She exhaled slowly and reminded herself to keep everything in check.

"Hey sweetheart." Alex purred just barely over a whisper as he ambled to Riana. Her eyes softened as her mind screamed out, *So not helping Alexander!* She smiled up at him, laid her head on his chest and wrapped her arms around him.

Riana couldn't halt the deep breath she drew in through her nose. She hoped to permanently imprint his scent into her brain. "So you ready to make some magic?" Alex wiggled his eyebrows at her. She mentally shook her head; *nope, no making magic. Not that kind of magic anyway.*

"You gonna show me what you got?" Riana provoked then mentally questioned why she felt the need to torture herself.

"I have skills you wouldn't believe." Alex's eyes turned the slightest bit steamy as he gazed down at Riana. She felt a flush run up her chest and neck, and she tried hopelessly to keep it from reaching her cheeks. Alex turned away from her and hollered, "MORE COWBELL!" Riana released a deep breath. *Too close.*

Alex took a seat at the keyboard, with a snare and a cymbal next to it and began to tinker. "Ah, Alex, the one man band." Derek laughed next to Riana.

"Impressive" she smiled.

Finally in a place where the hours didn't matter, they completely lost track of time. When the guys jammed together Lexi and Riana simply watched and relished being able to witness something indeed magical. Some favorite moments were when they'd have a nice melody in their heads but no words, so they would sing it out note wise and play with words. Some of which were totally ridiculous. Riana and Lexi were amazed as they watched a song unfold from the beginning. There was plenty of banter back and forth, teasing and laughter. There was a delicate balance of intense creative work and goofy, offbeat moments that brought Lexi and Riana to the brink of tears.

Late in the night Alex started to play on the piano with a tattered notebook by his side. The lyrics barely passed his lips but Riana was intimately aware of the underlying message. "She waits on the sideline...Just waiting...to be played....Pleading, breaking....Why won't he call?...Pleading, breaking....She needs it all." Riana watched Alex's eyes flick over to her and she nervously grabbed her vertical labret between her teeth and thought surely it wasn't as personal as it felt. "He won't give in...She stays...He can't love...She stays. ...She waits on the sideline." She pleaded with her eyes to Alex. She didn't want to think about it.

Alex didn't often voice his opinions of Ryan to Riana, as he knew she needed to come to terms on her own, but of course it didn't mean he didn't *have* opinions. Alex figured if he couldn't say it directly to her for fear of causing some form of rift between them, surely he could put it to music. The song was rough, but when he noticed the look of panic on Riana's face and the death grip she had on that piercing of hers; that sweet, feminine piercing that drew attention to her pouty lips, he knew that she knew. He frowned slightly when he saw her, his intention was not to make her feel badly. He only wished to get it out somehow; the deep annoyance he felt towards him. Along with the fact he knew if Ryan didn't shape up and treat Riana the way she deserved, someone would come and show her what she was missing. Someone would show her what it was like to feel valued, loved and special. Ryan certainly didn't make her feel that way. Riana felt lost and used when it came to him. She frequently called Alex, upset and confused. Alex despised how Ryan effectively crushed her time and time again.

Despite how badly she wanted to continue to watch the magic happen, Riana's eyes grew heavy and her vision blurred. She found comfort in the softness of the overstuffed chair and, without realizing, slipped into sleep. Alex came out of recording to find her there, curled up like a cat. He smiled softly at her sleeping form. "She really didn't mean to fall asleep." Lexi whispered.

"Oh, I know." Alex turned towards Lexi. She had been going over lyrics with Derek on the couch. "She's been so busy, we probably should have known better than to keep her so late."

"Nah, this is exactly how Ri would have wanted this night to end." Lexi laughed as she handed Derek's notebook back to him, got up and stretched. "I'll drive the car back to the hotel, but um, could you maybe *get* her to the car for me?"

Alex looked down at Riana again. "But then how will you get her to the room?" he pondered. "How about I get her to my car, follow you to the hotel and get her to bed?" Alex quickly saw the look on Derek's face, but knew he wouldn't actually say anything. Alex also saw Matt shoot Derek a quick, stern look.

"Yeah, I don't think we should force her to wake up just to get her to the place where she can go to sleep. Seems counterproductive." Matt commented. "We'll see you when you get back home." Alex gave Matt a small smile, then gazed back down at Riana. She looked younger, and incredibly sweet curled up with her hair wisped across her forehead and cheek. Alex squatted down and slipped his arms under her knees and her shoulders then pulled her to his chest as he stood back up. Riana gave a slight murmur as she snuggled into Alex's chest. He became acutely aware of how heavily his heart pounded and wondered if she could feel it too. He took a deep breath and reminded himself, again, to shove anything deep beneath the surface. He left Derek and Matthew in the studio as he followed Lexi out to the parking lot.

"This was such a wonderful day Alex, thank you again so much for inviting us." Lexi gushed as she walked along with Alex. "I know Riana loved every minute of it too." She grinned at Ri nestled securely in Alex's arms. Alex, too, gazed down at her.

"My pleasure, Lex." he assured as they got to his car. Lexi quickly unlocked the doors and opened the passenger side for him. Alex gently placed Riana in the seat and reached across her to do her seatbelt. Riana took a deep breath, attempted to burrow into the seat as she turned her body toward the center console. Alex backed out slowly and closed the door as quietly as he could. He watched the dome light dim over her. It left her illuminated only by the yellow lights scattered through the parking lot. He turned back to Lexi. She had an odd smile on her face. "What?" Alex asked as he nervously looked anywhere but her eyes.

"Nothing." She grinned. "It's just surreal you know?" She paused. "Yet, it seems so completely normal." Alex nodded.

"I know what you mean. Don't let D fool you though, he's far from normal." he teased. Lexi laughed and playfully pushed Alex.

She thoughtfully licked her lips and narrowed her eyes on Alex, "Say Alex?" She wrinkled her brow and contemplated how to continue. "That song, you know the one when you were at the piano, something about waiting on the sideline?" Alex's eyes grew a bit wider. It appeared he couldn't hide his feelings in his music as well as he thought he could.

"Uh huh." he grunted without commitment. He urged Lexi on without meeting her eyes.

"You had some special inspiration for that one, didn't you?" She knew the answer, it seemed frivolous to Alex to even ask. "I hate Ryan too." she declared quickly before he could answer the question.

"I don't even know him." Alex interjected shortly. He leaned back against the car and looked up, past the yellow light and attempted to find a star or two.

Lexi snorted a bit. "You aren't missing much." She twisted up her mouth. "It might be true that you don't know him, but you know how he treats Ri. That alone is reason enough to hate him. You're new you know? You've seen it for all of two months. Unfortunately, Sam and I have seen it for years." She frowned and sighed. "She'll be so close to finally walking away and somehow he always sucks her back in. She's totally deluded. She's not real with him, not herself you know?" Alex nodded though he really couldn't say one way or the other as he'd never seen them together. "She holds her tongue a lot around him--"

"Riana can hold her tongue?" Alex laughed quickly.

"Exactly!" Lexi exclaimed with a chuckle. "But it's true, she's not genuine and I try to tell her he can't truly love her if she doesn't show him who she really is." She paused and locked her eyes on Alex. "She's herself with you." his eyes shot up to hers and she swiftly added on, "And Derek and Matthew." Alex nodded. They stood in silence for a long moment. "Well, should we get the princess to bed?"

"We shall." he laughed. He followed Lexi back to the hotel, with sweet, softly snoring Riana in his passenger seat. Shortly after they started to drive Ri tossed a bit, reached out and found Alex's arm. She grabbed it, pulled his forearm to her face and snuggled into it. She breathed soft, hot air against his skin. Riana gave a little murmur and smiled in her sleep. Alex sighed. *Dammit.*

Alex was amazed by how deeply Riana slept. He picked her up again out of the car and carried her through the hotel, acutely aware of the perplexed expressions on the few people scattered in the lobby. He carried her into the elevator and down the hall to her room. All the while her heavy, rhythmic breathing assured Alex she was still asleep. Alex looked around her room and couldn't help but chuckle a bit when he noted he wasn't the only one with a sock issue. Except with Riana it wasn't just socks; she had jeans, pants, skirts, dresses, shirts and shoes strewn all over her room. He gently laid her down on a clear spot on her bed and whispered a "goodnight" in her ear before quietly letting himself out.

"I can't believe you're encouraging this." Derek accused Matthew after they got back to his and Alex's condo. "I have a bad feeling about this." he concluded.

"How so?" Matt asked. "About the girls? I'm pretty sure they've proven their trustworthiness." Matt knew that wasn't at all what Derek was talking about, but he felt Derek was just being overprotective.

"Seriously Matthew, don't play stupid. You know exactly what I have a bad feeling about. I think they're both getting into something messy." Matthew sighed as Derek sat down at the kitchen island.

"First of all, I'm not stupid." Matt snapped. Lexi's observation of Matthew's experiences in the public eye had been spot on that night in Chicago and being called stupid was definitely a sore spot. "I just realize they're both adults, D. And they're friends." *Friends that can't hide some obvious attraction, but friends nonetheless.* Matt grabbed a cold beer from the crisper in the fridge. It was Derek's turn to sigh. "Okay, fine, you might be right. They might be playing with some fire here. But I just don't think either one will push it right now. We have to trust them." Derek glared at Matthew. The moment did not pass without Matthew noticing. "Okay, I get it, you don't trust her completely with him. But if you don't trust her, you have to at least trust him, D."

"I do." he relented softly. "And I do really like Ri, Lexi and Samantha." Matthew grabbed a glass out of the cupboard, poured a shot of whiskey and handed it to Derek.

"Good, because I have a feeling they aren't going anywhere." Matt lifted his beer to Derek in a toast, he tipped his glass ever so slightly to Matt's beer and swallowed it quickly. Matthew sat down across from him and breathed deeply. He wanted to let Derek know the reason he trusted Riana so much was because he knew her, that he had known her for years. He just wasn't sure if that particular moment was the best time. The sound of a key in the door jostled both Derek and Matthew from their thoughts.

"Wow, that was quick." Derek jested as Alex tossed his keys to the granite counter with a clang. Matthew shot Derek another stern look.

"What?" Alex questioned. "Ri's hotel actually isn't far from here, and the lady sleeps like a damn rock so I just got her to her room and came back. Did you expect me to stay or something?" Alex looked confused as he ambled around the island to sit next to Matthew.

"No, Alex. We just know how you two can talk and we figured she would have woken up and y'all would get to talking again. That's all." Matt explained quickly before Derek could say something uncalled for.

Alex chuckled a bit. "Yeah, she is a talker, isn't she?"

"She always has been." Matthew noted offhandedly before he even realized.

"Always?" Derek asked. "We've known her for what, almost two months?"

Matt looked down at his beer. There went his plan of perhaps saving the information for a later time. "Yeah...about that..." he started. "I know it was a long time ago, a really long time ago, but do you remember the necklace I used to have? The black and red one? And you know how it came from that fan who always wrote me? The one all the fan club staff knew to pass along to me? Well, her name was Riana." A bit of clarity started to appear in Derek and Alex, but confusion still lingered. "I just had a feeling, you know? That it was her." Matthew rambled faster than he typically did. "I didn't want to scare her right off the bat though so I waited to confirm. Then today, when she and I went to get drinks, it all came out. Riana is *my* Riana. I mean, she's the one I knew all those years ago. It's unbelievable, but it's really her. All these years later." He finally took a breath. "So I know her. She's always been a talker. Her letters always drew me in, it was like I was there with her, living her life, keeping up on everything..." he trailed off, then looked at Derek. "Maybe that's why I trust her so much." Derek and Alex stared at him, both of their mouths agape as they tried to absorb it all. "I mean, you really get to know someone when you get a letter every few days for three years."

"Seriously!?" Alex blurted. "She wrote that often? Damn."

"She struggled Alex, a lot. If you think it's hard to hear her talk about everything she went through now, imagine how hard it was on her when she went through it. It seemed I was all she had at that point." he frowned.

"Wow." Derek whispered.

Matthew perked up a bit, "You know she and Lexi have been friends since they were 13? It's so cool to see her now and think back on silly stories Ri had told me about her. So it's almost like I knew Lexi too before we met." Derek and Alex still seemed shell-shocked. The sudden friendship with all of the ladies was hard enough to understand, but to tie it back to 1997 was, well, frankly ridiculous.

The groovy beat of Derek's phone pulled them away from Matt's endless rambling. "Speaking of." Derek laughed as he answered. "Hey Lexi. No, we're still up. Oh yeah, that sounds good....Sure. Okay... We'll meet you there at nine then. No problem. Bye Lexi." He set his phone down and yawned. "Alright, well I'm going to head to bed since we are now apparently having breakfast with Lexi and Riana before they leave tomorrow." he grinned.

"Sa-weet!" Alex hooted as he grabbed a bottle of water from the fridge and bounded up the stairs to his room. Matthew smiled after both of them, then moseyed towards the guest room he occupied when in New York with them.

CHAPTER SEVEN

Bad Day

Monday, July 24, 2006

"Son of a bitch!" Matthew yelled as he browsed the forums of the D.M.A. fan club website at his desk in the office.

"What!?" Derek commanded as he left his own desk and rushed over. Matthew's mind spun. *This is not going to be good. No, not good at all.* Both Matthew and Derek took in the pictures and the questions along with them.

"Who is this with Alex!? It certainly isn't Kim."

It certainly wasn't Kim. The image was Riana, peacefully asleep in Alex's arms, with Lexi beside him. There were more pictures that followed; of them at breakfast, walking along the street, pictures of Alex and Ri laughing hysterically.

"I've seen her before. They were in Chicago together."

"Who is the brunette with them?"

"Did Alex and Kim break up?"

"I wonder if Kim knows…"

On it went. It was taking on a life of its own. Matt and Derek knew it would be only a matter of time. "Dammit." Derek grumbled. Of course, this

89

wasn't the first time the members of D.M.A. had been pictured with other women, and the fans frequently blew things out of proportion. Then again, they weren't typically seen with other women, asleep in their arms, with a silly love-struck look on their face. "We have to do damage control. Now." Derek demanded. Matthew nodded and passed his laptop to him. Before Derek could start they heard Alex upstairs.

"Dammit Kim, she's a friend!" he bellowed. Derek and Matthew looked at each other, they knew they were too late. "It's not like she was a secret. I told you about her! Rebecca told you about her!" A slight pause and Matthew looked at Derek, worried. "You'd think after all these years you'd be used to stupid posts on the internet Kim." Matthew could only imagine the verbal assault Kim was laying on Alex. The look on Alex's face was easy to decipher, and Kim was no idiot. Derek could practically see the end of the road coming, like a brick wall magically placed in front of a speeding car. There would be no stopping this. It would be ugly, and painful.

Alex stormed into the office and straight to Matt's desk, as if he knew what they were looking at. "Okay, fine, I'll look at the damn picture, but I was there, I'm sure I know what was going on." Alex stopped next to Matt, but Matt didn't dare make eye contact with him. Alex opened his mouth, presumably to call Kim out on this unfounded freak out, but then he closed it as his eyes fell upon the look on his face as the still version of himself gazed at Riana. He knew he was caught. He turned around and silently left the room as Derek and Matt caught snippets from Kim's end of the phone. "...done Alexander...believe...I... stupid."

Matthew's pocket began a relentless vibrating and he looked down to see his wife's name and picture. He took a deep breath, he knew that somehow he would get in trouble for this. Being as Kim and Tabitha, his wife, were best friends he was sure Tabitha expected him to keep Alex in line and to prevent any pain to Kim. He slid his finger across the screen and answered.

"I'm so done Alexander. I can't take this anymore. I honestly thought I could trust you." Kim had proclaimed she was done at least a dozen times since Alex answered her call fifteen minutes prior. He was utterly exhausted. He tried to explain he was friends with Riana and nothing was going on but she wouldn't believe him. She continued to say it was so "obvious" there was more. Alex tried to tell her about Ryan and how he and Riana had been together for years. "Then I hope she's ready for the shit storm he's going to bring her too." was her reply. They went in circles, nothing Alex said calmed Kim down and he was beginning to think perhaps she was right. Maybe this was where it was supposed to end.

"I'm done fighting Kim." he sighed, defeated. "Maybe it is too much for us. Maybe it'd be better if you didn't have to worry anymore."

Silence.

"Are you serious?" she snapped. Before Alex could answer she screeched again, "Are you fucking serious!? I can't believe you would just throw this all away like that!"

"You're the one that keeps saying you're done!" Alex fired back.

"But you aren't supposed to just accept that. You're supposed to want to make it work!" Alex heard her voice break and he knew it was time.

"I don't want to make it work, Kim." There. Done. Alex felt as if a huge weight was lifted from his chest and he could finally breathe.

"You're serious." she gasped.

It wasn't a question, but Alex answered anyway, "Yeah, I am. I'm sorry Kim. I just don't think it's going to work."

Kim's next words were cold. "No. You aren't sorry." She hung up. Alex sat there for a moment, alone in his room and stared at his phone. A beautiful picture of Kim looked back at him while "call ended" blinked.

"Come on Ri, answer the phone." Lexi urged as she paced her office. There weren't remnants of a fire or explosion literally in front of her, but the internet had blown up with images of them from the night at the studio and of the next morning at breakfast. Lexi knew Riana was probably oblivious to it all at this point, so she figured she should be the one to clue her in.

"Hello my dear, sweet Lexi!" Riana chirped when she finally answered. *Yep, totally unaware.* Lexi swallowed the panic that clenched her throat.

"Hey honey. Say… are you near your laptop?" she asked cautiously.

She heard Riana shuffle in the background. "Um, I can be."

"Okay, when you get to it, go ahead and open up DMAfans.net or TMZ, or EOnline, whatever one you want." *Because it was all over the place.*

"Okay…?" Lexi knew Ri was confused as she heard the the keys and the mouse click. "I'm pretty sure if there was something important going on with the guys Alex…would…have…called." Lexi knew she found the pictures. "Dammit." Riana uttered.

"Yeah." Lexi sighed. "I figured maybe it'd be best if I were the one to let you in on the fact that apparently the whole world knows about you and Alex." The moment the words passed by her lips she knew it was the wrong choice in words.

"There is no 'me and Alex.'" Riana quickly corrected. "There is a me and Ryan and there is an Alex and Kim, but there is no me and Alex." she growled. *Okay, definitely the wrong choice in words.*

"Okay, Ri, I get it. I just… thought you should know...about this. Whatever this is." Lexi muttered carefully.

"This…" Riana started. "This is a friend, carrying another friend because she obviously can't hang with the big boys all night." She gave a light laugh, in an attempt to diminish the weight of the moment. "I mean, it's not a big deal. D.M.A. fans are crazy Lex, you know that." Lexi could tell Riana wasn't going to admit to noticing the look on Alex's face. She decided not to push it. "But..." Riana sighed. "Do you think I should call Alex?"

Lexi didn't know. It could help or it could intensify the whole situation. "I don't know Ri." she admitted softly. "Maybe I'll call D, test the waters."

Riana agreed and Lexi assured her she'd call back and let her know how she thought they should proceed. Lexi hung up and sat down in front of her computer. She looked again at a picture that should have been absolutely adorable, but was testing their new friendships instead. Lexi scrolled through her phone contacts, down to Derek and hit talk.

"You saw it." he assumed when he answered. Lexi was thankful she didn't have to break the news to him too.

"Sure did." She closed her eyes. "I didn't even think, D, that there might have been someone around."

She heard him take a deep breath. "Lexi, there's always someone around. It's something that we've known for years. You're...new. You don't think the same way. It's okay, we know this wasn't malicious." Lexi felt her shoulders relax. The last thing that she or Riana wanted was for the guys to think they purposely caused this situation. "Of course, it's not your fault Alex can be read like a damn book." There was a sharpness to his tongue that made Lexi realize maybe all wasn't as okay as he claimed.

"You saw that too, huh?" She instantly felt stupid for stating the obvious.

"It's hard to miss. It's just this was the first time it's been caught on film." Derek mumbled. "And posted all over the internet." he sighed.

"How's Alex doing with all of it?" Lexi asked slowly as she paced her office, then drifted to the window that overlooked the streets of Southside Chicago.

"Alex… well, Alex is currently partaking in World War Three with Kim." Lexi placed her forehead against her window. It quickly singed her skin and she gasped as she pulled back off it and closed her eyes.

"I'm sorry Derek." Lexi whispered.

"Not your fault dear. Really." Derek assured. "We'll make it through this too." Lexi could tell Derek was smiling. Somehow it did little to ease her unsettled soul.

Riana felt at times that her life had the worst timing. She couldn't wait for Lexi's call back after her water testing with Derek as she had to make it to the venue for her speaking engagement in Boston. She couldn't concentrate, yet she didn't dare call any of the guys. She took a deep breath, walked away from her cell phone and took the stage.

She went back to her things about an hour later and groaned when she realized she had no idea where to start.

> Missed call from Lexi Cell
> Missed call from Alex Cell
> 3 Missed calls from Ryan Cell
> 5 Text messages from Alex Cell
> 2 Text messages from Matthew Cell
> 4 New Voicemails

She shook her head in the darkness of backstage. She didn't bother to start yet, she figured it was a mess better dealt with alone, back in the hotel. Unfortunately, the hotel room came faster than she was prepared for.

Riana sank into the pillows at the base of her bed and took a deep breath, "May as well start from the beginning." she mumbled. Her first voicemail was from Lexi. *"Hey sweetheart, it's me. I know you're probably doing your thing at the U of M Boston but I just wanted to let you know I talked to Derek. Sweetie, they know it wasn't intentional, they aren't mad at you. But um, Alex was fighting with Kim when I was on the phone with D so you might want to wait just a bit before calling him. Okay, love you, bye."* Riana's phone continued to the next message. *"Ri..."* Alex started with a deep sigh. *"Listen... I know you know about the pictures and stuff. So does Kim. It didn't go well. Please call me."* Riana's heart tightened within the confines of her chest. Her last intention was to cause any stress between Alex and Kim. She couldn't dwell on it too

96

long because Ryan's voice broke through her thoughts. *"Riana, we need to talk."* Click. Then another. *"Ugh, seriously. Riana why aren't you answering? Oh I know, you're probably with your* **friend** *Alex."* Riana's teeth clenched together at the amount of hatred that oozed off of the word friend in Ryan's message. She slid off the bed and shuffled to the mini fridge to grab a mini bottle of wine before she dove into her text messages. "Okay, let's start with Alex." she decided as she opened her messages, as well as her wine.

"Riana are you free?"
"I really need to talk to you."
"You must be busy."
"Things...well...things are kinda crazy here."

About ten minutes passed between his last message and the next one. Right around the time he had tried to call.

"Kim and I broke up."

Riana sat there, dumfounded, and stared at his last message. *No, no Alex, why would you do that?* She was appalled he would tell her through a text message of all ways. Riana opened up Matthew's messages as she attempted to develop a coherent reply to Alex.

"I can only imagine you're having a hard time with all this too. Or maybe you aren't. I don't know. No one can reach you. I just wanted to say that y'know, we know this wasn't your fault."

Riana half laughed when she noticed Matt was long winded even in his text messages.

"I think you should call Alex."

Riana felt disoriented. She looked around her empty hotel room, and wished for some kind of support, comfort, or advice. She didn't know who to talk to first. She didn't particularly want to talk to anyone. It was too much at the moment. She had found three men, whom she had adored for years as a fan, and was lucky enough to have called them friends. Now, she wasn't sure what would happen. She knew she'd have to face it all eventually. She rationalized that eventually could be after she finished her mini bottle of Moscato, or perhaps after a second one. She really needed Lexi or Sam there, she couldn't fathom trying to figure it all out on her own. She realized she answered her own question of who to call first and picked up her cell.

One ring. A second ring. "Ri!" Lexi exclaimed as she picked up.

"Oh Lex, why aren't you here with me right now? This is terrible." Riana threw herself back, flat, but sideways on her bed. "Someone should have woken me up. Why would Alex have volunteered to carry me like that? Surely he knew about the stalker fans obviously milling about the studio." She sat up a bit to take another deep swallow of her wine.

"Ri, I don't think he cared quite honestly. He seemed perfectly happy to carry you." Lexi assured. Riana shook her head. *Why didn't anyone else see how bad this was?*

"But Lexi, they broke up." Riana whispered. She closed her eyes as the weight of guilt crashed on her chest.

"Who broke up?" Lexi demanded.

"Alex and Kim. I broke them up!" she gushed frantically. "Ugh, he's never going to want to talk to me again. Any of them. Can't blame them, really." she couldn't stop herself, she had a tragic habit where she would beat herself up for things she didn't have control over, or weren't her fault. It often explained why she took the blame for many of the issues in her relationship with Ryan.

"Ri. Shut up. This is not your fault." Lexi scolded. "Matthew texted you right?" Riana nodded even though Lexi couldn't see her. "I talk to them too you know." she teased lightly, a reluctant smile danced along Riana's face.

"I know." Riana mumbled softly. "And yes, Matthew texted me. So did Alex. But I'm just... I'm so embarrassed." Lexi continued to assure Riana it wasn't her fault, and the guys weren't upset with her and of course "everything happens for a reason." She finally filled Riana with enough courage--or perhaps the two mini bottles of wine Riana had, to get off the phone and call Alex. First she sent a quick text message to Matthew:

"Hey, sorry I didn't reply right away, was doing a lecture at U of M Boston. I'm not doing too well either I guess. About to call Alex if you still think I should?"

Matt responded quickly:

"Oh good! I thought you were avoiding me. Not good that you aren't doing well. If you need to talk just let me know. But yeah, I think Alex could really use a friend right now."

Alex knew he would probably hear that ringtone in the middle of a packed airport on Thanksgiving weekend with screaming children at every side of him--because it was her ringtone. Alex had locked himself in his room and refused to talk to Derek or Matthew. Immature? Probably. Needed? Absolutely. He swiped his finger across the screen and before he could say hello he heard her.

"Alex." she breathed. Just the sound of her voice made everything seem more manageable in his world. There was an odd calming effect she had on him without trying. He stared up at his blue ceiling and contemplated why anyone would actually paint a ceiling blue.

"Hey Ri." he replied, though he didn't quite sound himself.

"I'm so sorry Alex. I didn't mean for anything like this to happen." Riana quickly jumped into apologies and explanations, then more apologies. She couldn't imagine how to make this better, but she hopelessly tried to make sure he knew she didn't mean for things to go so horribly wrong.

"Ri. Ri! It's okay! This wasn't your fault. None of it is your fault. I offered to carry you and drive you to the hotel. I was well aware of the chances of there being people around the studio. And... I'm the one that ended it with Kim." he finished slowly.

"But I-- wait, you ended it with Kim?" Alex pictured Riana's face in his mind, the scrunched up nose, the squinted eyes. "I guess... I guess I just thought with the pictures and all that she... I mean..." Riana had a difficult time comprehending how it all could have gone down.

"Well, she wasn't exactly happy with the whole situation." he snorted. "No matter what I said to her she just kept going." Alex twisted the hem of his shirt around his fingers. "I guess she made the decision pretty easy for me."

Riana literally sat on the edge of her seat and continued to churn it all around in her head. "How are you doing though? You guys had been together for a long time." she murmured.

"Eh, I'm alright. I pretty much saw it coming. Things haven't been going well for a while. I guess this was just--"

"The straw that broke the camel's back?" Ri offered. Alex chuckled. "Really, have you ever wondered where that saying comes from? I highly doubt straw could break a back." Alex fully laughed at how wonderfully random Riana was.

"Yeah, something like that though. But please, Riana, don't take this on as yours okay? This was something that was going to happen anyway. I just feel terrible you're essentially in the middle."

"Stuck in the middle with you..." Riana half-sung and they both laughed lightly. She stayed quiet for a long moment, as she stared at her hands, then acknowledged softly, "People are going to think this is my fault." Despite her hard exterior, Riana was sensitive and truly hated it when people disliked her--for any reason. Her exterior kept her safe, though, so she maintained it well. Yet, there was something about Alex that brought honesty out of her, made her feel as though it was okay to be herself.

"I don't care what people think Riana, and neither should you." Alex retorted firmly. Riana took a deep breath and tried to etch his words into her heart.

"Okay." she relented, though he knew she would still blame herself and care too much about what people would assume about her, Lexi and the guys. Alex knew eventually Sam would be pulled into the mix as well, and he despised it. Everyone he associated with was instantly scrutinized, studied and pursued in order to get closer to D.M.A. "I have to go." Riana sighed. "Ryan called. I have to face that one too."

"Don't let him push you around, Ri." Despite what Alex had told Lexi, he did truly hate the man. Two months was more than enough time to see how poorly he treated Riana.

"I know." she agreed meekly.

"I mean it Ri." Alex insisted more sternly. "Don't. Remember, nothing happened, we aren't having some kind of *crazy* affair and my breakup with Kim was not your fault." Again Riana agreed, but it was obvious to Alex she didn't believe her own words. He hung up and prayed for the best for her talk with Ryan.

There may have been three, possibly four mini bottles of wine in the bathroom garbage. The warmth settled in Riana's stomach, and lightened her head. She finally had enough of a false sense of confidence to call Ryan. Even with the clouded sense of purpose, she didn't look forward to the call. She let out a small groan as she hit talk on the screen next to Ryan's name. As he picked up his voice made her sigh just slightly. She did still love him, and the sound of his voice reminded her of that fact. "Hey Ryan." she held her breath for a moment. "You wanted me to call?"

"Yeah, I wanted you to call three hours ago." he commented in a short, annoyed tone. Riana felt her eyes darken. *Love isn't supposed to be so dramatic, is it?*

"I had a speaking engagement at U of M Boston today. You knew that." Riana responded just as shortly as she went back to the mini fridge.

"How do I know for sure what you're doing anymore?" he snapped. "You were also supposed to be doing book signings and speaking engagements in New York but instead I find out via pictures on the internet that you were with damn D.M.A. again."

Riana's jaw became firm as she exhaled quickly through her nose. "First of all, they have names. Second of all, I did do book signings and speaking engagements while in New York. I'm also allowed to spend my free time anyway I want. I don't need to check in with you or anyone else for that matter for permission." *Dammit, no more wine.* "I mean, seriously, why are you so threatened by them?"

"I'm not." Ryan defended. "I just don't think it's a good reflection on us when there's pictures of you floating around the internet with *Alex* like that." Riana knew he emphasized Alex's name just to spite her after she called him out on not using their names. *He didn't have to emphasize it with so much disgust though.* Riana rolled her eyes as she stood in her window and watched the traffic below.

"I don't care what other people think." she replied flippantly, as she thought back on Alex's words. He would have been proud. A small smile danced along her lips.

"Not even me apparently." Ryan huffed. Riana narrowed her eyes to her reflection as she thought of how much of a whiner he could be at times. "We've been through so much and you don't even care how I feel." he said, his voice finally less worked up.

"Oh, that's rich Ryan. You don't even openly tell people we're together, but the moment it seems someone else might possibly want me around you lose your damn mind. Either you want me or you don't Ryan, I don't want to be a dirty secret." she growled.

A heavy silence lingered between them until Ryan dropped his voice to a tone Riana knew well. "I want you." Riana felt the flush of heat take over her body. *Damn you, body!*

"Ryan…" she breathed.

"I do Ri. I want you. I want you here, with me, in my bed." She hated how he did that. He could turn things around in a split moment. "I need to know you still want me, Ri. I need to know you're mine."

"I want you." she sighed. "I'll always be yours, Ryan."

CHAPTER EIGHT

Black Horse And The Cherry Tree

August 20, 2006

After the infamous Riana and Alex pictures got out and blew up, life was somewhat of a whirlwind for a while. D.M.A. fans were nothing if not relentless as they gathered information on D.M.A.'s personal lives. It only took about a week before they found out Kim and Alex were over, then it got intense among the fans. It appeared there were three sides; ones that sided with Riana, ones that sided with Kim, and the ones who didn't care either way. The third group was the most favorable to Alex, Derek and Matt. It was ridiculous, how quickly the fans presumed the breakup was because of Riana. D.M.A. didn't go out of their way to confirm or deny any of the rumors. They all felt it was none of the fans' business what transpired in their personal lives.

Riana had pulled away from them afterwards. She claimed it was because she was busy, but Alex knew it was mostly because she didn't want to add any fuel to the rumoring fires. Ryan had also successfully pulled Ri back in. She didn't tell Alex, but Lexi did. Both Lexi and Sam had hoped the whole situation would have driven Ri and Ryan apart, but somehow it brought them closer together. Lexi fumed over it.

"Have you talked to her lately?" Matthew asked as he and Alex sat in the studio while Derek laid down a track. Alex glanced down at his phone and frowned.

"Not for like four days." Alex answered, then chewed a bit on the inside of his lip. "I know she was just finishing up her tour though, I'm sure she's busy." he rationalized. He couldn't stand how she seemed to be slipping away. He had to attempt to explain it without admitting that maybe their friendship was suffering.

"Samantha said they were all going to be at the ranch for a while." Matthew started. "Maybe we could use a break too."

"Oh yeah?" Alex asked, his interest piqued. "What were you thinking?"

"Oh, I don't know..." He grinned at Alex. "How do you feel about horseback riding?" Alex couldn't prevent his laughter. The mental image of lanky, pretty Matthew on a horse was too much to take. "I'm serious!" Matthew laughed.

Alex stopped, save for a slight chuckle here and there. "I don't know Matt, I don't want to just... invite ourselves." He scribbled aimlessly in his notebook of lyrics.

"No need to." Matt assured proudly as he kicked his heels up on the table. "Lexi already invited us."

"Come on Ri." Lexi begged as she held the phone against her ear while she packed. "It's a couple of weeks with friends right? Who better to have with us than them?"

Lexi heard the frustration in Riana's sigh on the other end. "I just... I just think it could cause problems again."

"Riana." Lexi started firmly as she sat down on her bed. "Are you really going to pull away from these guys because of some shit talking by the fans? Seriously, we've always known the fans were crazy, and we always said we'd deal with it. Besides, your ranch is in the middle of nowhere, we're perfectly safe being ourselves without having to worry about what the fans might think."

The silence that followed reassured Lexi; it meant Riana wouldn't automatically blow her off with some kind of rebuttal. "I guess you're right." Riana yielded with a deep breath.

"Thatta girl." Lexi laughed. "I'll call Matthew."

Wednesday August 23, 2006

"Come along little doggies!" Derek drawled as he lugged his suitcase down the stairs. "We're going to miss our flight!" He heard Lexi giggle on the other end of the line.

"Derek, you're too cute."

"Ma'am you have no idea." he drawled again.

It'd been three days since Matt informed Derek and Alex they would take a small break and head to Riana's ranch in Arizona. Derek was super stoked, mostly to see how awkward Matt would look on a horse, but also to break free from the city for a while. Alex seemed nervous, which was unlike him. Usually he'd jump at the chance to get out of the city, but more than that, he'd usually be ecstatic to see Riana. "So you're good with the address and directions to get to Ri's place right? I know it's way out there."

Derek smiled at how thorough Lexi was with plans. "Yep, we're good. Trust me, 'out there' is exactly what we need. We should be landing at about eleven thirty, we'll grab the rental and head out, putting us at the ranch around three I think." Derek calculated as he lounged in the living room and awaited the other two.

"Perfect!" Lexi enthused. "I'm so excited to see you!"

"Us too Lexi." Derek smiled. "This will be great. I gotta run though, gotta wrangle up these city folk." He finished in another terribly overdone southern accent. Lexi laughed and bid farewell.

Derek turned around at the sound of heavy boots and an even heavier suitcase being pulled down the stairs. "Oh Matthew, you cannot be serious!" Derek chortled. Matthew definitely took the trip seriously. Derek took in his outfit: it started with some God awful red flame boots, a pair of jeans Derek was sure would prevent any further children from Matthew, and ended with what Derek was sure Matt thought was a "fashionable" button down plaid shirt.

"Derek!" Matthew gasped, offended. "This outfit is perfect." he defended as he rolled his suitcase down the hall. "Tabitha told me so." He grinned proudly.

Derek laughed again. "I think Tabs is just perfecting the art of making you undesirable to other women."

"Ha ha, D." Matt said dryly.

"They're still coming out on Friday right?" Derek asked. The guys had figured it wouldn't have been fair for them to take a break without having Matthew's family come out to spend time with him as well.

"Indeed." Matthew confirmed as he languidly slid into the armchair across from Derek. "Tabs is still at her parents' place with Spencer for a couple days then they'll head out." He glanced down at his watch. "You'd think Alex would have been the first one ready to go."

Derek felt the same way, but he knew something was a bit different between Alex and Riana since Alex's breakup with Kim. "I think he's actually a bit nervous to see her again." Matthew frowned at Derek's words. "I'll go get him." Derek declared as he stood up. He jogged up the stairs then knocked on Alex's door. "Alex, man, you almost ready to head out?"

"Umm, yeah, I think so." Alex pondered as he opened his door. His hair hung in his face, and his eyes seemed weary.

"Bro, you alright?" Derek asked quickly as he slung his arm over Alex's broad shoulders. Before Alex could answer his phone dinged. He pulled it out and opened a text that Derek quickly saw was from Riana.

"Can't wait to see you!"

Color returned to Alex's face and a smiled sparked in his eye. "Yeah, man, I'm good."

"Heeeeey Adonis." Riana cooed as she approached the stall of her favorite horse. She loved them all, but Adonis held a special place in her heart. He was a Friesian, adopted from a local rescue. The big, sweet boy was a reminder to Riana of how love could save someone. His rich, black coat was flawed by deep scarring from years of abuse. She adopted him when he was five years old; he had been skittish for almost a full year before he learned to trust Riana. She'd been told by her ranch hands that he was too unpredictable to ever trust and ride but she never gave up on him; she spent endless hours near him but far enough away to seem non-threatening. She waited patiently, day after day, until Adonis finally approached her. She spent another six months working with him to ease his nerves and prepare him for riding. They'd been inseparable ever since.

She heard his heavy footsteps approach his door, and his big black nose reached out and gave her a quick snort. She rubbed his velvet nose, then kissed it softly. "Wanna go for a ride?" Adonis jerked his head up, backed up and allowed Riana to step inside to grab him.

Riana had some time before the guys arrived and she decided to use it to clear her head. Riding typically worked for that, proven by the fact that she did much of her best writing after an exhausting ride with Adonis. However, on this day, she was a bit worried about what she might come up with after she cleared and organized her thoughts. She was on auto pilot as she tacked up Adonis and let her mind wander back over the last three months. She felt torn; being with Derek, Matthew and Alex brought her so much joy, yet being with them had also caused a lot of drama and hurt to other people as well as each other.

Adonis and Riana took off slowly. As they meandered through the front yard, Ri said goodbye to Lexi and Samantha, and assured them she'd be back in time to meet the guys when they arrived. She then urged Adonis to stretch his legs as they eased into a trot, and headed out towards the expansive eighty acres her ranch was settled on. The majority of her stress didn't come from the guys' arrival, it was that within days she would meet Tabitha. Riana could only imagine the amount of resentment Tabitha held towards her in regards to Alex's breakup with Kim. Matthew tried to assure Riana everything would be okay, but she knew if it were her in Tabitha's place she'd definitely blame the other woman. Even if nothing technically happened.

Riana leaned into Adonis and pushed him from a trot, past a canter and into a full gallop. She closed her eyes against the wind as her hair whipped around her. She heard Adonis' deep breaths and felt a thin layer of sweat form along his neck. She tried to focus on the ride, and not think about things like Alex's smile, because it led her to think of Ryan's smile. She then couldn't ignore the differences between them. Alex held a sparkle in his eyes when he smiled, but Ryan could close himself off emotionally and just give her the bare minimums. Ryan's smiles never seemed to meet his eyes. Ryan loved her though, didn't he? He'd always been there, inconsistently perhaps, but he always came back. She wondered, wasn't there a saying; "if you love something set it free, if it comes back to you it's yours"? Then surely Ryan was hers. Perhaps it wasn't love, though. Maybe he came back simply because Riana allowed it, much as Lexi and Samantha told her. Riana couldn't deny her draw to Ryan though; he was like gravity to her, a pull she was powerless to resist. He'd had that effect on her from the very beginning. Alex had started to have that effect on her as well. She had tried to pull away from him to prove to Ryan where her loyalty was, but it wasn't easy. She was frequently tempted to call or text Alex, she craved his voice and to hear the smile always behind it.

She felt selfish. She didn't want to bring any more stress or drama to them. Too many people knew about her friendship with him, Derek and Matthew already. Her social media followers had at least quadrupled after the pictures were posted. Most of the new followers were obsessed, not with her, but with D.M.A. and frequently posted to her questions about Alex, Kim, and the band. She huffed in annoyance as she thought about it. Ryan saw it too then hounded her with the same ridiculous questions.

Riana pulled back on Adonis as they approached the lake, she figured he could use a drink and she could stand to stretch her legs. She dismounted, not an easy task with how large Adonis was, grabbed his reins and led him slowly to the edge of the lake. She sighed deeply. She didn't know how the next two weeks would go, but she instinctively knew it would be intense.

Riana became immersed in her thoughts as she watched the hypnotic small waves move up onto the shore of the lake. Adonis brought her back to the present by how he pranced around anxiously. She noticed the sun sat lower on the horizon than she thought it should have been. She glanced at her watch, cursed, and leapt up from the ground. She scolded herself as she grabbed Adonis' reins. She knew she wouldn't have enough time to freshen up before the guys got there.

She led Adonis over to a large stump so she could hoist herself back into the saddle. She kicked him in the side and took off faster than they had run on the way out. She groaned and grumbled all the way back, angry at herself for having lost track of time.

Alex was glad the flight out to Arizona had been so uneventful, however, it had also left him with plenty of time to think. Sometimes, thinking wasn't the best thing for him. Especially when he found himself thinking about Riana, Sam and Lexi. The last three months were amazing, even if the last month had been tense. He felt Riana slip away. He never knew if he should push her to talk about things. Lexi had told him sometimes Riana would get defensive if people pushed too hard against her and Ryan. He worried he would end up pushing her further away if he voiced his concerns. He hoped some time essentially in the middle of nowhere with her would help work things out.

"Damn it's nice out here." Derek commented as they drove along the ridge of Arizona Snowball, a local ski resort. Riana's ranch was just northeast of it, towards Humphrey's Peak. Alex opened his phone, reread Riana's last message and smiled.

"It's crazy to think she's just as much at home here as she is in the middle of downtown Chicago." Matthew laughed. Alex gazed out the window and continued to smile. Riana was full of surprises like that. Just when he thought he knew what would come she'd change course and leave him shaking his head.

Derek mumbled about the GPS as he slowed down to find the side road that would eventually take them to Riana's. Alex perked up, they were definitely close. Derek took a left and brought them down a narrow road, tightly lined with thick trees. There were mountain peaks barely visible through the trees. Slowly, it started to clear. "No way." Matthew gasped slowly, his voice heavy with disbelief as the trees finally cleared. Their car was greeted by a wrought iron gate locked between two stucco pillars. He wasn't speaking of the gate; he was stunned by the house locked behind it.

"Damn Alex, did you know apparently Riana is some sort of multi-millionaire?" Derek laughed as he whirled his window down and pushed the buzzer.

"Yes?" Samantha's voice rang through the speaker.

"Housekeeping! We fluff pillow!" Derek called.

"Derek!" she squealed between giggles. The gate released and swung open. Derek turned to Alex and grinned, then slowly drove inside.

"This reminds me of your mom and dad's place." Alex observed to Matthew, who nodded in agreement. The house was up to the left, expansive but welcoming with its huge front porch and tall windows. To the right was a large stable, arena, what appeared to be a guest house and another pole barn. Beyond, nothing but picturesque scenery for as far as the eye could see. There were horses in the pasture and two dogs in the yard, who excitedly announced their arrival. Derek parked the SUV and they all exited. They stretched out their backs and legs. The dogs continued to circle, bark and dance happily around them.

"Guys!" Lexi yelled as she hopped off the porch and jogged to them. "How was the drive?"

"Great." Derek replied as he scooped Lexi into a hug. "It's absolutely beautiful out here."

"Right?" Samantha grinned as she hugged Alex then Matthew. She gave a little snort. "Nice outfit Matt."

"Hey! I thought it was fitting." Matt defended while he looked down at his attire with a small pout.

Alex shook his head and laughed. "I told you Matt." Derek teased.

"Riana should be here soon. She said she'd be back before you got here but, well, she loses track of time pretty easily when she's out with Adonis." Lexi explained as she helped the sulking Matthew unload the back.

A sudden rush of worry took hold of Alex, "Adonis?"

Before Lexi could reply the dogs started to bark as they ran towards the back of the house. Within seconds the thundering of hooves could be heard before Riana barreled around the corner of the house on top of a huge black horse. Alex stared in wonder, he knew that horses in general were large animals but this thing was massive. He smiled proudly when he took in how well Riana rode. She

117

pulled the horse in their direction, both she and the horse were sweaty, and hair a mess. Alex noticed it again, the heavy beating of his heart as he saw Riana smile. She pulled back on the reins and the horse slowed to a stop. He stomped his front hooves a few times as he caught his breath. "Adonis." Lexi stated simply. Alex nodded slowly in comprehension.

Riana went to dismount and Matthew quickly stepped behind her to assist her down. "Thanks." she huffed between her own heavy breaths. "I'm so sorry I'm late."

"Again my dear, the problem with punctuality." Alex teased. Riana grinned at him then moved closer to him, her monster horse in tow.

"Hey Alex." she greeted softly. Alex didn't move to hug her. He wanted to, but it didn't feel right at the moment. Something felt...different to him.

"This is a beautiful horse." Derek commented as he walked up beside Riana. She looked up at the horse and gave a deep and loving smile.

"Ah, yes, which is why he's so deserving of the name Adonis. Huh buddy?" she questioned as she rubbed his nose. "I hate to show up and then run off right away, but I have to get him cleaned up, rubbed down and put to pasture. Sam and Lexi can take you in and show you around. Matt, I figured you could hang in the house the first few nights then take the guest house when Tabitha and your son come if that works?"

"Sounds perfect, Ri." Matt agreed as he picked up his bags. He gave her a quick kiss on the cheek and followed behind Sam. Alex felt torn. He knew he should follow Matt and Derek but he felt like he needed a moment with Riana.

"Ri, can I come with?" Alex called out quickly. She turned and gave him a smile, as if she knew the question was coming, and nodded.

"Come on Sparky." Alex smiled as he remember she said essentially the same thing after dinner in Chicago.

Matthew and Derek followed behind Lexi and Sam, and tried to take it all in. There was a huge wrap around porch on the front of the house, complete with tables, chairs, and a swing. Derek imagined how easy it would be to sit there with his guitar, face the mountains, and come up with some new songs. Both he and Matt realized if they thought they were amazed when they pulled up to the house, it was nothing compared to what greeted them as they followed Lexi through the heavy, Mahogany, double doors.

They were met with a short marble hallway, painted light blue with silver accents, that opened up to the great room. The ceilings seemed to actually reach the sky as the horizon overtook the far wall created with floor to ceiling windows. To the right of the great room was a huge gourmet kitchen. Derek knew Matthew was going to love it as he was an avid cook and enjoyed experimenting with new things. It was filled with dark cherry cupboards, beautiful granite countertops and all stainless appliances. Off the kitchen was a small yet bright breakfast nook, behind was a large formal dining room, layered in reds. As they continued their tour Derek took in two more living areas, four bathrooms, a walk out to the huge in ground pool and hot tub. He quickly decided they might not want to leave in two weeks.

"Matthew, this will be your room." Samantha declared as she opened up one of the upstairs doors. Matt gave a low whistle as he stepped inside. There was a large king sized bed against the right wall, tall windows faced out to the mountains, an en suite and walk in closet. "At least until Tabitha and Spencer get here, then you can have the guest house if you'd like."

"The guest house." Derek chuckled with a small shake of his head. "I really had no idea Riana was... well... so well off."

Lexi gave Derek a small smile. "Yeah, she doesn't exactly like to talk about it. It was an inheritance. She rather people not know and like her for her instead of the money."

The guys nodded. "We know how that goes." Matt confirmed.

"Ryan doesn't even know about this place." Samantha commented.

"What? Really?" Derek exclaimed. "Wow."

"Yep, so you know, feel privileged." Lexi teased with a wink at Derek.

Matthew stood in the center of his room. He was still as he took it all in; the soft grey walls, the pristine white bedding and smooth hardwood floors. "Matt, you can drop off your bags, it might be wise to continue the tour with us." Samantha laughed. "I wouldn't want you to get lost."

As they proceeded down the hall Lexi pointed out where she and Sam stayed, another bathroom and a study. "D, this is your room." Lexi opened a door to another large bedroom with a similar layout to the one Matt would stay in.

"Very nice, thank you." Derek praised as he tossed his bags onto the deep blue comforter.

"Alex will be right across the hall, and Riana's room is downstairs." Sam explained. "She should be about done with Adonis by now. We can head down and I'll show you the back patio." She grinned and hopped up and down. "You're going to love it!"

"I can't imagine there'd be anything in this place we wouldn't love." Matthew laughed as he slung his arm over Samantha's shoulder.

<u>CHAPTER NINE</u>

Ordinary People

As Lexi and Samantha gave the tour to Derek and Matthew, Riana and Alex were on their way to the barn with Adonis. Alex walked next to Riana, but seemed distracted as he looked off into the distance. "You alright Alex?" she questioned. He looked over at her and smiled. Despite how she felt that something was off with him she still smiled back.

"I'm good." He paused for a moment. "I've missed you, Ri." Riana instantly felt the heaviness of his words and guilt gripped her. She had been selfish to pull away as much as she did after everything went down. She didn't stop to think if, or how, pulling away affected him. Riana stopped and grabbed Alex's arm when he didn't stop right away with her.

As his eyes locked on hers, the intensity of his eyes broke through his shaggy black hair. "I've missed you too, Alex." Riana admitted softly as she fell easily into his arms. He rubbed her back and she breathed deeply. She was quickly comforted by his scent. "I'm sorry I've been so busy, and distracted and just...I'm sorry."

122

"Hey, lady, it's okay." he assured as he grinned on top of her head. "We have a whole two weeks to try and catch up." He rubbed her back. "So, how about you show me how to clean up a horse after a ride?" Riana pulled away with a smile and nodded.

Alex helped her untack Adonis, and carried Adonis' saddle effortlessly to the tack room. *That man sure does have nice arms.* Riana thought quickly. Alex grabbed a bucket with some soap and a sponge. They talked aimlessly about the end of Ri's book tour, how things had been going in the studio, how Riana came to own such a "huge" horse, Samantha and Lexi. Riana was thankful he didn't bring up his breakup with Kim, how things were going with Ryan or how she came to have such an elaborate ranch.

As Alex rubbed down Adonis' front left leg and Riana rubbed down his front right, Riana suddenly had a face full of foam. She quickly sputtered and wiped her face then glared at Alex. All she got in return was a giggle. "Sorry?" Alex grinned.

Riana pursed her lips and slowly stood up. "Mmhmm." She quickly grabbed the hose and gave Alex a shot to the top of his head while he was still bent down next to Adonis. He gave out a scream and jumped up. Adonis jerked his head between the leads that tied him to the wash stall. Riana rubbed her hand down Adonis' neck to comfort him. She looked down and giggled at Alex. "Sorry?" She offered with the biggest grin she could muster between giggles.

"You are so dead." Alex threatened as he re-soaked his sponge. Riana still had a firm grip on the hose which provided her with a solid sense of who would win the fight. Alex darted underneath Adonis' neck and grabbed the arm that held the hose, and kept it turned away from him as he squeezed the sudsy water over Riana's head with his other hand. She gasped and laughed as she tried desperately, but unsuccessfully, to utilize her weapon. It carried on for some time, until Adonis' nerves started to get the best of him and became restless.

"Okay! Okay! You win!" Riana laughed in defeat. "Let's finish him up so he can go relax." she advised as she rubbed Adonis' chest and nose.

Samantha brought Derek and Matt out to the back patio where Riana had an infinity pool that overlooked the expansive desert, rolling hills and distant mountains. Also on the patio was a grill built into a solid stone bar, a wet bar next to it, a fireplace, fire ring, lounge area and hot tub. Matthew hastily decided he absolutely had to try the pool and proceeded to cannonball, completely clothed, into it. "You are insane!" Samantha laughed in shock.

"Aww, come on!" Matthew whined. "Come in, this is amazing!" he called as he floated on his back. His soaked clothing clung to his small, yet tone, frame.

124

"We know it is dear, but you know, typically we like to be wearing swimsuits when we go swimming." Lexi teased.

"Overrated." Matthew laughed and he sunk under the water one more time before he climbed out. The water rushed off him and he shook out his short, perfectly layered hair.

"At least now you can change out of that outfit!" Samantha exclaimed. She released the laughter she had successfully contained when they had first arrived.

"You guys are so mean!" Matthew complained light heartedly. Lexi tossed him a towel from one of the lounge chairs and he wiped his face quickly. They were torn from Matthew's dramatics by the sound of laughter inside the house as Riana and Alex stumbled out back.

"What the hell happened here?" Riana laughed when she took in Matthew's wet appearance and the laughter of the other three.

Matthew laughed, "Your pool is lovely Ri." He skipped over to her and wrapped her in a hug. "Thanks for inviting us." He pulled away and looked at her and Alex. "What happened to you two?" he questioned as he examined Riana and Alex's own wet, soapy look.

"It's Alex's fault." Riana declared as she shot Alex a stern look over her shoulder. Alex laughed deeply. She shook her head, "I have to get changed. Come on Alex, I'll show you to your room." she said as she turned and grabbed his hand. Samantha was the first to see it, a smile grew on her face as she watched Riana's fingers interlace with Alex's. Soon, quick glances were shared among Derek, Matt and Lexi as Riana and Alex headed inside.

"Um--" Derek started.

Lexi hushed him quickly. "It's fine." Samantha and Lexi found each other's eyes and smiled lightly. They both wanted Riana to see how toxic her relationship with Ryan was and they knew Alex was good for her, even if Riana didn't want him.

Alex's breath caught in his throat as he felt Riana's fingers intertwine with his. He gave her hand a gentle squeeze and Riana looked up at him with a shy smile. She didn't let go once they were back in the house and she pulled him behind her as she headed up the stairs. Alex fought the thoughts that rushed through his mind; how he wanted to pull her back by the connection of their hands and press his lips to hers as he tangled his hands in her long hair. His mind hastily scolded him. He focused on the grand house that surrounded him instead of his impractical fantasies. It was beautiful; modern, yet homey. It was practically an extension of Riana herself.

Riana took a left down the hall and stopped in front of a closed door. "Okay, here it is. Your room for the next couple weeks." She smiled as she grasped the brushed nickel door knob and pushed the door open. Alex was taken aback by the spacious room that greeted him. It was comfortable and inviting.

"Wow, Ri." he commented as he stepped inside.

"Is it okay?" Riana questioned as she hesitantly followed him inside. Alex turned to face her and barely shook his head in disbelief. She too often seemed to question herself and the things she had to offer the world.

"Okay?" he echoed as he looked around. "This is amazing!" he laughed as he spread his arms and threw himself back on the lofty bed.

Riana smiled down at him, her own mind was a flurry of mixed thoughts and feelings. "Well, um, I'm going to go get changed. There's a bathroom right next door, and Derek's room is across the hall." She turned to leave but stopped short. "Thanks for coming Alex, I'm glad you're all here."

"Of course, Ri." Alex answered softly. "I'm glad we're here too." She nodded then let herself out of his room and gently closed the door behind her.

Alex let go of a deep breath and tried to calm his thoughts. He looked down at the hand Ri had held and he flexed it slowly as he recalled the sensation of her petite hand. He didn't want to get tangled up in these conflicting feelings. He knew she had Ryan and, despite how much he wished she didn't, she wanted to make things work with him. The last thing Alex wanted was for things to get weird between them. However, he couldn't ignore the way he couldn't stop smiling around her, the way his breaths were uneven and his heart rate became heavy and fast. He couldn't deny the simplistic joy he felt in being around her. Buried beneath that he started to realize he also couldn't deny the fire she lit within him, everything about her was utterly irresistible.

After Riana closed Alex's door she leaned back and sighed. She was flustered. It had felt so right to have his fingers laced between hers, but she knew she shouldn't have done it. She allowed her eyelids to flutter closed and all she saw was his smile, his eyes, and the way he shook his head when he laughed at her. Her eyes shot open as she silently scolded herself. She set her jaw, walked away from his door and hurried back downstairs.

The sound of laughter greeted her as she reached the bottom of the staircase. The house felt utterly alive as Lexi, Sam, Derek and Matt discussed what to make for dinner. Riana smiled to herself then scampered down the hall to get freshened up and changed. She walked into her master suite and shut the door, determined not to think any more about the muddled mess of feelings within her. She quickly stripped off her wet tank top and her mud caked jeans. She scurried to the shower, stepped in under the steamy jets and let the water wash over her as she closed her eyes and attempted a quick meditation. The steam thickened the air and she slowly felt the tension in her muscles release. She reset her resolve to make things work with Ryan, and to re-establish her friendship with the guys.

Riana realized she was probably in the shower longer than she had intended and hopped out quickly. She wrapped a bath sheet around her and darted towards her walk-in to get some clean clothes. An impatient knocking stopped her halfway to her destination. She dashed over to the door and flung it open. "Ria--" Matthew stopped short and a quick blush crept up his cheeks. "Oh, um, sorry... We were just wondering if you were going to come hang with us while we made dinner." He refused to make eye contact with her, and at first Riana was confused, until she remembered she was fresh out of the shower and clad only in a towel.

"Oh my God, Matt, no, I'm sorry. Kinda, um, wasn't expecting it to be you at my door." she laughed as she held the towel a bit tighter to her body. "Let me get dressed and I'll be right there." Matt nodded and turned silently away. Riana laughed to herself as she slipped into a sundress, towel dried her hair and tossed it up.

As Riana approached the kitchen she heard endless laughter and conversation. The whole place just felt *right*. She heard snippets of things; "...No Matt, I'm telling you if you angle it like this..." "So this one time Matt had tried to make crème brule..." "No one told me how to use the torch!" "...you sure you want to trust him around an open flame?" More laughter.

"Hey kittens!" Riana chirped as she turned into the expansive kitchen. She was greeted warmly as she weaved her way through everyone and checked out the progress being made on dinner. Fresh veggies and steaks were spread over cutting boards on the island, and a pan of boiling water was on one of the six burners of the gas stove. "This looks amazing." she gushed.

"Just wait until it's finished. You won't believe your taste buds." Matt declared in a singing voice. They all settled into an easy rhythm as they brought ingredients out to counters and gathered place settings all the while they maintained comfortable conversation. Alex had come down just shortly after Riana and despite how hard Riana tried she couldn't keep her eyes off him. Whereas her eyes would often darken, narrow and feel more intense with Ryan; Alex seemed to lighten them. She could tell they often danced with amusement. He'd catch her here and there and he'd give a quick smile or wink.

Riana became overwhelmed and excused herself from the kitchen. She went to take a moment for herself outside and the laughter faded behind her. She debated on sending Ryan a message, just to say hi, and to keep her focus, but she knew it wouldn't help her situation.

"Hey sweetheart." Samantha's sweet voice called from behind. Riana turned and looked over her shoulder. She gazed at Sam for a moment. The mixture of the Arizona sunset and the fire Riana sat in front of brought out the contrast of the red in Sam's blonde hair. She gave Sam a half-hearted smile. "Oh I know that look." Samantha insisted as she sat down next to Riana. "That's the look of internal conflict you're undoubtedly going to try and suffocate and not talk about." Riana wanted to argue with her, but knew it'd be pointless. She dropped her head and sighed.

Alex brought down his camera and recorded Matthew as he cooked and Derek stood to the side to give a play by play. "Here we are, taking a much needed break from the studio, in an all secret location. It was a long trip and we're absolutely starving so it's time for another episode of 'Adventures In Cooking With D.M.A.'" Lexi tried to hide a giggle. "As you can see, Matthew is currently preparing the steaks, which have already been marinated." Derek did the best accents and it appeared that night he would be Australian. He poked the steaks. "Mmm...seems tender."

"Ugh, Derek, man, get your fingers off my steak!" Alex turned the camera on himself and twisted up his face. "Gross." Lexi giggled again. Matthew seemed to have perfected the art of ignoring the brothers as he cooked. Alex turned the camera back around and panned over the spread of food they had set up to be taken to the grill. "Looks delicious... We'll be taking the party outside here in a minute." he told his audience, which Lexi was sure would be the fan club members, as he walked out to the patio.

"Oh, I hope he doesn't get Ri on camera." Lexi moaned. Derek turned to her and questioned her silently. "She's not doing well with the fans guys. I know she has a hard-ass image, but she truly feels terrible about everything and doesn't want to cause any more problems."

Matthew finally turned away from the stove where he had started the rice. "All she has to worry about is us Lex. And trust me, we don't feel like she's causing problems."

"She's just such a worrier." Lexi sighed and rested her chin in her hands.

Matt smiled at her, "I know she is." he said, then turned his attention back to the stove.

Lexi knew Riana wouldn't want her to say anything further, but she felt Matt should know. "She's...she's pretty anxious about meeting your wife."

"What? Why?" Matt asked quickly and turned back towards her.

Lexi groaned, painfully aware of the wrath Riana would drop if she knew Lexi told Matthew. "Well come on Matt, think about it. She blames herself for Alex's breakup with Kim. She just... well she knows how much she loves Sam and I and she feels if it were one of us dating someone close to her partner and we ended up heartbroken, she'd blame the 'other woman' so to speak." Lexi sighed. "She feels like the other woman. She's afraid Tabitha already hates her."

Matthew released a slow breath. "I'm sure she doesn't." he assured. "But I can see why Ri would be worried she does."

Lexi slapped her open palms against the granite countertop. "Okay." she proclaimed. "Enough of this downer talk. Let's get those steaks on the grill. But don't either of you say anything about what I just told you." She shot both of them a stern look, then smiled as she grabbed a platter off the counter and left the kitchen.

Alex continued his narration as he walked out on the patio. "Now this is a grill. Can't wait to get those hunks of meat on it." he laughed a bit then panned the camera out to take in the sunset. "There's some spiritual handiwork. Seriously, you can't paint anything like that." He panned back over, across the pool and then saw the back of Riana and Sam's heads. "And there are two of my favorite ladies!" he called out.

Samantha turned her head, smiled and waved then gently nudged Riana. Riana glanced over her shoulder and gave a shy wave. Alex turned the camera back on himself. "Alright kids, this food isn't going to cook itself and we all know we can't trust Matt to be without adult supervision around open flame. See you next time!" He stopped recording and moseyed over to Riana and Sam. "Hey ladies, what's happenin?" He grinned. Riana rolled her eyes at him with a smile.

"Not a whole lot, just taking a break from all the laughter, my abs hurt." Samantha teased.

"Ah, yes, that is bound to happen." Alex agreed solemnly. "Great workout though." he teased.

"Hey!" Derek hollered. "Who wants drinks?" Samantha hopped up quickly and gave Riana's knee a small, reassuring squeeze.

"Oh you know one of those is coming this way." Sam laughed as she skipped over to the wet bar.

Alex remained next to where Riana sat for a moment he felt was too long. "You want me to grab you a drink, Ri?" She looked up at him and gave a small smile as she pondered the question.

"Actually, yeah. I think I'll have one." Riana had only confided a small snippet of the mass confusion in her head to Sam. She told her about how right it felt to hold Alex's hand. She told Sam how much she had missed him. There was even a confession of how Riana couldn't deny the difference between Alex's smile and Ryan's. She didn't, however, disclose how desperately she wanted to walk away from Ryan and straight into Alex's arms. She knew it was stupid to even think it, let alone say it. Even if it wasn't completely far-fetched, she couldn't imagine going there so soon after his breakup with Kim.

Alex reached his hand down to help her up and despite the warnings in her head; *Don't do it Riana, don't take his hand*, she smiled at him and easily slipped her hand into his. The stone bar off the built in grill was a short walk from the outdoor fireplace she sat next to and she quickly, albeit reluctantly, slid her hand from his as she hopped up on a bar stool.

Alex walked around and joined Derek behind the bar. Riana settled in between Lexi and Sam and grinned, first at them, then across the way at the guys. Derek dug through the mini fridge while Alex checked out the wide array of bottles which sat on the corner of the bar. Matthew kept a watchful eye on the meal. "See, now here's when I wish I would have paid more attention when I saw that horrible movie 'Cocktail'." Alex laughed while he attempted to spin one of the liquor bottles.

"Just remember, you break it you buy it." Riana teased.

"Alright ladies," Derek started as he came back up from the fridge. "It appears we have... Smirnoff coolers, Guinness, Mikes and a wide variety of wine and mixers. What can I get ya?"

Riana called for a glass of Asti, Lexi a glass of Moscato and Sam opted for a Guinness. Derek nodded as he accepted the glasses from Alex and provided the ladies with their drinks. Riana took a sip of her chilled wine and closed her eyes. She breathed deeply and attempted to process it all. Despite her internal conflict regarding Alex she couldn't have been happier. She was at her ranch, laughing with her two best friends and three men who had quickly become part of her elite private circle. Three men whom she never thought she'd meet, let alone form any kind of relationship with.

Matthew managed to finish the steaks with only three minor fires in the grill, which they all teased him about relentlessly. Riana had a second glass of wine with dinner and she started to feel the effect of relaxation take over her body. "This is quite delicious Matt!" Sam said excitedly.

"So little faith you have in me." Matthew laughed. They finished dinner, remained at the table and continued their naturally flowing conversation. Sam, Lexi and Riana told the guys how they came to be such good friends, Riana's trips to Canada, and how Riana and Lexi went to school together. They talked about each other's families, and things like their favorite vacation spots and the scariest rides they'd ever been on. It seemed to go on endlessly. Occasionally Riana would share a knowing smile with Matthew as he already knew much of what was shared. The haunting calls of coyotes began to fill the air and Riana noticed small yawns around the table.

"Why don't you guys head on to bed. I'll clean up." Riana offered as she stood. "We have a big day tomorrow, you'll need your rest."

"Oh yeah?" Derek asked as he reached his arms above his head and stretched as he stood from the table.

A mischievous grin slowly took over Riana's face. "Indeed." Her eyes jumped from Sam to Lexi then to the guys. "I'm going to teach you guys how to ride." Sam and Lexi giggled.

"I'm game." Alex declared with a puff of his chest. "Just...umm, give me a horse a bit smaller than Adonis, okay?"

Everyone laughed and Riana nudged his shoulder. "Adonis is the biggest horse I have, and he's mine." She winked. "You'll definitely get someone smaller. No go on, all of you, and get some sleep. I'll see you in the morning."

CHAPTER TEN

Ridin'

After a quick shower Matthew settled in to watch some TV in his room before he tried to get some sleep. As he flipped through the channels he heard a hesitant knock at his door. He hollered for them to enter. "Oh good, it is your room." Alex laughed as he entered and shut the door. "This place is so enormous I wasn't sure I had the right one." Alex grinned at Matt then took three long, quick strides and threw himself into Matt's bed. "Whatcha' watching?"

"Nothing yet." Matt laughed as he flipped through the channels. "What's up?" Alex leaned back against two pillows and the hickory headboard, took a deep breath then slowly exhaled.

"I'm…" He stopped and Matt could tell he was contemplating how to continue. "I'm thinking… maybe coming here wasn't the best idea." Matthew could feel his jaw drop but he was helpless to stop it.

"Alex, you seem happier now than you've been in weeks." he gushed.

"I know, Matt. That's it, though. I mean, I'm really… confused." Alex looked over half expecting Matt to laugh at him but Matt knew he needed a friend to confide in, and knew better than to belittle his feelings.

"About Riana?" Matthew didn't have to phrase it as a question. Alex nodded.

"There's just…" he sighed. "I know we're friends, right? She's probably one of my best friends, save for you and Derek. And I know she's with Ryan." Matthew almost smiled at how Alex said Ryan's name; as if it left a bad taste in his mouth. "And maybe…" Alex huffed and rolled his eyes. "Maybe I should process more how I feel about the breakup with Kim. But being with Riana, being around her, I just don't care about any of that. All these logical reasons not to feel things and yet…" Alex trailed off. It was apparent there were definitely some strong feelings taking a hold of him.

"She's a very lovable person, Alex." Matt assured as Alex nodded silently. "She's always been easy to love. That's just who she is. Even when she was younger, when she was so angry; I could still tell there was a sweet, loving nature below her tough shell. It's pretty amazing when you think about it. Knowing how hard things were for her; from her family life, her volatile relationships, to being assaulted so young, to the legal issues afterwards. She was put through so much more than anyone her age should have had to go through. Yet, she took it all and just…ran with it. She's owned her past and turned it into something… magnificent." Matthew seemed to forgot Alex was next to him as he spoke of Riana and her past. He slipped back into moments of when he would read her letters and wish there was something he could do for her.

"She's magnificent." Alex's simple proclamation reminded Matthew he wasn't alone.

"She is, I totally agree." Matt supported. "I think you're right though when you said maybe you need to take some more time to process how things ended with Kim. There's got to be some left over stuff there you need to deal with. If you really care about Riana, you'll support her in her relationship with Ryan." Alex didn't attempt to hide the disgust on his face as he groaned. Matt laughed a little and pushed Alex's shoulder. "I know, but I'm serious. Don't make things harder for her. She'll figure things out on her own, and however it plays out is exactly how it's supposed to okay?"

"Wow, Matthew, when did you turn into your mom?" Alex teased. Matt rolled his eyes at him and grinned. "She doesn't make it easy you know. She held my hand as she brought me to my room." he said. A slight blush crept into his cheeks, hidden behind his dark complexion.

Matt's grin grew. "I know. We all saw."

"It surprised me, but it felt good. Really good. Right." he sighed, then groaned again. "This will surely drive me insane." He scooted over and dropped his feet to the floor. "I'm gonna head to bed. Thanks Matt."

"No problem buddy. Remember, it'll all play out. Just enjoy being here." Alex nodded and left.

Matthew shook his head once the door was closed. "Poor Alex." he murmured.

Thursday August 24, 2006

Riana planned to get up early to make the guys breakfast before they headed out for the day, but when she shut off her alarm at 6am she thought she heard music down the hall, possibly from the kitchen. She lazily dropped her feet to the cool floor and stretched through a large yawn. She hurried to her bathroom, brushed her hair and teeth then went to investigate.

As she opened her bedroom door, it became apparent there was definitely music being played in the kitchen, and it smelt of waffles and bacon. "Who the hell is up this early?" she grumbled. Mornings had never been her strong suit and she was dumbfounded by those deemed morning people. As she got closer to the kitchen she realized it was The Temptations that flowed through the kitchen surround sound system, but she still heard voices that didn't belong to the track. She tiptoed to the end of the hall and peeked around the wall. The image that greeted her was too cute to ignore.

Matthew was at the stove, cooking bacon as he swung his small hips to the beat while Alex mixed waffle batter as he sang. Alex turned to Matthew, and Matthew turned to Alex and they sang into the spatula as a shared microphone. A little dance together and Riana simply couldn't help herself.

She jumped around the corner just in time to join them in the chorus of "Ain't Too Proud To Beg". She surprised them, but they didn't miss a beat. As the bridge played Matthew grabbed her around the waist and danced with her in the middle of the kitchen. She threw her head back and laughed. Matt passed her to Alex as the next verse started. Riana was acutely aware how Alex's grip on her waist was a bit tighter than Matthew's, and she felt her skin light on fire underneath his hands as he sang. His playful, dark eyes locked on hers. The music faded from Riana's ears and she felt a blush take over her face. The sound of Alex singing had always ignited her, but to have him sing directly to her was more than she could take. She turned away from him before she did something she wasn't sure she'd regret.

"This smells delicious." Riana complimented as she sat down at the kitchen island. Matthew turned down the music a little bit as The Four Tops started.

"We didn't wake you did we?" Matt asked.

"No." she laughed. "I was actually going to get up early to make everyone breakfast, but you apparently beat me to it. What are you guys doing up so early anyway?"

"Well, you know how jet lag is. Our bodies still think we're on New York time, and it's 9am there now. We've been up for a while actually." Matt explained. Riana nodded.

"Why don't you go get Sam and Lexi up." Alex offered. "Everything should be done in about ten minutes."

Riana hopped off her barstool. "Aye aye!" she laughed, then scampered down the hallway and up the stairs, unable to remove the smile from her face. She slowly opened Lexi's bedroom door and peeked inside. Lexi was still burrowed into her blanket. Riana flung the door open and leapt onto Lexi's bed. "Come on Lexi, get up!" Riana squealed. Lexi groaned and buried her head under her pillow. "Lexi...." Riana called in a sing-song voice as she curled up against her body. "You gotta get up. Matt and Alex made us breakfast."

Lexi stirred beside Riana and mumbled under the pillow, "He made breakfast? You should really marry that man." Riana knew Lexi was teasing her; Ri wasn't exactly a homemaker, and cooking definitely wasn't a strong suit of hers. She still didn't find the joke funny, given her development of conflicting emotions.

"Lexi!" she yelled. "Not funny." she mumbled with a pout.

Lexi finally sat up and rubbed her eyes. "I know, I'm just teasing sweetie." She slowly shuffled to her bathroom, but just as she closed the door she stuck her head out and said, "Still a valid suggestion though!"

"Argh!" Riana groaned as she threw herself back on the bed. "I hate you!" she yelled through laughter. She hollered at Lexi that she was going to get Sam up then made her way back down the hallway to Sam's room.

She knocked lightly then eased the door open. She didn't see her. "Samantha?" she called.

"In here!" Sam yelled from her closet. "Just getting dressed."

"Perfect, the guys are just about done cooking breakfast. I have a feeling we should hurry if we want any chance of getting any." she laughed, then hurried back downstairs.

As they strolled through the stables Riana pointed out some of her best horses for trail riding. Alex tried to pay attention, but found the way Riana's jeans hugged her curves distracting.

"Typically Lexi takes Chester and Sam takes Lilo." Ri explained as she rubbed each of the said horses noses. "Go ahead and tack up ladies." She walked a little further down as Lexi and Sam grabbed their horses.

Riana stopped in front of the stall that held a palomino Quarter horse and she smiled. "Matt, I think Sonny would be a great fit for you. She's super sweet and mellow." Matthew stopped at Sonny's stall and reached up to pet her forehead.

"Let's see…" Riana pondered as she walked out of the barn and stood by an outside corral. "Here's Daisy, Aphrodite and Ringo…"

Alex couldn't help but chuckle. "Ringo?"

Riana turned towards him, her eyes danced playfully as she laughed. "Yep. I named him that because he has bigger ears than most Quarters."

Derek walked over to the fence and spoke to Ringo in his best English accent. "Hi, I'm Ringo. I'm Ringo and I play the drums." Ringo appeared to nod as he walked towards Derek.

"Alright, D, he's yours." Riana laughed. Alex sighed at the sound, he absolutely adored her laugh. Riana opened up the gate and grabbed Ringo by his halter and led him into the stable to be tacked. She tied Ringo to a ring on the wall, then escorted Alex over to the stall next to Adonis. Inside stood a tall, lean, white Arabian horse with bright, large, dark eyes. "Alex, this is Adonis' best friend Apollo." She smiled shyly at Alex, and hoped he realized why she picked Apollo for him. Alex knew; he was able to read her better than almost anyone, save for Lexi and Sam. He felt it fit, as he considered her one of his best friends as well.

It quickly became apparent that Derek, Matthew and Alex weren't exactly cowboys. The start of their ride was delayed by the fact they weren't able to tack up their own horses; Riana, Sam and Lexi had to do it for them. Riana yelled at them to pay attention as she didn't want to have to be the one to always help them if they wanted to go out for a ride.

After the horses were tacked up the women grabbed two sets of reins each and led the guys' horses, as well as theirs, out of the barn so they could all mount and be on their way. It was embarrassingly amusing, how easily the ladies were able to mount their horses while the guys looked like hopping fools as they tried to finagle their feet in the stirrups and the rest of their bodies hoisted into the saddle. Even Riana, with Adonis, the massive Friesian, managed fairly easily once she utilized a small step outside. Of course, she had to then tease the guys, "Hey guys, you can use the step if you need to." Her eyes smiled as she laughed. Alex stuck his tongue out at her before he put everything he had into launching himself into Apollo's saddle. He succeeded, but not without some pain. He took a deep breath and awaited Riana's directions.

It wasn't that Derek, Matthew and Alex hadn't even ridden before, it just wasn't a regular occurrence. Riana made sure to arrange the group so there was a more experienced rider behind or in front of the guys, just in case. As they slowly moseyed away from the house it was apparent Riana didn't typically take Adonis out for such leisurely rides. He seemed antsy and pranced around as a request that Riana let him go. They rode in silence for a while and got used to their horses. As they became more comfortable they broke apart the line, and gathered side by side. Alex pulled Apollo up to Adonis and grinned over at Riana. "Having fun?" she asked.

Alex pretended to ponder for a moment. "Yeah." he eyed Riana. "Could be more fun if we raced." he teased.

She threw her head back and laughed heartily. "No, Alex, you don't want to race." she assured with a few more chuckles. "Adonis would own Apollo. I might emasculate you." Adonis seemed to sense the conversation as he started to dance around again.

"Alright." Riana conceded. "How about if Adonis and I lead you and Apollo into a trot first? See how you manage?" Alex shook his head slightly as he felt highly underestimated. He nodded though and readjusted in the saddle. Riana's eyes held the slightest bit of an evil twinkle as she seemed to settle deeper into Adonis' back before she gave him a quick kick.

Adonis responded instantly and sped up. Apollo followed suit without any encouragement from Alex. Alex tried desperately to find a rhythm with Apollo like Riana had with Adonis. He almost laughed at the irony; he was a drummer, it should have been easy to find a rhythm. Eventually he was sure he found the right rhythm as the jostle of the trot became less painful, so he gave Apollo a slight kick to get closer to Adonis. Alex pulled up by Riana and grinned foolishly. "You got it?" she asked.

Alex nodded. "Yep. Let's go." Riana shook her head at him, eased back on Adonis and brought him back to a walk. Alex did the same with Apollo as the rest of the group caught up. Alex and Riana looked back and couldn't prevent the laughter that followed. The look on Matthew's face as Sonny trotted was one of absolute panic. They both found it utterly hilarious. "Awww, Matt. Too much to handle?" Alex teased. Matthew shot him the finger then grasped the reins quickly as he and the others pulled up next to Alex and Riana.

"It's been awhile." Matthew explained. "I'm sure I'll find the groove."

CHAPTER ELEVEN

I Know You See It

Riana was wonderfully amused as she watched the guys attempt to get comfortable with the horses. Derek appeared to be a natural; the pairing of him and Ringo was a match made in heaven. He laughed and carried on with Lexi as they rode side by side. Matthew seemed nervous with Sonny, but Sonny being the sweet girls she was, didn't react to his nerves and simply kept pace next to Lilo. "Matt, honey, you have to trust Sonny." Riana called. "She won't let anything bad happen to you." He nodded apprehensively and she smiled softly. "I promise!"

They carried on, and played around with different gaits. Riana was drawn to watch Alex; his broad shoulders, strong arms, his hair tousled by the wind and his hips. Once he found a nice rhythm it was difficult for Riana to keep her eyes off the natural rocking motion of his hips as he eased off the saddle then back into it with the gait of Apollo. She bit her lip. The image incredibly sexy and she was sure it would drive her out of her mind. She gave Adonis a quick kick and looped back around to Lexi's side as she and Derek laughed together.

"Looking good D!" Riana hollered. He grinned over at her. "Seems you're quite the natural." She caught Lexi's eye and nodded her head to the side. A silent, yet understood gesture for Lexi to follow Riana away from the group for a moment.

"What's up lady?" Lexi asked once they were out of earshot of everyone else. Alex ran circles around Matthew and teased him relentlessly. Derek slowly followed behind and laughed at them. Samantha tried to reassure Matthew that Sonny would stay steady despite Alex's antics.

"Oh you know, checking out Alex, being overcome with naughty thoughts. The usual." Riana grimaced. Lexi laughed gaily at her.

"He is looking pretty good isn't he?" she teased.

Riana grabbed her vertical labret between her teeth and nodded. "He's looking *damn* good. Too good." She sighed. "I can't be thinking like this Lexi. He's too important to me." Riana paused. "Ryan is too important to me." As she looked over at Lexi she couldn't help but feel that as her best friend, Lexi could have at least attempted to hide how she felt about Ryan. However, the exasperated look on Lexi's face was easily understood.

"Ri, let me ask you a simple question." Riana knew Lexi's simple questions were never simple but she evened her face and awaited the challenge. "Why haven't you ever invited Ryan here?"

Riana quickly responded with her standard reason. "Lexi, you know why I don't share this place with many people. I don't want the judgment, or the change in treatment because of the money."

"Then why did you invite the guys?" Lexi asked quickly.

"Um, if I remember correctly it was you who practically begged me to invite them." Riana countered as she narrowed her eyes.

"Details." Lexi dismissed airily. "Why did you say yes?" she asked with a pointed look. Riana remained stoic. "Let me help. You said yes, Ri, because somehow you knew instinctively they wouldn't pass judgment, they wouldn't change how they act around you or treat you. Much like me and Sam. Now, given that, we have to wonder why it is you don't tell Ryan." Riana seethed. She really hated when Lexi had such valid points. "I don't really believe you trust Ryan as much as you say you do." she concluded as Riana scowled. "Just think it over a bit, Ri. There's something not right there, and you know it. You can't beat yourself up for seeing something good in someone else." She caught Riana's eye. "He sees the good in you." Riana's face quickly darkened with an embarrassed blush.

Lexi smiled sympathetically at Riana. She could tell that Riana's mind was overcome with too many conflicting thoughts. "Everything will be okay honey. Just enjoy the ride." She gave Chester a quick kick and took off. Riana gave Adonis the okay and they chased after them. Soon, the sound of thundering hooves was heard behind them.

Alex and Riana pulled away from the group after Riana coaxed Alex on to race. Lexi fell back and sighed. It was painful and frustrating for Lexi and Sam to watch Riana struggle with something that seemed so obvious to those who watched from the outside. The worst part was it wasn't new. Riana had struggled with the rollercoaster that was Ryan for years. Lexi hated that Riana couldn't see how much better she deserved.

"Everything okay?" a calm, deep voice questioned. Lexi looked over and smiled at Derek as he brought Ringo up to her and Chester.

"I'm sure everything will be okay."

Derek cocked his head to the side a bit. Lexi looked towards Alex and gave a little nod. "Ah." Derek comprehended. "I see."

"I think she's making it more complicated than it has to be." Derek nodded. Lexi watched ahead of them as Alex caught up to Riana. They both looked so happy. Matthew and Sam trotted along behind them; Matthew finally comfortable in the saddle.

"I was worried at first." Derek's voice startled Lexi out of her thoughts. "About Riana and Alex." he clarified. He appeared lost in his own thoughts for a moment. "I mean, you, Sam and Ri didn't worry me exactly. We felt at ease with you all right from the start. There was just something I could see when Alex and Riana would look at each other that worried me. Surely you remember our ride to dinner in Chicago and my commentary." Lexi smiled and nodded. "I guess...I mean, now that Kim is out of the picture I don't worry as much. I just don't want him to jump into something too quickly after her, you know?"

"I do. Of course, there's still Ryan lingering about in Ri's life." Lexi noted with obvious annoyance.

The group ahead of Lexi and Derek continued to play and chase each other as Lexi and Derek fell further behind. "What's going on there anyway?" he asked. "It just seems like there's some, umm, interesting dynamics."

"What a polite way to put it, D." Lexi laughed. "I think it's pretty much impossible to explain because it just doesn't make sense. They met in college. Riana was instantly smitten and it was good for a little while." Derek nodded as he followed along. "He plays with her now though. He can't seem to fully commit to her. He keeps her just barely holding on, giving her just enough that she has hope he still loves her. It pisses me and Sam off so much, watching her go through the same cycle of bullshit time and time again. She knows deep down it's not right." Lexi explained.

"Well she has to, otherwise why would she have kept this place a secret from him?"

"Exactly!" Lexi exclaimed. "She's a hopeless romantic though, and loyal to a fault. Makes for a bad combination when it comes to Ryan."

They rode in silence for a bit. They lost sight of the other four but neither of them seemed to mind. "What about you?" Derek asked suddenly.

"Huh?" Lexi questioned. She wondered if he was blushing or if sunburn was setting in.

"Do you...have...someone.." he trailed off and it finally clicked for Lexi.

"Oh!" she blurted. "No. I prefer to keep my life a bit less complicated." She smiled at him and he nodded with a small smile.

"Me too." He remained quiet afterwards. "Say Lex? Where did they all run off to?" Lexi scanned the horizon.

"No worries dear, I know where Riana took them. C'mon." she called as she had Chester take off in a canter towards the edge of the sky.

Alex enjoyed being able to run with Apollo after Riana decided she finally trusted him enough in the saddle to go all out. He was able to fully understand the appeal of horseback riding. Trail rides were nice, but letting a horse go full force was a thrill unlike many other things. There was an exhilaration in the sensation of so much power beneath him and the sun and wind against his face. Riana's time loss while riding finally made sense to him. Matthew and Sam cantered around as well, but Riana; she flew on Adonis and face was overcome by unadulterated happiness. Alex looked around and realized they had lost Derek and Lexi. He also noticed the barren landscape had gradually transformed into green. Suddenly Riana pulled up beside him; both her and Adonis panted heavily. "Hey Sunshine." Alex greeted.

"Hey." she breathed. "We're gonna stop for lunch right up here." She nodded towards a small lake. Alex pulled back on Apollo to slow him down to lazily walk along with Adonis. Matthew and Samantha trotted up to them, then also eased down to a calm walk.

"Break time?" Samantha questioned. Riana nodded.

"Awesome, I think my ass needs a break." Matthew grumbled.

The fact that Riana pretty much lacked a filter from brain to mouth was frequently entertaining and this moment was no exception. The laughter exploded from her mouth, "Matthew you don't have an ass!" Her laughter was contagious and Alex leaned into Apollo's neck as he, too, laughed heartily.

"Yes I do!" Matthew argued. Even Samantha snickered.

"Sure. Whatever you say, Matt." Riana chuckled. They eased up to a green clearing next to the edge of the lake. Samantha was the first one dismounted. She quickly looped Lilo's reins around a tree then turned to hold Sonny's reins as Matthew dismounted.

Alex followed suit and swiftly hopped off Apollo. He grasped his reins and led him over to Riana, where he stood by to assist her, much like

Matthew had when they first arrived. Riana gazed down at Alex and gave a small smile as she lifted her right foot from the stirrup and swung it up and behind her. As she started her descent Alex grasped her hips and eased her to the ground. Her feet hit the grass and she turned to face him. Alex assumed she would thank him, but she was silent. He was keenly aware of the proximity of their bodies, and how his hands still had a firm grasp on her hips. Her eyes had the slightest bit of veiled desire, or maybe he had only imagined it as he was sure his eyes held the same forbidden feeling.

Riana tried frantically to take control of the feelings that took over her as she became locked into Alex's beautiful and engaged stare. She was overcome by him; his intense eyes, the way his lip curled into his mouth as he nervously bit it, and the secure hold his heavy hands had on her hips. She couldn't stop the desperate pleas in her mind; *pull me closer, kiss me, I need you.* She barely noticed when her tongue snaked out and wet her lower lip as she closed her eyes and sighed. Alex unconsciously mirrored the same behavior.

"Hey lovebirds!" Samantha teased. "You going to unload lunch or what?" Riana shot her a vehement glare but turned away from both her and Alex as a deep and revealing blush overtook her face. Alex simultaneously relinquished the physical hold he had on her and took a step back. Riana was sure, however, the emotional and mental hold he had on her wouldn't be so easily broken.

As she went to remove everything they needed for lunch from Adonis' saddlebag Ri noticed her hands trembling. She sensed Alex next to her but knew she couldn't look at him, if she did she'd surely lose herself. His rough, calloused hand gently covered her quivering hand and fingers. "Let me help." he urged softly as he removed his hand from hers and proceeded to open the saddlebag and pull their cold lunches from it.

Riana slowly ambled around Adonis to get water from the other saddlebag. "Hey kids!" Derek hollered as he and Lexi trotted down the hill towards the clearing where Riana, Alex, Sam and Matt set up. Riana took a deep breath, thankful for another distraction. Derek and Lexi dismounted quickly and tied up their horses. Riana tossed a half-frozen water at Derek. "Thanks lady." he called out as he handed it to Lexi. Riana grinned as she saw first-hand his gentlemanly ways weren't just a public production.

They casually unpacked everything for lunch and ate while they chatted amongst each other. Riana, ever the wine connoisseur, packed a bottle of sweet red for all of them to split. The horses enjoyed their time in the shade and sipped at the lake's edge. Lexi decided she wanted to relax and close her eyes and Derek was quick to offer his chest as a recliner of sorts for her. Alex nudged Riana, nodded in their direction and wiggled his eyebrows. Riana held back a giggle and lightly pinched him.

"Ugh, it's so hot." Samantha moaned. She looked at Riana and grinned. "Want to go swimming?"

Riana startled Alex when she jumped up eagerly. "Hell yes." she confirmed as she stripped off her shirt and revealed her turquoise bikini top. The bright color offset her tan skin and brought out the depth of her cobalt eyes. She grunted as she pulled off her boots then shimmied out of her jeans. Samantha did the same, her off beat purple polka dot and tie dye bikini a perfect match to her quirky personality. The guys stared at them, completely bewildered. Riana suddenly became self-conscious. "Um, you guys coming?" she asked. Alex looked to Matthew.

"We didn't know we'd be going swimming." Matthew answered with a hint of confusion. Samantha giggled.

"If you're implying you don't have any swim shorts, you're wrong. We always swim in the lake when we ride, so we had Derek pack some shorts for you." she asserted. She skipped over to Lilo and pulled three sets of shorts from the saddlebag. "D, you can wait until Lex wakes up, but here ya go." She grinned as she tossed a pair in his direction. Next, she threw a pair at Matthew then Alex.

"We promise not to peek." Riana snickered as she grabbed Sam's hand and hastened to the water.

Matthew looked to Alex and shrugged. "At least they plan ahead." They left the picnic area and went to change by the horses; the hope being that the horses and the thicker trees would shield them from any prying eyes. "So...Alex..." Matthew ventured cautiously. "Seemed to be a little, um, moment between you and Ri earlier."

Alex's eyes turned playful yet a bit embarrassed. He cleared his throat. "I'm not exactly sure what happened there." he admitted as he slipped on his shorts and tossed his jeans and boxers onto Apollo's saddle.

"Alex," Matt started as he shed his shirt. "I'm not saying this to be mean, okay? I just want to look out for you--for both of you." Alex looked at him expectantly. "It's obvious you have some feelings for her. I also think it's obvious she has feelings for you." Alex snorted in disbelief but Matt continued. "You need to be careful Alex. She's a taken woman. I don't want to see things... get messy."

Alex tightened his jaw, then sighed in defeat. "I do. Have feelings for her, that is." He glanced up at Matt, his eyes smiled just a bit. "I wouldn't say it's obvious she has them for me. I can hope right?" They both chuckled. "You're right though. I know she's taken. I know I need to respect that. I just... He's just such an ass to her."

Matthew looked at him tenderly. He knew it couldn't be easy for him; to have formed feelings for a woman taken by someone who didn't treat her so well. "She needs to see a man can be kind to her. Be that man, Alex. Be there for her and she'll figure it out."

"Alex!!!" Riana called. "Matt! Come on!" Matthew laughed when he saw how quickly Alex answered Riana's call as he was already at least six steps ahead of Matt as he headed towards the lake.

CHAPTER TWELVE

Let Me Hold You

"Good. Fucking. Lord." Riana mumbled as Alex sauntered towards her and Sam. She quickly regretted the decision to go swimming, it was obviously a terrible idea to see the man half-clothed. She looked to Samantha, panicked.

"It's okay Ri, relax. You're friends. It's okay." Sam tried in vain to calm Riana down.

Riana gave her an urgent look. "It'd be easier to be friends if he wasn't so ungodly beautiful. Ugh, *look* at him." Alex's shaggy black hair was still disheveled from the ride, he smiled joyfully, his eyes were bright and alive. Riana's eyes continued to scan along his body; his broad shoulders, taut arms, and smooth, toned chest. He wasn't heavy by any means, but not quite thin like Matthew. He was strapping; strong and robust. Her mind went places she unsuccessfully tried to keep it from. She felt her body flush from the intensity of the images that flashed in her mind; her hands delicately tracing over his skin, his strong hands on her, their lips melding together. She told herself she could never have someone who exemplified beauty and sex in such a way. It was torture to entertain such silly fantasies.

161

Samantha couldn't very well blame Riana for having freaked out a bit. Alex was, indeed, unnaturally sexy. The best part was he didn't seem to realize it. He strolled towards the bank, then got an evil grin as he eyed Riana. Samantha grinned. She found it adorable how they already seemed able to read each other.

Riana started to back up with her hands in front of her, "Don't even *think* about it, Alexander!" Clearly she thought using his full name might deter him from what she could tell was a devious plan. Alex's grin radiated and he took off in a full run. Riana gave a delighted squeal and tried to escape. Alex got to her quickly, scooped her up effortlessly and flung her over his shoulder like a sack of flour. He gave a deep, hearty laugh and Riana giggled uncontrollably.

Sam felt movement beside her and she turned to see Matt watch the antics between Alex and Ri. He couldn't hide the happy amusement which danced on his face. "It really is pretty great, and terribly sad at the same time isn't it?" he mused. Samantha knew exactly what he meant and nodded.

She didn't want to ruin the mood of the day going over the dramatics of Riana and Alex. She typically avoided any negativity if she could so, instead of engaging Matthew, she hollered through laughter at Alex, "Hey! Let her go!" as she leapt towards him. Riana had been moved from over Alex's shoulder to cradled in his arms with her hands latched behind his neck. Samantha jumped on Alex's back but the next thing she knew Matthew had her slung over his shoulder. It was a blur of laughter and happiness.

Derek and Lexi remained on the shore. Lexi was still asleep against him. Derek eased his eyes shut as he drifted into his thoughts. Despite his initial apprehension regarding Lexi, Riana and Sam he couldn't deny the fun they'd had and the ease in which he talked with all of them; especially Lexi. He looked down at her as she rested between his legs, her head placed against his chest. He absentmindedly twisted her curls around his fingers as he watched Riana, Alex, Sam and Matthew play in the lake. He started to contemplate that perhaps the reason he hadn't found anyone to share his life with was because of his mistrust. It wasn't easy for him to jump in and believe things were real when he'd been treated as a commodity for the last ten years. Riana, Lexi and Sam didn't treat them like that, though. He loved how they teased the guys relentlessly but at the same time supported them completely. They had their own lives and didn't appear to be obsessed with D.M.A. like other fans. They shared personal stories, but never expected any in return. He knew he had unwittingly started to increasingly trust them. For once, it didn't scare him, he was excited to see what these honest friendships would bring.

Lexi stirred against him. She turned her head up towards his and smiled. "Did I actually fall asleep?" she inquired as she sat up.

"Indeed." Derek grinned. "Everyone else is swimming, did you want to join them?"

"Did you?" she questioned back. He couldn't stop smiling at her.

He nodded thoughtfully as he looked back out at the lake, "Yeah, I think I do."

"Sweet." Lexi yipped as she reached down and pulled her boots and socks off. She then hopped up, undid her jeans and danced around a little as she squirmed out of them. Derek leaned back against the tree and laughed at her; while he also took in her curvaceous form. His gaze panned up her legs, over her smooth stomach and along the swell of her breasts before his eyes suddenly found hers. Lexi had a bewildered, yet amused look on her face. He was instantly flustered at being caught checking her out. She raised one arched eyebrow, "You gonna get changed?" she asked with a wink.

Derek fumbled as he attempted to form words, "Umm. Yeah...I was... yeah...I'll get changed." Lexi giggled at him and reached down to offer him a hand to get up off the ground.

"Hey Matt? Does your son like horses?" Riana asked as they leisurely rode back towards the ranch. The sun had dipped into the horizon and casted long shadows ahead of them.

"Definitely." Matthew smiled. "He's only done carnival pony rides though. Tabs and I haven't taken him full blown riding yet."

Riana nodded thoughtfully. "I have a couple ponies. He could take one out." she rambled as she stared off into the distance. Lexi and Sam knew she was dancing around the issue of Tabitha's arrival the next day. "I mean, I'd keep them in the corral, but I think he'd really enjoy it. Sugar and Spice are both super sweet. Much like Sonny there." She nodded towards Sonny.

Matt reached down and patted Sonny's neck with a smile. "I think he'd love it Ri." he assured.

As they got to the ranch Derek noticed an extra vehicle in the driveway. "Umm, Ri? I thought this place was secure?"

A large smile formed on Riana's face. "Don't worry dear, those are my ranch hands. Jake and Dustin help out around the stables for me." she explained. "I'm especially happy to see them here now as I'm too exhausted to clean all these horses up."

"Right!?" Lexi laughed in agreement. They steered the herd towards the stable where two handsome, young, strong men mucked stalls.

"Hola Jake y Dustin." Riana greeted. The two men tipped their hats to her. "Puedes limpiar los caballos?" A look of astonishment appeared on Alex's face, then a proud, bright smile as Riana asked them to take care of the horses in beautiful Spanish. Jake, the shorter of the two with long, dark hair and shy eyes nodded and smiled at her.

"Hola Riana, si, vamos a limpiar los caballos." Dustin agreed to handle the horses as he approached Adonis and grabbed the reins from Riana as she quickly dismounted.

"Gracias." she smiled. "Estos son mis amigos, Matthew, Alex y Derek." she introduced the guys. Jake and Dustin removed their cowboy hats and gave a small nod. "You guys can go ahead and dismount, Jake and Dustin will clean up the horses." Alex, Matt and Derek nodded silently, still shocked by Riana's fluent Spanish. She beamed proudly at them.

As Alex walked back to the house he shook his head lightly, and wondered if there was any way Riana could stop amazing him. "Riana, I had no idea you could speak Spanish." Derek gushed, still in disbelief himself.

"Eh, it's pretty much necessary living out here." she said nonchalantly.

Matthew slung his arm over her shoulder. "You, lady, are full of all kinds of surprises."

"Man, I love the ache of a good ride." Riana sighed as she fell into a large armchair in the back sitting room.

"I don't think I feel quite the same way." Derek laughed as he attempted to stretch out his back. "I think I'm going to hit the hot tub if that's okay, Ri?"

"Of course my dear." Sam, Matt and Lexi concurred with Derek's idea and left to change. "I'm going to shower and lay down I think." Riana mumbled as she pulled her hair from her tie back.

Her blonde hair fell across her shoulders and she shook it out some. "Have fun kids!" she hollered as they disappeared. She got up and started down the hall. Alex remained in the sitting room and she turned to him. "I'm going to watch a movie after I shower if you wanted to join me." Alex noticed pinkness in her round cheeks as she offered and he nodded with a smile.

"Alright. I'm going to shower too then, would hate to stink up your room." Riana rolled her eyes and laughed. As Alex scurried upstairs he made a mental note to just let things go as they would. To be there for her like Matthew said. Despite how badly he may have wanted something more to happen, he had to resist.

Alex relished the feeling as he washed off the lake water, sweat and horse smells. He rushed through his shower and hastened downstairs. He stopped in the kitchen for snacks, then proceeded to Riana's room. He stood in the hall and chewed the inside of his full bottom lip, frozen. He suddenly felt about fourteen years old again. Not only did he feel fourteen, he felt stupid as well. He shook his head at his ridiculous apprehension, lifted his hand and knocked.

Riana was browsing her movies when she heard the quiet knock at her door. She swallowed over the slight lump in her throat and noticed her heart beat much too quickly. "Hey." she greeted as she opened her door to a shirtless, pajama pant clad Alex.

Alex held up his hand proudly. "I brought snacks!" he proclaimed as he balanced the bowl of popcorn in the palm of his large hand.

Riana snatched the bowl from him. "You know me so well." she laughed. She skipped over to her bed and sat cross-legged right in the middle. Alex stood in the middle of her room and looked around. "Um, Alex?" He quickly looked in her direction and she patted the bed. "Wanna join me?" He did one more scan around her room; he took in the city skyline prints, the endless papers strewn about on her desk, the clothes littered on the floor and the cases of books. He finally made his way to where she sat and munched on the popcorn. "You like comedies?" she asked with a huge grin. Alex loved how dorky she was, and loved that she allowed herself to be that way with him.

"Uh, duh?" he teased. "Whatcha have in mind?"

Riana hopped off her bed and scampered to her movie cabinet. She pulled a movie from the shelf and presented it excitedly, "Served!"

Alex applauded as he laughed, "Brilliant choice." Riana smiled proudly, tossed in the movie and leapt back onto the bed. Alex scooted back against the headboard and placed his sculpted arms behind his head. Riana took the spot next to him, with the bowl of popcorn between them.

Despite their exhaustion, they made it through the movie. Once they killed the bowl of popcorn Riana placed it on her bedside table and moved a bit closer to Alex. He watched her laugh at the disgusting jokes in the movie, and he couldn't contain his own laughter when a snort would escape through her nose. "Ah! It's funny because it's true!" she wailed through giggles. The bold statement intrigued Alex so, after the movie ended, they talked about how much truth the movie held in relation to Riana's experiences as a server. The truth was both hilarious and disturbing.

Alex loved Riana's stories; he loved to learn about her life and experiences. Especially when they were so entertaining. The best part for him was to know there had been more to her life than the heartbreaking basis of her book and speaking engagements. As they continued to chat Riana settled into the bed and naturally fell into Alex's body. Alex followed Matthew's advice and went with it. He didn't make any moves on her, but didn't push her away either.

Riana found something instinctually comfortable about Alex in her bed. It wasn't anything sexual. Given her past, any man in her bed made her exceptionally anxious; one might even use the word terrified. She realized, as she laid in the nook of Alex's side with his strong arm draped over her, that she hadn't even felt that at ease with Ryan. With Ryan, especially as of late, she knew there was an unspoken expectation of her, and she never let him down. Even as her heart and her mind knew that was the main, if not the only, reason Ryan wanted her there.

She found comfort and joy in being able to laugh with Alex about the inner workings of the restaurant industry. His sincere interest in her stories from everything from serving, to college and friends touched her in ways she didn't realize she'd been missing. Alex didn't bring up Kim, but he brought up Ryan as they talked about what their futures might hold. "Do you think you'll get married?" he asked as his hand ran up and down her arm.

"Maybe someday." she breathed. "Life is pretty insane right now. I'd need someone who could keep up."

She thought he would laugh, but instead he uttered two words she didn't want to hear, "To Ryan?"

Riana's breath and heart froze. She closed her eyes against the blatant reminder of her current position. "I always thought so." she whispered truthfully. The silence lingered around them for a long moment as she spun her vertical labret between her teeth. "I don't so much anymore." Alex's chest rose with a deep breath.

"Why don't you think it will be him?" he asked softly. He didn't want to push her, but he wanted to help her explore the change in feelings. She sat up, rested her elbow on his chest, plopped her chin into her hand, and gazed at him. She took in his heavy eyebrows, his deep brown eyes, the nose that she thought was absolutely perfect, the slightest bit of scruff under his nose and on his chin, and his strong jawline. In her mind he was the most beautiful man she'd ever seen.

Suddenly the words rolled off her tongue, "It doesn't feel the same. Sometimes… it doesn't feel right." Alex's eyes softened. "I guess, sometimes, I feel like he doesn't get me. Nor does he really try." Riana felt the start of tears in her eyes. She closed her eyes tightly and spoke through the darkness. "He's never read my book, never seen me speak."

She opened her glassy eyes to meet Alex's heartbroken face. "Oh Ri." he sighed. He pulled her back into his embrace. She despised getting overly emotional with people because it made her feel weak. She wanted to at least attempt to remain strong in Alex's eyes. Yet, there she was, overtaken by the pain caused by Ryan's inconsistencies.

"I don't want to talk about it anymore." she mumbled into Alex's smooth, bare chest.

Alex squeezed her. "You don't have to, Ri." he soothed. He felt his own chest tighten. He hated how Ryan treated her, how he played her, and how he didn't care about who she was; only what she provided him.

Despite the weight of the moment, Riana still felt it was right to remain wrapped in Alex's arms. She didn't feel the need to fill the silence, and neither did he. She simply laid there and listened to Alex's heart beat within his chest. She found comfort in the predictability of his breaths beneath her head. She sensed she could have stayed there forever and been perfectly content. "Alex?" she whispered.

"Yes dear?"

Riana contorted her head and neck to meet his eyes. "Can I ask you something?"

"Of course, anything." he replied certainly.

Riana suddenly felt it was silly for her to ask. Presumptuous even. She avoided his eyes, but proceeded with her question, "Would you.... I mean... You can say no. But would you... maybe... sing to me?"

Alex released a small breath and a modest smile played on his lips. He nodded as he sat up some. Riana went to move off him but he pulled her back. She settled her head back onto his chest and closed her eyes. She felt his smooth, deep, soulful voice roll through his chest, past his perfect lips and to her ears. She sighed blissfully, it was one of her favorite Snow Patrol songs. Alex's hand stroked Riana's arm again as he sang. It was a stark contrast between rough and smooth and it brought electric goose bumps to the surface of Riana's skin.

Riana smiled as the lyrics asked the listener if they would lay there and forget the world. She noted that was exactly what she was doing. She happily forgot everything that weighed on her. Riana felt her mind get heavy with impending sleep and Alex felt her breaths deepen. As she felt herself slip into sleep she vaguely thought to herself; *this must be what love feels like.*

CHAPTER THIRTEEN

Truth Is

As Riana and Alex bonded in Riana's bedroom the other four friends enjoyed their time easing their tired and sore muscles with both the pounding jets of the hot tub and the three bottles of wine they split amongst each other. "Shhhhh!" Lexi scolded as they snuck through the upstairs hallway. She grasped Derek's arm to steady herself.

"Ooh! Hold on, I want to see how things went with Ri and Alex." Matthew attempted to whisper as they neared Alex's room. He lightly knocked then slowly opened the door. "Oh Alex…" he cooed. The door swung all the way open, but all they saw was a confused look on Matt's face. He turned around, red faced and giggled. "Heeeey, Sam, is this Alex's room?"

Samantha burst out in laughter. "Uh, yeah."

"Guys!" Matthew again tried to whisper, but failed miserably. "He's not in here!"

"Ohmygod." Samantha breathed, her eyes widened in worry.

"Sam. No. Shhh." Lexi chided as she placed all her body weight against Derek. The floor seemed to run away from her. "I know what you're thinking, and you're wrong." she assured. "They're just still hanging out. Nothing's happening. Not like...that."

"Come on guys, Alex is a big boy, leave it alone." Derek lectured as he started to usher Lexi to her room.

"Woah, talk about a role reversal." Matthew quipped. Derek turned and shook his head.

"I guess I had a good teacher."

"That you did." Matt confirmed with a small nod as he closed Alex's bedroom door. "Ladies, I must bid you adieu, 'twas a lovely evening. We must do it again." Samantha and Lexi laughed at him and agreed. They called a sweet goodnight as he stumbled to his room.

Sam gave Derek and Lexi a quick hug as they got to the end of the hall. "See you in the morning!"

Lexi stood and wobbled in front of both her door and Derek. "I think...I should go to bed..." she pondered.

Derek laughed as he kept her steady, "I think you're right." He smiled down at her. "Goodnight Lexi." She leaned into him for a hug and was startled when she felt his warm lips press to her cheek. Her whole body increased temperature and she felt the need to get to her room instantly.

"I'll see you tomorrow!" she called as she quickly turned away from him and flung her door open. She caught a glimpse of mild confusion on his face as she shut the door behind her.

Riana had fallen asleep quickly once Alex started to sing to her, he could tell by the definite indicators of her sweet murmurs and light snores. He finished the song anyway, then laid there quietly with Riana cuddled into him. Even with the almost one foot height difference between them he couldn't help but smile when he realized how perfectly she fit.

Alex softly stroked her hair and sighed. Matthew's words replayed in his mind, *"She needs to see a man can be kind to her. Be that man Alex. Be there for her and she'll figure it out."* He shook his head lightly as his brow knitted together. He couldn't imagine anyone being unkind to her. The fact she'd had so many unkind men in her life enraged him. He looked down at her thoughtfully, felt his heart swell and made a mental promise that he would never be unkind to her. He scooted down into the bed, careful not to wake Riana, pulled the covers up and over them and kissed her forehead as he closed his eyes. His thoughts were prophetic as he drifted off to sleep; *Someday I could love her. Someday I will love her.* His concern was that "someday" quickly approached and he wasn't sure if either of them were ready for it.

Friday August 25, 2006

As Alex felt his body begin to wake he was keenly aware Riana was still snuggled into him. He kept his eyes closed and smiled. He had slept better than he had in months. He debated if it was all the fresh air and work of the ride, or if it was being with Riana.

He ventured it was her. He wished he could go back to sleep; he didn't want to wake up yet, he didn't want to leave that moment. Riana cuddled closer to him, if that were at all possible, and wrapped her arm tightly around his midsection. Her smooth, bare leg was tossed over his, her tank top had twisted up and revealed her bare back and side. Alex tried to stifle a yawn.

"No." Riana moaned, "Go back to sleep. I don't wanna get up yet." She didn't even attempt to remove her face from Alex's bare chest as she verbalized her desire to stay put. Alex squeezed her tighter and she murmured her approval.

"Did you sleep well?" he asked, his voice thick with the remnants of sleep.

She nodded against him. "The best." she whispered. "What time is it anyway?"

Alex turned his head to check Riana's alarm clock on the other side of the bed. "Umm, 9:45?"

Riana's head shot up, her hair a tangled mess. "Are you serious?" she challenged as she double checked her clock. "Damn." she muttered as she realized it was indeed almost ten am. It took Alex by surprise when instead of begrudgingly getting out of bed, Riana stretched out and then reclaimed her place cuddled into him. "Let's pretend that said 6:45 okay?"

Alex laughed deeply. "Aww, Ri, why are you resisting getting up?" Not that he could argue, he would have rather stayed exactly where he was all day as well.

"Many reasons." she mumbled against his chest again. "Like, the fact you're so warm." She giggled as she squirmed closer to him. Alex tried as hard as he could to keep calm. Reality was, she was a beautiful woman and he was a young man; despite how logical his brain might have been about the whole situation, his body reacted on instinct alone. "And..." She became speechless, which was quite unlike her.

"Ri?"

"I don't want to leave this yet. It's...perfect." she finished softly. Alex breathed deeply. "And if I get up I have to, you know, face things." She paused and frowned lightly. "Things like, the fact I shouldn't be wrapped up in you like this." she proclaimed as she ran her fingers along Alex's skin. There was beauty in the contrast of skin tone; Riana's much lighter skin with pink undertones against Alex's rich, darker skin. The sensation of her fingers along his skin drove his body insane. "Or the fact Tabitha is coming today."

"Alright." Alex declared as he sat up. "Let's address these." he offered. Riana sat up and looked at him with a mixture of a scowl and a pout. "I can't exactly argue against me being warm." He winked at her with a smile, and was happy to receive a smile in return. "But...about you being wrapped up with me." Riana's face flushed, she knew she went too far. It was inappropriate. She mentally scolded herself again. "Friends can cuddle Ri. I like cuddling with you." Alex admitted gently.

Riana looked up at him, her eyes unreadable. She wanted to blurt out that it was because she didn't want to be *friends* that the cuddling screwed with her mind so much, but she remained silent.

"I know that you're probably beating yourself up because of Ryan." Her heart dropped. "And if that's the case, I won't cuddle with you." It dropped even further. "I don't want to make things complicated Ri."

She stared at him, dumbfounded. Things were already complicated. She searched his eyes and tried to figure out his intentions. She wanted to throw herself back into his embrace, she wanted to kiss him. Instead she shook her head at him. "No."

His black brows furrowed as his eyes squinted. "No, what?"

"No, I don't want you to not cuddle with me." she informed with a firm pout on her face. "Because you're right. Friends can cuddle. I cuddle with Sam and Lexi all the time. In fact, studies have proven the positive effects of hugs and cuddling on both physical and mental health." *There you go Ri, take the emotion right out of it.* she thought proudly.

"Right." Alex quickly agreed. "As for Tabitha--" Riana groaned and Alex grinned at her. "It'll be fine Ri. I won't let anything bad happen to you." Riana was sure Alex had no idea the kind of weight that statement carried for her coming from a man. Men didn't protect Riana, they used her. They *were* the bad thing that happened to her.

Matthew, Sam, Lexi and Derek had been up for about three hours and had already finished breakfast, but hadn't seen Riana and Alex. They were outside about to relax in the pool when Sam voiced what they all thought. "Are you sure nothing was going on in there?" She directed the question to Lexi, being as Lexi was the one who said nothing would happen last night.

"Yes, I'm sure." she repeated firmly. "For knowing Riana for so long, you seem to have little faith in her. She's loyal to a fault Sam, she'd never cheat on Ryan. Even though if you ask me it wouldn't even be cheating as he can't commit to her the way she's committed to him."

"She deserves better." Matt observed sadly. He'd always known she deserved more, ever since she was a teenager. He'd read about how hurt she frequently was and he prayed every night she could find someone better, someone who would treat her the way she deserved. Part of him had even wondered if perhaps he should have been that person. Riana faded away though, and Tabitha came into his life. It didn't make it any easier to watch her still struggle.

"Understatement of the day." Sam grumbled as she slipped into the water.

"It's so weird though," Derek started. "She seems so smart--not just smart, brilliant. You'd think that she'd see how bad Ryan is for her."

Lexi gave Derek a small, sad smile. "Love doesn't know logic, D. Sadly, despite her healing

179

and her knowledge of the after effects of everything she's been through, it still made a huge impact on her. It changed how she views herself and her worth. She can't let go of the fact he was at one time good for her. She's desperate to believe it was real, and is still real. She thinks if she sees it for what it is now, it will change what it was."

Matt's heart broke as he realized the situation was much more complicated than Riana being taken. He wasn't sure if she'd ever be ready to see what was right in front of her in Alex. Matt's phone tore him from the conversation and his worry. "Good morning, my love." he greeted as he picked up Tabitha's call.

"Good morning honey. Just wanted to give you a call and let you know that we are at the airport, flight is on time and we should be landing around 4pm."

Matthew could hear his little boy Spencer in the background and it brought an instant smile to his face. "Perfect. I can't wait for you to get here. It's amazing. Riana has a surprise for Spence too."

He heard a sharp intake of breath, "Great." Tabitha snipped curtly. Matthew walked away from everyone else for a bit of privacy. He slipped through the sliding glass door and leaned against the kitchen island as he watched Sam, Lexi and Derek.

"Tabs, don't be like that. You're going to love her." Matt pushed firmly in a hushed tone.

"Much like Alex does I'm sure." she noted with a bite.

"Like we *all* do." he sternly corrected. "She's opening up her home to us, try being open-minded." Tabitha sighed on the other end.

"You're right, Matt. I'll try." she relented.

"There ya go. We'll be at the airport at four to pick you up. I love you, give Spencer hugs and kisses too." Matthew headed back towards the door to rejoin Sam, Lexi and Derek when he heard Riana's voice behind him.

"She doesn't want to come does she?" she looked utterly dejected as she stood in the entrance of the kitchen with her head downcast. Matthew hurried to her and pulled her into a side hug.

"No, Ri, it's not that she doesn't want to come..." he pursed his lips as he thought about how to handle this. "It's been hard on her... the breakup..."

Riana barely nodded her head. "She blames me for their breakup." she stated simply.

Before Matt could answer, Alex was in front of Riana. He placed his hand under her chin and brought her eyes to his. "That breakup was *my* decision." His eyes were fiery as he turned his face to look at Matthew. "Tabitha needs to understand that." His eyes instantly softened when he looked back at Riana. "Everything will be okay." he assured. She finally gave him a small smile then allowed herself to be pulled into his embrace.

Matthew knew, in no uncertain terms, that it was his job to make Tabitha understand Riana wasn't to blame for Alex's breakup with Kim. He had tried but Tabitha continued to resist. She loved Kim much the way Riana loved Sam and Lexi. Matthew hoped meeting her would help Tabitha understand she wasn't malicious and she didn't sabotage Alex's relationship.

"I'm actually really excited to meet Tabitha and Matt's son." Sam remarked as she floated around in her blow up lounge chair in the pool as Matt took his call in the house.

"Me too." Lexi smiled. "I just hope there isn't too much tension between Tabitha and Riana. She has a tough image, but Ri is a softy who wants people to like her."

"I've noticed." Derek commented as he took a shot to the water hoop. "She is likable though. She's super sweet, and funny. I find it hard to imagine people don't like her."

Samantha laughed. "She's also educated, articulate, assertive and hard-headed. A lot of people don't like that, especially in a woman." Derek raised his eyebrow in agreement.

"WATCH OUT!" Riana and Alex's voices echoed off the stonework around the pool. Sam squealed when a massive amount of water almost submerged her floaty as Riana and Alex did a double cannonball into the pool. Derek shook out his short, curly hair and Lexi quickly sputtered water off her face.

"You guys are ridiculous!" Lexi laughed once Riana and Alex re-emerged from under the water. They high-fived each other and laughed hysterically. Alex brought out the kid in Riana, something she desperately needed when one considered the childhood she had. Riana grabbed another floaty and pulled herself into it. She closed her eyes and sighed. Alex held on to the end of it and rested his chin on his arms as he gazed at her.

Their day was filled with a lot of lazing about, relaxation and attempts to take in as much vitamin D as possible without turning into crispy, burnt versions of themselves. Riana was oddly quiet as she attempted to manage the anxiety she had about meeting Tabitha.

Lexi found Riana around noon in her walk-in closet shortly after lunch. Riana tossed shirts, dresses and pants all over her floor. "Honey? Whatcha doing?" Lexi asked softly.

"Argh!" Riana wailed. "Trying to find something to wear." She huffed as she flicked through hanger after hanger. "I have to leave in twenty minutes and I don't have a damn clue what to wear." Lexi quickly went to Riana's side and placed her hand on her shoulder. "I want to look nice, but not too nice. I don't want to look sloppy though... ugh!"

Essentially anything looked amazing on Riana's tone, curvy body. "Sweetie, anything you wear will be fine." Lexi assured. Riana narrowed her eyes at her. "Seriously, I don't think it's going to make a huge difference what you wear."

"Right, she's going to hate me regardless." Riana pouted. Lexi grimaced at her and sighed. She walked along Riana's closet, grabbed a long, flowing, white skirt, a pink tank top and a pair of strappy sandals. She gathered it all in her arms and then flung them into Riana's.

"There. Now get dressed and get going! It won't be a good first impression if you and Matthew are late." Riana didn't bother to argue as she knew Lexi would win.

Alex sat outside with Matthew as they waited for Riana. It was a comfortable silence until Alex felt the need to break it. "I didn't break up with Kim because of Riana." he said simply.

Matthew quickly looked at him, shocked by his statement. Alex hadn't spoken at all to either him or Derek about his breakup with Kim. "I know."

"I don't think you do. I don't think anyone realizes while Riana is… special to me, she wasn't why I broke up with Kim." Matt nodded. "I always felt… pressured to make it work with Kim. You and Tabitha were so excited when Kim and I got along. I guess I felt it would make you both happy if Kim and I were together. Given the amount of time we always wound up spending together it just kind of happened. It didn't feel right though. It was okay, I guess, her company was nice, we had fun and she did really mean a lot to me…" Alex thoughtfully chewed his lip. "I guess… maybe Riana did play a part, kind of. She helped me realize what was missing with Kim. It wasn't working even before Riana though, you know?" Matt nodded again. He had no idea Alex hadn't truly wanted to be with Kim and he felt terrible for having played any kind of part in pushing him into something that made him unhappy. "Then when Kim went off the deep end when those pictures hit the internet, I took it as my out. Tabitha shouldn't be angry with Riana. If she needs to be mad at anyone it should be me."

"She shouldn't be angry at all." Matt stated. "I know she and Kim are close, but she shouldn't be so emotionally invested in Kim's relationships."

"Right?" Alex agreed with a small laugh. "Listen, I need your help in making this go well, Matt. Riana's not going anywhere if I have anything to say about it."

Matthew smiled brightly. "I know she isn't. I'll try my best to help this along Alex, I promise." The sound of the sliding glass door halted their conversation and Riana hesitantly stepped out.

She appeared to be agitated, nervous and unsure. She looked down at herself then up to Alex and Matthew. "Do I... look okay?" she questioned. Alex and Matt stared at her in disbelief. She was absolutely stunning in Alex's eyes, she always was. Alex approached her as he took her in. Okay was not a word he would use to describe her; pretty much perfect would be his choice. Her eyes locked on him and he saw just how terrified she was.

"Sweetheart, you look great." Alex assured. "Are you sure you don't want me to come with?"

Riana sighed. "As much as I want you to, I'm sure it won't help matters. Would probably make them worse I imagine." Alex twisted his lip into disappointed agreement.

"You're probably right." Matt agreed sadly.

Alex placed his hands on Riana's smooth upper arms. "Text me if you need to, I'll be right here—getting dinner ready." he smiled. Riana, however, didn't smile back. She swallowed thickly and nodded. "Hey…it'll be okay. You know I love you. I'll make sure she behaves."

Riana's eyes softened instantly; the moment Alex said he loved her. He chastised himself instantly, angry that he let it slip. He did love her though, she was his best friend. But he knew that was only the beginning.

Riana's heart jumped at his words. Even though she knew it was said from a place of friendship, the words grasped her soul and buried deep within her. Alex pulled her into a hug and she said "Me too." just barely above a whisper. He hoped she meant she loved him too, but he didn't dare ask.

Riana convinced herself to keep her feelings under strict observation, not to be admitted or acted upon. He didn't love her, not like *that*. She knew her love was in the process of quickly surpassing anything she could control. She pulled herself from his embrace and took a deep breath. "Alright, let's get this over with." she groaned reluctantly. Matthew came to her side and draped his arm over her.

"It will be okay dear, I promise. We all love you. Tabitha will too... eventually." He smiled down at her as they walked to the Jeep. Riana hopped into the driver's seat and Matthew jogged around to the passenger side. They rode in silence for a while, Riana's mind circled through different scenarios of how the meeting might play out. "Riana?" Matthew questioned. Riana turned and looked at him. She noticed his blue eyes were heavy with concern.

Matthew didn't have to finish his question. His eyes provoked her to speak. "Matt, I... I just want her to like me. I mean, she's your wife. I pretty much can't imagine my life without you guys, but if your wife hates me..."

"She's not going to hate you Ri." he said. It did nothing to ease her anxiety. "And considering how long I've known you," he smiled at her as he referred not to the last three months, but rather the nine years before. "I can't really picture my life without you either."

Riana pursed her lips, then continued to ramble; another nervous habit. "I didn't try to make Alex breakup with Kim." She kept her gaze on the road. She knew if she saw Matthew's look of compassion she'd surely cry. "My intentions were never romantic Matt. He's one of my best friends."

"I know honey." he assured softly. "Tabs is just protective of Kim, but because of that she was never really able to see what was missing between Kim and Alex." Riana glanced over at him, confused. "Alex felt obligated to be with Kim." he explained. "It seemed like a logical pairing. They had fun together and I know he cared about her. But he didn't love her the way he loves-- the way he should have." Matthew avoided Riana's quick look, he knew he almost made a huge slip up. "He saw an out and he took it, Ri. It just really sucks you got stuck in the middle."

"Tell me about it." she muttered. They fell into another round of silence. Riana was once again in disbelief that somehow her life ended up there. The fourteen year old inside her still danced around giddily when she looked at any of the guys.

She could tell something weighed on Matthew's mind but she was afraid to find out what it was. "How long have you and Ryan been together?" he asked suddenly.

Riana stumbled over an odd mixture of a laugh and a grumble. "It's complicated to say the least." she started. "We met fall semester of my freshman year at university in 2002. I think I loved him instantly. There was a magnetic, unnatural draw to him. He was hard to get though." She laughed as she remembered how frustrating their courtship had been. "We became official January of 2003 but almost instantly it became dysfunctional." She glanced over at Matt and smiled softly when she saw how intently he listened. "There were good things before the dysfunction; a lot of laughter, he taught me how to take things slow, how to love someone before being intimate. It didn't last long, we broke up in March. I was so in love with him, though. I couldn't let go. Neither could he. We continued to see each other and he became my rock after I was raped. He stood by my side, respected my choices in intimacy. He was good for me, Matt." Matt nodded. "But...here we are, three years later. I'm still ridiculously in love with him and he… still can't commit. He'll go weeks, even months, without speaking to me." Riana didn't miss the deep frown on Matthew's face. "But he always comes back Matt. I know he must love me."

Matthew shook his head. "No, Ri, he comes back because you allow it." Riana narrowed her eyes at him. "I don't doubt that he loved you at one point. But with being so disrespectful now, there's just no way he loves you." His words hit her hard. Matt reached over and held her right hand between both his hands. "Riana." he began sternly. "You are…" he looked up dramatically, "*amazing*. You've always been amazing. You're strong, intelligent, witty, compassionate, funny and assertive. You are worthy of love and respect. *Real* love and respect. If Ryan can't see that and treat you accordingly, then I think you need to walk away." Riana locked her jaw and tried not to cry. "Being with you is a privilege Riana. You should give the privilege to someone who deserves it."

Riana nodded silently. Shortly after though, the tears started. "What if no one else will want me Matt?" She quickly wiped the tears off her cheeks. "I'm… not easy to love. I'm complicated and moody. I'm always terribly busy. I overthink things,

I don't cook, I can be messy, I'm hard to please. I overreact, I'm territorial. I have… tragic baggage."

She glanced over and was shocked when she saw Matt wipe tears from his own face. "All the more reason you need out, Ri. You need to learn how to embrace these things as a part of who you are. I promise you'll find someone who will take all these things and love them because they are a part of you." He found her eyes. "I promise."

Somehow, she believed him.

CHAPTER FOURTEEN
Collide

Alex left the house to watch the horses in the pasture. The pasture was surrounded by a sturdy wooden fence, which he hoisted himself up on before he gazed out to the horizon. The pasture was sporadically green, mostly sand really, but Riana supplemented hay for the horses. It was stuffed into four feeders spread out as to not cause feeding congestion or fighting. There were also two, what looked to be carports, placed oddly in the middle of the pasture. Not barns, and obviously not carports but rather shelters for the horses to escape the hot Arizona sun. Alex's heart swelled; Riana took absolutely wonderful care of her horses. She rescued all of them, and said they deserved the best to balance out their rough beginnings.

Alex smiled and thought back, hardly able to believe it had only been three months. He felt like he had known Sam, Lexi and Riana for years. He felt like he'd known Ri forever; almost as if he'd known her before. He couldn't stop the flood of feelings for her that had quickly consumed him. No matter how many times he told himself she was taken, that he was freshly broken up, it was too soon, and he couldn't possibly know so soon or so certainly; despite it all, he loved her. She brought joy to him he hadn't known in years. He was comfortable with her,

191

yet at the same time always on edge due to the pull she had on him. He loved her smile and her laugh. He adored her quick wit and her passion. "Yep, there it is. I love her." Alex declared aloud.

"Good." Samantha remarked as she climbed up next to him.

"Holy shit Sam! Don't scare me like that!" Alex yelled as he attempted to keep his heart within his chest. He took a deep breath, "You weren't supposed to hear that." he mumbled quietly.

"It's okay Alex, I pass no judgment." she smiled gently and patted his knee.

Panic took a hold of him. "You aren't going to tell her, are you?"

"Absolutely not."

Alex examined her thoughtfully for a moment. She was stunning; a classic beauty within her quirkiness. "Why not?"

Samantha smiled warmly at him then out towards the golden sun. "A few reasons I suppose." she began considerately. "First of all, Riana is a people pleaser--shocking I know." she laughed. "If she knew you had feelings for her she'd likely feel obligated to jump into things I don't think she's quite ready for."

Alex's heart sank. "I don't want her to feel obligated to do anything." he admitted. He knew exactly how that felt and refused to make Riana feel the same way.

"I know. Which leads me to reason number two. She'll get there Alex. But she needs to get there on her own." Alex nodded silently. "You're good for her, like really good for her. Stick it out if you truly love her, she'll make it worth the wait."

Alex smiled as he imagined what it would be like to be Riana's partner. "I don't doubt that at all. I'll wait as long as it takes." Sam couldn't have smiled any bigger or brighter.

"That's what I like to hear. You should probably come inside in a few. We have to start dinner if you want it to be ready when they get back." She shot him a wink then hopped off the fence.

Riana and Matthew got to the airport with ten minutes to spare yet Riana couldn't stop the panic in her chest, or the trembling of her hands. They stood at baggage claim and watched for Tabitha and Spencer. "So remind me again, how old is Spencer?"

Matthew looked over at Riana and shook his head. "You really aren't anything like most fans." he laughed as he referred to what Riana considered to be the disgusting amount of information D.M.A.'s fans kept logged away in their obsessive brains. As the years had passed in Riana's life her love for D.M.A. the band never diminished but she grew up; and realized her pipe dreams of marrying Matthew Sullivan were ridiculous. She always loved the music which is why she remained a fan but she never understood the appeal of essentially stalking their lives. "Spencer is four."

"Okay, got it." she breathed deeply.

Matthew grabbed Riana's upper arm and pulled her from her distracted thoughts. "There they are!" he hollered. He pulled her along with him for a moment then let go as he and Spencer ran to each other.

"Daddy!" Spencer squealed delightedly. Matthew scooped him up and kissed his cheek. Tabitha approached behind and Matt turned and happily met her lips. Riana smiled warmly at the intense love in his little family. They chatted eagerly as Matthew brought them back to where Riana stood awkwardly.

"This is Riana." he started as he smiled at her and elicited a shy smile back. "We're going to be staying at her ranch for a while."

"Hi." Riana greeted softly. She looked towards Tabitha and noticed she stared at her with an intensity Ri wasn't prepared for.

"Riana." she stated coolly.

Riana would have been incredibly overwhelmed had Spencer's small voice not brought her back to the moment. "You have ponies?" he asked excitedly.

Riana laughed lightly. "I do." she replied as they started towards the baggage corral. "Do you like horses?" she asked. Spencer nodded quickly. "Good. I'll take you to meet all of them." Matthew started a juggling act as he held Spencer and grabbed bags. Riana noticed Tabitha seemed to be having difficulty grabbing the last two bags and Spencer's car seat. "I can take that if you'd like Tabitha." she offered hesitantly.

Tabitha looked at Riana a bit suspiciously but gave a small smile. "Thanks Riana." Riana let go of a breath she didn't realize she'd been holding. Matt gave her a reassuring smile, and she quickly rolled her eyes at him. She still wasn't looking forward to the three hour drive back to the ranch, but at least she didn't quite feel like Tabitha would strangle her from behind.

Lexi and Derek lounged in the sitting room deemed the theater watching some TV after they got their fill of water and sun outside. "So," Lexi started. "You think we're all ready for this?"

Derek intently stared at the screen of "World's Dumbest Criminals." He shook out his head and looked over to Lexi. "Ready for?"

"Tabitha." she stated simply. "Obviously it was only a matter of time before we all met her.."

Derek gave Lexi a smile then patted the spot next to him on the couch. She grinned and moved from the armchair to the place next to him. She curled her legs up under herself and turned to face him. He gazed at her for a moment then tucked a bit of her unruly curls behind her ear. "I think it's wonderfully sweet how worried you are about Riana and Tabitha." Lexi felt a light blush warm her cheeks as Derek's fingers barely touched the side of her face. "I think between Riana's assertiveness and Alex and Matthew's protectiveness of her, Tabitha will quickly discover any resentment towards Ri will not be tolerated." Lexi barely nodded. "Tabitha isn't all bad Lexi. She's actually very fun and sweet. She wants the best for those she loves and I think the more she gets to know Riana, the more she'll see she's good for Alex."

Lexi sighed uneasily. "I hope you're right."

Derek pulled her into his side and squeezed her. "Of course I'm right." he laughed. He didn't remove his arm from her shoulders and Lexi took a deep breath through her nose as she settled into him.

Alex remained on the fence for a bit after Samantha left. It was difficult to process everything; how he so effortlessly fell in love with one of his best friends, how terrified he was that she would find out, and how desperately he didn't want her to feel obligated to be with him just because he couldn't stop a progression of feelings that should have been kept in check right from the beginning. Yet, he wanted nothing more than for her to feel the same way, to know he loved her, and he wanted her to choose him over Ryan. He grimaced a bit, glanced down at his watch and figured it was about time to start on dinner if he wanted it ready by the time they got back. He smiled as he jumped off the fence and thought about how happy it made him to take care of Riana any way he could; starting with dinner.

As Alex entered the house and headed towards the kitchen he noted that he couldn't seem to find anyone else. He walked the halls in search of them. *This place would be absolutely epic for hide and seek.* He chuckled to himself. He found Lexi, Derek and Sam absorbed in terrible reality TV. Lexi and Derek were cuddled up together on the couch and Sam was in the armchair next to them. He cleared his throat, "Hey, anyone want to help me make dinner?"

Lexi smiled brightly at Alex. "Absolutely!" she yipped as she got up and out of Derek's embrace.

"Right behind you dear." Samantha called as Lexi and Alex hurried to the kitchen. "Come on, D."

They gathered in the kitchen as Alex slipped on one of Riana's aprons and started to search the refrigerator for ingredients. Sam giggled a bit. "Love the look, Alex." He turned his head and winked at her. "So what are you going to make her?"

"Stuffed Italian shells." he announced proudly as he turned from the fridge with a handful of cheeses, fresh spinach and milk.

"Ooh! She'll love it!" Lexi exclaimed delightedly. Alex hoped Riana would be pleased with what he made. He got to work, with the help of the ladies, while Derek made up drinks. They chatted happily, and Alex realized as his heart swelled and his smile radiated, that yes; this was exactly how his life was supposed to be. He was just getting the cheesy garlic bread ready to go into the oven when they heard the dogs begin to bark.

"They must be back." Lexi called over her shoulder as she scampered outside. Alex took a deep breath and looked worriedly towards Derek and Sam.

"It's going to be fine, Alex." Derek assured as he patted him on the back and headed outside. Alex relented and followed in the wake of everyone else.

The ride back to the ranch would have been tenser had it not been for Spencer's endless chatter. He kept Riana, Matthew and Tabitha terribly amused; and his questions of Riana were the beginning of Tabitha being able to get to know Ri without them having to directly engage. Spencer asked her all sorts of questions; how old she was, if she had kids, if she was married, what she did for a living. Though Spencer asked it as only a four year old could, "My daddy makes music, do you make music too?" Riana was all too happy to oblige him and answered all of his questions with a smile on her face.

Spencer fell asleep thirty miles from the ranch. The end of his rambling created a long, silent and awkward moment. Riana was relieved when they finally pulled up to the wrought iron gate. She reached out, swiped her card and drove through.

As they pulled into the ranch Tabitha's expression changed from one of indifference to one of awe. Matthew caught her eye and smiled knowingly at her. Riana parked the Jeep, they stepped out, and quickly stretched before they started the task of gathering the bags. Lexi and Sam were the first ones out of the house. "Tabs, this is Lexi and Sam." Matthew introduced. Tabitha gave them both a warm smile; so unlike her reaction to Riana.

"It's so nice to meet you." Tabitha gushed happily. Sam and Lexi both smiled but Matthew could tell they would keep their guard up until they knew their beloved Riana was in the clear in Tabitha's eyes.

Derek was shortly behind the ladies and jogged to Tabitha. He picked her up in a tight hug and swung her around. Tabitha laughed happily at him. "Hey D." she grinned.

The atmosphere shifted the moment Alex stepped out of the house. Tabitha locked her eyes on him and her lips transitioned from a happy smile to an intense, tight line. Alex was oblivious to her as he was instantly drawn to Riana. She stretched her arms over her head by the open driver's side door. Alex could tell she was exhausted. She looked in his direction and lit up. He increased the speed of his stroll and Riana met him halfway. She found instant comfort in his embrace.

Alex closed his eyes happily, only to open them to Tabitha's cold stare. Alex narrowed his eyes back at her, and Matthew knew, as he watched the exchange, things would get worse before they would get better between them. Alex squeezed Riana tighter as he kept his cold gaze on Tabitha. Matthew grabbed Tabitha's hand to break her concentration on. She turned her heated gaze onto Matt and he knew he would definitely get an earful once they weren't around everyone.

"How'd everything go?" Alex asked quietly.

"Okay I suppose." Riana whispered. She looked up at him as he kept his hands on her hips. "We'll talk later." He nodded and reluctantly let go.

Riana turned around and went to help unload the back of the Jeep. "So there's definitely room in the house for all of you if you want, otherwise I do have the guest house just past the stables." Ri explained as she grabbed two bags.

"I think we'll take the guest house." Matthew said. He knew perhaps for a while it would be best to provide Tabitha some distance from Alex. Riana nodded.

Tabitha surveyed the area as she slung a backpack over her shoulder. "I take it public speaking is going well?" she asked offhandedly.

Riana smiled, "Can't complain." Tabitha nodded silently. Alex hoped if Tabitha saw how well off Riana was, maybe she would realize she wasn't a gold digger who purposely sabotaged his relationship with Kim for her own selfish or financial reasons.

"D, can you keep an eye on Spence for a moment while we take all this stuff in? He's sleeping but I'd like him to eat before I let him punk out for the rest of the night." Matthew requested. Derek agreed as he leaned up against the Jeep and glanced in on Spencer.

Riana led the way to the guest house and gave Matt and Tabitha a quick tour. She offered open access to the pool and hot tub at the main house and invited them to share meals. "Speaking of meals," she started. "I'm going to go see if dinner is done. Come on in whenever you're settled." She gave a shy smile and Matt thanked her before she let herself out.

Matthew tossed Tabitha's bag onto the king bed in the master suite. "Are you hungry?"

"How can you say there isn't anything going on with Alex and that woman?" she snapped quickly.

Matthew took a deep breath, he had hoped to avoid this conflict until after dinner. "*That woman* is one of Alex's best friends. In fact, she's a great friend to all of us." he defended as anger built in his chest. "There isn't anything going on between them. Riana's remained faithful to her partner, just as Alex remained faithful to Kim when they were together."

"He may have been physically faithful to her, but it's obvious he wasn't emotionally faithful!" she yelled. "The way he looks at her hides nothing!"

"And why do you think he would have done that, Tabs? Can't you pull back for a damn minute and see he wasn't happy with Kim? There was something missing, Tabitha, and it's not fair for you to have some sort of expectation on him to make your friend happy!" Matt fired back. "He stayed longer than he should have." he finished.

"That's cold Matthew." Tabitha seethed sharply. "She's absolutely heartbroken and you're totally dismissing it!"

"I'm not dismissing it okay? I'm sure she's upset, but I rather focus on how much happier my best friend is!" he yelled exasperatedly. "If you just... stop looking at this through the lenses of Kim and see it for what it is, you might just see Alex didn't break up with Kim because of Riana. He did it because he knew something was missing. Riana is a good woman, Tabs. A sweet, funny, smart and witty woman. She's not looking for a fight, and she didn't want to cause any problems." he dropped the intensity of his voice. "She wants you to like her, Tabs." Tabitha dropped her head, she knew she was being unreasonable. "Now, let's go get some dinner." Matt urged as he reached out to take her hand.

<u>CHAPTER FIFTEEN</u>

Signs

Riana left Matthew and Tabitha and went back to the main house. She entered the door and was greeted by the mouth-watering aroma of Italian food. She hastened to the kitchen where Alex was pulling fresh cheesy garlic toast from the bottom oven. He turned around to put the pan on the island and grinned at Riana. "This smells absolutely scrumptious." she declared as she moseyed around the island to get her nose closer to the saucy, cheesy goodness.

"Thanks." Alex blushed. "I hope it tastes as good as it smells." he laughed as he cut up the loaf of toasty bread.

Riana snuck her head under his arm and stole a piece of garlic bread. "Oh, yeah, definitely." she mumbled around the hot, gooey toast stuffed into her mouth.

"Riana!" Alex laughed as he put down the knife and tickled her sides. "You can't be stealing food!"

"I bought it!" she argued as she squealed beneath his fingers. Alex playfully pinned her against the kitchen island and they both froze. Alex once again had a playful, yet urgent grasp on her hips. He was so close. She worried he was too close, especially when she felt him lean in. There was a faint scent of sweet, white wine on his breath and her

203

eyes unwillingly fluttered shut. Her hands, given a life of their own it appeared, reached up under his arms and grasped his shoulders as she sighed. She felt herself pull him closer, even though she knew she shouldn't. The sound of Derek clearing his throat tore them from their moment and Alex's dark skin quickly flushed.

"Um, sorry." Derek fumbled. "The table is set. Did you want me to grab anything?" Riana remained leaned up against the island and tried to slow her frantic heart.

"Yeah, sure. The bread is ready to go." Alex stuttered. Riana saw Derek nod out of the corner of her eye. She was unable to bring herself to look at him due to her mortification at being caught in a moment that surely couldn't happen--and definitely shouldn't happen. She heard Derek's footsteps move into the dining room and she barely had enough courage to look at Alex. He dropped his head, "Ri, I'm sorry."

Riana quickly turned around and started to clear the cutting board and knife Alex had just used. "Huh? For what? Nothing happened." she rationalized hastily. She refused to admit how close they had gotten to crossing a very distinct line.

She heard Alex take a deep breath before he muttered, "You're right." Her heart sank in her chest. She knew what almost happened, she should have accepted his apology. She turned to face him; she wanted to hug him and apologize but he was already

204

well into the dining room with two pans of stuffed Italian shells.

She sighed, defeated, and went to the theater room to get Lexi, Sam and Spencer. When Matt and Tabitha didn't come back out right away, Derek took it upon himself to wake up Spencer and bring him inside. "Hey, you guys hungry?" Riana asked as she entered the room. Sam was on the couch watching Lexi play with Spencer. Spencer looked up and nodded with a smile. "Well, come on then, Alex made some yummy stuff." she encouraged. Spencer quickly hopped up and ran towards the dining room. Lexi followed closely behind. Riana smiled softly as she watched her; Lexi had a natural maternal instinct like few others.

Samantha stepped in next to Riana as they followed behind Lexi. Riana leaned into her, "I can't wait for his night to be over." she grumbled with a small laugh.

As they approached the dining room Riana noticed Alex leaned up against the door frame. The brighter lights of the dining room illuminated him from behind. His jeans hung low on his hips, his hair fell into his eyes and his t-shirt clung to his brawny chest and solid arms. He literally oozed sex appeal. Riana's eyes traveled along his body, then landed on a glass of Asti in his hand. She smiled as she approached him. "I thought you might want this." he purred with a sly grin.

Riana took the cool stem from his hand. "You, dear, are absolutely correct." She took a sip and smiled around the sweetness. "Thank you." She eyed him suspiciously as she took another sip. "Wait… You aren't planning to liquor me up and take advantage of me are you?" she teased.

The blush that rushed to Alex's face was unexpected and he fumbled for a barely noticeable moment before he winked and replied, "Not unless you ask me to."

They gathered around the dining room table, Lexi dished up Spencer's food and Derek smiled as he watched her. Then, just as Derek voiced his curiosity as to where Matt and Tabitha might be, they came in from the back patio. "Sorry we're late, I was just showing Tabs the pool." Matthew explained as he pulled out Tabitha's chair.

"Oh good." Riana smiled. "Again, feel free to use it whenever. The main house is always open too, so don't be shy." She hated how she rambled when nervous, but she felt helpless to stop it.

"Thank you." Tabitha murmured softly. She looked across the table at Riana and smiled. "This really is a beautiful place, Riana."

"Thanks. It's a great place to take a break. I usually stay here to write or as a de-stressor after I do a long run of speaking engagements." *Rambling again*, she mentally kicked herself.

"I can see why."

"When can we see the ponies?" Spencer asked excitedly. Riana looked over at him and laughed. He was adorable; light blonde hair, big blue eyes and a smile that could melt the coldest hearts.

"Oh Spencer, it's already late tonight. I promise I'll introduce you to them tomorrow." Riana assured.

"In the morning?" Spencer asked as he clasped his hands together excitedly.

"Late morning." she confirmed with a laugh. While Spencer was nothing but joy, Riana couldn't help but notice how Alex and Tabitha didn't talk at all through dinner. Alex kept an eye on her though. He also kept his hand solidly on Riana's knee and when he sensed her anxiety increase, he gave it a small squeeze. It was a private way for him to let her know he had her back. Derek, Sam, Lexi and Matt kept the conversation going but skillfully kept topics away from anything that might cause conflict.

After dinner Matthew and Tabitha excused themselves back to the guest house with Spencer while Riana, Lexi, Sam, Derek, and Alex remained out back by the fire. Alex poured Riana another glass of wine and met her by the fire ring. There were a few lounge chairs, a patio couch and a couple more regular chairs placed around the ring. Derek and Lexi took the patio couch, Sam took a lounge chair and Alex got comfortable in the second lounge chair. Riana pursed her lips and clinked her nails against her wine glass. She met Alex's eyes and he smiled warmly at her.

He patted the spot in front of him, "Want to sit?" he asked. She nodded as she strolled over to him. Alex eased his legs open, Riana slid between them, and rested her back against his firm chest. His arms and hands comfortably found their place along her arms. Riana felt her whole body relax as she became surrounded by him. Alex placed his chin on top of her head, took a deep breath and caught the faded scent of her shampoo. He absentmindedly drew patterns on the bare skin of her arms and Riana barely heard the conversation that took place around her. The combination of wine and being so close to Alex left her head swimming.

An insistent buzz on the table next to them brought Riana out of her haze. She looked over and was mildly horrified to see "Ryan Cell" light up the screen of her cell phone. She picked it up and took a deep breath as she answered. "Hey Ryan." she said unenthusiastically as she leaned forward, away from Alex. Alex's face turned agitated.

"I haven't heard from you in a while." Ryan commented. Riana picked at stray strings on the cushion of the lounge chair.

"I know. I've been busy. Writing." she easily lied.

"Right." Ryan remarked sharply with obvious disbelief. Riana's jaw became rigid and she rubbed her temple with her free hand.

"What do you want, Ryan?" she asked pointedly.

"I want to see you." Riana knew it was not a request.

"I...can't." she stammered. She grabbed her vertical labret with her teeth.

Ryan quickly huffed on the other end of the line. "I haven't seen you in months Ri." he pointed out.

Her eyes narrowed. "Now you know how it feels." she snapped back. Over the years she had grown used to being abandoned by him, to wait around until he wanted her again. It was about time he chased her.

"Riana." Ryan started firmly. Her heart leapt at the tone of his voice and she fought to remain strong and not give in to his demand.

"No. No, Ryan. I'm not at your beck and call. I'm busy. Maybe I can make it up there in September. I don't know. I have to go." She didn't say goodbye before she hung up. She was barely aware of the tears as she got off the lounge chair and wordlessly went inside.

Alex was stunned, annoyed and heartbroken. It was a reminder, again, of how out of reach she was. Samantha quickly got up to follow Ri. She stopped behind Alex's chair and placed her hand on his shoulder. "Let me talk to her." she offered softly.

Sam entered the house and found Riana at the kitchen island staring blankly at the wall. "Ri, honey…" Sam started as she sat down next to her.

"I'm just so fucking tired of it, Sam." Riana blurted. "I'm so sick of how he expects me to drop everything to be with him, but I'm not allowed to have any expectations of him." Riana's face was red, her eyes intense and her hands were gripped tightly together.

"You have every right to be angry Ri, it's not fair." Sam assured.

Suddenly the intensity of Riana's face softened. "I don't know what I'm doing." she mumbled as she placed her forehead on the countertop. Sam reached over and rubbed her back.

"What do you mean?"

Riana kept her head down but turned her face in Sam's direction. She frowned a bit as she took in her dear friend's soft eyes. Sam had been with Riana for so many years, and faithfully took on the ups and downs of her life. "I... I don't think... that I love him anymore." Samantha could have sprung out of her chair and done a ridiculous happy dance, but figured it wouldn't be appropriate. She gave Ri a sympathetic half-frown and nodded. Riana sighed and turned her head back to the cool granite.

"It's okay not to love him anymore honey. You have to trust yourself." Sam paused. "You deserve better anyway." she said. She leaned into Riana and wrapped her arm snugly around her shoulder.

Riana again plopped her cheek against the countertop. "I know." she admitted meekly. "I've just... I've loved him for so long."

"Maybe it's finally come to its end Ri." Samantha observed firmly. Riana nodded as she pulled out of Sam's embrace and stood up.

"I'm going to go lie down." Sam frowned sadly but nodded. She watched Riana slowly proceed down the hallway and went back outside once she heard her bedroom door close.

Everyone looked up as she stepped out and slid the glass door shut behind her. "She's okay." Sam assured. As she walked behind Alex she leaned over next to his ear and whispered, "She's close, dear." He gave her a half-hearted smile. It was obvious he didn't want to be happy if Riana was in pain.

Riana entered her room and ambled to her en suite to run a bath. She lit a handful of candles, shut off the lights, clipped her long hair up and eased into the hot water. She closed her eyes as she felt sobs grip her chest. It tore her apart; to know how she and Ryan were three years ago, and to see how they were now. He wasn't the same. She wasn't the same. Ryan no longer made her happy. He didn't make her laugh anymore. She no longer looked forward to hearing from him; in fact, she dreaded it. It seemed to Riana the only positive reaction she had to him was physical. Yet, even that lacked the passion it once had. It was habit; a conditioned response.

Even as she attempted to keep her focus on Ryan and her mixed feelings about her relationship with him, images of Alex appeared. Moments with him replayed; hysterical laughter, honest heart to hearts, and intellectual discussions. Then those moments that lit her on fire; slight touches, gazes, a draw into him that she felt she was becoming powerless to resist.

Riana stepped out of the bath as she decided sleep might be her best course of action.

Riana looked down at him, his beautiful face was set in peaceful sleep. She lightly traced her fingers along his jaw, then his lips. They were perfect; soft, pouty, and kissable. His chest was bare and she deliberately drug her nails off his lips, and down the center of his chest. He gave a deep moan and she caved. She climbed on top of him and straddled his waist. She leaned into him and nuzzled his ear. His hands urgently grasped her hips as he whimpered her name.

"Riana."

"Riana. No." Another voice called. Riana felt a force pull her away from Alex.

"No!" she yelled. She frantically reached for Alex's hands.

"Riana!" Ryan hollered again as he ripped Riana away.

"No! Alex!" she screamed as she jerked from sleep. Her body shook as she repeatedly shot her eyes around her empty room. She felt the all too familiar sense of panic grip her heart. Her breath caught between shallow breaths. She glanced to her left and saw it was 3:12am.

Riana eased her door open and listened for any sounds of life. She didn't hear anything but coyotes so she ventured into the hallway then padded up the stairs. She crept down the upstairs hallway and stood anxiously at Alex's closed bedroom door. She turned the knob as she knocked lightly.

The room was dark but she was able to hear his heavy breaths. She nervously tiptoed to the open side of the bed, gingerly lifted the covers and slid in next to him. Her arms instinctively reached out and grabbed him across his stomach as she snuggled into him. "Ri?" he murmured. He felt her tremble against him.

"I had a bad dream." she whispered shakily. "I needed you."

His head was foggy as he tried to comprehend the moment. He reached across and pulled her closer, his hot breath warmed her cheek as she rolled into him. "You have me, Ri. You're safe." he mumbled, as he fought between sleep and consciousness.

Riana closed her eyes and breathed deeply, his scent permeated every cell of her body and created a sense of comfort. "I love you, Alex."

Alex's heart leapt in his chest. He brought his lips to barely touch her forehead. "I love you, Ri."

CHAPTER SIXTEEN

Dare You To Move

Saturday August 26, 2006

As the morning light crept into Alex's room he remained still and thought back to the night before. He hated when Ryan called Riana, though not specifically for selfish reasons; he hated how twisted he made her. Sam had told him she was close, she was getting to the point where she could see the end; he just wished the end could come without her having to face so much confusion and pain.

They had stayed outside for a few hours after Riana had taken her sudden leave. Alex loved to watch Lexi and Derek together, he loved how close they had become. They teased each other and were beautifully at ease in each other's company. Alex had found them off together often; in the pool, watching TV or movies, or cooking together. Lexi and Derek were almost as inseparable as Alex and Riana. If ever there was a woman Alex would approve of for his big brother, it'd be Lexi.

Alex smiled softly as he thought of them, then as he thought of Riana. He finally opened his eyes to gaze down at her. She was still asleep and curled into him. He sighed as he reluctantly accepted the fact that it'd be easy to get used to having Riana in his bed.

He pushed a wisp of hair behind her ear, closed his eyes, and remembered how she came to him. He felt terrible for her; she had been so terrified and shaken up. He was happy though, that she knew she would be safe with him after a bad dream. He had been absolutely beside himself when she said she loved him. Although he wondered if perhaps she only said it because she thought he was asleep. He had been, for the most part, but the moment the words passed by her lips they became etched into his mind and heart to hold on to forever.

Alex remained still and admired Riana as she continued to sleep. She had a slight flush to her cheeks and her typically tame blonde hair was tangled in a bed head mess. She wore a tight tank and flimsy shorts which twisted around and exposed her smooth, tan skin. "You're so beautiful." he whispered as he kissed the top of her head. Riana squirmed a bit then brought her hand up to the side of his face.

"No... you're beautiful..." she slurred. "Let's go... roller coaster..." Alex chuckled as he realized Riana was pretty much still unconscious, and dreaming about roller coasters.

"Uncle D!" Spencer yelled as he ran through the back patio door with Matthew and Tabitha shortly behind. He barreled into the kitchen where

Derek and Lexi worked on breakfast. Derek scooped him up with a quick laugh.

"How's it goin' little man?"

"Riana is going to show me ponies today!" Spencer gushed.

"I know!" Derek enthused.

Lexi smiled at them as she mixed pancake batter. "She's not quite up yet though." she said. "How about breakfast?"

"Yeah." Spencer grinned.

"Spence." Matthew scolded from the kitchen island.

"Yes, please, Lexi." Spencer softly corrected.

"Alright, go take a seat, I'll bring pancakes in a few minutes." Lexi promised as Derek put Spencer down. "I'm going to get Ri for breakfast. Matt, you want to wake Alex?" Lexi asked as she wiped her hands on her apron.

"Will do." He gave Tabitha a quick kiss then bounded down the hall and up the stairs.

"Looks like I'll bring breakfast to the table." Derek chuckled and winked at Tabitha. She gave a small smile as she eased around the kitchen island and approached him at the stove.

"I'll help you, D." she offered as she nudged his side.

"Thanks." Derek smiled as he pulled down a stack of plates. "Did you sleep well?"

"Wonderfully, actually." she said. "It's a very cozy guest house." Derek nodded. He discovered he slept better in the main house than he had in a long time.

"Spence seems excited about the horses." he commented. Tabitha laughed heartily.

She grabbed the stack of plates from Derek. "He's downright beside himself. He hasn't stopped talking about it since Riana mentioned it at the airport." she paused, "She is a nice woman, isn't she Derek?"

Derek sighed sympathetically. "She really is Tabs. I know this must be… hard for you. But maybe if you don't think of her as the woman who sparked the fight that ended Kim's relationship with Alex, but rather as one of our friends it'd be… easier for you."

She nodded thoughtfully but wouldn't give in. She smiled softly, "Lexi seems nice too."

Derek laughed as he thought about Lexi and how wonderful she was. "Lexi is *great*."

Matthew took the steps, every other one, and gave a quick knock before he opened Alex's door. "Hey Al--" he stopped, the scene that met him a bit of a surprise, and yet, not really.

Alex was still in bed, which wasn't a surprise to Matt, but as Alex lifted his finger to his lips to silence Matt, he noticed sweet Riana was asleep and curled into him. "She had a bad dream." Alex whispered softly as he gazed down at her and stroked her hair.

Matthew smiled softly as he got closer. "Well," he whispered, "breakfast is done if you want to come down." Alex nodded but didn't take his eyes off his sleeping bedmate.

Matt silently turned around, left the room and re-shut Alex's door. Just as he got to the top of the stairs he was met with Lexi on her way up. "Is Riana--"

"Yeah, she's with Alex. Still sleeping." he gently interrupted. "Alex is up though, I'm sure he'll bring her down in a few." Lexi smiled at him. "Let's go eat." They got back downstairs where Derek and Tabitha had already started to serve Spencer, who was in the middle of excitedly telling Derek, again, about how he was about to see the horses and how he couldn't wait until Riana let him ride one. Matthew was silently thankful that no one asked the whereabouts of Alex and Riana.

Riana felt his hands on her upper arm as he slowly rubbed her smooth skin. Then she heard his voice, "Ri...sweetheart... we should get up." she groaned but refused to open her eyes.

"No." she grumbled.

She felt the laughter rumble through him, "But everyone is downstairs waiting for us to join them for breakfast."

Riana groaned again as she stretched. "Fine." she conceded. "But I'm not happy about it." She cuddled into the blankets deeper in an attempt to delay the inevitable.

"Oh, I know dear. Me either. But you did make a promise to Spencer, and being as it's 9am, it's getting pretty close to 'late morning'." he laughed.

Riana sat up and eyed him. "Late morning by who's definition?" she blurted incredulously. "Certainly not mine." Alex grinned at her and she was once again struck by how beautiful he was. He crawled out of bed, stood up, and looked down at her. She suddenly felt vulnerable and overcome with desire. She wanted to lay back down and beckon him to her but instead, she grabbed his outstretched hand and got out of bed.

Alex laced his fingers through Riana's then pulled her to him. He was warm and comforting. "I hope you didn't have any more bad dreams last night." he murmured softly.

Riana flushed at the amount of skin to skin contact but shook her head. "Once I was... here, it was fine." She wanted to say once she was there, with him.

Alex kissed her forehead. "Good." He pulled back and led her out of his room and down the stairs. The downstairs was alive with the sounds of a family breakfast; chatter, laughter, clinking of silverware. Riana decided to head to her bedroom quickly to change into some more conservative pajamas before she joined everyone.

She sighed as she shut her bedroom door. Things were getting messy, and she knew she was getting careless. She knew if she didn't watch herself she would fall into something much too complicated. Things were rough with Ryan and she sensed things were developing for Alex but she had never been one to be unfaithful and she knew she owed it to everyone involved to sort out her relationship with Ryan before she felt like she was leading Alex on. Alex deserved better. She huffed and thought he might have even deserved better than her.

"Good morning Ri." Derek greeted as she walked into the dining room. She smiled at him and found a seat at the table. She made a point to take the open chair next to Sam rather than the one next to Alex. She had to try to distance herself a bit. She thought it might help her refocus. She caught the disappointment in Alex's face and frowned. She didn't want to upset him, but he had to know things were too complicated.

"Riana!" Spencer squealed. "We're going to see ponies after this right?" His face was lit up with a smile unlike any other Riana had ever seen.

"Shortly after, yes." His smile fell. "Don't worry, I'll eat quickly and get ready super-fast." He brightened back up and nodded quickly. Riana noticed Tabitha remained quiet as she thoughtfully observed the interaction between her and Spencer.

They sat around the table, chatted happily through breakfast and made plans for the day. It was decided they wouldn't make Spencer wait any longer for the horses. "Alright, I'm going to go shower and get dressed. Matt, make sure Spencer gets changed

into jeans and I'll meet you at the guest house."
Riana directed as she cleared dishes from the table.

Matthew and Tabitha got Spencer changed
quickly then waited outside. They sat on the front
porch of the guest house as Spencer played with
Riana's two dogs in the yard. Matthew held his
wife's hand lovingly in his. "You know I love you
Tabs."

She turned and smiled at him, "Of course I
do."

"I don't want this stuff with Alex--"

"The stuff with Alex is… my stuff with Alex.
You know I love him too. But Kim is my best friend,
it's hard to be here… watching him be so okay
without her." she admitted softly. "I feel like… If I
don't stay angry, I'm betraying Kim. She'd hate me
if she knew I somehow ended up liking Riana."

"You have free will, sweetheart." Matthew
reminded gently. "You can like or dislike anyone
you choose. You shouldn't allow others to dictate
that. Not even me." He nudged her and smiled. "As
much as I'd like for you to like Ri, or at least to see
she's not evil, I can't control how you feel. But…
neither should Kim." Tabitha looked out at their son
as she pondered his words.

Tabitha's attention was drawn away from
Spencer to sounds of laughter. She and Matt couldn't
make out anything being said, but the looks of pure
joy on everyone's faces was obvious as they left the
main house. Alex seemed to be picking on Ri. She
put her hands up and shook her head but after some

221

prompting from the others she seemed to relent. They stopped their advancement towards the guest house and Alex moved in front of her. She laughed as he bent down and she hopped on his back. Ri turned and pointed at Derek and Lexi as she continued to laugh. Lexi laughed and rolled her eyes but nodded, then Derek also bent down and Lexi hopped on his back. Some provocation took place between the guys as Sam moved ahead of them.

Matthew chuckled as he realized what was about to take place. Sam held her hands out and yelled, "Ready! Set! GO!"

Derek and Alex took off in a run as Lexi and Riana squealed through their laughter. Matt glanced over and saw Tabitha smile, just a little, as she too watched the race. Matt couldn't imagine Tabitha was unable to see the pure happiness on Alex's face. She had to realize he was happier now.

Riana relentlessly teased and provoked Derek as Alex took the lead. Lexi urged Derek on, "Go D! Run!! You almost got him!" In the end it was Alex who took the win as they got to the front of the guest house.

"I told you!" Alex laughed as Riana slid down off his back. He slung his arm over her shoulders and grinned proudly.

"Yeah, whatever." Derek laughed as he released Lexi to the ground.

"Riana!" Spencer yelled. Riana happily laughed as she turned around towards Spencer, well aware of what was coming. He got in front of her and danced around excitedly. "Can we see the ponies?"

Riana looked over towards Matthew and Tabitha. Matt gave a small nod. "Yes, Spencer, we can go see the ponies now." she smiled. Spencer turned, ran to the house, and clomped up the wooden steps of the porch.

"Mom, Dad, come on! We can see ponies now!" He grabbed both of their hands and pulled them down the stairs to where Riana, Alex, Sam, Lexi and Derek waited. As they approached, Spencer let go of their hands and ran up between Alex and Riana. He reached up, took both of their hands, and danced happily between them. Tabitha's smile fell, her heart tightened as she watched Spencer effortlessly treat Riana the way he used to treat Kim.

Riana was both happy and nervous to have Spencer take such a quick liking to her. However, the way she spun her vertical labret told Alex her anxiety was heightened. When she glanced over at him, he gave her a soft smile. She finally released the barbell and smiled back. "How many do you have Ri?" Spencer implored.

"There are ten horses and two ponies." she answered simply. As they got to the barn Ri released Spencer's hand and pushed the heavy door to the side. They were greeted with deep snorts and neighs. Riana stepped to the side to wait for everyone to get inside before she walked over to the first stall.

"I can't see." Spencer whined.

"Spencer." Tabitha warned sternly.

"Sorry Mommy. Daddy can you pick me up?" Spencer requested. Matt smiled and scooped him up, then walked closer to the stall.

"This is Adonis." Riana smiled. Adonis had his large head over her shoulder and gave her what looked to be a hug as she rubbed his neck. "He's my favorite boy, but don't tell the others." she laughed and winked at Spencer. "You can pet him." she urged. "He's a big boy, but very sweet." Spencer grinned as he touched Adonis' velvet nose.

Riana moved to the stall next to Adonis and smiled at Alex. "This is Apollo. He's Adonis' best friend." Spencer happily reached in to pet Adonis as well. Tabitha smiled and clicked pictures as she watched Spencer. Riana continued down the aisle and introduced Spencer and Tabitha to Aphrodite, Sebastian, MaTao, and Sonny. "Sonny is one of the sweetest horses I have. Your daddy rode Sonny the other day. What do you say, you want your dad to ride with you today?" Spencer quickly nodded. "Lexi, could you take Sonny and tack her up please?"

"Of course." Lexi obliged as she opened up Sonny's stall door. Derek quickly offered his assistance as he followed her. Alex caught Matthew's eye and grinned.

"I have a few more outside in the pasture, should we go meet them too?" Spencer nodded as he twisted his small hands together excitedly. Matt, Tabitha, Spencer, Alex and Sam followed Riana as Lexi and Derek hooked Sonny up to the wall to be tacked. Riana stopped near them, grabbed a bucket and dumped treats into it.

As they got outside Samantha skipped ahead, hopped up on the fence and gave a high whistle. Lilo's head lifted up and she began a quick trot to the fence. Chester, Ringo, Daisy and two ponies followed. "Thanks Sam." Riana laughed. She pulled a treat from the bucket and offered it to Lilo. "This is Lilo, the brown one coming up with the blue halter is Chester…" she opened her hand with a treat in her palm to Chester.

"Daisy is a little shy, but she's the shorter, dark brown one." she explained as she pointed to just beyond Chester. "And Ringo is my goofy looking boy." she laughed as she rubbed his large ear and gave him a treat.

"And the ponies!" Spencer chirped.

"Yes, Spence, here come the ponies." Alex laughed.

"This is Sugar and Spice." Riana introduced.

"The white one must be Sugar." Spencer said proudly. Riana giggled.

"Actually, no." Alex laughed and shook his head. Leave it to Riana to go against logic. "Spice is the white one. Sugar is the brown one." She laughed some more. "Don't ask me why."

Spencer gave her a small scowl. "That's silly."

"Spencer, that's not nice." Matthew chided.

"No, it's okay Matt, he's absolutely right. It is silly." Riana smiled. She grabbed a couple of treats from the bucket. "Spencer, would you like to give Sugar and Spice a couple of treats?" Matthew placed Spencer on the ground and he jogged over to Riana's side. She placed one treat in each small hand and directed him on how to open his hand flat to present the treat to the pony. As Sugar moved his lips over Spencer's hand to gather the treat he giggled. Tabitha took more pictures and smiled happily at Spencer's joy. "So which pony would you like to ride?" Riana asked as she easily climbed over the fence.

"Sugar!" he called delightedly. Riana stepped off the fence, grabbed Sugar's halter and led him to the gate.

"You got it mister." she laughed.

CHAPTER SEVENTEEN

Lips Of An Angel

As Riana had the rest of the group outside, Lexi and Derek remained behind to tack up Sonny. Lexi went to pull down Sonny's saddle but huffed when she realized Dustin put it on the peg above where it usually hung. "Let me get that, Shorty." Derek laughed as he lifted the saddle off the peg and made his way to Sonny. "You got a saddle pad?" Heavy dust infiltrated the hot, still air of the barn as the blanket Lexi grabbed came to rest on Sonny's back. They continued to work on Sonny, occasionally Derek's hand would brush Lexi's or he'd bump into her as they worked around the horse. Lexi would laugh lightly and try to keep the blush off her face.

"You think Tabitha is going to really give Riana a chance?" she asked quietly.

Derek skewed his lip. "It's hard to say. Sometimes it looks like she's making progress, other times I'm just waiting for the explosion, you know?" Lexi nodded in agreement. "Matt told me Tabs is pretty angry yet, but he's working on her. Trying to help her see it's not Ri's fault." Lexi stood on the other side of Sonny and watched Derek as he spoke. "It'd be a damn shame if we can't all work through this."

"Oh yeah?" Lexi asked, her interest piqued. "Why's that?"

Derek grinned at her then turned his attention to Sonny as he rubbed his hand down her golden neck. "Well...I'm pretty sure we all have this plan... to keep you ladies around for a long time. And it would just suck... if it was going to be tense every time we got together."

"You have a point." she teased with a wink. "Let's get Sonny out there." she said as she walked around Sonny and gathered her reins.

As they headed towards the barn door Riana and Alex approached with Sugar. "We'll be right there."

Lexi and Derek brought Sonny outside and over to Matthew. "Here's your lady, Matt." Lexi offered.

"Thanks Lex." he said as he grabbed the reins from her hand and slung them over Sonny's neck.

"Don't hurt yourself." Tabitha teased. Lexi and Sam tried to hold back their laughter but were unable. Matthew turned to his wife and childishly stuck out his tongue.

"His gracefulness really is astounding isn't it?" Sam laughed. Tabitha chuckled along with her.

"You've noticed, I take it?" she giggled but gazed at Matthew lovingly as her eyes softened with amusement and joy. Matt's eyes held the same amount of adoration when he gazed at her. Fans had often doubted their relationship, but it was obvious to Lexi and Sam the doubts were unfounded and likely fueled by jealousy; they were pretty much perfect together.

Riana and Alex exited the barn with Sugar in tow and Samantha beamed at how happy Riana looked as she walked along side Alex. "Spencer!" Alex called. "Come on cowboy, come get your pony." Spencer ran towards them as quickly as his short legs could manage. When he reached them Riana took his hand and led him around Sugar. She explained all of the tack to him; Sugar's bridle, saddle, the stirrups, and the horn. She made sure Spencer knew why every part was important and how they all worked together to ride properly.

"You think you're ready to take him for a ride?" she questioned with a smile. Spencer nodded and excitedly bit his lip. Riana grabbed him by his little waist and hoisted him into Sugar's saddle. Tabitha busily took pictures again with a proud smile. Riana adjusted Spencer's feet in the stirrups and showed him how to hold the reins. Alex stood in front of Sugar and watched them causing Riana to blush lightly under his gaze.

Riana led Spencer and Sugar through the gate to the corral where Matthew and Sonny waited. "Make sure you're holding on." Tabitha urged nervously.

"Riana will make sure he doesn't fall." Alex commented as he continued to gaze after Riana softly. Tabitha looked over at him with pursed lips and sighed.

Alex contemplated what kind of mother Riana might make as he continued to watch her with Spencer. He rationalized he wasn't actually thinking of having children with her. He just loved how she smiled at Spencer, and how they laughed together. He admired her patience and how she consistently watched to make sure he was safe. Alex noticed Tabitha seemed torn between having fun and trying to stay angry at Riana. He scowled and wished she would just get over it.

Alex moved back and leaned against the fence next to where Sam was perched on the top rail. She draped her arm around Alex's neck. "How's it going, dear?"

Alex took a deep breath. "It's going."

"Need to talk?" she pushed with a sweet smile. Alex pondered for a moment. There was a chance that if he talked about things it might make him feel worse, but he thought perhaps talking to someone who actually knew what was going on would help him feel less isolated in his emotions. He nodded silently. Sam hopped off the fence and Alex climbed up and over as well.

They meandered back towards the barn. "I don't even know where to start, Sam." he groaned. "All my logic seems to be slipping away. I can't keep my eyes off her, I can't stop myself for savoring every moment she touches me." They entered the hot, dusty barn and sat down next to Adonis' stall. "I feel like... Like I know she must know. It has to be pretty obvious huh?" He laughed a bit as he avoided Sam's gaze.

"Well, there's assumptions being made for sure." she confirmed with a wink. "Probably not by Riana, though. I can almost guarantee she thinks you'd never look at her that way, or feel that way about her."

"Wha--Why? How could she not know?"

"Well, you know, she's used to Ryan." Alex fought to contain a growl. "She doesn't know what it looks like, to have a man truly care about her. He used to be good for her Alex, and she can't let go of that. Even though it's so obvious to the rest of us he's just using her now... she still sees it as love."

Alex sighed and stared at the cement floor; waves of dirt and bedding created smooth patterns before him. "She came to me last night." he paused as he remembered the moment. "She had a bad dream and said she needed me."

"She does need you, Alex. More than I think you know." Samantha said softly as she wrapped her arm around him.

"I don't know how much longer I can keep it a secret, Sam." Alex confessed as he aimlessly picked at the bale of hay they sat on.

She pulled him into a side hug. "I know, but it's better for her this way." Alex nodded. He knew she was right, he knew Riana couldn't know how he really felt about her yet. If she couldn't see it, he couldn't tell her. He couldn't force her to make a decision she wasn't ready to make.

"You love her don't you?" A cold, even voice assumed from the entrance of the barn.

Alex snapped his eyes to Tabitha as she leaned against the doorway. Her face was still as her eyes narrowed at Alex. "That's none of your business Tabitha." he retorted in a low, threatening tone.

"I think it is, Alexander." Tabitha retorted sternly as she approached Alex and Samantha. "I want to know how you could claim to love Kim and then just callously toss her to the side once *she* came along."

"Leave it alone Tabitha." Alex warned. Samantha slowly got up and inched away.

Tabitha shook her head. "I won't Alex. I can't. Not after I stayed with her for days as she fell apart. I can't stand to see you... and... and how you don't even care!" she finally raised her voice as she stood over Alex. "I can't... I just can't understand!" Her eyes filled with a mixture of anger and pain.

"You don't have to understand!" Alex yelled as he stood up and towered over Tabitha. He glared down at her, "I loved Kim. I still love her--"

"Then why aren't you still with her?" she screamed. The horses paced nervously in their stalls as the tension built.

Alex took a deep breath. "I was never *in* love with her." he confessed simply.

"Bullshit!" she bellowed. "I can't believe you." she growled. "I can't fucking believe you!" she shrieked again. There was a muffled thud as

Tabitha's open palms connected with Alex's broad chest. "So what then?" she spat. "Now you're in love with someone you barely know?!"

"What the hell is going on in here?" Riana's authoritative voice echoed off the walls as she stormed into the scene. The horses snorted and danced around in their stalls anxiously.

Tabitha turned to Riana. "Nothing." she snapped, then turned her fiery gaze back to Alex.

Riana raised an eyebrow as she approached. Her boots scrapped along the floor, dust followed in her wake. Alex's heart swelled as he watched her, the intensity of her confidence alluring. "Really?" she asked condescendingly. "Because it definitely looks like something." Riana's typically playful blue eyes were icy as she scrutinized Tabitha. She had a good four inches on Riana but it appeared that didn't matter as Riana continued her approach.

"Back off, Riana." Tabitha warned. "This is between me and Alex."

Riana slowly shook her head. "No, I don't think it is." she observed with an eerie calmness. "You see, I think you seem to feel it was my fault that Alex broke up with Kim--"

"It was!" Tabitha interrupted and with cat-like reflexes Riana pinned her against the door of an empty stall.

"I wasn't done." The unnerving calm edge remained in Riana's voice. Tabitha swallowed and Alex was torn between breaking the confrontation up and waiting to see how it all played out. "I only have a few things to say about this and then I don't want it to come up again, understood?" Tabitha scowled at Riana without reply. "First of all, nothing has happened between me and Alex." Tabitha barely opened her mouth to protest. "Nothing." Riana repeated firmly and Tabitha closed her mouth. "Alex never cheated on Kim, just as I never cheated on Ryan. Alex isn't malicious and he'd never purposely hurt someone; especially someone he cared so much about. How we may or may not feel about each other is no one's business but ours." she glanced at Alex and barely smiled with her eyes. "As a guest to *my* ranch, I expect more respect from you; to both me and Alex." As Riana took a step back her eyes never left Tabitha. "This is done now, understood?"

The fierceness in her eyes made it clear it wasn't a question. Tabitha barely nodded in silent response. Riana nodded once, turned and wordlessly exited the barn. Alex watched her leave, stunned by her behavior. He had never seen her behave in such a way. He was taken aback when he realized he found it undeniably sexy.

Riana felt her whole body shake as she left the barn. She continued to seethe about how Tabitha had yelled at Alex. She was also terrified she had overstepped some major boundaries and might lose her friendship with the guys because she couldn't keep her temper in check. She glanced over and saw Spencer was still being led around on Sugar while Matthew rode behind him on Sonny. She hurried back to the house.

Just as she grabbed a bottle of water from the fridge she heard him. "Ri…"

Riana didn't turn to him right away. She dropped her head in shame as she shakily put her water on the counter. "Alex, I'm so sorry." she started softly. "I shouldn't--"

Her apology was halted by Alex's hands on her hips and his chest against her back. "Ri." he breathed against her ear. "You are incredible." He nuzzled into her as he inhaled her scent. Riana's logic vanished, she turned to face him without breaking the amount of contact between them. "Absolutely amazing." he whispered. His lips were just under her ear and they lightly brushed her neck. Goose bumps rose to the surface of Riana's skin under the sensation of his lips and the deep rumble of his voice.

Everything that told Riana not to continue was ignored as she leaned her head back and sighed as she tangled her hand in Alex's hair and brought his lips back to her neck. He pulled away from the soft skin of her neck and their eyes met. "Alex," she whispered.

"I'm sorry." he quickly stuttered. "I--"

"Alex." Riana interrupted firmly as she tightened the grip of her fingers in his silky black hair. "Kiss me." she commanded then pulled her lower lip under her teeth. "Please." she whimpered.

Alex tightened his hold on Riana's hips as he spun them around and pinned her against the kitchen island. She felt no fear or apprehension, only pure

235

exhilaration as she awaited his lip. Alex's own emotions rushed by him, he was nervous but only because he had wanted this moment for so long. Riana's hands grasped against the cool granite counter as she tried to keep herself upright despite her weak knees.

Alex gently placed his hand to the side of Riana's face. She leaned into it as she closed her eyes. He admired her for a long moment, the softness of her face, the blush in her cheeks and her pink, pouty lips. He licked his lip and pulled it under his teeth as he tried to calm himself. To Riana it felt like minutes--hours, passed by. She began to worry perhaps *this* was the boundary she shouldn't have crossed. She felt panic rise in her chest and squeeze the air from her lungs as she worried he wouldn't kiss her; that she just made a complete fool of herself.

Then she felt him, closer, his shaky breath against her lips. Alex felt his hand begin to tremble as he leaned in. Riana kept her cheek in the palm of his hand and brought her left hand back up to grasp the hair at the back of his head as she pulled him in to close the torturous gap between them. She was overcome with what felt like a full body sigh as Alex' full, soft lips finally met hers. She pulled him closer as she deepened the kiss.

Alex's mind raced as he relished the kiss. His hand drifted off Riana's cheek, only to be tangled in her hair with his other hand. Riana happily opened her mouth to the exploration of his tongue and she knew, in that moment, that she had never experienced a kiss so emotionally charged, or so raw.

Riana's mind swam as Alex pulled back and playfully bit her lower lip, her vertical labret gently pulled back by his teeth. She whimpered as her whole body lit on fire and the kiss finally broke. They panted heavily, their minds fogged with desire. Alex's eyes bore into Riana's and she felt utterly helpless and exposed. She trembled; an overdose of adrenaline, desire and conflicting emotions. She barely felt Alex back away but she grabbed his hips and urgently brought him back to her, desperate to continue the moment. She was completely consumed by him. Despite any warnings, she continued to move towards the flames he had ignited within her. Her limbs tingled as the fire spread, each touch of Alex's hands and lips caused a wave of cinders.

Alex again brought his lips to hers, the stubble on his chin rubbed against the sensitive skin of her face. She gathered the material of his t-shirt in her hands and debated whether or not she should just strip him right there in the kitchen. She decided against it, instead she feverishly used her grip on his shirt as a means to get him closer. He gently pulled back and gazed down at her. Part of him knew he shouldn't be there, kissing her. Riana gave a small smile as she pecked his lips, then his chin. She trailed kisses along his strong jawline to underneath his ear where she lightly nibbled.

Alex may have known he shouldn't partake, but as Riana's teeth gently grasped his skin he was overtaken by passion. He let out a throaty groan as he quickly grasped Riana just under her butt and effortlessly lifted her to sit on the countertop of the island. She quickly locked her legs behind him as she wrapped her arms around his neck. He rushed to meet her lips and moaned into her mouth as his lips crashed into hers. He broke the kiss and pressed his lips to her lower neck and gave a barely noticeable bite. Riana whimpered and bit her lip. Electric shocks of lust rushed through her.

"Mmm...Alex." she breathed as his hands dug into her hips. She yearned for him; every inch of her skin wanted his hands, lips or both.

Too soon, the guilt gripped her. "Alex." she choked out. The change in her voice forced Alex to instantly pull back. Riana's eyes pleaded with his. She wished it could be different. She felt her chest tighten. "I...can't..."

Tears formed in her eyes. Alex brought his hands to the sides of her face. His thumbs gently caught the first of her tears as they fell. "I'm sorry Ri." he whispered. "I should have known better."

"Me too." she sniffled as she placed her forehead against his. She brought her hand up to the side of his face and lovingly stroked his cheek with her thumb. Alex's eyes were deep, soulful and heartbroken. "If things were... different." He nodded against her. "I'm so sorry." she cried, then placed her lips softly against his. He took in a shaky breath then

238

hesitantly returned her kiss. Riana felt more tears break through. She closed her eyes tightly; it wasn't supposed to be like this.

"I guess..." Alex started. "I guess you know how I feel now, Ri." he confessed hoarsely. Riana opened her eyes and witnessed Alex fight his own tears. "You just..." he quickly wiped the first of his tears off his face. "...have to figure out how you feel." he finished and took one full step away from where Riana still sat on the island.

Riana's heart and soul crumbled the moment he stepped away. She swallowed thickly. "It's not... It's not that easy, Alex."

"Ri..." he sighed. "You're... with Ryan." She winced. "You can't have us both." Riana turned away from him and let go of deep sobs as she nodded. Alex squeezed her knee, then walked away.

Riana wrapped her arms around herself as she heaved out broken sobs. She was overcome with a sense of nausea; she had never been unfaithful to anyone, especially Ryan. She shook her head against the knowledge that she was more than willing to cross lines with Alex she knew she shouldn't. She couldn't deny the rush she felt when embraced and kissed by him. It was unnatural. How she felt with him was different than anyone else in her life. She had never been so overcome with passion and emotion.

<u>CHAPTER EIGHTEEN</u>
Not Ready To Make Nice

Samantha quickly approach the corral and urgently motioned Lexi over. Lexi caught Derek's eye, "Hey dear, could you take over for a minute?" Derek agreed as he stepped off the fence and took the lead from her with a smile. She hopped over the fence, jogged over to Sam and noticed her eyes were wide and terrified. "What's wrong?" she asked quickly.

"Lexi!" Sam quietly exclaimed. "I think Ri is about to kick Tabitha's ass." Thankfully she didn't say it loud enough for anyone else to hear.

"What?" Lexi hissed as she pulled Sam further away from the corral.

"I was in the barn, talking with Alex when Tabitha came in. She was questioning him about how he felt about Ri. He told her to let it go, but she started yelling…" Sam tried to catch her breath. "I didn't exactly want to be in the middle of it so I left… But as I was leaving I ran into Riana. Before I could even fully tell her what happened she stormed into the barn." Sam gave a look Lexi understood all too well, and her next words confirmed it. "She was on a fucking mission Lex."

"Ah, dammit." Lexi muttered. "Sam, go hang with D and Matt." Sam didn't argue as she didn't particularly care for conflict and Lexi went to attempt to defuse what she was sure would be a confrontation to end all confrontations. Once Riana loved someone, be that friendship or otherwise, she would fight to the ends of the earth to defend them. Tabitha had no idea what she got into.

However, as Lexi approached the barn, she didn't hear any yelling. She looked in and saw Tabitha, alone. "Tabitha?" she beckoned. She looked up, startled. "Um, Matthew was wondering where you ran off to." Lexi covered.

Tabitha gave a weak smile. "I'll be right there."

Lexi nodded and backed out of the doorway. She scanned the surrounding area in a search for Ri and Alex. Chester greeted Lexi at the fence as she rounded the barn, but there was no sign of Riana or Alex. She was sure they hadn't gone out past the corral or surely Matt and Derek would have convinced them to stay. The logical conclusion of their whereabouts was the house.

Lexi didn't find them out front, or outside in the back, but when she reached the patio door to check inside she was halted by the scene her gaze fell upon. Alex had Riana backed against the kitchen island and their hands were tangled in each other's hair as they kissed. Lexi blushed at the intensity of their moment and smiled to herself as she turned to walk away. "Good for you, Ri." she murmured with a smile.

Lexi rushed back to the corral and hopped up on the fence with Derek and Sam. Tabitha had taken over with Spencer and Sugar. Lexi nudged Sam. "Did Tabitha say anything?" she whispered.

Sam shook her head. "Not about anything with Alex and Ri. What did you run into in there?" she quietly asked.

"Nothing actually, only Tabitha. She seemed a little shaken up, but physically unharmed." Lexi grinned a bit. "Um, Alex and Ri weren't in there… they were… umm… busy, in the house." A blush kissed her cheeks as she remembered the scene. Samantha's eyes grew wide.

"Are you serious?" She grabbed Lexi's knee quickly. Lexi looked around to make sure no one else had heard, then nodded. Sam took a deep breath. "She's going to need us." she surmised softly. "She's not ready, Lex."

"I know. But maybe this will help the process along, you know? I mean, she wasn't exactly seeming to mind it." Lexi grinned devilishly. Sam rolled her eyes.

Lexi felt the fence flex and suddenly Alex was next to her. "Ugh! Alex, don't scare me like that!" she scolded. She tried not to look him in the eyes as she was sure she'd blush; the image of him and Riana still fresh in her mind.

"Sorry." he mumbled as he looked out at Spencer and Tabitha. Lexi realized something must have happened between him and Riana; there was no reason he should be back outside with them. She glanced over at Samantha.

She reached for Sam's hand and pulled her off the fence. "We're going to... see if Ri needs any help getting things ready for lunch." Derek smiled and nodded while Alex continued to glaze over.

Lexi took a deep breath as they reached the front door. "Okay, we'll have to... probably not say that I saw them. We have to hope she opens up right away. By the way Alex looked whatever happened in here did not end well." Samantha frowned and nodded in agreement. Lexi eased the door open. "Ri?" she called.

Riana gathered herself enough to slide off the kitchen counter after a long moment. She shuffled to her room, overcome by a choking sensation. She couldn't breathe, and couldn't see through her tears. She eased herself onto her bed and buried her head into her pillows as she wailed.

A light knock broke through the sounds of her sobs and the door eased open. "Ri?" Sam beckoned.

"Yeah." Riana croaked. Sam pushed the door all the way open and stepped in, Lexi close behind her. Once they saw the pain in Riana's face they rushed to her side.

"Ri, oh honey, what's wrong?" Lexi murmured as she hastened to Riana and wrapped her in her arms. Riana was unable find any words, but her wails intensified as she melded into the embraces of Lexi and Sam.

They tried to hush her, but Riana was inconsolable. "I'm so...stupid." she choked out. "I don't know what I was... thinking. He's gonna..." she fought to catch her breath. "He's gonna hate... me." Her breaths continued to be choppy and forced.

"Shh... no, honey, you're not stupid." Sam assured. Riana watched the fabric of Sam's shirt darkened as her tears came to rest on her shoulder.

Riana sniffled and swallowed thickly as she glimpsed towards Lexi and Sam and fought to find her voice. "He will. They both will. Ryan and Alex." she clarified. "They're both going to hate me." Her friends sighed and patiently waited for her to elaborate. "I'm not a cheater, you know that." Riana affirmed through her shallow breaths. Lexi and Sam nodded and assured her that they knew she wasn't. "But...but I kissed Alex." Riana winced and waited to be scolded but the scolding never came. "Like, really kissed him." she made her eyes wide and serious. "You know... tongue and all, pulling hair... ugh, it was... unbelievable." she finished and closed her eyes. Images of Alex flashed before her and her eyes fluttered open. She was met with mild looks of amusement on Lexi and Sam's faces.

"Oh yeah?" Sam urged as an excited spark danced in her eyes.

"Argh! You guys suck." Riana yelled with a light laugh. "Can't you see I'm in emotional turmoil?" Riana flung herself back and covered her face with a pillow.

"Ri, sweetheart…" Lexi began with a deep breath. "I think, that maybe, you need to stop worrying so much about Ryan."

"He's my boyfriend, Lex." Riana bemoaned into her pillow.

"Is he, Ri?" she challenged. "Think about it. Does he support you in your career? Does he care for you or make you laugh? Is he the one here right now? Any time you ask him for more commitment he pulls further away. You've never met his family, and it's been what, almost four years? You give and give to him and he gives you nothing in return except mixed signals and consistent heartbreak." Riana scowled in the darkness under her pillow. She hated when Lexi made such valid points.

"Alex…" Samantha prompted softly. Riana felt her chest tighten at the sound of his name. "Alex is everything Ryan isn't, Ri."

Riana uncovered her face. "He won't love me. He can't love me." she reasoned through her tears.

Samantha twisted her mouth and her hazel eyes narrowed. "Why not?"

"He just can't. He deserves better. I'm not good enough for him." Riana grumbled.

"Did he kiss you back?" Lexi pushed.

A blush rushed to Riana's cheeks as she lightly touched her lips and smiled softly. "Yes." she whispered. "it was phenomenal." she breathed. "It was sweet, yet the sexiest thing I've ever experienced." The tears welled up again as she remembered. "He... He said to me after I stopped it... He said, 'I guess you know how I feel now.' and I don't!" Lexi and Samantha sighed in frustration.

"Really, Ri? Come on honey, you're a smart woman. Do you really think it would have been so intense if he didn't care about you?" Sam pressed.

"Who knows." Riana mumbled. "Maybe he's like every other man--"

"Shut your face. You know damn well he's not." Lexi scolded with a quick swat to Ri's arm. Riana knew she was right again. Alex was unlike any man she had ever known; he was silly and fun yet deep and compassionate, he was beautiful yet humble. He had provided her with safety and comfort whenever she needed it.

"I don't know what to do." Riana whined as she burrowed back under her blanket.

"Whatever you do, honey, be honest with Alex." Samantha urged as she rubbed Riana's back.

Riana nodded and sighed. "I think, I just want to stay here for a while."

Lexi frowned. "You can't hide in here forever, Ri." If Riana didn't love her as much as she did, she may have found Lexi's mothering annoying.

Riana turned her head and glared at Lexi. "I know." she snapped. "Just give me awhile. I'll come out to untack the horses once they're done."

"I'll get them to finish up and we'll start lunch for you." Sam offered as she kissed Riana's cheek and crawled off the bed. Lexi followed shortly behind. Riana sighed as more tears escaped her eyes.

She knew Lexi and Sam were frustrated with her. She also knew they saw the good and happiness Alex brought her but she couldn't seem to break free from Ryan. Despite the moment she had with Alex, she still couldn't convince herself that he could want her, love her, or treat her any differently than the other men she'd been with. She was acutely aware of the sick comfort being with Ryan brought her.

Alex had a hard time fighting his own tears as he walked away from Riana, and everything she represented in that moment. He wanted to hold her, wanted to tell her it was okay, that he was there for her and that he loved her. As painful as it was for him, they had to stop, and he had to walk away. Riana had to make a decision.

He wandered back outside and watched silently as Spencer enjoyed his ride. Tabitha refused to acknowledge he was there, and Sam and Lexi left shortly after he arrived. He felt the heaviness of being alone while surrounded by those he considered family. Matthew glanced over at him and furrowed his brow as he mouthed the question, "Are you okay?" Alex barely shrugged in response. He wasn't okay; he had fallen desperately in love with a woman he knew he couldn't have. He snorted at the irony of how so many D.M.A. songs dealt with love yet there he was; realizing he'd never truly been in love. He'd loved before, but he'd never wanted to give himself so completely to anyone. Alex wanted to bare his soul to Riana; present himself more honestly than he had before and hope somehow she could love him too. She was unlike other women he had known over the years; she wasn't consumed with his status, wasn't star-struck or dumbed down in front of him. He took solace in knowing that if she did love him, at least it would be authentic.

"Hey Matt?" Lexi hollered as she and Samantha reached the corral. "Want to start on lunch?" she asked as she opened the gate and jogged to him on Sonny.

"Absolutely." He pulled back on Sonny's reins and brought her to a halt. Tabitha stopped Sugar and assisted Spencer out of the saddle.

"What should we do with the horses?" Tabitha asked.

"I'll take them back to the barn. Riana will be out in a minute to take care of them." Sam said as she walked over to Tabitha and Sugar. She grabbed the lead from Tabitha and gave her an apprehensive look. Alex watched the moment and wondered when everyone would find out about the confrontation in the barn. Sam also grabbed Sonny's reins after Matthew dismounted. Alex hopped off the fence and ambled towards her.

"I'll take Sonny." he volunteered. Sam placed the reins in his hand as she nodded. They moseyed through the gate silently. Matt, Derek, and Lexi headed to the main house while Tabitha took Spencer to the guest house to change. Once everyone was out of earshot Alex spoke, "I'm sorry about what happened in the barn."

"It's okay Alex. It wasn't your fault." she assured. She placed her small hand on his broad shoulder. "We knew something was going to give before things would get better right?"

"I suppose." he mumbled as he shuffled along.

"That's not what's really bothering you, is it?" Sam assessed. They entered the barn and stopped at the rings on the wall to tie up the horses.

"No." he sighed. "Riana came in here, when Tabitha and I were getting into it. She... She downright owned Tabitha. It was outrageous. And wonderful. But..." Alex stopped and twisted Sonny's leather reins around his hands. "She was beautiful when she did it. There was something... irresistible in it." He finally looked at Sam. "I messed up, Sam. She knows how I feel. I went against everything you told me, everything I knew I shouldn't do."

"I know." Sam interrupted unpretentiously. "Things are going to be complicated for a while. But... she doesn't know how you feel Alex." Before he could debate it or question her, she continued, "She's pretty much in denial that you feel anything for her. She's terrified Alex."

"Yeah. I messed up really well didn't I?" he commented sarcastically. Her eyes softened.

"Like I said before, if you really love her, stick it out. She'll make it worth it. She might not be able to fully admit it yet Alex, but she loves you. I can see it, Lexi can see it. She'll get there." Alex gave her a half-hearted smile. He turned to Sonny and started to undo her bridle.

"You don't have to do that." Riana's soft voice remarked from the barn door. "I'll untack them." Her voice lacked the assertive power it typically had, she sounded weak and broken.

Alex was unsure if he should argue with her or not. Everything was new now, different--awkward even. "Alright honey." Samantha complied as she pulled on Alex's upper arm. "Come on, Alex." Alex's eyes sadly traveled to Riana's face. Her eyes were swollen and bloodshot, her cheeks and neck splotched with red. He realized that she had been crying and wanted to stop and gather her in his arms, but knew he shouldn't. He sullenly followed Sam out of the barn.

Matthew was at the grill and happily watched Spencer in the pool with Tabitha. Derek sat at the side of the pool sensing that something wasn't quite right so when he saw Lexi leave the bar and head into the house he decided to follow. "Hey D." she greeted happily when she saw him enter the kitchen.

"What's going on, Lex?" Derek asked deliberately. Her eyes shot around nervously.

"Just, um, getting Matt some seasoning." she replied uneasily as she turned to the cupboard.

"Not that." he retorted. "Why is everyone acting so... weird?" The energy among almost everyone had been thick and tense. Derek saw Lexi's shoulders fall and she slowly turned back to him.

"There was a bit of a... confrontation between Alex and Tabitha earlier." she explained. Derek sighed as he lowered himself onto one of the stools at the kitchen island. "I don't know any details. Sam was there for part of it. Riana...she, um, finished it."

"Well, that explains how quiet Tabs is being." Derek reasoned as he ran his fingers along the cool granite top. Lexi moved around the island and sat next to him, her unruly curls drifted into her face.

"Alex is going to need his big brother, D." she presumed. He nodded. "Things also got... intense with him and Ri."

"They're fighting?" Derek questioned in disbelief. Lexi wet her lips, then bit her lower lip softly.

"Well, not exactly. They, um, became a little intimate afterwards." she blushed lightly. "Just kissing, but it's messing with Riana in an awful way."

"Damn, I imagine." Derek mumbled. "I'm sure Alex is a bit confused right now as well." Lexi nodded.

"I think I'm going to suggest a girl's day out tomorrow. Just me, Sam and Ri. We'll go riding, maybe camp out for the night. I'm sure you and guys could handle a night without us." she smiled.

Derek draped his arm over her shoulder. "Oh, I don't know." he teased.

"Uh, Lexi? I kind of need that seasoning!" Matthew hollered from the patio.

"Ah, dammit." Lexi cursed as she jumped up, grabbed the seasoning off the counter and jogged back outside.

CHAPTER NINETEEN

Upside Down

Riana took her time as she untacked and cleaned up Sonny and Sugar. She wasn't in any particular hurry to be back in the presence of everyone else. She was sure Tabitha wouldn't keep their confrontation a secret for long and figured Matt would hate her for being so aggressive with his wife.

And Alex.

Riana let out a long sigh as she dropped her head to Sonny's neck. Alex would want her to make decisions she wasn't ready to make. It took every ounce of resistance she could muster not to rush into his arms, find his lips and confess it was him she wanted. She thought it would be rash of her to assume there could be an actual relationship with him. They had a weak moment, she rationalized, where attraction took over. Attraction didn't equal love; which had been a hard lesson for Riana to learn and come to terms with. Alex was one of her best friends, she felt it was stupid to jeopardize the friendship with such reckless behavior. Stupid and selfish.

His words replayed in her mind; *"Now you know how I feel...you have to figure out how you feel...you can't have both of us..."* She figured one might logically conclude that Alex had feelings for her. She wasn't exactly a logic driven person however. Riana knew the world expected a beautiful, classy, passive and accommodating woman on Alex's arm and she wasn't any of those things; she was short, curvy, aggressive, and she cussed too much.

Riana took a deep breath and continued her task, desperate to block everything out of her mind. She attempted to distract herself with ideas for her next book, a new speaking engagement schedule, she even considered spending some time in Canada with Sam. Eventually the monotony of untacking and rubbing down Sonny and Sugar calmed her. She didn't feel quite so on edge, so terrified or anxious. For a moment she felt alone on the ranch with her horses. After she finished with Sonny and Sugar she put them out to pasture and hopped up on the fence to watch them. She closed her eyes against the sun and felt herself slip into a peaceful moment. She wondered if perhaps it wasn't about being good enough for Alex. Maybe it was about being herself and being able to find someone who could handle her. Someone who could love her despite her past, her aggression, and her cynicism. She couldn't say for sure if that person was Alex, though she definitely wanted it to be. She couldn't get past how terrified the possibility of losing him made her.

She couldn't forget Ryan either. She attempted to comprehend how it all changed. She wondered if it had ever been real. Had he truly loved her at one time or had she been duped for the last three years? She thought back over the years and remembered the look in his eyes; playful and compassionate. She shook her head, and questioned how they got to where they were. How did she get to the point where she knew deep down that he didn't love her, yet she couldn't walk away from him? No matter how much time passed between when she'd hear from him or saw him, she was a willing, spineless puddle the moment he came back.

Ryan had helped her in her healing journey, she figured that had to mean something in all of this. He was the only man to have asked permission to touch her intimately. He was the first man she was present with during intimate moments. For years she had disassociated from every sexual encounter she had. It was easier for her to emotionally leave the moment than it was to face how each encounter brought her back to being assaulted. Ryan was the first man she truly hadn't been afraid of. That, too, had changed. There was an apprehension deep within Riana's gut lately when Ryan came back. It was a desperate whisper that yelled at her not to do it. Riana snorted at the cruel irony; how passionate, assertive and strong she was in her speaking and writing about sexual violence and healing yet there she was; a passive, weak, and quiet woman willing to be used in order to fool herself into believing she was loved. She hated that she was willing to change herself in order to appease him. She buried her passion and became soft spoken as to not intimidate him.

A smirk spread across Riana's face as she thought of Alex. He apparently liked her aggression and how brutally blunt she was. She blushed at the memory of their kitchen encounter, then groaned and hopped off the fence. Brushing it under the rug would not be as easy as she had hoped.

Riana unenthusiastically ventured back to the house. As she approached the back she smiled at the sound of laughter. She was glad that at least everyone else was having fun. She straightened her back and put on a brave face to make it through lunch.

"Ri!" Matthew hollered as Riana turned the corner. "Where the hell have you been lady?"

"Just, taking care of some things." she covered as she quickly glanced at Tabitha and Alex. She found Matthew's blue eyes and smiled. "So what masterpiece did you whip up for lunch?" His smile brightened as he led Riana to his spread of delectable meat, fruit and side dishes. As they took their places for lunch Riana noticed that Tabitha couldn't look her in the eyes; much the way Riana couldn't look at Alex.

"So Ri, Sam and I decided that we should take a day ride tomorrow. Maybe even camp out for the night." Lexi declared from across the table. Riana kept her eyes on her plate and pondered the idea. She figured it couldn't hurt to be away from Alex for a day.

Riana nodded as she finally looked at Lexi. "Okay." she relented. She excused herself from the table early; stating she wasn't feeling well.

Riana spent the remainder of the afternoon in her room. Samantha checked on her, but Riana urged her to keep with the original plans for the evening. About the time the sun started its descent to the horizon there was another knock at the door. She yelled for them to enter and was graced with Matthew's sweet smile.

"Spencer was wondering if you were going to join us for our movie." he beckoned softly. Riana avoided his eyes. He slipped further into her room and sat on the edge of her bed. "He really likes you, Ri." She smiled despite herself.

"I really like him too." Matthew placed his hand on Riana's calf and gave a gentle squeeze.

"I know about what happened in the barn, Ri." he revealed simply. Riana groaned. "I'm not upset with you." She quickly lifted her puzzled face to him. "She needed to hear it. She wouldn't listen to me when I'd tell her." He paused for a moment and studied the patterns on Riana's comforter. "And... And I really think it's great how you defended Alex."

"I just couldn't let her talk to him like that." she explained softly. "I shouldn't have gotten so aggressive though." Matthew gave a quick shrug.

"She's tough Ri, she'll handle it. Like I said, it had to be said. I'm glad it was you that said it." he smiled warmly at her. "So what do you say? You coming out for a movie?" He was almost impossible to say no to. Riana gave a quick roll of her eyes but conceded to his request. She slipped into some sweat pants and a hoodie, hoping to cocoon herself outside and avoid any further confrontations.

Riana found Sam in the kitchen, producing massive amounts of popcorn. "How are you doing, love?" she asked as Riana slipped in beside her and stole a handful of the buttery goodness.

"Oh, you know, perfecting the art of denial and avoidance." she mumbled. Sam wrapped her arm around Riana's waist.

"Oh Ri, let's go watch a movie." Riana nodded and followed Sam outside. Riana was stunned at how hard everyone had worked to set up the outdoor theater. The patio furniture had been taken from the back yard and placed in front of the makeshift movie screen hung on the barn wall. There were a few hay bales stacked and layered with heavy blankets to form more seats. Spencer was snuggled between Matthew and Tabitha, and Derek was on the ground backed against a hay bale with Lexi next to him. Alex sat in one of the lounge chairs and turned his head to Riana. She smiled hesitantly as she approached.

She couldn't stop herself, she nervously advanced further then asked softly, "Can I sit with you?" His smile was sweet and understanding as he nodded. She crawled over one leg and settled in between the other then leaned back against him. She

258

turned her head just a bit and breathed in his scent. "I'm sorry." she murmured.

Alex ran his hand along her arm. "I'm sorry too." She closed her eyes and snuggled into him. Despite their forbidden encounter she didn't want to lose the comfort she felt with him; it was all encompassing. She was a wreck inside as she cried in her bed, but the moment she was within Alex's embrace the emotional whirlwind settled.

The next thing Riana knew she barely noticed being scooped up off the chair and carried. She vaguely heard voices around her, "She really can sleep anywhere can't she?" his deep voice rumbled. She then heard a light laugh beside her; Lexi.

"She really can. Good thing she has you around to carry her back to bed." Riana's drifted back into her slumber.

Sunday August 27, 2006

Lexi was dancing in her room to some old school 90's music as she packed for her ride when she heard a deep laugh from her door. She jumped around, startled, and found Derek leaned up against her door frame. He shook his head and chuckled at her. Lexi blushed at being caught in her guilty pleasure. "Nice, Lex." he laughed.

"Oh, come on. You know you love it." she taunted as she turned up the music and sashayed over to him. She grabbed his hands and pulled him all the way into her room. Derek finally gave in and showed her just how perfectly he could bad man-dance.

"What time are you ladies taking off?" he asked as he followed Lexi into her closet where she pulled down her sleeping bag and a change of clothes.

"Well, that depends on our sleeping beauty." she giggled. "I figure we'll head out around noon. She needs some time just us girls. I know her. She's beating herself up and thinking in circles." Derek nodded thoughtfully.

"So I heard this rumor…"

"It's not good to listen to rumors, D." Lexi teased as she stuffed her clothes into her bag.

"Right." he grinned. "I think I should listen to this one, though. I heard it was your birthday soon." Lexi turned and beamed at him. "And I was wondering if, maybe, you'd like to spend your birthday with me in Prescott?" Lexi's smile grew. She found it adorable, how apprehensive he seemed to be. "We could find a little hole in the wall restaurant, maybe take in some theater. Whatever you'd like."

"I'd really like that, Derek." she assured. She couldn't think of a much better way to spend her birthday than being with him. He was sweet and funny, articulate and caring. An all-around honest, nice guy. Derek smiled and nodded.

"Sweet. Then I guess I'll pick you up Wednesday, say 8am?" Lexi giggled and nodded. "Have fun with the girls, Lex." he called as he left her room. Lexi grinned to herself then squealed just a bit as she bounded out of her room with her bag and down to Riana's room.

Riana's dreams had been twisted and heartbreaking and left her exhausted. She had wanted to find a sense of safety with Alex again, but knew if she did, it would only make things worse. As she woke up she stayed burrowed within her blankets and cynically thought that her bed was much too large to be alone in. She closed her eyes and willed herself to remember what it felt like to be held by him; his warmth, the protective nature of his embrace. As her mind trailed further into the comforting image she was ripped from it when she realized it wasn't Ryan her mind envisioned, it was Alex. She growled as she flung her blankets off and stormed into her en suite for a shower.

Riana barely spoke two words to Alex as she and the girls got ready to leave, and had been short with everyone else. Alex looked absolutely crushed. Sam frowned as they walked through the door and to the barn. Riana silently tacked up Adonis and loaded his saddle bags. She led him outside, mounted, then looked back to Lexi and Samantha expectantly. Lexi took a deep breath and hoped the tension wouldn't last long.

The first fifteen minutes of the ride were painfully silent. Riana's gaze was hard and cold to the horizon. Her jaw was rigid. Lexi knew she was

261

close to bursting from the emotional turmoil within her. She also knew an intense run would probably help work out some of the frustration. Lexi leaned forward into Chester's neck as she gave him a solid kick. Chester lurched forward and they blasted past Sam then Riana. Lexi glanced back, just quickly enough to catch a mischievous grin spread over Riana's face. Lexi knew Chester wouldn't maintain his lead for long once Riana let Adonis free so she whooped and cheered as they led the charge and left dust flying up behind them. Too soon, the sound of powerful, heavy, pounding hooves not belonging to Chester caught up to them. Samantha and Lilo approached from the left and then Adonis shot out in front of them on the right, Riana's laughter trailed behind the black streak.

Lexi turned her head to Sam and smiled. Chester and Lilo tried desperately to keep up, but Adonis was by far Riana's strongest and fastest horse. Riana continued on, then looped Adonis back around to Lexi and Sam. The racing, chasing and playing continued. The horses were covered in sweat and fought to catch their breath. Riana finally eased up on Adonis and allowed Lexi and Sam to catch up. "That was great." Sam commented as she and Lexi reached Riana.

"Indeed ladies." Riana agreed. She took a deep breath and frowned lightly, the weight of her issues hadn't faded away like the dust behind them.

"Ri," Sam called. "Let's get the horses some water." Riana nodded and veered right. They trotted towards the river that fed into the lake and Lexi started to debate on how to get Ri to talk.

Riana pulled back on Adonis, halted him, and dismounted. Sam and Lexi followed suit. Lexi was acutely aware that Riana probably picked the river rather than the lake due to memories of Alex. They led their horses towards the bank where they pulled off their boots and socks, rolled up their pant legs and proceeded to wade into the water; horses in tow.

"So," Lexi began. "Derek sort of asked me out."

Riana's head quickly snapped in Lexi's direction, excited. "Seriously?" Lexi nodded.

"What did you say?" Samantha asked quickly. Lexi grinned and bit her lip, a blush barely showed through her creamy, olive skin.

"I told him no."

"Lexi!" Riana screeched, startling Adonis. She instinctively reached up to stroke his nose.

"I'm kidding." Lexi laughed. "Of course I said yes. I mean, he didn't actually call it a date." she rationalized.

"Well, what did he call it?" Samantha impatiently implored.

"He said he heard a rumor my birthday was coming up..." Lexi shot a stern eye at Riana and she dropped her mouth in exaggerated offense.

"Why do you automatically assume it was me?" Riana laughed, fully knowing Lexi was right in her assumption.

Samantha giggled as she led Lilo further into the current. "Ri, you're such a terrible liar."

"Anyway!" Riana laughed. "So *somehow* D found out your birthday is coming up."

Lexi smiled lovingly at Riana. "So he invited me to spend the day with him in Prescott. Catch some theater, dinner. Just some nice one on one time." Her blush finally deepened. Sam gave a delighted squeal.

"And how do you feel about this?" Riana probed. Lexi furrowed her brow, wasn't she supposed to be the one asking Ri that question?

"I'm pretty excited I guess." Lexi replied as she stroked Chester. "A little nervous maybe." she admitted reluctantly. She adored Derek. She found him alluring, intelligent, compassionate, funny and definitely easy on the eyes but she despised the drama of relationships.

"Aw, miss independent, it's okay to like an awesome guy like Derek." Riana assured as she snuggled Adonis' face.

There it was, Lexi's chance to turn the attention off her and onto Riana. "Much like it's okay for you to like a wonderful man like Alex." Samantha heard the growl that rolled through Riana's throat and shot Lexi a worried glance. Samantha hated confrontation, but worried especially about confrontations that included Riana, her temper had its own reputation.

Lexi was a seasoned professional when it came to confrontations with Riana. It was one of the things that made their friendship so strong. "That was uncalled for Lex." Riana seethed as she pulled on Adonis' reins and started to lead him out of the river.

Lexi tightened her jaw. "Was it?" she snapped from behind Riana as she too led Chester from the river. "I thought it was a perfectly logical thing to say."

"You would." Riana snarled. Sam reluctantly followed behind with Lilo as Lexi continued her pursuit of Riana.

"And why is that Ri?" Lexi pushed. "Personally, I think anyone who saw you with Alex would feel justified in saying it."

Riana spun on her heel and faced Lexi, fury burned in her eyes. "No, Lexi, they wouldn't." she retorted. "They wouldn't carelessly encourage me to cheat on my boyfriend!" She turned her back on Lexi and tied Adonis to a tree before she sat to put her socks and boots back on. Her cheeks flushed with frustration. "You're so damn insensitive!" she yelled.

"Fucking hell, Riana, you know that's not true." Lexi countered as she stood over her. "I love you, Ri. I want you happy. But I don't think Ryan truly makes you happy."

"Even if that were true," Riana started, despite the fact that Lexi spoke the truth; Ryan made her miserable. "it wouldn't give me the right to cheat on him." Lexi and Sam both sighed. Riana, even with her temper, was a loyal and loving person; whether or not the recipient deserved it.

"You don't need to cheat on him, Ri." Lexi murmured. "I'm just saying you don't have to ignore all the good in Alex or the feelings you have for him."

"I don't have feelings for him." Riana snapped with cold eyes. Lexi was tempted to expose that she had seen Riana and Alex in the kitchen and that it had been more than obvious she had feelings for him. She knew, though, that given Riana's current level of resistance she'd chalk it up to a moment of weakness in physical attraction.

"Riana." Sam pleaded softly.

"Stop. It doesn't matter how I feel about Alex, I'm with Ryan." Riana's eyes finally softened as she looked to Sam and Lexi. "As my best friends I need you both to support me in that. Can you do that for me?" she finished softly.

Lexi approached her and pulled her into a hug. "Of course honey." she assured. "I just want you happy."

"Me too." Samantha whispered as she snuck in between their hug. Riana kissed Sam's forehead.

"Thank you." Riana mumbled before she pulled out of the hug and untied Adonis. "So, where are we setting up camp?"

<u>CHAPTER TWENTY</u>
Unpredictable

Alex felt completely rejected by Riana as she gave him the cold shoulder before she, Lexi and Sam departed. The last twenty-four hours had been the most intense and emotionally draining twenty-four hours of his life--or at least close to it. It exhausted him. However, he couldn't justify giving up. He loved her, and he knew it wasn't easy for her either. He imagined it was likely much more difficult for her given her commitment to Ryan. He groaned as he threw his head back against the pool lounge chair. He heard the sliding glass door open then close, but didn't bother to turn his head.

"Alex, man, what's up?" Derek asked as he claimed the chair next to Alex and slid his sunglasses onto his face.

"Dude, you don't want to know." Alex moaned with his eyes closed against the sun. He heard the crack of a can being opened, then felt the chill of metal against his bare arm. He opened his eyes and looked at Derek over the top of his sunglasses. Derek lifted the can of beer and tipped it towards Alex in offering.

"Things not going so well with Riana lately, huh?" Derek presumed as Alex accepted the can and took a deep swallow.

"Not so much." Alex admitted with a sigh. "She's... confused."

"Well, let's not dwell on it. Let's just sit back and relax. I'm sure things will work out." Alex pursed his lips and wondered how it was everyone seemed so sure about things between him and Riana; first Sam, now Derek.

"I don't know Matt, I don't think he's going to forgive me so easily." Tabitha brushed out her hair and watched Matthew get dressed. Matt sauntered to her as she stood in the bathroom doorway.

He grabbed her small hips and kissed her softly. "He loves you Tabs. He'll appreciate you going to him. Although, he might resist until he knows Riana's in the clear." He smiled a bit and Tabitha nodded. "I imagine the hardest part will be apologizing to her."

Tabitha pulled away and turned back into the bathroom. Matthew followed her and found her eyes in the mirror. "That woman scares the hell out of me Matt." The fear in her eyes spoke louder than her words.

He didn't want to discount his wife's feelings but a smile still played on Matt's lips and in his startling azure eyes. "Her bark is worse than her bite."

She gave a nervous laugh, "Oh, I don't know. You fail to remember she had me pinned against a horse stall."

"Oh honey," he soothed. "Riana's a softy. You'll see." Matthew had decided months ago to keep his history with Riana from Tabitha. He was well aware of how she blamed Riana for Alex's abandonment of Kim, so he could only imagine how paranoid she'd be about him and Riana. Of course, he worried that keeping it from her might end badly, but he hoped to help out Alex and limit Tabitha's reasons to dislike and mistrust Riana. Surely she would understand when he finally told her; considering he didn't even let Derek and Alex in on her nine years ago. He figured he'd tell her once she was over the Alex and Kim drama.

Tabitha approached tentatively to where Alex sat at the bar. "Alex," she started softly. Alex snapped his cold, chestnut eyes to her. "I... I didn't mean to get so angry yesterday." she confessed. Alex wanted to stay angry at her, but the look on her face convinced him she was authentic; she looked heartbroken and scared. He didn't know how to respond, he knew it couldn't say it was okay, because it wasn't. She had been out of line. "I just wanted to... understand more, but it escalated so fast..."

Alex placed his hand on top of Tabitha's as he found her soft cognac eyes. "I know the whole breakup was a shock to you, to her-- to almost everyone really. But it was a long time coming, Tabs. It was a decision I had to make, and Riana just got thrown in the middle."

Tabitha gave him a weak smile. "Riana... She's a feisty one."

Alex couldn't stop the laughter that rolled out of him. Matthew quickly looked over from the pool and smiled when he saw that Tabitha joined Alex in his laughter. "She certainly is." Alex chuckled.

"It's obvious she cares about you, and it's clear she makes you happy." Tabitha dropped her eyes for a moment as she wrung her hands together. "That's all I really want Alex," she admitted quietly. "for you to be happy."

"I am, Tabs. I'm much happier."

Tabitha nodded. "Okay then."

Alex pulled her into a hug. "I love you, Tabs." he mumbled as his chin rested on her petite shoulder.

"I love you too, Alex."

Lexi, Samantha and Riana rode past the lake and up towards where the trees thinned into rocky edges and decided to set up camp. They weren't exactly girly-girls but they weren't candidates for "Survivor" either. Riana hated tents, truly and honestly hated them. It seemed to her there were never enough pieces to make it all work. Lexi was her hero in this regard, as she was a bit rougher around the edges when it came to outdoor endeavors. While Lexi and Riana fought with the tent, Sam gathered kindling for their fire. "I'm sorry for pushing the Alex thing." Lexi deplored as she threaded a pole through the loops on her end and pushed it through to Riana's side.

"I know." Riana sighed. "It's just...It's becoming too complicated." she bent the pole down and attempted to slide it through the last loop before she pushed it into the ground.

"It doesn't have to be." Lexi started again. Riana felt tension form in her temples.

"I feel like I owe it to Ryan to talk about things. I mean, we've been together for three years." Lexi walked around to Riana's side of the tent with the rubber mallet to finish securing the tent.

"You've been with him for three years. I don't see that he's been with you for those three years. He's left you totally alone and questioning for months, yet you still hold on and love him. You deserve so much better Ri. If you give Ryan the chance to talk about things, he's going to say he wants you. But you have to really think about what that truly means. You two don't even date anymore. You don't go out, you don't hang out with friends together. He keeps you a secret; isolated and alone." Riana dropped her head and took a deep breath.

"I love him." Riana whispered.

"You love who he was, Ri. Not who he is." Lexi declared. "There's a difference." Riana narrowed her eyes at Lexi. She was so tired of this same conversation they had all the time. She wondered if she would ever believe Lexi, or if she would ever truly be able to see her relationship with Ryan for the twisted, manipulation it actually was.

She was sure Lexi was tired of it as well. She couldn't understand why Lexi didn't just give up on her, she was a lost cause when it came to Ryan.

After they finished the first bottle of wine, Riana, Sam and Lexi were finally relaxed and laughing. "No, I'm serious!" Riana laughed. "He honestly thought it was a picture of a horse! I have to show you the video when we get home because it's hilarious!" Riana was happy to be back with her girls and not talking about Alex.

After the laughter subsided, they silently watched the careful roasting of their marshmallows. "So, I guess Matt already knew about my encounter with Tabitha." Riana blurted. Sam quickly looked over at her. "I felt like an ass of course, but he assured me that it needed to be said."

"He's absolutely right." Lexi interjected.

Samantha brought her marshmallow up and gently touched it to gauge the center gooeyness. "If she knows what's good for her, she'll get over it." she observed with a small laugh.

"What if she doesn't?" Riana groaned.

"She will. But, for argument's sake, even if she doesn't, I don't think you'll lose the guys. D's made his intention to keep us around absolutely clear. And, well... I don't think Tabitha could sway Alex when it comes to you." Lexi assured as she rotated her marshmallow.

"I know." Riana relented. She spun her stick and inspected how evenly her marshmallow was toasted. She brought the golden brown, toasted, gooey mess to her mouth. "I just hate how much she despises me without even knowing me." she mumbled around the sweetness.

"You're such a delicate flower, Ri." Sam teased. Riana swiftly gave her the finger with a laugh.

"Alright." Riana declared as she poured herself another glass of wine. "You have a point. Why the hell should I care if she likes me?" she laughed as she raised her glass in a toast.

"You and Alex make up?" Matthew asked against his wife's ear as he wrapped his arms around her from behind.

Tabitha hummed happily at the sensation of his lips. "Yes we did." she confirmed. "I might not ever fully understand, but he's happier now. As much as I wanted him to be as miserable as Kim; it's obvious he's happy." Matthew kissed her just under her ear and turned back to the grill.

Alex had Spencer on his shoulders in the pool as they played water basketball with Derek. A smiled danced along Tabitha's lips as she watched them. "Uncle D! I got you!" Spencer yelled happily after Alex had lifted him higher to dunk over Derek's head.

"Alright little dude, time to swim. I need a break." Alex laughed as he lifted Spencer off his shoulders. He and Derek exited the pool and proceeded to the bar where Tabitha chatted with Matt.

Derek leaned in behind Matt and grabbed waters for himself and Alex. "So," he started, as he leaned back against the bar. "I sort of asked Lexi out."

"Way to go, D!" Alex whooped. Derek chuckled.

"That's great, Derek." Tabitha smiled. "Lexi seems wonderful." She glanced at Alex, "They all seem really great." Alex smiled softly at her, he knew she meant Riana. "So what's the plan?"

Derek took a quick drink of his water. "Well, her birthday is coming up. I figured it'd be a nice opportunity to spend some time with her…"

"Without actually making it a date?" Matt jabbed playfully.

"Kind of." he laughed.

"Honestly, D, from what I've seen, I don't think you need to test the waters or anything." Alex offered. "You both seem plenty comfortable with each other."

Derek pursed his lips and nodded. "I know. But I also know she thinks relationships complicate life." He took another, slower drink.

Tabitha rubbed his arm. "It's all about finding someone worth the complication." Matthew glanced over his shoulder and winked at her.

CHAPTER TWENTY-ONE

Everybody's Changing

Monday August 28, 2006

As Riana, Lexi and Sam approached the ranch Riana's heart grew heavy. She knew without a doubt that things were falling apart with Ryan but she also knew she would have to see him to know for sure and to put things to rest. Or maybe work them out. She thought perhaps when she voiced her concerns in person to Ryan he'd finally prove he wanted to be with her. The heaviness in her heart was because she knew she had to tell Alex.

"So, considering how well I know you," Lexi broke Riana from her thoughts. "I'll take care of the horses and gear. You go find Alex." Lexi knew the longer Riana waited to talk to Alex about what she felt she needed to do, the less likely she was to actually do it.

Riana felt nauseated, her palms were sweaty, and she would have sworn she had the beginning of tunnel vision. "Hey Ri." Matthew called from the pool as Riana turned the corner into the back yard. "How was your ladies' night?"

"Really good." she smiled as she scanned the back quickly. "Have you--"

"He's inside, playing video games." Derek

275

offered quickly.

"Thanks, D." Riana hollered over her shoulder as she hurried inside.

Riana checked the theater first to no avail, she peeked into two more empty sitting rooms then figured he was probably in his room. She started up the stairs quickly, skipping one each stride. Halfway up she stopped and wondered why she was in such a hurry. It wasn't as if he would find this to be exciting, or even happy, news. She had missed him, though, and wanted to see him. Remembering what she had to tell him forced her to slow her progression. She took the steps one at a time and willed herself to remain strong.

She reached his door and knocked lightly. He didn't answer, but his door wasn't latched so she pushed it open a bit. Her heart skipped a beat when she saw him. He sat on his bed, cross-legged, in only a pair of cargo shorts. His gaze was locked intently on the screen, controller in hand while he talked smack to his cohorts via his headset. Riana grinned as she leaned against the doorframe and watched him. She fought to control the desire to saunter in and pin him to the bed.

Alex glanced around quickly, almost as though he felt her as she watched him and he smirked when he saw her. "I have to go." he declared quickly into the mic of his headset. He pulled the headset off and powered down his game. "Hey."

Riana straightened her back. *I can do this.*
"Can we talk?" Alex nodded and patted the spot next
to him on his disheveled comforter. Riana licked her
lip then grasped her labret ring as she ambled to his
bed. She crawled up slowly and sat opposite of him.
She crossed her legs and stared intently at her hands
placed in her lap.

She refused to meet his eyes, she knew if she
did they would surely melt her resolve. "Alex," she
breathed softly, his name rolled easily off her tongue
and spiked her heart rate. "You're one of my best
friends. I--I was stupid, and selfish, on Saturday."
she took a deep breath. "I'm not an unfaithful
partner." Her voice shook and she still refused to
meet his eyes.

Alex's hands reached out and she sighed
when they covered her own hands. "I... I love Ryan,
Alex." His hands tensed. "At least... I know I did.
Maybe I still do." Riana shook her head as she tried
to clear some of the confusion. She finally lifted her
eyes to Alex. "He's still my partner, Alex, I need to
respect that. I need to know for sure where I'm going
with him." Alex's face was still as stone and
unreadable. "I love you, Alex. I need to know I
didn't lose my best friend." she pleaded. The idea of
being with Alex terrified her.

Alex pulled his hands from hers and Riana
felt the beginning of her chest caving in; certain she
had ruined everything. Before the sobs could
consume her, the bed shifted and Alex's strong, bare
arms wrapped around her. "I will always be your

best friend, Ri." he promised, his chin on top of her head. Riana wrapped her arms around him and sighed over his shoulder. "I'm sorry about Saturday." he whispered.

"You only did what I asked you to do." she discerned sheepishly. She pulled back and dropped her head again. "It was my fault."

"I have a feeling we could fight forever about who to blame for that." Alex teased with a smile.

Riana laughed a bit. "So true. I mean, I may have asked, but it's your fault for being so sexy." Riana's brave admission warmed her cheeks.

Alex's dark eyes lit up playfully. "I'm sexy?"

Riana shoved him backwards as they both laughed. "Shut up. Don't pretend like you don't know you are."

"I don't know Alex, do we really want to let Matt grill again?" Riana laughed as they rummaged through the refrigerator for dinner.

"Well, you know, aside from the fires he actually is a talented cook." Alex jested as he pulled chicken quarters from the shelf.

"Valid point, dear." Riana giggled as she shut the fridge door, only to be met with Tabitha on the other side. She jumped, startled, and tried to force her heart from her throat back to her chest where it belonged. "Holy shit!" she gasped as she braced herself against the cupboard doors.

"I'm so sorry Riana!" Tabitha stammered quickly. "I didn't mean to startle you." Riana heard

Alex put the chicken on the counter, then felt his hand on her back; he provided long, comforting strokes and Riana took a deep breath.

"It's okay." she replied, her heart finally slowed. *Damn PTSD, never fails.*

"I, um--" Tabitha stuttered. "was wondering if we could talk?" Alex stopped stroking her back and the pressure of his hand increased as he grasped her side. He stepped in behind her while he pulled her to him. Riana suddenly realized Alex was being protective of her and her heart swelled. There had never been a man in Riana's life that did anything of the sort. She placed her hand on top of his, thankful to feel so loved and safe.

Riana then searched Tabitha's face in an attempt to figure out her motive. "Sure." she answered simply.

Riana watched as Tabitha's eyes passed by her and glanced at Alex. "Alone, maybe?" Alex's grip tightened and Riana's knees weakened.

Riana nodded as she turned to face Alex but he didn't remove his hand from her side. She placed her free palm to the side of his face. "We'll be out in a few." His eyes narrowed past Riana to Tabitha. Riana squeezed the hand that was still placed protectively on her side. "It's fine." she assured. "Go. Bring the chicken to our grill master." She smiled and released both of her hands from his skin. She watched as he picked up the chicken and went out back. After Alex closed the door Riana turned to Tabitha, deliberately stone faced.

Tabitha shifted her weight and avoided Riana's eyes. Their last confrontation replayed in her mind and she wondered if her request to be alone was such a good idea. "I was out of line on Saturday." Tabitha admitted. "Things just… escalated so quickly with Alex." She glanced to Riana. "I wanted to blame someone instead of accepting that he and Kim weren't well suited for each other. I—I was wrong to blame you. I'm sorry Riana." Riana knew Tabitha probably wanted her to say something, but she was only able to nod. "He's like family. I want him to be happy. You make him happy Riana." Riana's throat tightened. "I haven't seen him this happy in years."

Riana finally found her voice. "He makes me happy too." she croaked softly.

"You seem like a wonderful woman. The guys love you, Spencer loves you. I'm actually pretty upset with myself for being so bullheaded, because I have to leave tomorrow and I didn't get to know you at all." She gave Riana a weak smile.

Riana finally conceded and smiled back. "I know what you mean."

"I have a feeling, though, we'll have a lot of time to get to know each other." Tabitha glanced out back to where Alex played with Spencer.

Riana led the way to the sliding glass door. "I do believe you are correct." Matthew turned at the sound of the door and as he saw smiles grace both of the women's faces his own smile danced along his lips.

Riana and Tabitha took two seats at the bar and Tabitha quickly jumped into conversation. She felt ridiculous for missing so much time to get to know Riana, and was determined to make the most of the time she had left with her. She asked Riana about where she grew up, her schooling, and her career. Riana finally felt she was being given a chance to be herself and happily answered. "I truly despised growing up in a small town." Riana explained. "It seems I have to have one extreme or the other, I can't do the middle ground crap." she laughed. Tabitha agreed and told Riana stories of her own growing up in a small Southern town and how great it had been to travel with the guys.

Tabitha also admitted how in awe she was of Riana's writing ability. Tabitha had been featured in some online blogs but couldn't imagine actually writing a book. Riana beamed proudly. "I'll have to find a copy of it when I get back home, I'd really love to read it." Tabitha revealed with a shy smile.

"Really?" Riana blurted. She didn't miss Matthew's huge grin, or Alex's. Tabitha assured her she was serious. "I have extra copies in my office. Follow me." Riana offered as she hopped off her barstool.

Alex nudged Matthew. "Nice." he commented as the women entered the house. He felt it had to have been Matt who pushed Tabitha to come to her senses.

"That was all Ri, Alex." Matt chuckled. "Tabs resisted me the whole way, Riana was the one that finally made her see she was being unreasonable." He turned a chicken leg. "Riana... She seems to have an authority about her few have the ability to resist."

"Tell me about it." Alex laughed.

Tuesday August 29, 2006

Matthew decided to take the Jeep alone to bring Tabitha and Spencer to the airport. Riana supposed it was hard on him, to be away from them so often. The fact that he would stay at the ranch for another week brought insurmountable guilt to lie upon her heart. Tabitha gave Riana a hesitant hug as they packed up and apologized again for the heated encounter. Alex stood by and kept a watchful eye on them but Riana could read the relief in his face--as well as in Matt and Derek's faces. Yet, there was heaviness in Riana's heart caused by conflict she didn't want to face.

After Matt pulled through the gate and onto the road Riana breezed by the group and headed into the house to make a quick call. She knew if anyone found out who she was calling she'd get all kinds of lectures so she hastily made her way to her room and quietly closed the door. He didn't pick up and Riana sighed as she felt the familiar sense of rejection.

Alex stood at Riana's door and his heart dropped as he heard her leave Ryan a message. "Hey Ryan, it's Ri. Just wanted to call and say hi. Haven't talked to you in a while. Hope things are good. Love you, bye." Riana's chest tightened as she said she loved him; almost as if her body revolted against the words.

Alex chewed his lip and debated on his next step. He wanted to rush in and ask her what she was thinking, how could she still want to be with him when he was right there and wanted to give her everything Ryan wasn't? Sam and Matt's advice replayed in his mind and he figured allowing his pain to come out as anger wouldn't help his cause. He lightly knocked on her door. Riana hollered for him to enter and he gently pushed her door open. "Hey Ri."

It seemed ironic that after being rejected by Ryan, even if was just a phone call, that Alex would appear. His voice hit her, made her heart jump and her breath catch. She couldn't stop the spread of a smile as she turned to face him. "Hey." Alex was lost in the joy that filled her eyes and wondered if it was him or the call to Ryan that brought her happiness.

"I have a craving for cookies." he declared. Riana's grin grew.

"Oh yeah?" she teased as she leaned against her cluttered desk.

Alex threw himself back on her bed. He dropped his head back over the edge and gave her a lopsided grin. "Wanna come bake with me?"

Riana gaze down at him, struck once more by how lucky she was to be friends with him and how beautiful he was. "Oh, I suppose." she laughed. "But only if they're chocolate chip." Alex pulled himself upright and beamed at her. She approached the bed and extended her hand out to him. "Let's go."

Alex wove his fingers through Riana's and followed her out of the bedroom and into the kitchen. Her mind ran multiple directions as she savored the connection in their hands. She contemplated how Ryan would react if he knew and she lightly snorted when she concluded he wouldn't even notice. She glanced to Alex nervously and wondered if he could read how badly she wanted to kiss him again.

Riana let Alex's hand slip from hers as they entered the kitchen. "First things first." Alex declared before his arms were suddenly around her from behind as he slipped an apron around her waist. She took a deep breath. "We must dress appropriately." he quipped.

Riana turned to him. "What about you? We wouldn't want to ruin that sweet shirt." she jested as she trailed her hand along his crisp, light blue, button down shirt. Alex smirked at her and reached for the second apron that hung on the wall. He kept his eyes intently on hers as he draped the apron over his head and tied it behind his back. She gave a weak smile.

"Alright. Time for bowls and ingredients." Alex declared with a clap of his hands. Riana watched as he happily dug through the cupboards and drawers to find all the necessary equipment for their adventure. She skipped over to the surround sound system and found the Motown station on satellite. As the simple beat of Sam Cooke flowed through the room she couldn't help but notice how Alex's hips began to sway. Alex turned to her and danced towards her with his hands outstretched.

Riana easily slipped into his embrace. He held her hand in his and placed it on his chest as his other hand grasped her hip. His voice quietly sang the beginning lines of "Bring It To Me" to her. *Why must Motown be so damn romantic!?* Riana's mind cried. She continued to dance with him, her head laid on his chest as he swayed and sang. Riana ached to bring it to him, she truly did, but she was paralyzed by the fear that it was too large of a risk. As the song trailed off Alex pulled her tightly to his chest and kissed her temple. He left his lips there for a long moment and Riana's knees weakened, along with her resolve.

The ring of her cellphone tore them apart. She glanced to the counter and saw it was Ryan. She looked up at Alex, bit her vertical labret and pulled away from him. She snatched the phone and turned her back on Alex as she answered. "Hey honey." she greeted artificially. Alex swallowed the pain and put on a brave face. He let her be and continued to dig out their ingredients. Riana's side of the conversation was easily heard and Alex pretended not to eavesdrop.

"I just hadn't talked to you in a while, wanted to see how you were." she explained. Alex wondered if all of her conversations with him were so painfully forced. There was no authenticity in her voice when she talked to Ryan, nothing like how she was with him. "Yeah, things are good. I'm starting to put together a schedule for more speaking engagements." Alex's brows knitted together, he hadn't heard anything about a new schedule. He then wondered if Riana frequently made a habit out of lying to Ryan as well. "Of course I'll make some time to stay with you before I start traveling again." Alex sighed as he grabbed the eggs. "Now? No… I'm with Lexi and Sam." Alex contained a snort, loving how she conveniently left out him, Derek and Matthew.

"Speaking of, we're actually about to get cooking, so I should probably go. Okay, yeah, call me later. Or I'll call you when I have more time to chat. Okay, yep, bye."

She placed her phone back on the counter, but didn't turn back to Alex right away. She finally turned to him, her head downcast. "Alex…" she started. Alex could have picked a fight, but he remembered that he had to support her and show her what it really meant to be cared for.

He approached her and rubbed her upper arms. "Hey, it's okay. I get it. It's fine." She glanced up at him, her eyes full of disbelief. "Ready to bake?" he asked with a playful grin. Relief overtook Riana's disbelief as a smile grew on her face as well.

"They are adorable, aren't they?" Derek commented from Sam's side as she watched Riana and Alex in the kitchen from the front hallway. She turned to him and Lexi.

"They really are." She leaned back against the wall. "They've been dancing and singing for a while. I find the current song wonderfully fitting." she giggled. Sam had never seen Riana so happy or so at ease. Alex brought life to Ri that had been missing for years; if she ever had it at all. They played like children as they laughed together and teased each other. Alex was appalled by Riana's willingness to steal clumps of cookie dough to eat, but squeezed her from behind as he stole a taste himself.

"Absolutely. 'You Can't Hurry Love' should be their anthem or something." Lexi laughed. "I just wish she was able to really see what was in front of her." she mused. Sam nodded.

<u>CHAPTER TWENTY-TWO</u>

Wanna Get To Know You

Wednesday August 30, 2006

Derek didn't often share much in D.M.A. interviews; he wasn't outwardly goofy like Alex or exuberantly charming like Matthew. As he and Lexi drove to Prescott, Lexi found Derek was these things, and more. There had been hints to this conclusion, but once it was just them alone it seemed Derek was more at ease. He was profound without being stuffy and funny without being crude. "So did you always want to be an editor?" he asked as he glanced over at Lexi.

She gave a light laugh. "Not particularly." Derek raised a brow. "I just sort of fell into it. Riana was very possessive of her writing--she still is. She didn't trust strangers to be looking at her work." Derek nodded. "So between our relationship and my English minor she asked me to take it on. Her publishing company took notice so now I'm a contract editor for them."

Derek grinned, "That's pretty neat how that worked out." Lexi agreed and mentioned how she felt the best part was how the set up left plenty of time for her to volunteer in areas that brought her heart happiness. Lexi loved to volunteer in group

288

homes and blocked out weeks at a time to help with the Special Olympics. "That's incredible, Lex." Derek gushed. "I do believe we found three of the most amazing women out there." Lexi fought the blush that tingled in her cheeks. Derek brought the car up to a park surrounded by beautiful, golden and red rock formations.

"Picnic?" he offered.

Lexi felt that Derek was an exceptional study in regards to what she would like. "Perfect." she confirmed with a wink as she stepped from the car.

Derek jogged to the back and pulled out a blanket and tote of snacks and drinks. As they strolled through the park he draped his arm over Lexi's shoulder and she leaned into him. He led her over to a lightly shaded area and spread out their blanket.

They continued their endless chatter and relaxed in the sporadic protection of the Joshua tree they were under. "Mm, so as glorious as this is," Lexi started, her head dipped into her chest as Derek massaged her shoulders, "do we have any other plans?"

"All up to you dear. There's a couple of art galleries, a museum, some sightseeing tours.." he trailed off as they contemplated what to do with their rest of their day.

Lexi and Derek found a small family owned Italian restaurant in Prescott after they had explored three small art galleries. They were led to a secluded table in the back by an older gentleman who could barely speak English through his thick Italian. "Derek, this day has been perfect." Lexi sighed.

Derek bravely reached his hand across the pristine white tablecloth and slipped his fingers through hers. Lexi's cheeks instantly filled with an excited blush. "You deserve it." He waited until her eyes met his. "Happy birthday, Lexi."

Lexi watched Derek in a different way through the rest of the evening. She thought perhaps it wouldn't be a bad thing to consider the possibility of being with someone like him. Despite her conclusion, she also decided she would not be the one to present the idea to him.

Fortunately, she didn't have to. As they neared the ranch late that night Derek once again enclosed Lexi's hand with his as he felt it was pretty much now or never. He knew once they were around everyone else he'd likely lose his nerve. "Lexi, I had a wonderful time with you today." he confessed as he glanced over at her. "A really wonderful time. I know you like to keep your life... less complicated," he silently cursed his nerves when he noticed his palms were sweaty. "but I thought, maybe, it might be cool if we, you know, decided to see each other. Nothing serious, just, hanging out." He cursed himself again for his lack of eloquence.

Lexi silently nodded as Derek slid Riana's card and drove through the gate. He let go of Lexi's hand as he parked the car. She met him at the back of the car where she reached for both of his hands.

"Derek," she murmured softly. "I would be happy to complicate my life with the likes of you." She grinned and raised up on her tiptoes to gently place her lips to his.

"As would I." he breathed against her lips before he kissed her again.

Saturday September 2, 2006

Lexi curled up against Derek as everyone gathered around the fire; they'd been essentially inseparable since Lexi's birthday. Alex prepared drinks and Riana was obviously torn between him and Ryan as she once again pulled her phone out. It seemed cold to Lexi; how Riana rubbed Alex's nose in the fact that she was with Ryan. Ri seemed to always wait until Alex was around to send Ryan a message or call him. Often times her motivations to behave in certain ways were way off and this was a perfect example. Lexi felt Derek sigh and she turned her head up towards him. "I know." she sighed.

"I just worry Lex, if she keeps pushing him away, eventually he's going to listen." he whispered.

"I really, really hope not." Lexi bemoaned.

"Riana, stop calling him." Alex groaned as Riana placed her phone against her ear.

She narrowed her gaze at him. "Why, Alexander? He is my boyfriend after all." She knew it was cruel of her, but she was hopelessly trying to prove a point. The amount of emotional discourse she had dealt with over the last few days seemed to have created a type of Dr. Jekyll and Mr. Hyde within her. She loved the time she spent with Alex, but that was why she felt she had to reach out to Ryan more frequently. She tried to keep herself in check by pushing Alex away with reminders of Ryan.

"He's an asshole, Ri." Alex muttered under his breath. Before she could snap some witty comeback Ryan's voicemail picked up--again. Riana sighed angrily as she hung up and stormed over to the fire pit to simmer in her frustration. "No answer again, huh?" Alex commented as he stood over Riana. Sam anxiously looked to Lexi, the tension in the air quickly thickened.

"Just stop." Riana mumbled as she rubbed her temples.

"There's a reason he doesn't answer, Ri. It's because *this*," he motioned around her "is for his pleasure at *his* convenience. You are expected to be available when *he* wants you, not the other way around."

Riana clenched her teeth together. His words hurt, but only because they were true. "Shut up, Alex." she demanded.

"No! Dammit, Riana, you're insufferably stubborn! You are, at this moment in time, one of the dumbest smart people I've ever met!" he yelled exasperatedly.

Lexi glanced over at Derek, who watched the scene worriedly and braced herself for the storm that was surely about to erupt. "Did you seriously just call me dumb?" Riana snapped as she jumped up and attempted to stand off against Alex, who stood a good foot taller than her.

Alex evened his face. "Yep. Sure did." Riana flicked her eyes over his face and contemplated how to proceed. She knew everything he had said was true, but she wouldn't openly admit it. He lowered the intensity of his voice, "I just don't get why you put yourself through this."

"I've been through worse." she mumbled as she brushed past him. Alex widened his eyes at Lexi, Derek, Matt and Sam in vexation, then turned quickly on his heel and pursued Riana. Matthew moved to follow, with the intention to mediate, but Sam grabbed his arm before he could stand.

"It'll be fine. Well, maybe not fine. But they have to do this Matt." she assured.

Alex caught up to Riana in the hallway to her bedroom. "Ri." he called. She barely paused before she flung her door open. "Ri!" he called again more urgently.

"What?" she yelled as she turned back to face him, tears welled up in her eyes. "Did you want to call me ugly too? Maybe irrational or gullible? Come on Alex, give me what you got!" she growled.

Alex reached out, grabbed her arms and pulled her to his chest. The moment their bodies met Riana's tears spilled over. She was hurt and angry, but at herself more than Alex. "It doesn't matter that you've been through worse, Ri." he explained softly. "The fact is, you're better than this, you're better than him," he smoothed her hair. "and you're definitely not ugly."

She snorted and smiled just a bit as she finally wrapped her arms around Alex. "You're right though, I am stupid." she mumbled into him.

"You just love him is all." he choked out. "I hear love makes you stupid."

"Yes, yes it does." she agreed. It was a reference to her love for Alex but refused to elaborate.

Derek, Matt, Lexi and Sam murmured amongst themselves as Alex and Riana handled their confrontation inside. "Trust me, if Alex can stand his ground with her like that, he's pretty much golden." Lexi assured.

Matthew shook his head in disbelief. "I just can't imagine them fighting like this is a good sign."

Lexi smiled just a bit. "Riana... Well, she needs friends that can stand toe to toe with her. She's aggressive and emotional. If Alex can deal with it, he'll be great for her."

"Lexi would know." Samantha quipped and Lexi laughed lightly. "Lexi knows that true love for Riana includes providing a little tough love on occasion. I'm pretty sure she and Ri get closer each time they have a big blowout." Sam poked at the flaming logs. "I guess the biggest thing with this is for Riana to learn that just because they fight, doesn't mean he cares any less about her. He probably got so upset *because* he cares about her so much."

"I just worry it's going to take too long. She'll keep purposely hurting him. He won't stand for it." Derek mused.

"Yes he will." Sam replied. Her knowledge of how much Alex loved Riana fueled her certainty. "The best part is soon Riana will realize she doesn't have to keep hurting him. This fight might actually be the moment she gets it."

Monday September 4, 2006
2:51am

Riana was shaken awake once again by tormented dreams. She didn't try to fight it; the internal battle of what she wanted, what she needed and what she should do. She slid out of bed and padded silently out of her room, up the stairs and down the hall. She shuffled through his door and climbed under his covers. As she wrapped herself around him she cried against his neck, "You can't leave me in two days, Alex."

"Ri?" he questioned hoarsely as he pulled out of sleep. "Honey, what's wrong?"

She clawed at him, desperate to get closer. "I don't want you to leave me." she sobbed. Alex quickly awakened further and sat up. He gathered Riana in his arms and brought her into his lap.

295

"Sweetheart, it's okay." he soothed. He held her tightly and kissed the side of her face. She heaved sobs into his neck and he allowed her to cry. He silently provided her with the comfort she so obviously needed. "Come back with me." he blurted after a long moment.

Riana's breath caught, she pulled back and found Alex's face through her blurry vision. "What?"

"Come back to New York with me." he urged.

Riana barely shook her head. "I… can't."

"Sure you can. You can stay with me and Derek. Hang out in the studio, inspire me." He bit his lip softly.

Riana crawled out of Alex's embrace as she hung her head. "I can't. I need to go see Ryan." Alex's eyes narrowed, the pain evident. "I know, it's stupid, but I have to Alex."

Alex nodded. "I know." he whispered. They remained quiet in the awkward moment. Finally, Riana scooted back towards Alex.

She was uneasy and anxious. She glanced up at him as she kept her head low. "For tonight can we not talk about it? Just… Let's just… pretend you aren't leaving me."

Alex reached out and pulled Riana to him as he laid back down. "I'm not leaving you Ri. I just have to go home." She trailed her hand down his sternum and around his waist. Her hot breath tickled the side of his neck before she placed one, sweet, yet desperate kiss to his skin. He fought to contain both the groan in his throat and the urge to turn and envelope her lips with his. She snuggled closer, closed her eyes and drifted off to sleep.

Alex wasn't able to fall asleep so easily. He remained awake as he stroked Riana's skin and replayed everything since May. He wondered how much longer he could take this roller coaster. He couldn't comprehend how Riana was so oblivious and resistant. However, she was his best friend and he loved her. He knew that he would remain as long as she wanted him to.

He gazed down at her and lowered his lips to her temple. "I love you, Riana." he whispered. "I wish you could understand that."

CHAPTER TWENTY-THREE

Say Good-bye

Wednesday September 6, 2006

Lexi couldn't seem to erase the pout on her face as she helped Derek pack to go home and he felt horrible. "Lex, you just let me know and you can come visit any time you want." he assured as he kissed her softly.

"I just feel like, so much time was wasted. I've only been able to be with you for a week. I have a feeling I need much more time than that."

Derek laughed as he tossed a few shirts in his suitcase. "I know exactly what you mean. It's been an amazing break Lexi, we definitely needed this. Thank you again for convincing Riana to invite us."

"Of course. Speaking of, I should probably go check on her. I imagine she's having a hard time processing Alex leaving." Derek nodded solemnly.

Riana chose to hide in her office as she attempted to stuff all of her emotions to a depth she hoped to never reach again. She was overcome with despair, anger, and confusion. Alex had attempted to console her, to no avail as she fiercely pushed him away. "Hey sweetie." Lexi's soft voice beckoned as she entered the office. Riana turned to the sound of

Lexi's voice. Riana's face did nothing to hide her pain. Lexi fully entered the office and leaned against Ri's cherry desk. She didn't say anything, just patiently waited.

Riana's couldn't seem to grasp the rationale for any of her emotions. She dropped her head to her desk. "I can't believe it's been two weeks already." she mumbled.

"I know, honey." Lexi soothed as she rubbed Riana's back. "Derek said to just let him know if I wanted to stay in New York with them. I'm sure Alex would love if you visited too." She ran her fingers through Ri's hair as it was something she knew relaxed her.

"I can't, Lex." Riana moaned. "I have to go see Ryan."

Lexi sighed but knew it was something she had to do. "You're still going to ride with us to the airport, right?" Riana was hesitant but nodded as she stood.

As she and Lexi exited the office Riana was suddenly tackled in the hallway. Strong, lean arms wrapped around her and lifted her off the ground. A sweet, innocent kiss was placed to her cheek. "I'm going to miss you so much, Ri."

"Oh, I'm going to miss you too, Matt." Ri declared sadly. Matthew set her down, but kept his hands on her waist.

"Please promise me you'll stay in touch this time." Riana blushed under Matt's sweet, Persian blue eyes and nodded. He watched her for a moment and wondered how things might have been different had Riana continued to write to him. He was suddenly overcome with the desire to place his lips to her skin again, but instead he pulled his palms from the subtle curve of her waist.

Alex knew it wasn't easy for Riana to accept he was leaving, it was difficult for him as well, he just wished she'd talk to him about it instead of pushing him away. He escaped the house, dropped his bags on the ground behind the Jeep and jogged to the barn. The heavy door creaked as he pushed it to the side. He smiled softly as he saw Apollo lean his head over his stall door.

"Hey buddy." he called. Alex sighed as he climbed up to sit on the front wall of Apollo's stall. He reached out and rubbed Apollo's cheek. "I'm going to miss you dude. We had some fun, huh?" Alex snorted. "This is what it's come to? Talking to a horse?"

"Hey now, I talk to my horses all the time." Riana chuckled from the barn entry. She approached Apollo's stall and folded her arms on the top of the door. "Sometimes I think they understand more than we give them credit for." she mused. "I know Adonis has heard more about my life than most people. I feel less crazy when I can talk it out, you know?"

"Sure do." Alex sighed. He gazed down at Riana. Her eyes seemed to be focused off in the distance. There was so much left unresolved. "Ri..." he murmured.

"Alex, please, don't." she bemoaned. "This is hard enough already, isn't it?" she commented as she lifted her head, turned around and leaned against Apollo's stall door.

Alex swung his legs over the wall then hopped down. "It is. But don't you think it's this hard because of things left unsaid?" Riana snapped her eyes to him.

"Like what, Alex?"

He searched her eyes and debated if he should say what truly needed to be said. She was blatantly in pain. His jaw tightened and he shook his head lightly. "Nothing I guess." he sighed. He reached for her hands and locked his deep brown eyes on hers. "I'm going to miss you, Ri." Riana's lip quivered as her eyes welled up with tears. "If you change your mind... About coming to New York, just call me okay?"

Riana barely nodded. Alex raised her hands to his face and nuzzled them. He placed a soft kiss to the inside of her right wrist. Riana's chest tightened and she fought to control the tears that threatened to spill over. "I will." she whispered. Her typically ultramarine eyes had transitioned to a dovetail grey as they glanced up to his solemn face. Alex realized that her grief was so deep it literally changed her. "It's time to leave." she choked out. He swallowed thickly and nodded.

Riana and Alex trudged out of the barn to find Derek, Matt, Lexi and Sam by the Jeep. They had everyone's bags already loaded. Riana took a deep breath. She was determined to make it through the three hour drive and the departure at the airport without tears. The way Alex squeezed her hand in urgent desperation did not help her plan. Lexi found Riana's eyes and gave a sad smile. Riana approached her and let Alex's hand slip out of hers. "Lex, could you drive? I'm not exactly feeling up to it."

"Of course, Ri." she agreed as she took the keys from her. She turned and opened the driver's door as Derek climbed into the front passenger seat. Riana turned back around and took Alex's hand once more to be led to the seats farthest back in the Jeep.

Matthew and Samantha chatted as they took the middle seats and even though there was plenty of space for Alex and Riana to sit on opposite ends, she chose to nestle in next to him. Alex had no complaints, he wrapped his arm around her shoulder and pulled her into him. "Oh, I'll be staying with Riana for a while yet." Samantha told Matthew when he asked about upcoming plans. "I don't have anything planned until mid-September, then I'll be heading to the New Orleans area." Riana's mind turned the chatter between Matt and Sam into nothing but an incomprehensible murmur. Alex rubbed her arm as she snuggled further into him. She wanted to savor the last three hours she had.

"Now, before you all leave, I think I speak for all three of us when I say; you're not getting out until we get a private concert here in the Jeep." Lexi laughed.

"I totally concur." Riana agreed, her eyes finally sparkled when she looked up at Alex. He grinned at her; it warmed his soul to know how much she loved when he sang.

"Oh, I suppose." Alex laughed. The guys did a couple soulful Motown classics and two of their own. The energy finally got to Riana and she rocked and danced in her seat as the guys sang. Sam reached her hand over the seat to Riana, they clasped their hands together and swayed to the rhythm.

The break in tension and sadness was embraced by everyone. Riana smiled at Alex and instead of having to fight tears when she leaned into him she fought laughter as he continued to tell hilarious stories of Matthew's misfortunes over the years. "Oh my God, I totally remember when he did that." Samantha howled after Alex finished the story of Matt's seasickness when they performed on a cruise. Matthew was unaware of his inability to handle the sea and it turned out to be a horrible time for both D.M.A and the fans.

"It's okay Matt, we still love you. We just won't take you on any cruises." Lexi laughed from the front.

Riana became quiet again as they penetrated the city, it wouldn't be long until they reached the airport. Her heart rate increased and her palms formed the slightest layer of sweat. She despised goodbyes. Everyone else slowed their chatter as well. Matthew gazed over the seat and grimaced sadly at Alex. Alex glanced down at Riana, nestled once again in his side, and frowned.

The Jeep slowly made some turns as Lexi pulled into the parking garage. Riana mentally shook her head and tried to deny that within minutes Alex would be ripped from her and flown thousands of miles away.

Lexi and Derek got out first, followed by Matt and Samantha. Alex sighed deeply underneath Ri. "We have to go." he whispered hoarsely. Riana nodded against him, pulled back and allowed him to climb out. She swallowed the beginning of her tears and followed.

"Holy shit, Matthew, what's in here, your hair products?" Derek bellowed with a laugh as he pulled an unusually heavy bag from the back. Riana snorted.

"Actually, I think those are his shoes." Samantha teased.

"Wow, Matt, I don't even have that many shoes." Riana nudged him with a wink.

"Ha, ha. Whatever, just give it to me." he commented dryly as he grabbed the bag from Derek.

Everyone loaded up and proceeded to check-in. Riana, Lexi and Sam stood by the side as the guys checked their luggage. "You hanging in alright honey?" Sam asked. "Both of you, actually." she added as she watched Lexi gaze sadly at Derek.

"Yeah, it's okay. I mean, we're not serious or anything." Lexi rationalized. "I'm sure he'll call once they land in New York." She forced a smile to Sam.

"I'm fine." Riana attempted to declare, but her tight voice revealed she was anything but fine.

The guys turned from the counter and slowly approached Sam, Lexi and Ri. Before they reached them they looked at each other, and placed their bags on the ground. Matthew softly counted out with three snaps of his fingers.

Riana, Lexi and Sam's smiles grew as they watched the corniness unfold in the guys' spontaneous rendition of Peter, Paul and Mary's "Leaving On A Jet Plane." "Are they seriously doing this?" Riana hissed to Lexi.

Lexi giggled, "They sure are." The small crowd that had gathered in the terminal while the guys sang burst into applause when they finished and picked up their carry-ons. They sauntered back to the women, who were still full of grins and giggles.

Lexi wrapped her arms quickly around Derek and met him in a full kiss. "I'm going to miss your craziness." she laughed.

He squeezed her tightly and kissed her again. "And I'm going to miss everything about you. I'll call when I get in, okay?" Lexi nodded as a quick tear escaped.

Matt squeezed Samantha and gave her a quick kiss on the cheek. "You are by far one of the most entertaining and random people I know. You're fantastic, Sam, I can't wait to see you again."

"Me too, Matt." she sighed as she squeezed around his waist. He pulled back and smiled sadly at her.

Matthew turned and found Riana saying goodbye to Derek and waited patiently for his turn. She fought against her tears as Derek released her and Matthew stepped in. "Ri." he breathed. She bit her lip and rushed to his embrace. "Remember what I told you, Ri. Be true to yourself. You deserve amazing things, and I promise you'll find them." She nodded against him without a word. "I love you, Riana. So much."

"I love you too, Matt." Her voice broke but she still refused to let her tears fall. "Call me later?"

"Of course." Matthew placed a solid kiss to Riana's forehead as he closed his eyes. Images of her letters to him flashed before his eyes, memories of things he always wanted to say to her but never could overtook him and he held her a bit tighter.

Matthew, Derek, Lexi and Sam proceeded towards security while Alex said goodbye to Riana. Riana watched them walk away and felt sobs creep up her throat. Alex walked up behind her and draped his arms over her shoulders and chest. He squeezed her from behind and she sighed. She turned to him and was unable to fight the anguish any longer when she was met with his tear-streaked face. "It's not fair." she wailed as she reached her arms around him and grasped his shoulders. "I don't want you to leave." she mumbled.

"I don't want to leave either, Ri. But I asked you to come with, you said--"

"I know what I said!" she cried. "It doesn't make it easier." Alex tightened his grip on her. He placed his head on top of hers and took a deep breath.

"I love you, Ri." he whispered, desperate for her to get it, to realize what he meant. Riana froze for a quick moment, then allowed the tears to fall. Slowly at first, but then it seemed they came faster and faster until she was unable to control them. "Let me know if you need anything. I'll call you as soon as we land."

Riana nodded as sobs overtook her body. She twisted his t-shirt in her hands and felt as though she would lose complete control. Her knees were about to give out and she couldn't catch her breath. Alex pulled back and found her eyes through their tears. He caressed her face as he watched her cry. His tongue snaked out and wet his lip as he leaned into her. Riana closed her eyes as Alex placed his lips softly against hers. "I love you." he whispered again.

"I love you." she breathed against his lips. Her chest tightened and her mind went black. She cried harder as she wished he loved her the way she needed. It was too soon for him to leave, she was still confused. She needed him there to help her figure it out. As he took a couple steps from Riana, Lexi and Sam hurried to be at her side. Alex continued through first class security and felt his heart break as Riana fell into Sam and Lexi, overcome with despair.

Samantha sat in the far back with Riana as Lexi drove back to the ranch. Riana was inconsolable. Her tears had dried, but the painful wails remained. Sam's heart broke as she watched her while Lexi fought her own tears in the front. Riana eventually cried herself to sleep, but was in a fitful rest. Her heart attempted to show her what she needed through her dreams, but she fought it endlessly.

"Sweetheart, we're home." Samantha whispered as she rubbed Riana's arm. She opened her eyes, but when they befell on the empty Jeep the sobs started again. "Shhh.... oh honey." Sam soothed as she held Riana close to her chest. "Want some tea?" she offered softly. Riana nodded as she pulled back. "Alright, let's go in. Settle in on the couch and I'll make you some."

Riana did as she was told. She found her feet were heavy and her shoulders seemed to bear too much weight. She shuffled into the theater and burrowed underneath her Sherpa throw. She glazed over, refused to talk to Lexi and Sam, and sipped her tea.

They let Riana be and sat together outside. "I'm glad you'll be staying with her for a while, Sam. I don't think this is going to go well for her."

Samantha frowned. "I know. I wish I could say I'll stay as long as she needs me, but I already had that trip planned. Plus, I know she plans on leaving soon to see Ryan."

"God, that's essentially the last damn thing she needs right now." Lexi grumbled.

Riana got up, after she struggled to finish a quarter of her tea, and drug herself to her bedroom. She opened the door and shuffled in, but instantly noticed something out of place. She skewed up her face as she looked at her bed. She bit her lip as she approached her light lavender comforter. Placed gently on top of it were three t-shirts. *Alex.* She hurriedly climbed atop her bed and brought a light blue t-shirt to her face. His scent infiltrated her senses. She curled into a ball and clutched the small piece of him to her chest. Each time she would take in his scent her exhales turned into deeper and more heart-wrenching sobs. Everything had gone so horribly wrong. It wasn't supposed to feel this way.

Riana's phone called to her. She didn't recall falling asleep but she rubbed her eyes quickly before she reached for her phone. Alex's t-shirt was still clenched in her hand, she lifted it up and inhaled deeply. She swiped her finger across the screen. "Hello?"

"Hey." Ryan greeted. Riana's heart instantly fell. She should have known Alex hadn't landed yet.

"Hi." she mumbled.

"Listen, I have some time off in a week, I thought you could come see me." She grimaced when she noted how he didn't ask her.

"Um, yeah, I think I could do that." she relented. "I'll check out some flights and let you know. I'm... not feeling well right now though, I have to go." He accepted her excuse and quickly got off the line. Her heart tightened, she knew had it been Alex on the other end he would have at least asked if she was okay. She groaned and threw herself into her pillow.

"Hey honey, it's me. I know it's super late, I figured you'd be asleep by now. I just wanted to let you know we got home safely." he paused and took a deep breath. "I miss you Ri." Alex ended the call and placed his phone on his bedside table. He laid back and chased elusive sleep.

Sunday September 10, 2006

"I'm only going for a few days." Riana attempted to assure Samantha that her trip to Minnesota would be fine but Sam didn't want her to go. Her fear was that Ryan would successfully twist Riana around his finger again. The two weeks with the guys had been so good for Riana, even with all the drama. She worried that going back to Ryan would ruin all the progress Riana had made.

"I don't want you to go at all, Ri." Samantha grumbled as they sorted through Riana's closet.

"I know Sam, okay? I get it. I just… I have to do this. I need to know what he wants from me." Riana explained.

"You know what he wants." Sam mumbled snidely.

"Samantha!" Riana gasped. "That's enough." she warned.

CHAPTER TWENTY-FOUR
I Go Back

September 12, 2006

Riana was overcome with anxiety as she flew back to Minnesota to see Ryan. She didn't know why she felt the need to see him, but she had always been a bit powerless when it came to his requests, and this one was no exception. Even though she knew the whole thing was in pieces she decided to go. She figured it would either help her figure things out with him or complicate her life further.

Ryan said that he'd pick her up from the airport but he had told her that before and never showed, so she had her doubts. She tried to distract herself from her worries with writing but she spent most of her time at odds with a blank screen. She was acutely aware that a couple of young women frequently examined her from three seats over. D. M. A. fans, she figured. If that were the case she knew she probably shouldn't shoot death beams from her eyes at them--no matter how badly she wanted to.

Her flight was right on time; landed at 2:03pm. 82 degrees and sunny. *Not bad for September in Minnesota.* Riana thought. As she grabbed her bags she noticed the women staring at her again. She forced a polite smile and let them move ahead of her in line. One gave her a small smile while the other attempted to cause Riana's spontaneous combustion through her evil glare. Riana snorted as she figured that one must have been Team Kim. She sighed and followed them out to the gate.

She saw no sign of Ryan so she proceeded down the corridor, took the elevator down a level and then approached the car rental station. Which was exactly when she heard him; cool, calm, almost indifferent, "Riana." He lacked the barely noticeable southern accent and playfulness that Alex had. Ryan's voice was like home to her though; a home that suddenly made her nervous.

She turned to him and felt tremors in her hands and her heart. "Ryan." she smiled artificially. He smiled back as he came closer to embrace her. Riana's heart broke a little when she noticed that his smile didn't meet his eyes the way Alex's smiles always did.

Ryan barely spoke to her as they drove from the Minneapolis airport to his place in Plymouth, save for generic small talk. His hand was possessively on her thigh, she knew what he expected, and oddly enough she found herself still willing to give it to him. She wasn't sure if it was a physical need, or because it was the only time she felt anything from him. She frantically fought to balance the internal battle of desire and resistance.

As she shut Ryan's apartment door behind her he kissed her neck and murmured that he had missed her. Riana's stomach knotted. Ryan's lips lacked the tenderness Alex's had. Yet, she allowed him to bring her to his bed as she tried hopelessly to believe there was more to their relationship than that.

Ryan was detached; cold almost. Riana clenched her eyes closed and fought to keep the tears at bay. She felt used, dirty, and unloved. After he finished her heart crumbled and the tears broke free. "Sugar, what's wrong?" *Wow, he actually noticed* she thought snidely.

"I just missed you so much." she easily lied. "I'm actually pretty tired. Is it okay if I catch a quick nap?" Ryan smiled and nodded as he got out of bed, dressed and left her alone. Riana held herself tightly and sobbed. There was no question that she shouldn't have been there.

Riana's ringtone called out to Alex and he quickly pulled his phone from his pocket. "Riana, dear, I take it you made it safely back to Minnesota?" he assumed quickly.

"Yes, she did." a male voice replied. Alex stopped short in the kitchen and his eyes turned cold. Matthew and Derek noticed the instant change and tried to catch his eye to figure out what was happening. Alex pulled his phone from his ear and changed it to speaker.

He took a deep breath and attempted to calm himself. "Ryan." he stated simply. Matt and Derek exchanged worried glances.

"You're damn right, Alex." Ryan confirmed, his voice thick with indignation. "Listen here, boy, I want you to stay away from Riana."

Alex's jaw clenched as his hand reached for the kitchen counter. "I don't think you have the authority to dictate who Riana spends her time with or who she talks to." he retorted as calmly as he could manage.

"Of course I have the authority." he growled. "She's *mine*, Alex. I refuse to allow this to continue, and you will respect that." he threatened.

Alex's knuckles whitened from the intense grip he had on the counter. "Respect?" he bellowed. "Do you even know the meaning of the word? I won't respect your insistence that Riana and I don't talk considering you don't even respect *her*. If you respected her at all you wouldn't try to control her the way you do. You'd treat her the way she deserves."

"You know nothing about how I treat her." Ryan spat.

"I know more than you think." Alex replied simply. "I won't stay away from Riana until the request comes from her, you got that?" he muttered. "I won't disregard my friendship with her just because some asshole is on a power trip."

"Don't worry, I'll make sure the request comes from Riana." Ryan vowed coolly. Alex didn't like the way Ryan was so sure of the control he had over Riana.

Alex's jaw tightened again. There was a muffled shuffling and then he heard her. "What request?" she questioned. Alex looked to Matt and Derek. "Ryan? Who's on the phone? Wait—is that *my* phone?"

"There you go Ryan, why don't you try to explain this to her?" Alex taunted.

"Go to hell, Alex." he grumbled before the call was disconnected.

Alex gently put his phone down, then turned and punched the wall as he yelled, "I can't fucking believe him!" Matthew was quickly behind Alex. He pulled Alex's arms back to his sides. Alex's fist had left a hefty hole in the wall and pieces of drywall fell to the floor. "I'll fucking kill him." he threatened as he shook against Matthew's hold.

"Alex?" Riana questioned. "Why were you talking to Alex?" Her eyes were intense and her brow furrowed deep into her forehead. Her breaths quickened and her hands trembled.

Ryan narrowed his gaze at her with a level of coldness she had never seen before. "You aren't to talk to him anymore Riana." he fumed as he threw Riana's phone at her. She caught it and stared at the blank screen.

She shook her head in disbelief. "You're kidding right?" Ryan's still face told her he wasn't. "I cannot believe you Ryan! You can't tell me who I can and cannot talk to!" She felt the hot flush of anger infiltrate her cheeks.

"If you love me, you'll understand why you have to stop this." he retorted evenly.

Hot tears welled up in Riana's eyes. "That's not fair." she whispered between ragged breaths. The thought of ending all contact with Alex put her in a panic. She sank into Ryan's old, brown couch as he approached her.

"Do you love me?" he questioned as he stood in front of her. His frame was much smaller than Alex's but it didn't make him any less imposing to her.

She refused to raise her eyes to his. "That's not the point."

He scared her when he slammed his hands into the wall behind her as he yelled, "That *is* the point Riana! You can't say you love me then be with *him* all the time!" Riana flinched. Ryan had never been like this before, his chest flushed and he kept pounding his hands against the wall. Riana's body began to tremble. She was both terrified and enraged. "You need to call him and tell him all this consorting is over." he snarled.

"I won't." she uttered.

"Dammit, Ri!" he yelled as he hit the wall again. "If you want us to work you need to call him." He stormed away from her and paced the living room. Riana surveyed the disarrayed room and found her bag next to the door.

"No." she retorted firmly as she furiously wiped tears from her eyes. She jumped off the couch and sprinted to the door.

"Where are you going?" he called after her. Ryan pinned her to the door, his face red and eyes bloodshot. "If you walk out that door, we're done." Riana tightened her grip on the handle to her bag as Ryan's hands tightened their grip on her upper arms.

She took a deep breath and gathered all the courage she had. "Then I guess we're done." She twisted out of his grasp and flung the door open. She didn't bother to close it as she rushed down the hallway.

"You are such a fucking bitch, Riana!" he screamed after her. "Run off and be the whore you are!"

His words cut right through her and turned everything they once had into a vicious, dirty lie. She ran down the stairs and out the main door, only to realize she didn't have a car with her. "Fucking hell." she muttered as she shakily dug out her phone. She looked up a local taxi service and called for a ride to the nearest car rental business. She provided them with an address four blocks away as she decided she had to burn off the adrenaline somehow. She also had to get as far away from Ryan as possible.

Riana kept herself together long enough to get to the car rental business, pay the taxi driver and process a rental agreement on a car. She quickly lost it the moment she sat in the driver's seat and cried hysterically. She couldn't breathe and couldn't see through the tears. Ryan had terrified her; brought her back to moments of being hurt by so many other men. Her heart felt like it had been ripped from her chest and tossed into a blender set to puree. Three years of her life, gone in an instant. Alex had tried to call her at least a six times since she left Ryan's. She couldn't answer; she knew she couldn't hear his voice without being in the safe embrace of his arms.

Eventually she settled enough to put the car in drive and leave it all behind. She finally pulled over at a rest stop in Nebraska when she decided she should probably contact someone to let them know she was okay. She shut off her phone shortly after she started to drive six hours ago, she just couldn't bring herself to deal with anyone. Riana thought the best when she drove; music turned up, windows down, and a tight grip on a leather steering wheel.

She got out of the rented Jetta and turned on her phone. She groaned and ignored the numerous notifications of text messages, missed calls and voicemails. She went straight to Lexi's number. "Oh my God, Ri!" Lexi blurted when she picked up the phone. "What the hell is going on? Are you okay? D called me, Alex is totally freaking out. Ri!?" She finally paused enough for Riana to speak.

Riana closed her eyes against the breeze. "Lexi." she sighed. "I… can't talk about it yet. I just… I need you to call Alex and let him know I'm okay. Please?"

"Where are you, Ri?" she asked quickly.

"I'm…driving. Can you call Alex?" Riana didn't want to dive into everything quite yet.

Thankfully, Lexi knew Riana well enough not to push. "Yeah, Ri, I'll call him." she complied. "Please be careful." she whispered softly. Riana pursed her lips as she dug a small trench in the dirt parking lot with the toe of her shoe. "Let me know if you need anything."

"Of course, Lex. I'll talk to you… later." Riana turned her phone off and got back into the driver's seat.

Lexi took a deep breath after she hung up with Ri. She wasn't doing well, that much had been blatantly obvious. She wished Riana would have told her more about what happened. All she had gotten from Derek when he called what that Ryan had called Alex from Ri's phone and demanded that Alex leave her alone. Alex was losing his mind. Lexi highlighted Alex's name and hit talk. "Did you talk to her?" he asked instantly.

"I did." she acknowledged simply.

"What's going on? Is she okay? Where is she?" he fired rapidly.

"All I know is that she said she's okay. She asked me to call and tell you she's okay. I wish I could tell you more, dear, but she didn't say much aside from that." Lexi explained quietly.

"Where is she? Please tell me she's not still there… with him." he pleaded desperately.

Lexi's heart broke for him. "She said she was driving. She thinks well when she drives Alex. I'm sure she's okay." The truth was Lexi knew Riana had to be an absolute wreck. She didn't want to say that to Alex though, he wouldn't be able to handle knowing that Riana was falling apart and he wasn't there to help pick up the pieces. She knew he'd feel that way, because that was exactly how she felt. Lexi looked around her apartment and considered packing her own bag and leaving to be with her, but she wasn't positive as to where Riana would end up. "We just have to give her some time and space."

"She needs me, Lex." Alex argued. His voice broke as he fought to contain his emotions.

"You're right, Alex, and when she's ready to see that, you'll be the first to know. I'll let you know if I hear from her again."

CHAPTER TWENTY-FIVE

Wake Me Up When September Ends

Riana was flooded with memories and emotions as she drove. Some made her laugh, but most brought stinging tears back to her eyes. She had to be careful of the music she allowed to rush through the speakers, as too often music was a bigger trigger than anything else for her--next to smells. Anytime the system would select a D.M.A. song she frantically found the skip button before Alex's voice met her ears.

Unfortunately, even things that should have been neutral, weren't. The moment The Temptations spilled from the speakers Riana was brought back to the morning with Matt and Alex as they made breakfast; how she danced and sang with them, the sensation of Alex's hands on her hips rushed back to her mind. Suddenly the intrusive memory of them in the kitchen as they shared their first kiss surged to the front of her mind. She could have sworn she could still feel his lips meld against hers, the slight burn of his scruff against her chin. She fought the image but it wouldn't disappear. As her hands slid over the steering wheel her palms seemed to recall the feeling of Alex's strong arms underneath them. Her body betrayed her mind.

As the soulful strums of Jonny Lang's "Leaving To Stay" filled her ears she decided to pull over. Sometimes one just had to give in to emotions. Jonny's voice called out to her. She had been deceived for years. Riana finally saw a side of Ryan she never thought existed. The anger, the contempt, and the unrealistic demands to keep her isolated. It was time, for Riana to leave to stay. She vowed not to be led back into Ryan's twisted web of confusion and maltreatment. Her resolve didn't lessen the pain, however. The end of her relationship with Ryan ended a whole part of her life. He had been intricate to so many things. It was almost impossible for her to accept that the good parts had been valid, even if it had eventually changed into something different and hurtful. Ryan had made her better at one time. Her laughter with him used to be genuine. She used to see herself through his eyes; beautiful, funny, smart and worthy. Unfortunately, she could see herself through his eyes now too; disposable, vulnerable and controllable. She didn't want to be those things.

She just wanted to be herself.

She wiped the tears from her eyes and put the car back in drive. Nebraska was monotonous but the further away from Minnesota she got, the better she felt. She scanned through her music files and settled on a heavy mix of Marilyn Manson, Korn and Tool. At least they didn't bring back any overwhelming memories.

Wednesday September 13, 2006
1:03am

Studio time for D.M.A, or any band, can be difficult at times, but downright impossible if one of the members was emotionally distracted. Alex was a wreck and couldn't focus on anything, and his distraction angered him. He was generally pissed off about everything, but beat himself up over the fact he couldn't get the music right. Matthew had assured him it was okay, that they could take a break. They were independent artists and didn't have such a strict schedule to adhere to anymore. He shot Matt down and fought harder to push through. A buzz on the table caught Matthew's attention and was shocked to see Riana's name on the screen. He stood up quickly and excused himself to Derek as he walked out of the studio. "Hello?" he questioned.

"Hey Matt." she greeted softly.

"Ri." he murmured as he gently closed the door behind him.

There was a long moment of silence, but Matt didn't attempt to fill it. They hadn't heard from Riana at all since Ryan called Alex and Matt didn't want to push her. "I, um, thought maybe I should call." she paused. "I didn't expect him to do anything like that, Matt." she confessed as he heard her cries break through.

"Oh, Ri, I know you didn't." Matt assured as he sat down in the quiet hallway.

"He…" her voice caught, "he scared me Matt." she sobbed. A mixture of pain and anger shot through Matthew. He couldn't help or rescue her nine years ago, but he'd be damned if he wouldn't try now.

"Ri, are you safe now?" he asked. "Do you need us to come get you? We can get a flight yet tonight." he offered hurriedly. The thought of anyone scaring or hurting her drove Matt into protective dad mode. He knew how much she had loved Ryan, and how much he meant to her, he couldn't imagine the pain and confusion she must have been dealing with.

"No. No, Matt, I'm fine. Well… no, I'm not fine. But I'm safe, Matt, I promise. You stay there." she thwarted his offer. "I left. I'm… driving. Somewhere, I haven't decided where yet. I just need some time to think."

"I understand." he conceded. He felt defeated and helpless. "Alex… is worried about you." he pushed quietly.

"I can't, Matt. I can't hear his voice right now. I feel horrible about the things Ryan said to him. I'm so angry. I feel so… stupid for not seeing the truth earlier."

"You're not stupid, Ri. So far from it. You're loyal and loving. Ryan took advantage of you. It's not your fault." he heard her breaths get choppy. "Ri, do you want me to come? I don't have to tell Alex where I'm going. I feel terrible you're alone in this right now."

Riana caught her breath. "That's… sweet Matthew. It really is. But no, I need to be alone. Please, just assure Alex I'm okay. Tell him…I'm sorry. And…and that I… miss him."

"Of course I will. But Ri? I think you need to tell him too. I know you can't talk to him, I get that. Maybe just a quick text message? He needs something from you, I don't think he can take this much longer. I know it's only been about ten hours, but I think it's been the worst ten hours of his life quite honestly." Matthew knew he was pushing his luck by saying it, but someone had to. He couldn't allow his best friend, who was more like a little brother, suffer much longer. If he could assist in giving him something to settle his heart and mind, he would.

"Okay." she choked out.

"Ri, honey, please let us know if you need anything. Anything at all. Any of us would be there in an instant if you asked." he promised.

"I know, Matt. But you guys are busy. You have an album to finish. Don't worry about me, I've been through worse things than this." She attempted to give a small laugh but failed miserably.

"I love you, Ri." Matt whispered though he'd never admit the depths of his statement.

"I love you too, Matt." she sighed. She hung up and Matt remained in the hallway, alone, as he cried.

Alex sat at the piano and fumed at how nothing came together, nothing felt right. He stared at the discordant keys and ground his teeth until he felt his pocket vibrate. Typically D.M.A. had a rule of no cellphones in the instrument area of the studio, but Alex had to keep it with him--in case Riana called. Derek and Matthew didn't argue.

He pulled his phone from his pocket as he turned his back on the keys. One new text message. He swiped his finger across the screen and opened his messages.

Riana.

Alex breathed a sigh of relief before he even read it.

"Alex, I'm so sorry. I'm okay. I miss you."

He held on to his phone tightly, unsure of how to respond. He was just happy to hear from her.

"I'm sorry too. I miss you. Please let me know what I can do to help."

There was so much more he wanted to say; *I love you, please come to me, I'll take care of you.* He didn't dare say it though.

"You have nothing to be sorry for. I just need time right now. Please don't call me. I'll call you when I can."

Alex's face twisted up in confusion. He got up and entered the main area of the studio. "She doesn't want me to call." he mumbled distractedly.

"You heard from her?" Derek asked quickly. Alex nodded.

"She just texted me, apologized and said she missed me. But she told me not to call her." Alex looked to his big brother. "I don't understand, Derek.

327

Why won't she talk to me?" Derek got up and sat on the arm of the chair Alex was hunched over in.

"I think, it might be too much for her to talk to you right now." he guessed gently.

"Why?" Alex blurted, pain evident on his face.

"She…" Matthew started hesitantly. He focused his eyes on his water bottle and thought of how to continue. "…is processing the loss of something… huge and intricate in her life. And… she has a lot of conflicting feelings right now. She just needs time, Alex." Matt finally lifted his eyes to Alex, and he could tell instantly.

"You've talked to her." he accused quickly. Matt dropped his eyes from Alex's and nodded. Anger rose within Alex. He felt Riana had to have known he would do anything for her. Why would she have turned to Matt instead of him?

"Alex, please don't take it personally." Matt started softly. "She just wanted to let us know she was okay, without being faced with how she feels about you right now."

Alex narrowed his eyes at Matthew. "She doesn't know how she feels about me." he grumbled.

"You're absolutely right." Matt confirmed. "And talking to you right now is only going to make it harder for her to figure out."

Riana decided to stop for the night in Colorado as she was completely exhausted. Too much emotional pain, too much thinking, too much to figure out. She warily made her way to the front desk of the hotel with her shoulders drooped from having to bear too much weight. After she got her key she shuffled down the hall to her single room. It was all she needed at that point, a place to shower and attempt to sleep. She didn't need anything else.

Except Alex.

She needed his smile, his safe arms, and the assurance that everything would be okay. She wasn't sure if she was just spun around by Ryan and feeling so lost that she craved something familiar or if Alex was truly what she needed. She worried she would accept the deceitful comfort of anyone's arms at that point. Instead of dwelling on it she took a shower and crawled into the stiff coolness of the bed.

Riana woke up surprisingly refreshed. Usually when she and Ryan would go through one of their "off" times she'd slip into a depression that grasped every inch of her and brought her fighting beneath the surface. She didn't feel that way this time. It still hurt, there was still a loss she felt, but she knew that she had to keep pushing forward. Further away, to where she could find herself again.

Arizona. She decided to head back to the ranch. Part of her said not to, that there would be too many vivid memories of Alex there. The memories were vivid regardless of where she was so she dismissed the warnings. She headed south on interstate 25 to New Mexico before she went west, back home. Her phone remained off, and she relished being alone in her thoughts. Even if her thoughts were a bit tormented at times.

A full twelve hours of driving would exhaust most people, but Riana loved it. She loved the freedom she felt while she drove and the southwest was one of her favorite places to be. Despite her lack of religious beliefs, there was undoubtedly something wondrous about the mountains, the canyons and beautifully layered rock formations. As she found her way through New Mexico there was a peacefulness to the barren expanses of landscape with little civilization.

Riana pulled up to the gate of the ranch as the sun finished it's decent to the horizon. A mixture of oranges, pinks and purples welcomed her home. The warnings were correct though; the moment she drove through the gate every image that faced her brought another memory of Alex. She felt her chest tighten and her eyes tear up. She stayed in the car, attempted to gather herself, and erase the images. She heard his voice in her mind, his laughter, and she finally gave in to the tears. As the floodgates of emotions overtook her she yelled out with her head against the steering wheel. It was excruciating. She couldn't remember the last time she had felt so much pain. She had successfully held it together pretty well when it happened, and all the way back to the ranch, but once she didn't have to keep it together she fell to pieces. She couldn't decide what hurt more; how she finally saw the truth about Ryan, or having to face the pain without Alex at her side.

She furiously wiped at her bloodshot eyes to dry the tears as she gathered her things to head inside. The house was hauntingly quiet and still; the only soul there was her. Riana ached to hear the laughter of Alex, Matthew and Derek, or the delighted squeal of Lexi as Derek got his hands on her. She wanted to hear the relentless teasing that would undoubtedly take place after Matthew started yet another fire in the grill. Instead, all she heard was the ticking of clocks, the water being filtered through the pool, and the call of coyotes. The same calls she had heard the night she found comfort in Alex's bed after her nightmare. Even silence couldn't stop the memories.

Riana made herself something to eat as she fought more memories; of every meal they had made together. Suddenly, she lost her appetite. She cursed as she tossed her half eaten sandwich away and trudged down the hall to her room. She decided to finally turn on her phone as she ran herself a bath.

The barrage of notifications brought out a throaty groan as Riana scrolled through them. Lexi and Alex were the main culprits, but she also saw Sam, Matt and Derek. She was thankful not to see anything from Ryan.

As she slipped into the steamy water she dialed Lexi's number and closed her eyes. "Hey Ri." Lexi answered gently.

"Hi Lex." Riana breathed. "I just wanted to let you know I got to my destination." She swished the water around.

"Where'd you end up?"

Riana leaned her head back against the ledge of the tub. "The ranch." she replied simply. "It's hard, being here. Everything reminds me of... him. Which is weird, isn't it? I mean, shouldn't I be preoccupied with what happened with Ryan?"

"What exactly *did* happen with Ryan?" Riana had tried not to think about it, but she supposed she'd have to process it eventually.

"You know, Lex, I'm not exactly sure." Riana started with a deep breath. "I don't even know why I went to see him. I already knew that it had reached the end, you know? But there's always been something about him, something I couldn't resist. The moment I saw him I knew I shouldn't have gone. It's as if I saw every difference in him I'd been blind to the last three years. He was so... detached. I felt so used by him, Lex. And then..." She closed her eyes and flashes appeared. "Then when I found him on the phone... he said something about a request coming from me. He told Alex to go to hell when I realized he was on my phone." Lexi felt the pieces of what Derek had told her come together. Riana's heart twisted and fought to keep beating as she was brought back to the moment. "He... He yelled at me. He's never really yelled before. He told me I couldn't see or talk to Alex anymore and I had to be the one to tell him." Her breaths got choppy. "And when I told him I wouldn't... he..."

Lexi interrupted quickly, "Did he hurt you, Ri? So help me God if he touched you I'll kill him." Riana smiled weakly at Lexi's overprotectiveness.

"He didn't touch me, not...really. He terrified me though, he was so angry and demanding. He told me if I loved him I had to stop 'consorting' with Alex. He grabbed me..." Riana ran her hands along her upper arms and fought to remove the image of Ryan's flushed face from her mind. She heard Lexi mumble something about him being a bastard. "He said if I walked out the door we were done. So I left." Riana released a long breath.

"Oh Ri." Lexi sighed.

"I'm kind of... confused, Lex. I mean, not about what happened with Ryan, it is what it is I guess. But all of this has brought up such a rush of feeling about Alex. I feel like I don't know if it's real, or if I'm just craving that instant gratification of being wanted by someone. Because we all know I've been down that road before." she grumbled.

"You're a different person now, Ri. You're strong and independent and understand the emotional reasons you used to do that. If you think about it, I'm pretty sure you'll find these feelings for Alex aren't new. Don't you think maybe your heart is trying to tell you what you really need?" Lexi urged. If that were the case, Riana wondered if she could trust her heart. After all, wasn't it her heart that kept her with Ryan for too long?

Riana reluctantly agreed. "You might be right. I'm going to go though, it was a long drive and

I have to get some sleep. I love you, Lexi." She removed her Bluetooth from her ear, tossed it on the ledge of the tub and deliberately lowered herself completely underwater. Behind her eyes she saw his; dark, deep and playful. She broke through the surface and wiped her face. She looked around and was reminded of her solitude.

CHAPTER TWENTY-SIX

What's Left Of Me

September 21, 2006

It was going on eight days and Alex still hadn't heard anything more from Riana. Of course he relentlessly gave Matthew the third degree every chance he got. Matt assured Alex he hadn't heard anything else but Alex wouldn't believe him. He had come to terms with the fact Riana and Matt had a relationship long before she and Alex did. He couldn't blame her for reaching out to Matt. He just wished he knew what was going on, where she was-- anything.

Lexi flew out to New York to be with Derek, but Alex thought perhaps another reason was for her to provide him with a little bit of support. Alex was thankful that she was at least honest with him and let him know when she heard from Ri. She didn't give him much for details, but it helped him to know Riana wasn't completely alone. "Hey buddy." Lexi beckoned softly as she nestled in next to Alex on the couch. He looked over and gave her a half smile, he felt absolutely pitiful. "I just got a message from Ri." Alex's eyes lit up and she smiled when she saw the quick change. "She's starting to do a little better. She asked if Sam and I would go see her next week."

"That's great! You think she might talk to me soon?" Lexi's eyes softened. She leaned into Alex and rubbed his arm.

"Oh sweetheart. I know this is really hard on you."

"It's more than hard, Lex." he blurted quickly. "I...I love her." The only one who knew was Sam, but he needed Lexi to know as well, he needed to not feel so utterly desolate. He felt perhaps if he had them both in the loop they might help Riana figure out how she felt about him. He hoped she loved him, but he didn't know for sure. He was fairly certain that he'd be okay if she didn't love him the way he loved her, he just wanted his best friend back.

"Really?" Lexi asked as she excitedly turned towards him and pulled her feet up and under her. "I mean, you know, I had hoped you did, and it seemed like you did, but do you really? Like, *really* love her?" she rambled.

Alex knew she was trying to ask if his love for Riana surpassed her being his best friend. He locked his eyes on hers. "I love her more than I've ever loved anyone in my life, Lexi. And to not be with her now, to know she's hurting and I can't fix it. It's probably the most intense pain I've ever felt." Alex's eyes darted away. "Sam's known for a while. Since the ranch. I knew I couldn't tell Ri, I knew she had to work through things first. I probably still shouldn't tell her. I mean, I've said it to her, but she thinks she's my best friend. She is, but I love her beyond that." Lexi nodded.

"Maybe it's best not to share with her yet. But… I'll keep this in mind when I go see her, okay? I won't tell her, but I can at least help her work through some things knowing this in the back of my mind." She then narrowed her eyes at Alex. "She needs something real, Alex. Don't mess with her."

"Honey?" Derek called. Lexi gave Alex a quick smile and a tight squeeze as she whispered assurances that things would work out. "Lex, come on, we're going to be late." Alex smiled as Lexi got up off the couch and met Derek with a sweet kiss.

September 27, 2006

"I think Apollo misses you."

Riana had slowly started to reconnect with Alex. She couldn't bear to cut him completely out of her life. She had also slowly regained some resemblance of normal functioning after about four days. The first week definitely wasn't her brightest, she was inconsolable and disheveled, she had dishes everywhere, and she barely got out of her pajamas. She spent a lot of time, probably too much time, with a glass of wine and a notebook at her side. She eventually pulled it together some, showered on a regular basis, started cleaning up the house and found some joy in music again. Her notebook didn't always bring tears now, sometimes it brought moments of clarity. She even started to ride again. Which led her to her most recent text to Alex.

"Oh yeah? He probably wants to race again."

Riana was thankful that he didn't push her, or try to call. He didn't ask about Ryan or how she was doing. Riana figured it would take a long time for them to get back to where they had been, if they ever got there at all.

"Yeah he probably does."

Riana looked at her screen and debated on finally changing from small talk to something more. A whisper in the back of her mind told her she needed to hear his voice and before she could talk herself out of it, she clicked on his name and pressed talk. When she heard him pick up she considered hanging up.

"Hey sweetheart." his deep voice greeted smoothly, gently. Goosebumps rolled over almost every inch of her body as his voice reached depths of her she didn't think existed. Her breath caught in her throat and for a moment she wasn't sure what to say.

"Hi." she whispered softly as she watched her hands shake. They stayed quiet for a moment, yet she felt that with her calling him things were being said that didn't need words. "Alex, I'm sorry I haven't called." she uttered carefully. "It's been a rough couple weeks." Alex remained quiet on the other end. "I just… I needed to process things."

"I know, Ri." he assured. Riana wished she was curled up in him with his strong arms around her. She missed how safe she felt with him.

"I didn't listen to him you know. I wouldn't let him tell me who I could talk to." She wasn't sure how much Lexi or Matthew had shared with him over the last fifteen days. "It ended that day."

"I'm sorry it ended like that Ri." he whispered carefully.

Riana didn't want him to feel the way she felt when he and Kim broke up. "It wasn't your fault, Alex. It was mine. I... I wasn't faithful to him." She referred not only to the one kiss they shared--that one, magical, soul twisting kiss, but also her emotional attachment to Alex.

"Ri." Alex started firmly, but gently. "He didn't deserve you. He didn't love you." She dropped her head.

"I know." It had taken a long time for Riana to come to terms with it, but Alex was right, Ryan didn't love her. The part about not deserving her though; that was harder to accept. The silence that lingered between them was thick, with words that desperately wanted to be shared. "I miss you, Alex." she whispered. She braced herself for the rejection she feared.

"I miss you more." he murmured. She didn't think it was possible; how could he need her the way she needed him? Did he wake up numerous times a night and search his bed for her the way she searched for him in the middle of the night?

"I have to go." she proclaimed hastily before more secrets passed by her lips. She hung up and tried to calm down. His voice grasped her heart and refused to relinquish its hold. She stuffed her notebook, phone and pen into Adonis' saddle bag and mounted for a mind-clearing run.

It had been wonderful to hear his voice again. There was a comfort to it for Riana that she couldn't describe. He calmed her, yet drove her crazy. She felt the power of Adonis under her and was thankful for the rush, the distraction, and the revitalizing moment. She hadn't felt so alive in weeks. She actually found that she smiled against the sun and wind as Adonis took off to the end of the horizon.

September 28, 2006

"I'm so glad she's finally ready to be with people again." Sam commented from Lexi's side on their flight to Arizona. "I think that's the longest she's gone alone."

"I know. But what happened with Ryan was... huge. She needed the solitude. I agree though, I'm happy she finally asked us to come." She absently flipped through the inflight magazine. "Honestly, though, I don't think we are the ones she needs." Samantha gave her a knowing look.

"I know. She needs him." Lexi raised her eyebrows and nodded.

"That shall be my mission, Sam. I mean, after supporting her through whatever else she has to process. I swear though, she'll see it. I imagine she already has, she's just in massive amounts of denial." Sam nodded, both of them well aware of Riana's unfortunate habit of self-deprecation.

"Things are going well with D?" Sam asked quietly as a smile danced on her lips.

"Things are going wonderfully." Lexi confirmed. She and Derek falling for each other had happened so subtly she hardly noticed that it happened, yet once she did, Lexi knew it was right. "The record is coming along well, they're all stoked about it. I was actually just helping him plan a surprise party for Alex's 21st next month."

"Oh super fun!" Sam squealed. Lexi leaned in closer, perfectly aware of the risk of being overheard any place she was.

"I'm really hoping to bring him the best present ever." Sam met Lexi's eyes and they both smiled as they whispered, "Riana."

Their flight landed at 6:40pm and Riana patiently waited for them at baggage claim. Sam and Lexi ran to her and wrapped her in a tight, suffocating hug. Lexi noticed that a few young women took note of their reunion and knew it would soon be shared with the D.M.A. fan community. They didn't discuss anything serious in the airport, they all knew how quickly anything they said would be taken out of context and spread online with the fans. Sam could tell Riana's happiness at their arrival was genuine; how her eyes lit up and danced was proof enough for both her and Lexi that Riana was doing much better.

As they left the airport and headed into the vast landscape that would lead them back to the ranch, they caught up. Riana didn't share anything right away, but was eager to hear how Sam and Lexi had been. She was glad to hear that Derek and Lexi had slowly become more serious; taking casual dates and phone calls to more regular dates when they could and daily calls when Lexi wasn't in New York with him. Sam had done a lot of traveling and shared entertaining stories of crazy locals in the remote areas she visited.

Finally, Riana started to share. "I've been writing a lot." she offered. "I'm not sure if anything will come of it, in the way of publishing, but it's been helpful." Lexi smiled at Sam and nodded to Riana. "I felt a need to put into words where we started and where we ended up. I think as a way to grieve the end, you know?" Lexi continued to nod, at least Riana hadn't buried everything. "Apparently the end was much earlier than this month." Riana mumbled. Lexi frowned a bit, the realization had to hurt. She placed her hand on Riana's arm and stroked her in silent comfort.

They got back to the ranch late, all of them fairly exhausted, but they stayed up for a while and relaxed in the hot tub with a glass of wine. After some laughs of times past, Riana got quiet. She looked over at Lexi hesitantly. "Lex? How's… how's he doing?" She didn't have to specify of whom she spoke.

"Alex is doing okay. He's hanging in there, hoping maybe once you get through your grieving he'll get his best friend back." Riana nodded slowly. "He's gotten better since you started talking to him again." Lexi continued. Riana started to spin her vertical labret and Lexi knew there was more on her mind.

"It's been really hard without him." Riana admitted. "I miss him. It feels like a part of me is missing. It doesn't feel the same yet." Lexi glanced at Sam. It was so obvious to them, she couldn't understand why Riana fought something so right. She felt the same way Alex did.

Wednesday October 4, 2006

Riana couldn't help but wonder why she had suffered alone for so long. Having Sam and Lexi there with her made things so much better. Not exactly easier, but better. She smiled to herself as they took a ride with Chester, Lilo and Adonis. She felt a sense of comfort and relief she hadn't felt since the whole thing with Ryan happened. "Do you ever wonder how differently things might have played out in life?" she pondered. Lexi and Sam looked at each other, then at her. Riana knew they hated it when she asked vague questions.

"In what regard?" Sam asked. Riana twirled her barbell and wondered what she meant.

"I don't know really. So many things, I guess. I mean, what if Ryan and I had gotten married, what if I hadn't had a meeting with my publisher that day in May? What if we had decided not to get coffee? What if I hadn't taken Alex's number?" she was rambling and knew it, but those were the things that cluttered her mind.

"Well, thank God you and Ryan never got married." Lexi chuckled. Riana gave a twisted half-smile. "The rest...well, we've always believed everything happens for a reason, right?" Riana nodded. "Things just played out right that night."

"Did they?" Riana pushed. "I mean, look at everything that's happened since then. Alex and Kim broke up, I got in a fight with Tabitha, Ryan and I broke up, and now, here I am, questioning if it all really happened for a reason."

"Did you really want to stay with Ryan?" Sam probed as she moved Lilo closer to Riana and Adonis. Riana frowned and shook her head. "And you know Alex didn't want to stay with Kim, that one was falling apart well before you. Just as you and Ryan were falling apart well before Alex." She definitely had a point. "Maybe... you're supposed to end up together." Sam offered. Riana felt her shoulders sag.

"I don't know..." Riana trailed off.

"You said you felt like something was missing, right?" Lexi asked as she looked to Riana then to Sam. Riana nodded. "What if that something isn't a thing... it's a someone. Maybe it's Alex."

"What if it is though?" Riana blurted. "What if what I need the most is him? But what if he won't have me? I know I'm not easy to put up with, I mean, you two would have to be the first to admit it." She gave a quick chuckle. The truth was, she was terrified that it was Alex. She ran the risk of losing her best friend. "I already told Matt I'm not easy to love, I'm...complicated to say it nicely."

"Alex has seen that, though." Sam justified. "He's seen you at your best, and has held on through your worst. He has wanted nothing more than to be by your side through this, Ri. He knows your terrible humor, your crassness, your passions, your mean streak, your sarcasm. He *knows* you, Ri." Riana thought perhaps Alex did know her. Perhaps he had successfully gotten within her walls without her realizing it.

"And you know him." Lexi finished. Riana smiled at the thought. It was true, Riana knew Alex in ways she never thought possible. She quickly realized she wanted to know him in every way. Her cheeks felt the burn of a quick flush at the thought.

"What is this, some sort of intervention to get me to admit I love Alex?" Riana laughed. Lexi and Sam didn't laugh with her, however. Riana's eyes flicked from one to the other. "Oh my God, it is! You can't be serious." Riana laughed again. She hoped her laughter would imply how absurd she thought the idea was. Except, it wasn't absurd.

"We just… We think you're running from something, well, obvious." Lexi explained as they brought the horses up to the barn and dismounted.

"It's not obvious." Riana argued. "It's presumptuous, risky. Stupid even." she huffed as she tied Adonis up to be untacked. Lexi followed Riana's lead and tied up Chester.

"I know you've spent weeks going over everything between you and Ryan and undoubtedly comparing it to you and Alex." Riana huffed, she hated how Lexi knew her so well. She narrowed her eyes at Lexi. "What did you come up with, Ri?" She tilted her head in expectation. Riana sighed angrily.

"That… Ryan didn't love me anymore." Lexi pursed her lips and silently told Riana she expected more. "And….and that… maybe Alex did." Lexi and Sam couldn't stop the smiles that spread across their faces. "Stop smiling!" Riana demanded.

"So, you can see Alex treats you better, right?" Riana nodded, despite not wanting Sam to be right. "And you liked when he kissed you, right?" Riana groaned.

"Yes! Okay, fine. Yes, Alex treats me better than anyone else ever has. Yes, I absolutely love the feeling of his lips on mine and his hands on me. And yes, I can imagine being with him all the time. But he's one of my best friends! What if, what if I somehow thought it would be a good idea to tell him this and he totally rejected me? I couldn't take it." Riana sat down on a bale of hay and tried to catch her breath. She wasn't ready to admit these things. "I can't imagine my life without him." she confessed softly. "After everything happened with Ryan, the majority of my pain wasn't the end of my relationship with Ryan," she looked up and bounced her eyes between Sam and Lexi. "it was that Alex wasn't by my side to help me through it."

"Ri, listen to yourself." Lexi urged softly as she sat down next to her. Riana nodded as large tears welled up in her eyes. "What are you really trying to say?"

Riana's vision blurred as she met Lexi's large, carob eyes which were softened with the unconditional love she held for Riana. "I'm...I'm trying to say... I'm in love with Alex." Riana completely broke down as she let the words finally come out instead of burying them as deeply as she could. She fell into Lexi's embrace as Sam came in behind her. They both hushed Riana as they held their arms tightly around her. "I'm so in love with him." she cried. "I need him."

"He needs you too." Sam whispered. Riana closed her eyes tightly and hoped Sam was right, because she knew she was barreling down a road she wasn't sure she could stop on.

The ring of Riana's cell phone tore them from the moment. It wasn't Alex's ringtone so she wasn't sure who it could be. She pulled her phone out and was mortified to see Ryan's number on the screen. Lexi saw it too and ripped the phone from Riana's hand before she could decide whether or not to answer. "You aren't to call her anymore." Lexi snapped angrily when she picked up. She didn't give him any time to respond and promptly hung up. "Tomorrow we're going to town and changing your number." she declared firmly. Riana nodded. Her heart raced just at the sight of Ryan's number, she had deleted his contact from her phone but his number was permanently engrained in her memory. If Riana was to succeed in walking away, she needed to be able to completely disappear from him.

"Come on honey, let's get you inside. I'll come back out and take care of the horses." Riana nodded again against Lexi and slowly got up.

"Why would he call me?" Riana grumbled. She felt herself tremor and despised the way he had any effect on her.

"I'm sure because he's used to you waiting for him to come back to you." Sam guessed. "All you have to remember is you don't have to put up with getting the bare minimums from him anymore because there is a wonderful man on the other side of the country willing to give you everything you deserve." Riana sighed, frustrated with Sam and Lexi's certainty when it came to Alex. She supposed they could feel that way, it wasn't their life and friendship on the line. She started to think that sharing her feelings for Alex with them had been a bad idea.

CHAPTER TWENTY-SEVEN

You're Beautiful

Friday October 6, 2006

There was a sense of closure that overtook Riana after they changed her cell number. She had Lexi text the guys as she knew they'd never answer a call from an unknown number. Suddenly, she started to feel she might actually be able to move on.

"So," Lexi started as they sat out by the pool. Riana turned her head in Lexi's direction expectantly. "Alex's birthday is coming up."

"Oh my God, you're right!" Riana exclaimed as she sat up. "I have no idea what to get him." She couldn't believe in the midst of everything that had happened she forgot his birthday.

"Well, maybe it's not so much about what you get him, Ri. I was hoping maybe you'd think about coming back to New York with me and Sam for Alex's surprise party." Riana laid back in her lounge chair and closed her eyes. "I think seeing you there would mean more to him than any gift you might get him." There she was again, overly confident about the dynamic of Riana's relationship with Alex.

"I'd really love to." Riana admitted. She didn't miss Lexi's obnoxiously huge grin. "I'm just not sure I can." Lexi's smile faded instantly.

"Yes you can, Ri. I promise, you have nothing to be afraid of." Sam assured.

"Trust us." Lexi said sternly. "Don't forget, I have someone on the inside. If I thought at all it wouldn't bring Alex immense joy to see you there I wouldn't push you to go." Riana glanced at Lexi over the top of her sunglasses. She knew Lexi would never purposely lead her astray.

"Okay." she sighed. "I'll go." Lexi and Sam both squealed happily and rushed to envelope Riana in an excited hug.

Monday October 9, 2006

Alex discovered that perhaps Riana had a deeper effect on him than he originally thought. He already knew she was buried deep within his soul, he just didn't think anyone would be able to effect his musical side the way she did. Once she had started to talk to him again the music was no longer difficult. He was able to let go, find the groove, and have fun with Matt and Derek again. D.M.A. was back on schedule, planned a November release date and a winter/spring tour. Things started to feel right for him again.

Alex laughed heartily with his phone nestled between his shoulder and ear. "Tell Lexi her boyfriend is an idiot." he urged as he watched Derek man the controls and make Matthew sound like a chipmunk on speed. Riana's own laughter was back to normal. Alex was happy that apparently having Lexi and Sam there had helped her heal and move forward.

"I'm glad you guys are having fun." A smile radiated through her words.

"We really are. It's just final mixing now. Everything is looking great for a November release." Alex replied as he leaned back and tossed his feet on the table in front of him. "We're going to have a big party for it, you should come." he blurted, then instantly regretted it. He wasn't sure if she was ready to see them yet. More specifically he wasn't sure if she was ready to see him.

"Oh, but whatever would I wear?" Riana teased. Relief swept over Alex and he laughed deeply at her over the top demeanor.

"Something hot for sure." he declared. Riana giggled madly on the other end.

"You, mister, are terrible!" Alex grinned, it seemed he would end up with his best friend back.

Matthew yelled at Alex to get off the phone, but did so with an amused, playful grin on his face. "Ri, honey, I have to go. The diva is having a conniption." Matthew's eyes grew wide and Riana laughed. "I'll talk to you tonight. Love you."

"Love you too." she echoed before she hung up.

Saturday October 14, 2006

Riana felt as though she was out of her damn mind. She had to be to think this was a good idea. She was on a plane with Lexi and Sam to fly out to New York for Alex's birthday party. They had all kept it a secret from him, seeing how Riana had made the ridiculous decision to finally tell him how she truly felt about him. She had fought it for a long time, too long, but had discovered a lot about herself in her solitude after the blow up with Ryan. The main thing she had discovered was somehow she had found love; real, honest, be the brutally raw version of yourself and still be loved kind of love. She had shown Alex the darkest parts of her soul and he had stayed. She wanted him to stay forever, which is exactly why she thought this plan was completely ludicrous. She knew it was one thing to handle her as a friend, she still doubted he'd want more.

There was something between Riana and Alex which had defied logic from the very beginning. It seemed the rest of the world saw it well before she did. Which led her to another downfall of falling in love with Alex; she knew the fans would watch and judge their relationship. They'd done it consistently since July--before then really. Considering they had pictures from their first night together in Chicago, they had apparently been watching from the first moments.

"Lex, what time did D say we should be at the restaurant?" Derek was the mastermind behind the surprise party to be thrown at the prestigious 230 Fifth restaurant. The knowledge that they would be with at least fifty of Alex's closest friends and family was certainly not helping Riana's anxiety.

"Party starts at eight my dear."

"Yay..." Riana groaned unenthusiastically. "That gives me five hours to freak out." She dramatically thumped her head against the tiny window next to her.

"Oh, stop." Samantha laughed. "Everything will go swimmingly. Besides, the time will fly by. We booked appointments at the John Barrett Salon. Hair, makeup, massages. You'll be absolutely perfect."

Riana chewed her lip and groaned internally. She was not typically one to get all gussied up, and Alex knew it. He'd suspect something was peculiar. She knew it wasn't worth the fight now; Sam and Lexi had destroyed any and all of Riana's arguments as of late. They did it out of love, of course, but it didn't make it any less annoying.

They landed just before three and hightailed to baggage claim. Riana hoped to avoid fans at all costs; not because she minded them, but because she truly wanted her arrival to be a surprise. Her anxiety increased as doubts crept in and scenarios of it all going horribly wrong played in her mind. She scanned the carousel as she spun her vertical labret.

Lexi came up next to her, grabbed her hand and squeezed it reassuringly.

Riana glanced over and smiled nervously at her. "Everything will be okay, Ri. More than okay. I really believe something great is going to happen tonight."

"You need to stop stressing, Ri. We have the hotel booked, your beauty appointments booked, and your outfit picked. All you have to do is show up." Sam said as she quickly grabbed her luggage from the carousel. Somehow, her words didn't do much to calm Riana's nerves.

They hailed a cab and hastened downtown. Memories of Riana's last time in New York promptly hit her. First, memories of her book signing, which warmed her heart and brought a smile to her face. Then she remembered dinner, the studio, Matt, Alex and the pictures that started it all. Again she questioned if this was truly the best decision. Then the thought of Alex came to her, just Alex, without the opinions of anyone else or his status. She thought of their time together, and the way he made her feel. The plan, the decision to tell him, no matter how crazy it seemed, was right. She needed him. Not just the way she had him, she needed all of him. She knew she had to do this in order to finally find lasting happiness. For once, she believed that perhaps she deserved it.

Their hotel was only two blocks from the salon, so they checked in, dropped off their bags then enjoyed a quick walk downtown. "I don't want anything over the top." Riana demanded as they took the elevator up to the penthouse where the John Barrett Salon was located.

Lexi shushed her, "We only asked that your natural beauty be accentuated." Riana sighed. She relented and figured it'd be nice if she did look her best as she made one of the biggest decisions of her life. She snorted and thought perhaps that was a bit dramatic, but it wasn't as though the decision was insignificant.

They were greeted warmly by the receptionist of the salon and quickly ushered to a private room to change in anticipation of their massages. It was a calm and serene environment that provided Riana with a slight sense of relaxation as she laid on the table and awaited her massage therapist. She was thankful that her therapist didn't feel the need to partake in small talk; Ri simply wanted to lay there and forget everything for a moment.

A moment turned into forty-five minutes. The next thing Riana knew she was told she could take her time getting up, and that her stylist would be waiting for her. She took a deep breath and kept her eyes closed. There was an air of anticipation and excitement as she slowly got up, slipped on her robe and headed out to meet her stylist. As she opened the door from her private room she was met by a young woman with a glass of spa water and some fruit.

Riana smiled graciously as she accepted the water and fruit from her then followed her lead to where Francisco, her wonderfully entertaining stylist, waited. He was tall and thin, with beautiful green eyes against olive skin and silky black hair.

Francisco was nothing but lavish and spunky right from the beginning. He told Riana how happy he was to work on such a superb canvas. She laughed and blushed as she sat down. He turned her from the mirror and stated she was not allowed to watch him perform his magic. Lexi, Sam, Francisco and Riana gabbed happily while Riana was doted upon and Sam and Lexi were fawned over by their own stylists. "Mm, so what is this special occasion for which I have the honor of preparing you?" Francisco asked with a thick Argentinian accent. Riana's blush deepened. "Ah, is for someone special, yes?"

Riana nodded as the blush deepened so much she could feel tingles within her cheeks. "He doesn't know I'm here." she disclosed softly.

Francisco gave a small squeal and radiated joyfully. "Oh, sweetheart, you shall make a grand entrance." He brushed a deep red lipstick over Riana's lower lip quickly. Riana glanced over to Lexi and Sam. They were both captivated as they gazed at her. Francisco continued to work and provided last minute teases and pin backs to her hair.

"I'll go grab your dress." Samantha squealed.

"You're putting me in a dress?" Riana exclaimed, but Sam had already disappeared to a back room. Riana laughed and shook her head. A dress was definitely not her everyday style.

356

Professional pencil skirts and flattering tops, maybe, but not typically dresses.

"Oh hush!" Lexi scolded. "You're going to look amazing. Like you always do, only better." she winked. "He won't be able to resist."

It wasn't that Riana never wore dresses, she just had an inkling the kind of dress her two lovely best friends would pick for her would be drastically different than what she might choose for herself. Sam reappeared and Riana shook her head as she took in the very short, slinky black dress with lace cap sleeves. "Are you serious?" she laughed. "No way."

"Yes!" Samantha exclaimed. "You're going to look amazing in this. I mean, really, have you seen yourself?"

Francisco stood in front of Riana with his hand on his hip and nodded thoughtfully. "Mm, yes, that will do marvelously." he agreed. Riana groaned and snatched the dress from Sam.

"Fine." she huffed. She got up from Francisco's chair and proceeded back to the private massage room to change. Francisco hollered for Lexi and Sam to keep Ri from any mirrors. They went into the room with Riana and assisted her as she stepped into dress.

Lexi and Sam then presented Riana with the shoes they expected her to wear. Stilettos. Riana groaned loudly and rolled her eyes. Though she figured at least with how vertically challenged she was, the dress wasn't right under her butt cheeks as it was designed to be. And perhaps the stilettos would make kissing Alex easier. She quickly chastised herself for presuming he would kiss her. Though she couldn't stop the excited smile that passed over her face at the thought.

Riana shimmied around a bit and attempted to get used to the feel of the dress then looked to Lexi and Sam. "Alright ladies, how do I look?" she asked as she bit her lower lip.

"So hot." Lexi proclaimed. Sam giddily agreed. "Let's get you back out there so Francisco can see, and so you can finally look in a mirror." Lexi urgently ushered Riana back out to the main area of the salon.

As Francisco turned to face them he gave a quick gasp and covered his heart with his hand. "Girl, for real. Damn." he gushed as he motioned Riana over to him. "You must see yourself now." He gently guided her to turn and face the mirror and for a moment, she didn't recognize the stunning woman before her.

Riana's hair was brilliantly teased into beach waves, with the sides pinned back just a bit to present the face Francisco transformed from ordinary to unearthly exquisite. Her smoky eyes were rivaled only by her pouty red lips. The dress Sam and Lexi picked out accentuated her curves perfectly. Riana did a slight turn as she checked everything out. *Whew.* She figured if she was going to do something huge like this, she may as well look damn good as she did it. She turned and grinned at Lexi and Sam, then turned and hugged Francisco as she whispered a heartfelt thank you.

Lexi and Sam changed into their own dresses, a bit toned down from Riana's because they wanted to keep the attention on her, but fantastic nonetheless. Sam was in her typical atypical style; a black and white polka dot vintage look with a red patent leather belt, red heels and thick black framed glasses. Lexi had her curly hair tossed up in a messy yet classic French twist and had slipped into a chic white A-line dress with strappy flats. Riana sighed in envy and wished she had flats. She wasn't a stranger to stilettos, however, and knew she'd adjust quickly.

Riana glanced up at the clock, considered the traffic downtown and knew they'd have to leave quickly in order to make it to Fifth in time. "Alright ladies, let's do this." She was ready. Ready to tell the man she was in love with that... well, that she was in love with him.

CHAPTER TWENTY-EIGHT
Ain't No Other Man

Derek and Matthew arrived at 230 Fifth around six to meet guests who came early and to make sure everything came together as planned. "Alright, seems the ladies are on their way." Derek called with a smile from where he chatted with the DJ.

"Ri didn't bail last minute, did she?" Matt asked as he waited for the manager to come back so they could go over the custom menu one last time. Derek confirmed she didn't, and that she was happy to have decided to come.

Matthew felt an insistent vibration in his pocket and he quickly pulled his phone out. "Now why didn't your girlfriend call you?" he mused to himself as he slid his finger across the screen to answer. "Lexi, love, what's going on?"

"Well, Matthew, dear, Derek didn't answer his phone and the maitre'd won't let us into the private room." she quickly explained. "Would you mind either sending my lovely boyfriend out here or coming out to let this fine gentleman know we are indeed guests to such a lavish private party." she teased.

"I'll be right there." Matt slid his phone back into his pocket and went out front. He spotted Lexi right away, she looked ravishing. His eyes then caught Samantha in her quirky off-beat style. Finally, he saw Riana. She had her back to him at first, but as she turned he was rendered speechless. His mind quickly reminded him he was married and that he was pretty sure Alex was hopelessly in love with the woman.

"You ladies look...amazing." he gushed as he approached. He leaned into the maitre'd and assured him they were VIP guests to the party. He apologized quickly and Matt patted him on the back to calm his anxiety about having denied them access.

Lexi hurried to Matthew and gave him a quick kiss on the cheek and a tight squeeze. "You look dashing as well, Matt." Matthew was simply mesmerizing without much effort. Black slacks, and a pinstripe button down shirt was all he needed to appear perfectly put together. Riana smiled shyly at him. "Riana." he murmured softly as he approached her. She blushed as he wrapped her up in a tight embrace. "I'm so happy you came, and that you're doing better... and you look..." He pulled back and shook his head as he gazed at her again.

"It's too much isn't it?" she assumed quickly as she fought to pull her dress down to a more modest length.

"No," he corrected. "You look...absolutely enchanting." Riana released a breath. "Come on, I'll show you to our room." He wrapped one arm around Sam and the other around Riana as they proceeded to the back of the restaurant. "Hey D!" he hollered. "Look who I found!"

Derek turned from the DJ and grinned brightly as he took in the beauty of their best friends and his girlfriend. He reached for Lexi's hand, pulled her to him and then met her in a heavy kiss. "You." He kissed her. "Are." He kissed her again. "Gorgeous." One last time for good measure. "Sam, looking classic." he beamed. He then rested his eyes on Riana. His smile softened. "Oh, Ri. You look stunning." He released Lexi's hand and embraced Riana. "How are you doing?" he asked quietly. While Alex was the one who struggled the most with what happened to Riana and how isolated she'd been, all the guys had been concerned.

"Much better, D, thank you." she answered as she hugged him. Matthew and Derek ushered their VIPs around and introduced them to a few friends and cousins who had arrived already. They went through the rough game plan of Alex's surprise party; Frankie would bring him in for dinner at eight, where they'd all greet him at the main entrance of the private room. It would then essentially be game on; plenty of free flowing food and drinks, dancing and moonlighting. "That leaves us with how much time?" Ri implored nervously.

"Twenty minutes." Matt replied as he watched more people come in. First family, Matt's parents, Derek and Alex's parents, Rebecca, then Tabitha and Spencer. A quick rush of friends followed. Some well-known, others were private friends who weren't in the celebrity spotlight. Riana continually pulled at her vertical labret. Matt could tell the anxiety of meeting everyone was getting to her. Lexi tried to comfort her, which was logical, being as she was Derek's main squeeze she had met his family and a fair number of their friends.

"Good lord Riana, you look hot!" Rebecca exclaimed as she ran to her. Riana laughed as she hugged her, happy to see another face she knew. They excitedly chatted about Rebecca's schooling as they awaited Alex. Spencer also quickly found Riana. As he wrapped his little arms around her leg Sam could literally feel Riana's nerves relax.

"Hey buddy!" she grinned as she looked down at Spencer latched to her leg. "Hi Tabitha." she greeted as Tabitha came up behind Spencer. She smiled warmly at Riana as she took Matt's hand.

"Alright ladies and gentlemen!" The DJ called. "The man of the evening has arrived. He's down in the lobby, I figure we have two minutes!"

Oh hell here we go. Riana thought as every ounce of her soul panicked. She hid herself in the back of the crowd; she didn't want to be the first person he saw. Everyone anxiously turned to the door and as it swung open there was an overwhelming cry of, "HAPPY BIRTHDAY ALEX!" Riana laughed as Alex dramatically grabbed his heart and pretended to be surprised. His smile was grand and bright, his laughter genuine and contagious.

Alex made it through the crowd and made sure every person knew how happy he was they were there. Then, as the handful of people in front of Riana parted, he saw her. His eyes met hers and the world instantly melted away. There was no one else in the moment but the two of them. Riana could hear her heart in her ears, her tongue felt like it had swollen up and taken over her whole mouth, and the heat of the room had to have at least doubled as she took him in. His hair had grown out some, and his button down shirt was undone slightly underneath his leather jacket. She sighed as she determined that Alex pulled leather off like no one else in the world. She grasped her vertical labret with her teeth and waited for him.

Alex couldn't believe she was there. She was absolutely enticing. There were no words he could find to describe the radiance she put out. He found her unnaturally blue eyes first, then her dark crimson lips, accentuated by her small silver barbell. Her hair was messy, like she had just spent the day at the beach. And her dress... Alex swallowed hard as he tried to mentally burn the image into his memory. His eyes traveled along her body and he became mesmerized by how her curvy legs were displayed. He quickly scolded himself to keep his dirty thoughts repressed.

He felt like it took forever to reach her. In her heels she was a good four inches taller but still melded perfectly into him. It was almost too intense for Riana. She wasn't sure if she could go through with the plan as she waited for him but as she fell into his embrace, and found comfort in the feel and scent of him she knew she had to. Just not yet.

"Ri." Alex breathed. He squeezed her tightly, perhaps too tightly. His hands instinctively ran along her back and rested at her hips. Riana reached her arms around Alex's neck and twisted her fingers into his hair. "Oh my God, Ri." he mumbled by her ear. "I've missed you." The vibration of his voice weakened her knees.

Riana turned her face into his neck as she murmured, "I've missed you more." Alex couldn't bring himself to release her yet, and Riana wished they were alone. Alex knew he didn't need anyone or anything else that night except for her. He was also mildly aware of the hushed questions among his guests, yet he didn't care. He didn't worry about who was saying what, if they wondered who she was, or if they wondered what her relationship to him was. All he cared about was having her remain in his arms for as long as possible.

Riana knew she wouldn't be able to tell him what she had to tell him in front of everyone. Lexi approached, and with one small sentence from her lips, he was ripped from her embrace. "I provide pretty good birthday presents, huh Alex?" Lexi teased. Alex reluctantly let go of Riana but instantly grabbed her hand as he turned to face Lexi. Riana sighed, thankful she could still touch him.

Alex looked over at Riana as he replied, "The best." Lexi smiled at Riana and gave her goofy eyes full of excitement and expectation. Without a word Riana widened her eyes to tell her that no, she hadn't told him yet. They chatted for a moment as Riana tried to regain her composure.

"Ri, let me introduce you to some friends." Alex urged excitedly as he started to pull her through the crowd. She pulled back on him, knowing it was now or never.

"Actually, Alex…" she looked around nervously. "could we step outside for a moment? It's kind of hot in here." He nodded and placed his hand on the small of her back as he ushered her out to the top floor balcony. "Wow, it's beautiful!" Riana gasped as she took in downtown New York City from the 52nd floor. Alex rested his head on her shoulder and hummed in agreement as his hands rested protectively on her hips.

Riana turned to him as she placed her back along the glass railing. "Alex," she started as she wrapped her arms around his waist. "A lot has happened recently." She paused and he patiently waited for her to continue as he read her expression and deduced she had a lot to say. "I didn't do so well for a while. Ryan…had terrified me…and it brought up a lot of stuff." Alex's eyes darkened quickly as Riana confessed she had been scared. She rubbed his lower back to ease him. "I had to understand my past, what happened, where I was going. I was in a lot of pain." His eyes softened as he tightened his grip on her. "But… I wasn't in pain because of him, Alex. I was…but I just… I wanted you there so badly." He started to speak but she hushed him. "I wasn't ready to ask you to be there. I'm...I'm ready now, Alex. I want you....with me." she swallowed hard. "I love you." She looked up and finally met his eyes. "I'm *in* love with you." she confessed softly. "And I know you're my best friend so I understand if that's weird...or whatever, but I...I just had to tell you--"

He didn't interrupt her with words, but he immediately pulled her to him as he crushed his lips against hers. It was a desperate, soulful kiss that brought everything to a screaming crescendo. Riana pulled her hands from his waist and tangled them in his hair at the back of his head. She whimpered against his lips as every emotion she had tried to deny broke through. Alex pulled away, just enough to speak against her lips, "I'm so in love with you, Ri." Tears rushed down Riana's cheeks as his lips embraced hers again.

As Lexi watched Riana and Alex head out to the balcony she hoped this would be the moment Riana would tell him. She grabbed Derek's hand and quickly pulled him over to Sam and Matthew. "Listen, okay, I know it's wrong to spy, but something huge is about to happen." Matt and Derek looked at her like she'd grown a second head but Sam's eyes grew excited.

"Now?" she asked. "Where are they?" Lexi headed over to table by the window and drug Derek behind.

367

"They're outside. Now if we just hang--"

"Who's outside?" Matthew interrupted. Lexi groaned loudly. Sometimes, Matthew was frustratingly oblivious.

"Riana and Alex. Now, if we just hang out here all nonchalantly we could probably see how this plays out. Though, of course, I know it's going to play out wonderfully." Lexi tittered.

"Lex, what do you know that we don't?" Derek probed. She smiled at him innocently then turned and looked out the window. Riana faced Alex with her hands around his waist. She was talking, which was good. The way Alex looked at her, Lexi couldn't understand how Riana couldn't see it. The whole group intently took in the scene. Riana continued to talk and then, mid-sentence, Alex pulled her into a quick, intense kiss.

"Yes!" Sam and Lexi squealed happily.

"Good job Ri." Lexi beamed.

"You knew she loved him." Derek concluded simply as he pulled Lexi to his side. She nodded.

"I also knew that he loved her. It took a while for Riana to admit it and gain the courage to tell him, but I twisted her arm." she laughed.

Derek kissed her cheek. "I'm glad you did." he murmured. "He's absolutely ecstatic. Thank you, Lex."

<u>CHAPTER TWENTY-NINE</u>

Inside Your Heaven

Alex was soaring; Riana loved him. She was *in* love with him. Finally, everything they had gone through became worth it. She was finally in his arms, where she belonged, and he didn't have to deny how he felt anymore. He couldn't stop kissing her; small, short, sweet kisses, and long, deep, intense kisses. Every inch of his body reacted to her touch and he desperately wished they weren't at the party. He knew eventually they'd have to go back in and mingle but until the decision was made, they devoured each other. Riana pressed herself into Alex, each of them attempted to get closer to the other.

Alex's hands traveled off her hips, to just under her butt, and grasped hungrily. Riana moaned against him then tossed her head back with her eyes closed. He kissed along her neck as she sighed. "I love you." she whispered again.

He released her slowly, brought his hands up and cupped her face. "Ri," he started cautiously. "Are we together now?" Riana nodded as tears welled up in her eyes and a smile spread across her lips. Alex brushed two large tears from her cheeks then kissed her softly. "Well, then I think we should

make the rounds and make sure everyone knows it."
His heart had swelled to the point of bursting and he
couldn't wait to share it with the world.

"I'd rather just stay out here and kiss you."
Riana teased as she reached her lips to the side of his
neck.

Alex groaned and bit his lip. "Ri... You're
not making this easy." Her idea did sound much
better than his, but he knew they had to go back in.

"It's not supposed to be." she purred as she
continued to kiss his neck. He laughed deeply as he
pulled away from her tender lips. She gave him a
pout but accepted his hand and followed him back
into the party.

Lexi was the first one to meet them. Alex
slung an arm over Lexi's shoulder but kept his other
hand still firmly locked in Riana's. "Best. Birthday.
Ever." he proclaimed. He kissed Lexi's cheek then
pulled back. "Lexi, I'd like you to meet the lady of
my life, my *girlfriend*, Riana." Lexi couldn't contain
the squeal that escaped her as she danced around
Alex and wrapped Riana in her arms.

"I told you." she teased as she continued to
hold Riana. Alex arched his eyebrow. *So this had
been planned. Nice job ladies.*

Riana smiled and nodded against Lexi.
"Thanks, Lex." she sighed. "I would have stayed
alone--and miserable--forever if you hadn't helped
me along."

"This I know." Lexi laughed.

"Lexi, Lexi." Alex interrupted excitedly as he pulled his phone from his pocket. "Would you do me the honor of documenting this momentous occasion?" Riana couldn't stop the eye roll as she laughed at his corniness. Lexi smiled and grabbed his phone.

Derek approached just as Alex pulled Riana back to him and Lexi got ready to snap the picture. "What's up guys?" Derek asked with a smile and a wink in Riana's direction.

"I'm about to introduce the world to my girlfriend." Alex declared proudly. Riana's mind was swimming; *I'm his girlfriend. And he's going to tell the world.* Panic abruptly gripped her and Alex noticed instantly. "Ri, sweetheart. It's okay, I promise." Riana took a deep breath and locked her eyes on him. His eyes were sweet, caring and genuine. "You love me?" he asked slowly.

"I love you." she answered quickly with firm certainty.

"Then smile." he urged as he pulled her into him again and Lexi snapped a picture. He faced Ri and stroked the side of her face before he kissed her and Lexi took another. Alex pulled away, accepted his phone from Lexi and examined the pictures. "Perfect."

Alex thoughtfully chewed his lip as he filtered the picture, captioned it and posted it to the whole world via online social media. Riana's own phone pinged her and she opened her notifications; D.M.A. had posted a new photo. She grinned as she opened it. The image of them in a sweet kiss greeted her with the caption: "Best birthday ever. I love you Ri. -A" Riana looked up at him and smiled.

Before she knew it they had bid Lexi and Derek farewell and started their rounds. As friends and family stopped Alex he quickly and happily introduced Riana as his girlfriend. Riana was sure she'd never be able to erase the blush imbedded in her cheeks.

Rebecca made the comment that she "knew it" and hugged Riana again. Alex's mother was incredibly sweet and gushed about how much she had heard about Riana. She had even read her book, which had been shared by Tabitha with her. Riana's heart was touched to know Tabitha had passed her book along to others.

After the stress of confessing to Alex was over, they fell into the party. They shared drinks and danced to the heavy beats the DJ spun. Riana was acutely aware of more pictures being taken, but she figured she had to get used to it. She had him now, nothing else mattered. Riana couldn't get enough of Alex's lips, and she was sure their constant displays of affection drove most of the guests crazy. "Alex." she mumbled against his lips, the sweetness of drinks lingered between them. "Stay with me tonight?" He hummed in contemplation against her lips.

"Only if we can leave now." he replied with a mischievous spark in his eye.

Riana licked her lips, then grasped her barbell for a moment. "Mmm, that is indeed tempting." she purred as she gazed at him. "But wouldn't it be rude? I mean, this is your party after all." Alex groaned dramatically and twirled Riana around. She faced him again and he pulled her quickly to his chest.

"You might have a point." he agreed. "But yes, I will stay with you." Riana and Alex danced the night away, though they both stopped their drinking. Riana didn't want to lose her bearings, and Alex wanted to be sure he remembered every detail of the night.

They couldn't count how many times they told the story of how they met, but his friends found it hilarious. Everyone sang "Happy Birthday" then Riana took great pleasure in smashing a large piece of chocolate cake in Alex's face. She laughed loudly with a snort then attempted to run away in her stilettos. Alex caught her quickly, scooped her up and painted her nose and cheeks with chocolate as well. He then slid her down, and kissed off the frosting. If it hadn't been her, she would have found the display horribly adorable.

"Finally!" Alex laughed as he found a place next to Riana on one of the lounge couches. "Guests are leaving, I think it's time for us to go." He winked at her.

Suddenly, Riana felt suffocated under fear and uneasiness. Despite her certainty that Alex loved her, the fear came from how so many before him had either taken it forcefully from her or used her under the pretense of love. She took a breath and reminded herself that she could do this, that she wanted to do this. She wanted it to be right though, honest and full of love. Alex stood and extended his hands down to her to assist her. She laced her fingers through his and allowed him to pull her off the couch.

They wove through the remainder of the guests and bid their farewells. Alex lovingly led Riana out of the restaurant and down to the pulsating streets of New York. She couldn't stop gazing at him, he was breathtaking. He gripped her left hand firmly and she couldn't help but wonder what she had done right in life to deserve such an overwhelming moment. A swift breeze hit them, the cold fingers of late fall swept over Riana's bare skin. A deep shiver ran down her spine and she cursed herself for not demanding some sort of cover up from Sam.

Alex halted his strides, released Riana's hand and pulled his leather jacket off. "Here baby." he cooed as he swung the jacket behind Riana. She stepped in closer to him as she snuggled into the warmth and became engulfed in both the heavy leather and Alex's soothing scent. Alex briskly rubbed her upper arms and attempted to warm her up as he kept his eyes locked on hers.

"Thanks." she whispered. They remained still on the sidewalk, droves of people quickly cut left and right to avoid colliding into them. Alex drifted his hands off her arms and around to her back. Riana's eyes fluttered shut as he pulled her to him. His lips were cool from the October air, but she still burned for him. The connection of their lips created sparks to the consuming passion deep within her. He slowly released her and she found his hand again before they continued their short walk back to her hotel.

Riana knew she wanted to explore every inch of Alex, and give every bit of herself to him but she worried it might be too soon. It was more than a physical need that grew inside her, it wasn't strictly about a primitive expression of desire. She was irrevocably in love with him and she wanted it to be perfect. She didn't want to ruin things by allowing her body to trump her logic.

Alex noticed Riana seemed unusually pensive as they traveled down Fifth Avenue. He worried that she was nervous about inviting him to her hotel. Alex chewed his lip and knew he'd have to provide her with support and reassurance for any decision she made. There was no way he would pressure her to do anything she wasn't absolutely ready to do.

Riana stayed at the historic RomaBelle Hotel when she was in New York. Twelve stories of imposing beauty. As they entered, the concierge tipped his head in greeting. The sound of Ri's heels echoed off the marble tiles as they ensued to the elevator. She pulled Alex through the golden doors, selected the tenth floor then leaned back against the mirrored wall. She smiled at Alex, but uncertainty clouded her brilliant eyes.

The vintage bell announced the elevator's arrival at their floor. Alex followed Riana out of the elevator and down to a corner suite. As they stepped inside they were greeted by crisp white walls, dark woodwork, a panoramic view of Broadway and a conservative living space.

Riana bit her labret, "Well, here it is. It's my favorite hotel to stay at in New York. I love watching the people down on the street." she rambled quickly as she strayed to the window. Alex frowned slightly as he followed behind her. Riana had slipped out of Alex's jacket and he gently placed his hands on her arms. He watched her smooth shoulders drop with a deep exhale.

"Ri?" Alex beckoned. She turned to him, the lights of the surrounding buildings framed her sweet face. "How long have we known each other?"

Riana twisted her face a bit, confused as to why he'd ask. "Since May." she replied simply.

"Since May 25th." he specified. She raised her brow and widened her eyes as she questioned the motivation of the question. "It's been four months, two weeks and six days, Ri. It wasn't an easy journey we made, was it?" Riana shook her head lightly. "Even with the complications, the other people, the fights; I've been in love with you for each and every one of those days, Ri." Her eyes softened and Alex noticed her hands tremble slightly. He clasped both of her hands in his and brought her fingers to his lips.

Alex moved back and took a seat at the small dining table. "I read your book." He found her eyes and found a mixture of love and pain reflected through them. "And even though you are undoubtedly by far one of the smartest, strongest and bravest women I know, I know the damage those men did isn't completely gone." She swallowed thickly. "I love you more than I ever thought possible, Riana. I don't ever want you to feel obligated to do anything. I am yours. You control this."

Riana didn't want to cry, but as she realized just how fully Alex understood her she couldn't stop. Alex instantly got up and gathered her in his arms. "Honey, you okay?" he asked softly next to her ear.

Riana nodded. "How do you know me so well?" she mumbled.

"I pay attention." Riana couldn't see his face but she could tell he was smiling. "Because I care about you and want to do this right. All of it right."

She pulled back from him and turned around. She lifted the messy waves of hair off her back and neck. "Unzip me." she whispered. He placed one hand on her hips as the other pulled the zipper. He stopped about halfway and pulled Riana backwards as he found his chair again. He sat and picked up where he left off with the zipper, except he placed slow, sweet kisses on each newly exposed inch of skin. Riana closed her eyes and felt love wash over her body. The pressure of Alex's hands instructed her to turn around.

She admired the striking man before her, who was so gentle and deliberate. "You're okay?" he questioned. Riana nodded silently. *Could I possibly love him more?* "Can I keep going?" *There it was, I officially love him more.*

"Yes." she breathed. Alex brought his calloused, yet tender, hands to the lace cap sleeves and gently coaxed them down her arms. Soon her dress fluttered down, off her arms and chest, and gathered at her hips. Alex leaned forward and simply placed the side of his face against Riana's stomach, his late night stubble tickled her sensitive skin. He released a long breath and attempted to relax his excited nerves.

Alex's hands embraced Riana's hips as he barely lifted his head, his endless dark eyes beheld her as he murmured, "You're the most beautiful woman I've ever seen." Riana knew he had to have seen tens of thousands of women in his career so she took the compliment seriously. He then placed his perfect lips against her skin, just above her belly button. She closed her eyes and sighed. No one had ever taken so much time with her.

Riana gathered the bunched up material of her dress and pushed it off her hips. It landed in a soft pile around her heels. She stood there in only her heels, panties and strapless bra. She was completely exposed, yet she had never felt more comfortable. She took one small step out of the dress and flung it away with the toe of her heel. She playfully grinned at him. "Come with me?" she questioned as she stepped back with her hand outstretched.

Alex took her hand and stood, "I'd go anywhere with you." She led him towards the back of the suite and through the door to the bedroom. She faced the bed with Alex behind her. She turned back to him and grasped the sides of his face as she crashed her lips into his. She pulled back as her heart raced, and started to undo the buttons of his shirt. He stepped out of his shoes as Riana finished, and he shrugged out of his shirt.

Riana pouted when she was met with a white undershirt. "Really Alex? Layers? You're really going to make me work for this aren't you?" she teased.

His deep laugh eased the rest of Riana's anxiety. "Had I known this was how tonight would end, I wouldn't have worn anything at all!" Riana couldn't keep her composure and she snorted as she broke into laughter. Alex wrapped his arms tightly around her as they both laughed. "I love you so much." he chuckled.

"I love you more." she declared as she kissed his neck. "Alex," she breathed, then hesitated. "You know my past. You know how I've been hurt and used." Her breath got choppy and she kissed his neck softly. "Would you do something for me?"

"Anything." he whispered.

"Will you teach me what it means to make love?" Riana's heart transitioned from a steady beat to a deep thunder as she tried to calm herself. She felt virginal again. She was scared but absolutely thrilled at the possibility of being able to experience him completely.

Alex eased Riana back, just to arms-length. His eyes were intense, but sincere. "I would be honored, my love." he kissed her sweetly, then peeled his t-shirt from his firm, smooth chest. Riana sighed as she trailed her fingertips over his skin.

Riana was stunned, and couldn't believe what she'd been missing. Alex was sweet, patient, funny and utterly sexy. He loved every inch of her, praised every curve. As he read Riana's book he learned how triggering moments like these could be for her, so he paced himself and made a point to keep her from disassociating. He teased her and kept her present as he brought waves of sensations to her she honestly hadn't known existed.

They were tangled up in each other, sweat formed in crevices of elbows, knees and in their hair. Alex talked through every moment that had the potential to trigger Riana. He made sure she was still with him and okay. Even in her most vulnerable state, he made her feel safe.

It was the most impassioned, beautiful and all-consuming moment of Riana's life. As she pulled Alex to her and found the last of the ultimate peaks he brought her to, she felt nothing but love explode out of every pore of her body. She dug her nails into his broad shoulders as she cried out his name. Alex kissed along her face as she laid there and panted. His body trembled as he whispered, "I love you so much Riana, you're so beautiful." Riana held the back of his head and stroked his dampened hair as her chest heaved underneath him. Her body rode aftershocks and she quivered with her eyes closed as fireworks exploded in the darkness.

"Ri, baby." Alex's voice called out to her. "Baby, open your eyes." Riana found the strength to open her eyes slowly and found his tender eyes. She realized that hot tears rushed down the sides of her face; but they weren't just hers. She was astonished to realize their making love had been as earth shaking for him as it had been for her. She wiped the wetness from his cheeks as she kissed him.

"I want you forever, Ri." he breathed against her lips.

"Forever." she confirmed.

Made in the USA
San Bernardino, CA
20 September 2015